BACK IN THE DAY:
TALES OF NZ'S OWN PARADISE ISLAND

Mike Johnson

99% Press

Published by 99% Press,
an imprint of Lasavia Publishing Ltd.
Auckland, New Zealand
www.lasaviapublishing.com

ISBN: 978-0-9941015-7-0

Dedicated to the memory of Simon Val Johnstone
1956 – 2009

THE 52 TALES

Preface   9
MoJo Mayhem and the Dope Patch   11
Horrowitz and the Furious Fantail   16
How Sid Vicious got his Name   21
Bobby and the Bunkin   26
Wally and the Wolf Spider   31
A Theatrical Production   36
Garrison Ford and the Merry Mercenary   41
Ricky and the Rowdy Rooster   46
Kendell and the Killer Chemicals   51
A Queer Rooster   56
Art is a Way of Looking   61
Houdini and the Holiday Hotties   66
Stumpy and the Bunny Rabbits   71
Millie Millicent and the Spider Man   75
Chainsaw Travis and the Sleeping Ugly   80
Charlie and his Chop Suey Wife   84
Tricksy Claw and the Demon Rat   88
Dennaray Darko and the Primordial Twins   92
Petrolhead Pinkie and Stock Car Sally's Last Ride   97
Short Cuts   102
Willard and the Wine Tasters   107
Xena and the Zombie   113
The Artist and the Apple Tree   118
Pippa and the Placenta Tree   123
Harry the Hobbit and the Hidden Treasure   128
Hettie Harper and the Indigo Children   133
Polly and Playcentre   138
Little Thieves   143
Cess Claw and the City Slicker   148
Revenge of the Dish-Dog   152
Suzie, Sarah and the School Uniform Shemozzle   158
Manny and the Men's Group   163
Petra and the Peculiar Painting   168
The Man who Couldn't Stop Walking in Circles   173

Lady Nicotine and the Nicolettes, or, Last Gasp
gasps his Last Gasp   178
The Suitcase that Walked by Itself   183
Standing or Squatting?   188
Crusty and the Canny Cat   193
Tina and the Taniwha   198
Kendell and the Talented Typewriter   203
Northrop and the Frog Man   208
Sammy and the Septic Tank   213
The Man who Mistook the Moon for a Street Light   218
Sue Lake and the Sizzling Sausages   223
Tina and the Ten Cents   228
A Place Apart   233
How Greedy Nan got her Name   238
A Mortgage and an Orange Tree   243
Pear Shaped in Paradise   248
The Recluse   253
Boatie Ben and the Mists of Unbeing   258
Garrison Ford and the Morning After   263
Acknowledgements   268

PREFACE

There was and there was not, an island called Paradise...

These stories were written between February and September, 2014. I followed a few simple rules.

The stories were not to exceed two thousand words. Hence, no story would outlive its welcome.

I would resist the novelist's organising impulse to mesh the stories together; each story must stand on its own.

There would be no swearing, even though that meant the sacrifice of a certain realism.

The stories should remain easy to read so they might be enjoyed during a summer hour on the beach, or while taking a ferry to all the paradise islands of the world.

Finally, I would not obsess over the stories or engage in endless revisions, which is the habit of the perfectionist. I didn't see this as a literary exercise. I live in a homemade house. The beams are exposed and you can see the nail holes. These are homemade stories, and I don't mind a few nail holes. They are all part of the fun.

I pretty much kept to my brief. The stories can be read separately, but there are rewards for the reader who starts at the beginning and works forward, with characters reappearing and new vistas opening up. The last story should be read last. However approached, the reading of each story should inform the reading of the others. However independent each may be, the stories as a whole are a composite picture.

Some are tall tales, some are not, but there are a couple that require special mention. '*Bobby and the Bunkin*' is derived from a children's book with the same name by D Barbara Muir, and features the same characters, based on dim childhood recollections of that book. My story might therefore be seen as a shameless rip-off, a loving tribute, or an exercise in that most modern of genres, fanfic, in which stories are written within worlds created by other writers. Nowadays it's called intertextuality. One perceptive reader also pointed out that the rat in the freezer motif in '*Tricksy and the Demon Rat*' is something of a cliché, an urban myth perhaps, but I decided to leave the story in because it did actually happen. A poor excuse, I know. A case of life imitating cliché perhaps? What looks like the most 'made up' story of them all is actually one of the most real.

There is a certain necessary fuzziness to the sense of place, also. I have lived on three islands. Formentera, a small island off the larger Spanish island of Ibiza; Skiathos, a Greek island in the Northern Sporades, and Waiheke Island in the Hauraki Gulf. Since I have lived on Waiheke Island for thirty-four years, island readers will naturally seek a reflection of Waiheke in the stories, which is fair enough, but those other two islands are there, almost like palimpsest texts, beneath the surface.

There was a time when I was sustained by the idea that these stories, in keeping with the holiday of the imagined reader, would be largely light and whimsical. And some are. But there are some which, again, one perceptive reader pointed out, are 'jarringly different.' I've left these stories in. After all, life back in the day wasn't always light and whimsical, even if Paradise Island is memory's paradise, and the jarringly different could strike at any moment. Just like now.

Mike Johnson, September 2014, Waiheke Island.

MOJO MAYHEM AND THE DOPE PATCH

What is an island but a place to run in circles?

A place to meet your neighbour from hell?

MoJo Mayhem had done running in circles, but didn't meet his neighbour from hell until he stayed at home and started noticing things.

The first thing he noticed was a bright young pohutukawa tree planted on his side of their boundary, a good two metres, he estimated, judging from the bottom surveyor's peg, clearly visible behind the trellis his neighbour had built right along the boundary. He tried to remember when that had happened. The second thing he noticed was that his neighbour had mown right around a trellis onto MoJo's side, quietly swallowing a patch of land by making it a part of his lawn.

On Paradise Island, boundaries became blurred and surveyors' pegs tended to vanish into vigorous regenerating bush or even more vigorous weeds. In the early, carefree days, nobody cared too much anyway; nobody wanted to build fences, and everything in the garden was organically lovely.

As much as anybody else, MoJo shared that philosophy, but the pohutukawa tree gleaming in the morning sun, and the smug patch of mown grass on his side of the trellis, got under his skin. Pohutukawas turned into mighty big trees, quickly too when they were young, and he'd been eyeing-up that mown patch for a little garden, since it was north-facing and had the neighbour's trellis to support runner beans, passion fruit, or some other climber.

So MoJo approached his neighbour and asked about the tree.

'No,' his neighbour said. 'The tree is right on the boundary. Look,' and he lined his eye up behind his outstretched arm and drew a bead up the gently sloping bush to where the far peg might be. At that high end of their properties, any visible boundary had been dissolved in chaos of bush and weeds.

'You've got a bent elbow, mate,' MoJo said. His trigger finger was itchy for the axe.

'You can't cut it down,' his neighbour said.

'Why not?'

'It's over three metres. Council will fine you $400.'

'If they find out.'

His neighbour said nothing but got a grim look on his face.

'You wouldn't,' MoJo said.

'Somebody might.'

'And why are you mowing right around the trellis?' MoJo gestured to the incursion.

'I can hardly use the trellis on my side if honeysuckle and wandering jew are invading from your side, can I?'

The way he said it, it sounded unreasonable not to agree.

MoJo's wife Ella didn't think it was reasonable at all. She made disapproving noises that made him feel guilty. 'He'll keep pushing and pushing, because that's what he does,' she said. The implication was clear. MoJo should stop being such a wimp and do some pushing back.

So MoJo consulted his two oldest mates on the island, Chainsaw Travis and Boatie Ben, over a beer. 'I've got trouble with Numbnuts next door,' he told them.

Chainsaw Travis made chainsaw type motions.

'I can't, he'll dob me,' MoJo said.

'I wasn't thinking of the tree,' Travis said with an evil grin. 'His house is on poles, isn't it?' MoJo liked Travis because he wasn't a wimp and he didn't think too much. If he said he would chainsaw the foundations from under your house, he would do it. People didn't mess with Travis the way they messed with MoJo.

'I'm glad all over again that I live in a boat,' Ben said. 'All I need is my mooring. No rates, no neighbours, no boundaries...'

'...no wife,' Travis said. A big plus as far as Travis was concerned.

'All I have to do is jump the next tide,' Ben said.

'You guys are a hell of a lot of help,' MoJo said. He knew how a situation like this could develop. There used to be a TV series about just this very thing. *Neighbours from Hell.* Both sides caught in an escalation plot that ends in general ruination. Tit-for-tatsville. Couldn't go there. Not healthy.

MoJo finished up his beer and left them to it.

'I asked our neighbour today to remove the tree,' Ella said when he got home.

'Did he come over here?'

'No. I was looking at the tree. He came over trying to be friendly. So I asked him outright. You know what he said?'

Obviously MoJo didn't, but refrained from saying so.

'He said that it was too late. That he planted it four years ago.'

The implication was clear. It was MoJo's fault. He should have got onto it years ago. All that running in circles and he'd missed it. Island life! He looked around the property and found the spade Ella had left out to rot, and dug up the mowed piece of grass on their side of the trellis. He pulled up the honeysuckle and wandering jew and dug out the kikuyu grass. His neighbour wouldn't be bringing his mower around here any time soon. And MoJo might get to plant runner beans and passion fruit using his neighbour's trellis. A non-escalatory way of dealing with that situation. He felt quite pleased with himself.

'That'll teach him a lesson,' Ella said.

'What do you mean?'

'You've done just what he wanted you to do. He's been onto you to clean up that patch for ages. Now you oblige.'

'I can't win,' MoJo said.

'But he can,' she said. 'He's smarter than you are.'

That day MoJo went hunting for the top boundary peg, the one his neighbour had lined up behind his bent arm. After half a morning of cursing and swearing and getting his clothes ripped and his skin scratched, he finally found it. A little oblong peg that had once been white for visibility. He got a piece of bamboo, tied a white cloth to it, and stuck it in the ground next to the peg. Looking down to the lower peg, any reasonable person could clearly see that the pohutukawa was well inside the boundary.

'You can't trust the peg,' his neighbour said when MoJo showed him. They stood at the bottom looking up at the white cloth waving above the bush like a signal of surrender.

'Old Stumpy could have moved it any number of times. He does that, you know.'

Stumpy Stewart had been the previous owner of the neighbour's property. It was said he could create a section out of nothing, just by moving other people's pegs around. Made a fortune in property speculation. Not bad for a guy with one arm. You don't need two arms to have an eye for the main chance, Chainsaw had commented.

'We could get it surveyed.'

'That'd cost you six hundred dollars,' his neighbour said. 'But look. You can see the pohutukawa on the boundary. Clear as day.'

'I can't do anything with him,' MoJo later complained to Ella. 'He can't see straight.'

'He's got you by the short and curlies,' Ella said.

MoJo fumed. He sat by the bottom peg and looked up along the line to the revealed top peg. Stumpy Stewart would have had to move that top peg a massive distance to take in the pohutukawa. His neighbour was so crooked he couldn't lie straight in bed. As his eye roamed along the imaginary boundary he saw evidence of further boundary pushing. There were signs of activity about half-way up the gentle slope, in the most impenetrable part of the bush. On his side.

After struggling through bush for ten minutes he found it. The game changer.

'I've got him,' he said to Ella.

'How?'

'He's got a dope patch – on my side. He takes out the pohutukawa or I call the cops.'

'And what? Bust us? The patch is on our side. He denies it, and we go down. He doesn't even have to be smart to do that.'

MoJo fumed some more. There had to be a way of turning the dope patch to advantage without calling the cops. It was still a few weeks off cropping. Best wait until it was ready and steal it. He was partial to a little of the old buffalo sacrament himself. But that was another step up the escalation plot he'd vowed to avoid. That's what all this was about – meeting the challenge on a spiritual level. Easy enough to get the axe and wreak havoc upon trellis, tree and crop, which was what Chainsaw advised. That would leave him with a neighbour from hell bent upon revenge instead of just a neighbour from hell. Ella was goading him. 'You're too weak to stand up to him,' she said, and that hurt. There was something like admiration in her voice. He didn't like it.

His neighbour had to be stopped right away. There were other boundaries at stake.

It was Boatie Ben who gave him the idea. 'I'll steal the crop for you,' he said. 'Creep in one night and take the plants. Every one. A clean sweep.'

'I might take you up on that,' MoJo said, although it was hard to see how anybody except Ben benefitted from the scheme.

He approached the neighbour. They met on the boundary by the pohutukawa.

'Here's how it's going to work,' MoJo said. 'You remove the tree,' he brushed one of the slender branches, 'and nobody gets to hear about your dope patch. You might like to sweeten the deal. Perhaps half an ounce.'

'You wouldn't,' his neighbour said.

'Somebody might. Lot of strangers wandering around with backpacks at harvest time,' MoJo said. It was true. Ripping off dope had a long tradition on Paradise Island back in the day.

His neighbour said nothing. There was nothing he could say.

As MoJo was turning to go his neighbour said, 'You really are the neighbour from hell.'

MoJo laughed. The boot was on the other foot now.

Ella stood by the kitchen window watching the neighbour cutting down the pohutukawa tree.

'I can't believe it,' she said.

MoJo had picked a few leaves from his neighbour's crop, dried them, and was now testing them out. Not bad. Lots of promise. He was sitting on his deck with his feet up on the railing looking down over the tranquil bush, the quiet boundary line. A kingfisher flashed blue. A thrush gave the air its song.

'He finally saw reason,' MoJo said, blowing smoke on his fingernails. 'Everybody has their good side.'

HORROWITZ AND THE FURIOUS FANTAIL

When Horrowitz arrived on Paradise Island he was a man with a past. A deliberately unspecified past. He wasn't the only one, he discovered, who preferred not to look back. There were many escapees of one kind or another, those with memories they couldn't live with and who wanted to create new ones.

He arrived with quite a packet of money, the fruits of a criminal past, apparently. He didn't talk about it but word got around in the magic manner of gossip. He used it to buy himself a little A-frame cottage in the bush and a small grocery business and got on with keeping his head down and his nose clean.

Even Garrison Ford, reporter for the local *Paradise Island Times*, who had a boyish way of getting people drunk and ferreting out their secrets, couldn't make any headway with Horrowitz. Horrowitz drank but didn't get drunk, talked but only of current concerns. 'There is no emotional spillage,' Ford complained to Yvonne, the girl he wanted to marry. There had to be emotional spillage. A spilling for a grilling. His life was built on it.

Horrowitz, he concluded, was hiding something.

Which was true, but Horrowitz didn't want to think about it. He preferred to think about his garden. He'd never had a garden, but soon discovered the secret that all gardeners know – there's nothing quite like a garden for keeping a person busy and focused on immediate tasks. Weeding he found particularly soothing. Like cleaning up. His house was always immaculate too. His little shop was tidy and his accounts were in order.

'There's something behind it,' Ford said to Yvonne. 'No man is naturally that tidy.'

Maddie hesitated before a range of sarcastic rejoinders, most of them involving Ford's underpants. What she loved about Ford was how trustingly he would open himself to comment.

Everything was going fine for Horrowitz until he was visited in his garden one bright and cheery morn by a furious fantail, a piwakawaka, who followed him around chittering its little head off. Horrowitz was unused to the ways of the Paradise Island bird life, and fantails in particular, and wasn't to know that fantails often do this because they are insectivores and have learned that when humans are gardening the inhabitants of Insect Street are disturbed and scattered.

Horrowitz thought there was something personal in it. The hyper little bird had a message for him. He knew it was silly to think that way but at the same time it wasn't. He'd been waiting for a message for some time now, with no idea how it might arrive.

'Danger danger danger danger danger danger,' the fantail chirruped.

'What do you know about anything?' Horrowitz said.

'I know I know I know I know I know I know,' the fantail said, its body twitching from side to side in excitement.

'You can't know anything,' Horrowitz scoffed.

This island was making him soft in the brain, he decided. Come to Paradise Island and end up talking to the birds. At the same time the persistent creature made him uneasy.

It was laughing at him, he was certain of it.

Horrowitz was not well read, and knew nothing of the piwakawaka's reputation for laughing at foolish mankind. At the same time it seemed to Horrowitz that the bird was chiding him, reminding him of all his sins. It flipped from branch to branch, scolding him all the while.

'Get away,' he said, taking a swipe at it, which the bird easily evaded.

The bird was making him think about things he didn't want to think about. Its high-pitched laughter filled the garden. Horrowitz surveyed his garden. What did he have here, but a thin defence against his great fear. His garden would be no use to him when the time came. The weeds would quietly grow back, that's all. After a time the garden would forget him. Just as the island itself would. There would be little trace of his passing.

The fantail was surely mocking him, and the dream he had that he could get away and be safe.

He took a few steps towards the bird, maybe to take another swipe at it, and the bird retreated towards the fence that separated his property from some undeveloped land that had reverted to bush. He took another couple of steps and the same thing happened.

'You want me to follow you, is that it?'

'Yes yes yes yes yes yes,'

He felt stupid following the bird, which stayed just out of reach, especially when he clambered over the fence into somebody else's land. If he'd read more he might have been acquainted with a range of fairy tales in which a 'king' would be led astray by some animal only to discover his true destiny. Sometimes it was a graceful white deer, not a flitty little bird. If he'd known the tales he might have been forewarned.

As it was, without knowing or understanding what he was doing, he clambered the fence and followed the bird. It was a random act in an otherwise tightly controlled life. A childish scribble on a colouring-in picture, spilling over the lines. The scribble of the irrational. This was not exactly Ford's emotional spillage, but it was getting there.

He cursed himself and the bird, which seemed to be leading him in a wide semi-circle.

'You're not leading me anywhere, are you? Just up the garden path.'

'Little faith little faith little faith,' the bird said, an answer that didn't mean much to Horrowitz.

Several times he almost turned back. This was altogether too foolish. At the same time it made him feel like a child again. It reminded him of a time before... before everything. Before the noose of his life tightened. Before the deal went down.

He had now gained some height, and took a rest at an open spot that had a view of the road. The bird fluttered around his head, making a terrible racket. He grabbed for it. If he could snatch it out of the air, he would cheerfully wring its neck.

Below him, on the road, a Black Explorer crept past. A big shiny beast like that was rare on Paradise Island, and its darkened windows looked sinister. When it went past and disappeared from view, he found himself giving a sigh of relief. This is how it was for him now, his new life on the island. Every day gone by was another sigh of relief, because one day they would come for him and the pretence would be all over.

He was about to get up when the Black Explorer returned, travelling the other way, slowly. Checking letterboxes. Feeling very exposed, Horrowitz crept into the bush, trying to keep a watch on the vehicle at the same time.

He looked around for the bird but the bird was gone. Just like that. Lead him up the garden path and leave him there. Where? There in the silence of the bird's absence. Distant, familiar sounds were abruptly punctuated by the sound of doors slamming. Big solid Explorer doors. He adjusted his position to get a better view of the road.

There were three of them. He recognised Sammy in the black leather jacket. And the killer they called The Burner who liked loud Hawaiian shirts that made him look like a tourist. The third was a woman he didn't know but surmised was Sammy's girlfriend. She wore a matching leather jacket and black jeans. Like a bikie. He'd heard of her, how she stayed by Sammy's side while he did time, remaining loyal. Seeing them made him lose all the heat in his body. He felt dizzy, as if he'd just been running for a long time, which in a metaphoric sense was true. Horrowitz, however, was not in a position to appreciate the niceties.

The fantail returned briefly to check him out and flew on.

'I thought I might've had a bit more time,' he said as it went past.

The bird laughed hard at that.

The three on the road below were checking out the letterboxes. No mystery, which one they were looking for.

Fear froze him where he was, and when the fear wore off he stayed put. Flight or fight. Or hide. He could see it in his mind's eye with awful clarity. The three of them fronting up to his door, Sammy fingering the flick-knife in his pocket. Sammy was a knife man. The Burner preferred knuckle-dusters. The girl would knock on the door and call out his name. When he didn't come, they'd shoulder open the door and toss the place. It wouldn't take them long. They'd probably find the stash he'd put aside for this very day, but it wasn't what they were after. It was him they were after. Wet work was their business.

'I thought I'd get more warning,' he said to the absent fantail. He thought he heard the echo of laughter.

Sammy would have a look around the garden. He probably wouldn't get that Horrowitz was the gardener; the Horrowitz he knew never had his hands near the soil. Not that kind of dirt, anyway. Sammy would look around without understanding what he was seeing.

Knowing Sammy, they would hang around a while waiting for him to return. The back door had been open. He'd left some groceries on the table. It would look like somebody had just popped out for the moment. The Burner would find his cognac and help himself to it. They would wait. They had waited long enough, a little longer wouldn't daunt them.

Horrowitz had a choice. He could either stay hidden here where they would never find him, not even think of looking for him, until they gave up and left. Or, he could use the delay, while they were waiting for him, to get away, go somewhere. The fantail had given him his window of opportunity.

He waited and it was a good thing he did. They didn't stay as long as he thought. He watched them approaching the Explorer. Sammy had his shoulders hunched and his arms stiff, walking the way he did when he was ready for murder. Before they got in the car, The Burner, paused and took a good long look around, as if aware he was being watched. The very paranoid Burner, not as stupid as people thought. It might have occurred to him that Horrowitz was hidden nearby watching them.

As the Explorer drove slowly off, Horrowitz began to shake. For ten minutes he shook like a man in fever. Then he was on his feet. He couldn't go back to the house. He couldn't walk any roads. He had nothing but a shirt, a pair of gardening slacks and some old shoes. He took off overland, climbing fences and crossing over people's property with hardly a second thought.

There was only one place he knew to go. Garrison Ford. The inquisitive reporter wouldn't be able to resist.

And so it happened. When Ford arrived home from work there was the miserable Horrowitz huddling in his back doorway.

Ford produced a bottle of vodka. 'Why were they after you?'

'I snitched. I put them away for a long time. The parole board never told me they were getting out, Sammy and The Burner.' He drank his vodka down and Ford promptly refilled it. It didn't warm the cold in his stomach.

'How did you know to leave the house? I mean, you got out just in time.'

Horrowitz grinned. 'A little bird told me,' he said.

Ford didn't believe him. You could never get the truth out of a guy like Horrowitz.

HOW SID VICIOUS GOT HIS NAME

Two roosters came to prominence on Paradise Island back in the day. One was Ricky the Rooster, who gave his life in defence of his liberties, and the liberties of his kind, and the other was Sid Vicious who hung onto his, despite the best efforts of some to hunt him down and wring his scrawny neck.

It would be nice to think that Sid was not born vicious, that he had been a cute, corn pecking little ball of feathers, but it wouldn't be true. Sid was born vicious and stayed that way, clawing his way up to the top in a chicken run half full of roosters.

The chicken run was looked after, in a fashion, by an overweight man called JJ 180, or just JJ for short. JJ's bulk gave the impression of largesse, but that was merely camouflage because, it was generally recognised, JJ was as mean as the proverbial meat axe. Anyone who did business with him was warned. Watch for the rip off! Stay clear of Miser Mickey. His most famous act of miserliness was his cost-free wedding. The venue was a local beach, the most beautiful spot under the sun, who could ask for more? There was no wedding dress or hired suits as everybody was invited to be naked, as were the bride and groom – what could be more glorious than the god-given human form?

His interest in having a chicken-run was entirely motivated by the prospect of free eggs. His theory was that chickens did not need to be fed expensive grains or mashes, that they might thrive on kitchen scraps and worms and other bugs they could scratch out of the ground. But he didn't have much in the way of kitchen scraps – he didn't hold with waste – and as the chickens pretty much ate all the worms and bugs in their chicken run in the first few days, the number of eggs they produced declined, along with JJ's interest in the venture.

What was the use of having hens if they didn't produce any eggs?

He didn't bother culling out the roosters.

So he let them out of their run to fend for themselves. Among those liberated was a young rooster of fine white and ginger plumage who was larger than the rest and ruled them with a capricious nastiness that brooked no opposition. While still behind mesh, the young Sid had developed his style, herding the other roosters into multiple rapes and harassment of the hens and giving the evil eye to any human that might intervene. JJ had conveniently forgotten that the reason people cull roosters is that, in the hen-house, there can be only one cock. Sid's answer to being incarcerated with other cocks was to viciously sodomise them and peck at their combs until they submitted. At that point, in Sid's mind, they were no different from hens.

Letting them all loose simply allowed Sid, who had not yet been named, a larger field of operation.

JJ was tickled by the antics of this now large, handsome rooster. He would laugh as the magnificent bird chased after a browbeaten hen, and slap his thigh in triumph when Sid mounted the poor hen and did his brief business. For a while things seemed to go okay. The birds were not as hungry, since there was all kinds of vegetation and snails and slugs around.

And there was always the garden.

Not that JJ had a garden, but his neighbours MoJo and Ella did, and that's where the trouble started.

Every morning, after dawn and after Sid had blessed the neighbourhood with his gargling cry, he would lead the charge through the inadequate wire fence into MoJo and Ella's garden.

MoJo complained, but JJ couldn't see what the problem was.

'Hens are good for the garden,' he explained to the sceptical MoJo. 'They eat all the pests, caterpillars, slugs, green beetles. It's a win-win.' Win-win was a big thing back in the day; everybody wanted one. In this case there was an extra win for JJ, who might breakfast on the eggs formed by the nutrients from the neighbours' garden. Win-win-win. If he could find the eggs.

'What about lettuce and cabbages and broccoli and…' and all those greens that hens relish, he thought. Just about everything.

'Okay, I'll put them back in the run,' JJ promised.

But he never did. Because if he put them back in the run he'd have to feed them, and that would cost money.

In the meantime, Sid set the pace for the return of his little flock to a feral state. He was the first to roost high up in the trees, higher up than even rats would care to go. He encouraged the hens to lay their eggs in places the clumsy human would never find, and was soon rewarded by a new generation of chicks that had no memory of life behind the mesh.

Sid, having full control over his flock, now set his sights on bigger game to subdue. A human being.

This human being was MoJo's niece, Clementine, staying with them in their caravan sleepout for a while. Every morning, the half-asleep teenager would have to make the trek from the sleep-out to the house, not any great distance, but the path wound through a patch of kanuka and ponga trees, and it was there Sid would lie in wait.

The first time MoJo and Ella, in the kitchen preparing breakfast, heard screams they rushed outside. Clementine was rushing towards them, still screaming while behind her, in the bush, there was a flash of white and ginger.

'Sid Vicious is after me,' she shouted.

Sid, now properly named, was flushed with his success and stalked arrogantly through his flock of subservient hens and cringing males. Cock of the walk, he was, and he made sure everybody knew it, even the humans. His first successful attack on the little female human was something of a revelation to Sid. He did not have to be afraid of the humans. He was in charge here. He could stand his ground and meet them in the eye. No longer would he, and his flock, be terrorised by humans; he would be the one doing the terrorising now. He signalled his change of status by strutting up and down outside the house, eyeballing the humans inside and, at regular intervals, letting forth his gargling cry.

The next morning, however, he received something of a rude shock. He lay in wait for the little female human, and along she came, but this time she was carrying a stick, and when Sid leapt into the air in front of her, squawking and flapping his magnificent wings, she batted at him and forced him to retreat. But not very far. He learned that by just staying out of range of the stick he could still engage in a variety of menacing activities, like circling around behind the girl, or moving beside her as he fixed her with his evil eye.

That day the larger male human came after him with a bigger stick and tried to swipe him but Sid easily evaded that attack. He simply retreated to his roosting tree, sat on a high branch and laughed at the impotence of his attacker.

He began to stalk the girl all the time, not just in the morning but whenever she was around. When she was in her caravan, he would wait outside for her, his chest puffed up. If she ventured into the garden, which he now considered to be his legitimate territory, he would track her and launch an attack when he saw that she was occupied with something else. He kept a firm eye on her stick, which she put down at her peril.

He also began to keep a sharper eye on the house, since inside there was another female, and Sid sensed that this older, larger female was more frightened of him than the young, stick-wielding one. He could see it in her eye and sense it in her uncertain movements when he approached.

At first this larger one was too big to attack directly, but his menacing tactics worked like a wonder. He developed an aggressive little dance which saw him hopping from one leg to the other while keeping an eye fixed on the object of his attention. It looked as if he was readying himself for an attack. One day the bigger, fatter male from next door came over and Sid kept his distance while the three older humans stood around and shouted at each other while every so often the young female would wave her stick warningly at Sid. After the shouting match, the big fat one made a pathetic attempt to catch Sid, trying to run after him with a bit of rope looped on the end of a stick.

Sid did not, however, forget the older female, and was only waiting for the right opportunity. That came one day when the woman was sitting outside in a chair reading. Sid approached, doing his little dance, and launched his attack, rising into the air and flying at her, claws first, screaming like a thousand hens.

The woman shrieked and shouted and ran inside, Sid scratching and flapping at her as she went. He was so given over to his triumphant fury that he nearly followed her all the way inside the house. He knew there was food in the house and sooner or later he would have to conquer this territory as well. Following the woman inside was the first step in that direction. When she finally slammed the door on him, Sid strode up and down in front of it, daring her to come out.

The next day disaster struck. The fat male from next door left out a whole lot of brightly coloured wheat for them to eat. Sid ate his share, but was there to observe some of the hens and smaller chicks fall over. Before long Sid felt dizzy too. He tried to crow but the gargle died in his throat. The world began to tip this way and that and Sid staggered to stay upright. The other roosters were going down now, keeling over. Sid was the last one left standing. Still pecking at the brightly coloured wheat.

When he awoke he was in a strange place. He was in the middle of dense bush with no sign of any humans. He could hear the sound of his own kind nearby and staggered to his feet. The dead bodies of his flock lay about him. Sid stalked among them, pecking here and there, but there was no response. He moved on and soon encountered another rooster. Weak as he was, Sid immediately attacked to establish his dominance.

In this place, the wild, he sensed an even larger field of operation, an infinitely greater world to subdue. But he was equal to the challenge. Oh, yes!

He puffed out his chest and let forth a long gargling cry.

BOBBY AND THE BUNKIN

Bobby had a little friend nobody else could see. He looked a bit like a dog, like a spaniel perhaps, but that was just a disguise. He was really a bunkin. Bunkins have some special powers, like being able to talk. Or turn into what looks like a burnt stick. That was very handy, especially when there were people around he didn't want to see him, which was everybody except Bobby.

That was how the bunkin had come into Bobby's life. He had been helping his father clean up their property and burn off all the sticks and leaves. Bobby was tossing some stuff on the fire when a stick in his hand spoke to him.

'Me burn don't,' the voice said.

The stick, which already looked half burned, wriggled in his hand and a sharp little face with a doggy snout peered up at him. 'Bunkin am I,' it said.

That was his introduction to the funnest pet a boy could wish for. He was better than a dog because he was more intelligent, but best of all he had two flying friends, Wumps and Woggie. Wumps was long and skinny and looked a bit like a mosquito gone wrong, whereas Woggie was short and tubby, like a flying teapot, and had problems staying up in the air.

The crazy things they did made Bobby laugh. When they got excited, which was often, they would bump into each other and nearly knock each other out of the air. They were completely faithful to the bunkin, and went everywhere he went. They were very shy. It took them ages to show themselves to Bobby. Even after he'd glimpsed them, they liked to hide behind the curtains in his bedroom or in his father's garden shed. He wasn't allowed to tell his parents about them, or about the bunkin.

One of the bunkin's peculiarities was that he liked apples. 'Apples want I,' he would declare when he got hungry, which was often. Bobby's mother was pleased that her son was apparently eating fruit at long last.

'Have as many apples as you can eat,' she said.

Their favourite activity was having adventures. They went everywhere and did all sorts of things. If people came along, Wumps and Woggie could vanish in an eyeblink and the bunkin could always turn himself into a burnt stick. And there was nothing more innocent than a boy wandering along with a stick in his hand.

A couple of times his parents nearly caught him out. They got to know the funny burnt stick he sometimes carried around.

'What's with that stick?' his mother asked him.

'It's not a stick,' he said. 'It's a wand.'

'Ah...' she gave her son a knowing look. 'What kind of spells can it do?'

'It can make nosy mothers disappear.'

'Ah! A useful stick.'

Although the bunkin could only speak a few words at a time, and Wumps and Woggie couldn't speak at all except to chitter to each other, they managed to have a fine time and Bobby learned stuff. He couldn't turn himself into a burnt stick, but he learned to lie so still he hardly existed at all. Wumps and Woggie taught him how to laugh. They had chirpy little voices that sounded like laughter anyway. From the bunkin he learned how to steal without anybody noticing.

Eventually however his mother figured out something was going on – it's hard to fool mothers long term – and she began to ask him some pointed questions. 'I think he has an imaginary friend,' Bobby heard his mother say to his father. 'Maybe more than one.'

'Is that bad?'

'I don't think so.'

Bobby thought it was handy to have people think he had imaginary friends; it was further camouflage for the bunkin and Wumps and Woggie. But it wasn't quite so handy when his mother began enticing his human friends home after school with fresh baked scones, and bought board games he was expected to play. He liked his friends and enjoyed the board games, but it wasn't as much fun as being out and about with the bunkin and his flying friends.

For his part, the bunkin refused to be introduced to Bobby's parents, or even his best friends. 'Seen be won't I,' he declared when Bobby suggested it, and Wumps and Woggie fluttered around in agreement. His mother didn't give up, and after a time took him to see Tina Tuppa who was known for her wisdom and psychic ability.

Tina sat with Bobby alone in her friendly garden, and Bobby told her about the bunkin and his friends. 'They won't show themselves though,' he said.

'There's one of them over there,' Tina said, pointing to her apple tree. 'He's hiding in the branches.'

'That's Wumps, he's the skinny one.'

'And the plump one is over there,' she said, pointing to her woodpile.

'That's Woggie. He enjoys playing with spiders and beetles.'

'He's got little fat wings.'

Bobby stared at the woman. 'Can you really see them? No one else can see them. I mean, they won't let other people see them.'

'They can't hide from me,' Tina said, and she pointed back to the apple tree. A furry snout was appearing above the grass around the base of the tree. Bobby grabbed Tina's hand. 'It's the bunkin,' he whispered. 'He loves apples.'

'I can see,' she whispered back. 'Ask him if he will let me see him.'

'He won't,' Bobby said, but ran over to the tree where the shy bunkin was hiding, and asked him.

'Seen be will I,' the bunkin declared, and stepped out of the grass so Tina could see him.

Tina clapped her hands. 'What a grand little creature,' she said. She sealed the friendship by offering the bunkin an apple. Even though it was still green, the bunkin polished it off in no time. 'Apples want I,' the bunkin said, and Tina gave it another one. Wumps and Woggie came out of hiding and were soon flitting and swooping around Tina Tuppa's garden twittering joyfully, annoying the blackbirds who were used to having the garden to themselves. The bunkin trotted about quite unselfconsciously putting his nose into this and that and making cryptic comments.

They were having so much fun, they didn't notice the arrival of Bobby's mother until almost too late. Bobby's mother glanced at the burnt stick in his lap.

'How did we get on?' she said.

'Wonderful,' Tina said. 'We've had a great time.'

After that, Bobby always knew he could go to Tina's place and let the bunkin and his friends roam free and do what they liked as long as they stayed in the garden and the little orchard, and they were never short of laughter. Their only concern was to ration the bunkin's consumption of green apples, as he had a tendency to get a belly ache.

One day Tina said to him, 'You know, Bobby, a day will come when you will lose the bunkin. You'll turn around and he'll be gone.'

'Why would I lose him?'

'A moment's carelessness,' she said. 'Little bits of the world can slip away in moments of forgetfulness.'

'I could never be that careless,' Bobby said.

Summers on Paradise Island can be long and hot, but after a time the apples ripened and fell from the tree, and the pumpkins, which had crawled all over the place, began to die back. Bobby started going to a quiet nearby beach and enjoyed swimming in the warm water. The water was always warmest late in the summer.

The beach didn't suit the bunkin. He got sand in his hair and had to sneeze a lot to get the sand out of his snout. Also, he wasn't too keen on the water; it wasn't his natural element. Wumps and Woggie didn't mind too much, as long as there was air they could fly, but they did get flustered if the wind got up.

The bunkin made it clear that he would rather be back in Tina Tuppa's garden. 'Garden want I,' it said, but Bobby had other, boyish things to do. The bunkin could always stay at home and pretend to be a burnt stick if he wanted to.

A couple of his friends, Robo and Whizz discovered his quiet beach. He liked them because they did exciting things at night like breaking into empty baches. They'd talk over their plans on the beach and made Bobby jealous. Sometimes they brought Whizz's dog with them. He was a terrier, and catching rats was his speciality.

'You know how he kills them,' Whizz enthused. 'He throws them up into the air and they land on their backs and snap their spines. Or he just rips their throats out.'

'Amazing,' Bobby said.

The bunkin didn't like dogs, terriers in particular. At the sight of a dog he would instantly turn into a burnt stick. This apparently worked, as Bobby had seen a dog sniff at the burnt stick and walk away.

Robo and Whizz could tell the most amazing lies. One day they arrived at Bobby's little beach full of excitement. They told him some fantastic story about breaking into a house and finding some bad videos and a tramp had jumped out at them and the police came. The story didn't make much sense, and while Whizz was trying to explain it, Robo wandered along the beach throwing things into the sea for his terrier to fetch.

Bobby was so busy trying to get the story straight he didn't notice Robo pick up a half-burned, bent stick and throw it into the water. What roused him was an alarmed twittering from the branches of a nearby pohutukawa tree. He jumped up and ran down to the water just in time to see the burnt stick lift on a wave and the terrier determinedly peddling in pursuit.

The three boys, and two unseen little creatures, watched intently as the terrier reached the point where the stick had been, but no longer was.

'Where is it?' Robo said.

'Maybe it sank,' Whizz said.

Those two quickly got sick of watching the dog swim around and Whizz called him back in. Only reluctantly did the dog obey, looking back over his shoulder all the time.

After the dog had arrived, Robo and Whizz left in search of further mischief, but Bobby stayed, staring at the spot where the burnt stick had vanished. Then he went into the water and started looking all around, going under looking around too, and feeling the seabed with his feet. He kept on doing that until it got dark. He didn't see Wumps and Woggie, and after a while he didn't hear them, but he knew they were there, watching him.

Eventually he had to give up and go home. It was just as Tina Tuppa had said.

That night he didn't eat any supper, and his mother was worried about him. All night he could think of nothing but the bunkin drowning.

The next day he went to see Tina Tuppa in her garden. Tina assured him that the bunkin was not dead. 'You can't drown bunkins,' she said.

She had seen Wumps and Woggie. Wumps was in the now bare apple tree, and Woggie was in the woodpile. That made Bobby happy.

With those two flying friends here, the bunkin could never be far away.

One night Bobby woke up to the sounds of a strange yowling noise. He was out of bed and half way to the window to see what he could see when he realised it was just a cat. Now it had become a more familiar growling sound, rising and falling as happens when a cat faces down an enemy. He peered out the window but could see nothing but the vague shapes of the night world.

As he turned to go back to bed he thought he heard a little piping voice say, 'Fierce she do seem,' but doubtless he just imagined it.

WALLY AND THE WOLF SPIDER

Wally was afraid of spiders. Even the word, arachnophobia, with its harsh sounds, conjured up visions of rapidly moving legs and clacking mandibles. Even pictures of spiders made him afraid, as if the spider was about to jump out of the picture at him. As far as Wally was concerned, the only good spider was a squashed spider.

Except he could be afraid of even squashed spiders. A couple of intact bent legs were enough.

To make matters worse, he had to listen to the pious preaching of his buddy, Mainland Mike, who was so unafraid of spiders that he could let one run up his bare arm, even run over his face, without flinching. He offered to show Wally how to overcome his fear. 'Just imagine it's a leaf tickling your skin. You're not afraid of leaves, are you?'

Wally wasn't afraid of leaves but he declined anyway; he didn't have that good an imagination.

'I had a friend once,' Mike, who seemed to have had a lot of friends, said, 'who was also afraid of our eight-legged friends. One time, in India it was, my friend was with a group of people who had to take refuge in a cave one night. The cave was full of spiders. My friend was terrified but had no choice. And you know what? Only one person was bitten by a spider that night and guess who that was?'

'I don't have to,' Wally said miserably. The story had only one moral, and here it comes…

'It was his fear, you see,' Mike went on, in case Wally hadn't gotten the point. 'The only person afraid was the only person to get bitten.' As far as Mike was concerned, this story illustrated some wonderful cosmic principle.

'I get it,' Wally said. Mike would go on about it till the cows came home.

Being arachnophobic was a distinct disadvantage on Paradise Island back in the day because the island was paradise for spiders too. Every garden, every woodpile, every unattended space sprouted spiders of all kinds. There were the fat black ones that made their webs in the eaves and on the windowsills, there were what people miscalled daddy-longlegs, the skinny ones with tiny bodies that swung with an awkward, mechanical gait all over everywhere. There was the shy but nasty white-tail.

And then there was the brown wolf spider looking for all the world like a smaller, slightly smaller, cousin of the fabled tarantula. Wolf spiders came big, and were rare enough to give someone like Wally a helluva shock when they appeared. Their favourite spot for suddenly turning up included the bath and the sink. Shame was his when he found one once stuck in the bath, unable to scale its smooth sides, and had to call his wife, Sweety Ann, to come and remove it for him so that he could take a bath. Sweetie Ann showed him just how easy it was to scoop the poor, lost spider into a jar and empty it into the garden unharmed.

'What's to stop it from coming back?' Wally asked.

'You're a lot bigger than it is,' Sweetie Ann said. People who didn't know what they were talking about often said that. As if sweet reason would make any difference.

'It's not a question of size,' Wally said.

'Mmmm.'

'We'll have to move back to the City,' Wally said.

'Not on your sweet life,' Sweetie Ann said.

He talked to Doctor Lovejoy about it. Lovejoy knew all about such things. He told Wally about Gautama the Buddha who had overcome his fear of death by meditating on a dead animal for some weeks, observing every stage of decay.

'Can't you just give me a pill?' Wally said.

Lovejoy asked him to write a list of all the things he found frightening about spiders, but he got too frightened to finish the list. In fact, even attempting it made him more aware of the spiders around him, and hence more afraid.

The crisis had to come, and it did, but not in the way Wally anticipated, which was that he would wake up one night, his face crawling with wolf spiders, trying to get into his mouth or up his nose.

Wally was a gib-stopper, and had some night work in front of him costing out a job. He'd done some painting on his own spider-infested house, whitewashed the wall with an undercoat. He loved a freshly whitewashed and conspicuously spiderless wall. He seldom ventured anywhere without his trusty can of white paint and tube of polyfill. The smell of the paint was pleasant, but the work was tedious. His mind drifted. Sweetie Ann was determined to stay on this accursed island, which had somehow got her in its grip. He'd seen it happen with others. They'd come to the island and suddenly, boom! they never wanted to leave, clung on for dear life. It wasn't an island, it was a lifeboat for the Sweetie Anns of this world.

While he was thus pleasantly engaged, Wally became aware that he was not the only presence in the room. There was another awareness in here with him. He went very still and listened. Sweetie Ann was out for the night, the house was very quiet. He looked up from his papers and there, starkly outlined against the white of the undercoat, sat a very large brown wolf spider. It had appeared from nowhere, he couldn't imagine it getting halfway across the wall without him seeing it, and it had been heading in his direction. No window was open, no obvious point of entry.

As soon as he saw it, it tensed its legs. It knows I'm aware of it, he thought, with the prescience of the terrified. It knew the moment he became aware of it. He was too struck to move, even to run, he could do nothing but sit there like an idiot and stare.

The spider stared back. There was no other way to describe it. Maybe that's the scariest thing about spiders, he thought, absurdly thinking of Dr Lovejoy's silly list – it's their *awareness*. This arachnid knew he was looking at it. It's a lot more frightened of you than you are of it, Sweetie Ann would say. But that was not necessarily reassuring; a frightened spider was no less scary. Anyway, Wally doubted that the spider was frightened. It didn't know fear as mammals did. It knew caution and calculation, but hardly fear. It knew when to attack and when to retreat and when to hold deadly still, as it was doing now. And that was another scary thing about spiders: their uncanny stillness.

It's waiting for me before it makes its move, he thought. I've interrupted its stealthy movement.

Since his desk was separated from the wall, it might crawl right past him at arm's length if it continued its course. But where was it marching off to? He imagined it leaping off the wall onto his desk.

Very slowly and carefully he moved his chair back a little and got to his feet. If he'd thought he'd feel better standing up he thought wrong. The spider didn't move, but the room throbbed with its presence.

'Okay buddy,' he said. 'What are you doing here?'

If he thought his voice would break the spell he thought wrong. His voice sounded quite unnatural in his ears, like a piece of movie dialogue. '*Okay buddy… time to meet your maker.*'

Except he'd never be able to kill it, not like this. Or would he? Lying handy, one of those thick *House and Garden* magazines suggested itself. It would make a helluva mess on his lovely pristine wall. Just thinking about it made him shudder. More undercoat would handle the mess, but whether he could deliver the blow or not was another matter. The idea was there, however, lodged in his brain. The image of a squashed spider on a white wall kept repeating.

Instead, he took a step closer. And another step. With each step the spider grew larger and more scary. It was a beauty, he had to give it that. A spectacular example of its genus. On closer inspection, he saw that its body was slimmer than the rounded shape of the dreaded tarantula. A sleek hunting machine. He could imagine how fast those long spiny legs might carry that sleek body to its prey. Even from the respectful distance he was keeping, he could see the nightmare elaboration of its mouth.

Then he did an incomprehensible thing. He took a step even closer. The creature shifted slightly in recognition of the move but did not break the spell. He was easily able to reach out and touch it. He didn't think it would leap off the wall at him. It wasn't that sort of spider. From its point of view, he would be hanging in its sky. He'd heard once that spiders don't see well, but one way or another it sensed him, and his every movement. Possibly his every thought. He hardly dared breathe. But he kept staring.

It was his fear he was looking at, and testing. He was testing himself without any idea why. A vague idea at the back of his mind that he was, mentally at least, doing Dr Lovejoy's ridiculous list, but that wasn't really it. For some incomprehensible reason he wanted to fill his vision with the horror of it. And he did, by leaning forward until he was a mere handbreadth or two away. He could savour every detail of it, perfectly outlined against the white wall.

A wild creature, no shy house spider. A bush spider, strayed into the house. Still it made no move. It had decided to wait him out, it seemed. Perhaps it sensed that he wasn't going to kill it. Imagine what he could tell Mainland Mike. That he stood there and had a telepathic communication with a spider. Mike would no doubt say how happy he was for Wally, finally overcoming his fear.

But Wally wasn't overcoming his fear. If anything he was feeding it.

Enough, he thought. I can't kill it so I'll have to do what Sweetie Ann would do and manoeuvre it into a jar and throw it outside. How he could get it into the jar was to be faced when he had one in his hand. A little trip to the kitchen and back. No more than twenty seconds. Then inspiration and courage would come.

He backed away, then quickly ran to the kitchen, grabbed an empty Agee jar and rushed back to his office.

The spider was gone. The wall was empty. It might never have been there. So now the question was, where was it?

He looked around him with growing dread. It might have made its way outside as mysteriously as it had found its way inside, but he couldn't bet on that. It was in here with him. Somewhere. He knew it and it knew it.

Now he faced a brutal choice. It was getting late. He was tired. He could go to bed and try to sleep or he could stand there all night watching for a scuttling movement in the shadows. Or he could completely play coward and go sleep in the car. A lovely sealed environment, but hardly comfortable.

The choice was his. How he responded would define him as a person, and his relationship to the arachnids of this world, his relationship to Sweetie Ann and Paradise Island and his life and everything.

The choice was his.

A THEATRICAL PRODUCTION

There comes a season in every small town where the minds of the young and the old-but-frivolous begin to turn towards a dramatic production of some kind. No serious drama, please, this is Paradise Island, after all. One year some brave soul staged Beckett's *Waiting for Godot* which Garrison Ford of the *Paradise Island Times* cruelly called, *Waiting for an Audience*. 'Godot never came, nor did the audience,' his review began.

Light Opera will do fine, thanks. If singers can be found.

This didn't stop the Island's theatrical luminary, Jean Jeanie, from harbouring ambitions. Jean Jeanie, the very same one immortalised by David Bowie (she would tell people in tearful moments), who had once had fame and stardom almost in her grasp (it was carefully rumoured), and who had aspirations that went beyond yet another enthusiastic production of *Annie Get your Gun*.

A way to realise her aspirations *and* cater to the Island's theatrical tastes came her way at a BBQ put on by retired politician Big Buster, the very same BBQ at which Sue Lake encountered some Sizzling Sausages. Rob Malarky, who didn't drink, was talking to Garrison Ford and Kendell, both drunk, when Jean Jeanie, playing herself for a change, attached herself to the group. She had to wave her blonde hair about a bit to pull the men's attention, but she managed to get Kendell aside and the writer, close-lipped about his work when sober, let slip that, purely for fun he hastened to say, he had done an adaption of Gilbert and Sullivan's famous light opera *The Pirates of Penzance*. Shorter. Modern setting. Leaning towards the absurd.

Jean Jeanie didn't hesitate. Straight away she started talking about funding. Before the BBQ ended she had pitched Sue Lake for Council funding and asked Garrison Ford, who apparently had a good voice for Leonard Cohen songs, if he would play Fredric, the lead male role. Ford had examined her as if she were a particularly small insect wriggling on the end of a particularly sharp pin and informed her, in a rumbling voice, that there was quite enough drama on the island as it was, thank you very much. All for free.

Well, he wasn't quite right for the part anyway. Perhaps he could do the Sergeant of Police, which called for a bass.

Soon the Café Résumé was buzzing with news of the play, the latest hot goss and shenanigans. At first it was all to do with the casting. Jean Jeanie reserved the role of Mabel for herself, being the only member of the cast who could really act and, at a pinch, sing, although describing her as a soprano was a bit hopeful. But it meant that she would swan about in the arms of Sean Bootcamp who would play Fredric. With the shoulders of a rugby player, because he was a rugby player, and the waist of a dancer, all he had to do was take off his shirt and nobody would care too much about his acting. An additional bonus was that the whole of the Paradise Island rugby team would come to leer and jeer and help pack out that important opening night.

Jean Jeanie had chosen the part of Mabel's sister Kate with equal care. The Doctor's wife, Melanie, was smart and pretty, and her legs would command attention as soon as they appeared on stage; shapely, provocative legs that they were. On the same grounds, she fancied Millie Millicent for the part of Mabel's second sister, Edith. Melanie and Millie would look wonderful with their arms around each other's waists, throwing their legs naughtily into the air in the 1930's style can-can dance scene Kendell had inserted into the script. Millie, however, proved incapable of any kind of singing and had to be relegated to the purely speaking role of Isobel, Mabel's third sister. That way she still got those legs in the air in the can-can scene. For a long time the role of Edith remained unfilled.

Jean Jeanie's big triumph was to convince Billy McCloud, the self styled Colonel, to play Major General Stanley. He was perfect for the part, even though it was only with generosity that his voice could be described as comic baritone. Keen to show what a good sport he was after his ritual burning of some modern art works, the Colonel threw himself into the part with gusto. He approved of the play because it was written in the 1870s; nothing good came after, that's for sure.

His inclusion meant that the Lions Club, of which Billy McCloud was a leading light, would attend the opening night in force.

The play was already in rehearsal when Jean Jeanie finally produced an Edith, and something of a sensation. The scheming sister was to be played by a schoolgirl, Xena. Word in the Café Résumé was that Jean Jeanie only took her on after she demonstrated her special 'zombie' dance, during the number, '*Stay, we must not lose our senses.*' And all the silly zombie dance consisted of was Xena chasing around the stage after a pirate, with her arms outstretched and her mouth open, croaking 'Brains! Brains!' to the brisk music. Could you believe that? Only on Paradise Island. Jean Jeanie must have lost her mind.

Still, Xena was a spunky kid and looked pretty good in the chorus line with Millie Millicent and the Doctor's wife Melanie, even if she did tend to miss the beat and throw her legs in the wrong direction. And besides, her inclusion ensured the attendance of half the school who would turn up to root for their popular classmate.

Jean Jeanie herself carefully cultivated the impression that she had indeed lost her mind. It put an edge into the rehearsals. Kept the excitement going. When she swept into the rehearsal room everybody paused and wondered, what's she going to do next, which was just the way she wanted it.

After warning that he did not have a baritone so much as a barista-tone, Rob Malarky agreed to play the Pirate King, adopting his new title with all the pride of his profession. He could learn his lines okay, and although he was no great actor, he knew how to enunciate, he knew how to throw his voice to the back of the room and he did so with every speech. Jean Jeanie found him rather litigious, however, always questioning the script and asking why people did things. Why would the Pirate King want to burst into song and sing '*Oh Men of Dark and Dismal Fate...*' at that point in the story, and so on.

The part of Ruth, 'a piratical maid of all work' was played by the indomitable Mavis Stretchly, who thought that making a fool of herself on stage would do no harm to her political career. People liked to laugh at their politicians; it eased their consciences at the polling both. She couldn't act to save her life, but she could boom and bluff and that was enough. Her supporters would turn up to clap and cheer. More willing bums on seats. Jean Jeanie just about had the whole community covered. Just about. She had a plan to take care of the rest.

Once the rehearsals had started new explosions of gossip went off in the air at the Café Résumé like bursts of anti aircraft fire. Believing that the character of Kate lacked interest, Kendell had inserted a scene in which Mabel discovers Fredric in bed with her sister. He assures her he only did it to make her jealous. She accepts his apology and together the three of them sing, '*Oh Happy day with joyous glee...*' Scandalously, this little addition of Kendell's involved Sean Bootcamp being in bed with Melanie on stage, in front of everybody, and the word was that they were doing a little rehearsing in the Doctor's rooms at night while the good Doctor was at home looking after their poor wee bairn.

Jean Jeanie was happy with Kendell's cunning little script change, but she was overjoyed at the rumours swirling about Sean and Melanie. Her plan was working. *Everybody* would be there on that first night; *nobody* would be able to resist the allure of seeing the alleged lovers in bed together in public. Oh happy opening night.

The only fly in the ointment from Jean Jeanie's point of view was that the rugged young Sean Bootcamp did indeed seem to be paying the pretty Doctor's wife a lot of attention, distracting him from his central role, which was to woo her, Mabel, aka Jean Jeanie.

Opening night went off with a bang, just as Jean Jeanie had hoped, with plenty of clapping, whistling, stomping and cheering, and a satisfying hush during the bedroom scene. Xena had swung her legs in the wrong direction and collapsed the chorus line into a tangle of limbs but everybody clapped furiously and the show went on. For some it was the highlight of the evening. The main problem was that Sean Bootcamp couldn't remember his lines. The prompt behind the curtain had plenty to do. The loud whispers, audible to all, made it appear that the doughty Fredric was hearing voices, some hissing demon, and there were those who thought this added interest to his character. A schizophrenic Fredric.

After the show, Jean Jeanie was all smiles, but she harboured a viper in her bosom. What she hadn't foreseen was that Melanie and her shapely legs would upstage and outshine her. That was not in the script, nor was the obvious chemistry between the lovers. Her plan, right from the start, to use the play to seduce Sean Bootcamp into bed for a hearty romp, had to be abandoned, and she did so with such thoroughness that she would have been offended at the suggestion she ever harboured the idea in the first place – but a bad taste, the venom of the viper, lingered. Her stratagems had been all too effective. Now she would hate the Doctor's wife for years to come. Forever.

It was all Kendell's fault.

She was not the only one bruised by the experience. Once he had discarded Major General Stanley for the night, Colonel Billy McCloud confronted Kendell, telling him in no uncertain terms that his rude cuts and additions had reshaped the story such a way that nobody could follow it. In fact, Kendell had deliberately sabotaged Gilbert and Sullivan's wonderful work, turning it into a travesty, and he wished he'd never had anything to do with it. Kendell was a pirate and a scoundrel.

'Things are more complicated now,' Big Buster said to him. 'It's all this jolly postmodernism that's to blame. Stories don't start and end properly. Everything has to be terribly clever. Nothing's sacred anymore, not even Gilbert and Sullivan.' Big Buster had a son who was doing a thesis on 'Politics in a Postmodern Age', so Buster was an authority on the matter.

'Then I've been conned,' the Colonel said. He looked like a man facing a firing squad.

The next day the Café Résumé exploded with stories. In a fit of pique Jean Jeanie had gone off with Garrison Ford, who was later to deny everything but wrote a suitably indulgent review. The Doctor had left the theatre looking very pale. Rob Malarky advised everybody to sue. Kendell was seen skulking off into the night. Xena had finally got her teeth into the neck of her pirate…

… everybody was looking forward to the second performance.

GARRISON FORD AND THE MERRY MERCENARY

Garrison Ford first ran into Ernie the Mercenary in the Paradise Island pub. Back in the day there was only one pub and everybody drank there. And, effectively, the pub only had one bar, and everybody drank there.

The Wednesday night crowd was pretty thin in the off-season, but the large, stout Ernie, sitting like a monarch on his throne before a frothing pint of Guinness, would have stood out in any crowd. Ford was immediately curious. He loved ferreting out the stories of visitors to the island, and the winter ones were always the most interesting. Sometimes he got a story out of them fit for the *Paradise Island Times*, the esteemed weekly for which he worked, and sometimes he didn't, but it didn't matter because he got plenty of drinks whatever. If he needed one, pretending to work was a good excuse for drinking.

He didn't feel confident about approaching the large stranger, until the man was joined by Boozy Buck and Johnny Rotten, and the pints multiplied on the table before them. The big man was chugging pints as if they were five-ounce glasses. Garrison knew Johnny Rotten as he knew just about everybody on the island through one connection or another, in this case the pub itself. Johnny had hammered his ear one time about how they should go into partnership and set up a new publishing business and newspaper; Ford would do all the work while Johnny drank all the profits. Great idea.

Johnny and Boozy Buck welcomed Ford to the table and introduced him to Ernie. Just Ernie. He wasn't giving out any second names. The men were blathering about something, Ford hardly paid attention. Ernie fascinated him. The man was big and going to seed, in his late forties or early fifties, with a round, whiskery face and a merry smile. Ford could see that at one time he had been a powerfully built man. Despite the pints, there was an alertness about him, in his scrunched up eyes. He was on his guard. So Ford sweetened things up by buying the next round, which hurt his pocket but then again, that was what booze always did. An occupational hazard.

Ernie accepted the pint with a gracious inclination of his head. Foaming Guinness just the way he liked it. Glasses were raised. 'To the quick and the dead,' Ernie toasted in a broad Irish accent. They drank to that. Boozy Buck and Johnny Rotten would drink to anything, whether it moved or not. Ford managed to get a bit of conversation going with Ernie, the usual thing, how did he enjoy the Island, how did he come to be here, how did he know these boozers and so on. The standard gambits with his usual jokes thrown in. They might have worked well with women, given that Ford was tall and dark and a little dopey around the edges, but it cut little ice with Ernie.

'He's suspicious of writers. Especially journalists,' Johnny Rotten said in his wheezing, tobacco cracked voice while Ernie was saying something to Boozy Buck about the fine art of concreting.

'Why?'

'You'd better ask him yourself,' Johnny said with twisted grin.

So Ford did. Indirectly. He began by asking Ernie what he did for living.

'I'm retired,' Ernie announced. He had way of talking which turned everything into an announcement.

'Lucky you. From what?'

Ernie looked at Ford for a long time before answering. Ford had the sensation of being picked apart and put back together again.

'Special Forces,' Ernie said. He didn't elaborate.

For Ford, a number of things fell into place. The reticence. The posture. The alertness. He glanced up at Johnny Rotten for confirmation.

'I thought you'd be interested,' Johnny Rotten, with his twisted grin, said.

Ford stood up and headed for the bar.

It was time to switch to gin.

The next day, after a late breakfast, Ford dropped in on Boozy Buck. Boozy, who was a bricklayer and a hard working as well as hard drinking man, owned a modest little house on a back road, a place he kept up with some pride. Ford figured that if anyone was to give him a straight answer about Ernie it would be Boozy, who didn't revel in secrets the way Johnny Rotten did. Ford could smell a story.

He found Boozy Buck, sitting outside on his deck with Johnny Rotten, a mate of theirs called The Duke, and Ernie, drinking red wine out of a cardboard cask and passing around spliffs. That was The Duke's main occupation, the careful mixing and rolling, fitting a piece of rolled up cardboard filched from the cigarette paper packet into one end, and getting it lit. As soon as one was away it was time to roll another.

They were talking politics and dealing to their hangovers.

'I'm not voting for anybody. Put 'em all up against a wall and shoot 'em,' Johnny Rotten said.

'Why spoil a good wall?' The Duke wanted to know.

'I didn't say it had to be a good wall.'

Boozy Buck was at his stereo putting on some Pogues.

'Is this Ernie guy for real?' Garrison asked quietly. The big man was waving away the spliffs.

'Try going at him with a weapon and see what happens,' Boozy said. 'Would you like a little snort of Tequila?'

'Don't mind if I do.'

Later, Ford managed to talk to Ernie alone while the other three were ra-rarring. The big man had abandoned the reticence of the night before and seemed happy to chat to Ford. 'Special Forces pulled me off the streets of Belfast when I was just a kid running around with a gun shooting Sinn Féin and filthy Papists. They trained me up to be a good killer. I was sent to assassinate Idi Amin, but he got away from me. Too smart.'

'That was Angola, wasn't it?' Ford asked, setting a little trap.

'Uganda,' Ernie corrected him. 'He really was a cannibal, you know. He ate schoolkids. Nice and tender. The nearest I got was twenty clicks. He knew Special Forces had sent someone. He kept on the move, and had doubles. You know, guys that looked just like him set up as decoys. He wasn't just in one place, he was everywhere.'

'I guess you've killed people. What's it like?'

'It's easy enough to point a gun and pull a trigger,' but the big man seemed uneasy, breaking out in a sweat as he quaffed his glass of Chateau Cardboard. Maybe a memory, Ford thought. Memories can be persistent.

'I got out of the Specials because they were killing too many Irishmen,' Ernie said, looking out over the peaceful Paradise Island landscape. 'I worked as a mercenary. Went all over. Laos, Afghanistan. Wherever the Yanks go there is plenty of wet work.'

Wet work! Ford was thrilled to meet someone who could casually use that expression, one which Ford had only encountered in American thrillers. At the same time he wondered if this was an elaborate joke. The way Johnny Rotten kept looking at him and nodding his head as if to say, *you see, you see* seemed suspicious to Ford, but then again, he did have a tendency to paranoia when he got stoned. A little drink was the answer to that.

A couple of days later, Ford got a call from Boozy Buck. Would Ford like to visit? They had an issue to discuss. The scene was at Boozy Buck's again, and the cast was the same. This time they sat inside around a low coffee table on which sat a large bottle of Glenfiddich.

'The thing is,' Johnny Rotten said in his wheezy voice, 'Ernie wonders if you could vouch for him.'

'How?'

'With Immigration. They're sending a guy to interview him.'

Ford tossed back his whisky and set his glass down. As the spliff came his way he wondered if this was not a set up. 'Why?'

'The thing is,' Ernie said, 'I'm having a bit of a breakdown. That's what I'm doing here. Paradise is a good place for a nervous breakdown.' The big man laughed but Ford could see the sweat on his forehead. God knows what it was costing him just to sit there and talk like this, with apparent calm. 'My visa's still good for another three months but they want to deport me.'

'Why?'

'Because I'm classified as a lethal weapon. I'm trained. I could kill someone with my pinky.' He wriggled his little finger. 'If I went berserk, I could kill a lot of people.'

'Will you go berserk?'

'Naaa. That's not where this is heading.'

It wasn't until a few days later, when Ford drove Ernie somewhere in his car that he had the opportunity to dig deeper.

'What's this really about? What's happening here?'

'Death has never bothered me. In Laos a mate of mine was blown to pieces right beside me and it was just another day at the office. I've been in places where the air is full of flying shrapnel and never turned a hair. I didn't care. I had no fear. That's what made me a good mercenary. I was able to make a lot of money. I've got a bunch of gold bars in Jo'berg for body-guarding a guy everybody wanted to kill. Now, now I can't walk outside without having a panic attack. Just getting on the ferry the other day was worse than any shoot-out. As soon as I walked on board I knew exactly how many people were there, and who looked dodgy. If I wanted to, I could hear a conversation from the other side of the room, even with the ferry engines booming. I held on to the table so hard it just about broke apart.'

'Maybe it's all catching up with you.'

'No, it's the kid. He was dying of cancer and I had to sit beside his bed and I couldn't do it. I'd seen women and kids die plenty of times. But I couldn't sit beside one kid's bed while he died and that was the end of me. I was finished, washed up. I came as far as I could to get away.

'Who was the kid?'

'That doesn't matter. What matters is I couldn't sit with him while he died, which is all I had to do.'

A week later the Immigration guy arrived and Ford turned up to vouch for Ernie as best he could. A boring set of questions that Ernie fielded well enough. The only moment of excitement was when the official asked Ernie how often he drank.

'Every night,' said Ernie.

'How much?'

'About twelve pints.'

The official wrote it down.

Ernie wasn't deported, but left the island soon after. Boozy Buck heard that he was up north working as a security guard. Ford tried to write up the story in some way that would make sense, and perhaps sell to one of those glossy periodicals, but it didn't quite work. There was no data, no chequerboard of facts that underpinned any good story. For all he knew, Ernie might have been a compulsive liar. And maybe Johnny Rotten knew. Was in on the joke.

There were all kinds of nutters floating around. Paradise Island seemed to attract them. Ford wondered if he himself was not one of them.

And he never stopped wondering what would have happened if he'd put Ernie to the test, gone at him the way Boozy Buck suggested.

As it was now, he'd never know.

RICKY AND THE ROWDY ROOSTER

While God's paradise may be eternal and unchanging, the same can't be said of Paradise Island. Even those who arrived first, and gazed upon its wonders, were quick to set about changing it. Paradise can always be improved.

If our town planners ever get to heaven, which is unlikely, their first thought will be that the place needs some kerb and channeling. And some street lights. And that straight gate and narrow way could do with tar-sealing. Even those Pearly Gates, impressive as they are, need a makeover.

Gentrification is the word local *Paradise Island Times* reporter Garrison Ford pulled out of the thesaurus. A seeping, insidious process seemingly beyond human control in which the landscape and surrounds becomes smartened, trimmed and tamed – with lashings of concrete. Street lights, footpaths, hedges and lawns with short-back-and-sides cuts, tar-sealed roads with shiny SUVs driving on them, all appear like some creeping alternate reality. Suburbanisation is another word Ford pulled from his wellspring of inspiration.

We are gentrifying the ex-burbs, he wrote, then crossed it out. Words like these bothered Blackbeard the editor, especially two in one line.

Because of its insidious nature – a street light here, a piece of footpath there – the process was never dramatic enough to arouse public protest or anything more than the usual grumbling and a letter or two to the *PITs*. There was the case of the lone resident of a back street, Yani Yanos, who claimed that the garishly orange street light, recently installed, infringed his human rights, in particular his right to the dark and unsullied night sky. Light pollution became the buzz phrase of the hour, and that was worth a few columns, but the issue had no legs. Even a few spirited letters as to whether street lights deter or encourage intruders, and the information, ferreted out by the intrepid reporter Garrison Ford himself, that the Council had picked up the street lights cheap from a pile the City airport discarded, couldn't fire the issue. Cheap and gaudy from the start, Yanos said, and nobody disagreed much, but nobody cared much either.

Those who came to live on Paradise Island from the City, tended to bring the City with them, much in the way plague victims spread the disease by fleeing from it. Town planners and developers could see a time coming when the whole of Paradise Island would be one big suburb, there was money to be made and they wanted a piece of it.

Then along came Ricky and his rebellious rooster and Ford had what he wanted. Ricky himself was perfect. Born on the island back in the day when automobiles were a rare sight, it seemed, and a hardcase old bugger for sure, Ricky Roundtree was a perfect poster boy for the old Paradise Island, the one in people's imaginations; but it was his rooster, Bert the Bold who really caught the public imagination.

Now there was a bird who just loved the camera.

Sitting on his favourite fence post, with his head held high, his wattles puffed up, one suspicious eye on the camera, he was very photogenic.

It is said that pets and their owners will often, over time, come to resemble each other. A constant mirroring effect, perhaps, Ford thought. In any case it worked for Ricky and Bert. Put them side by side in a photo, get the angle right, and you have the Rooster Rebels, two brave souls, their beaks set against a cruel and heartless City Bureaucracy.

It was the irascible Bert who was the cause of all the trouble. He liked to crow at dawn, announce the day to all and sundry. He was a one-bird dawn chorus. Somebody had complained to the Council and the Council was in turn obliged to investigate the complaint. Bob Knox, the suit who landed the job of sorting it out, was a decent sort of fellow and not the least bit cruel and heartless. He loved his children as much as Ricky loved his rooster, but when he investigated district statutes he discovered that it was illegal to have poultry within suburban zones, and the street where Ricky and Bert lived now fell into that zone. Whether he was a decent bloke or not, he had to find on behalf of the complainant.

He decided on the softly-softly approach and so began with a couple of mild letters to Ricky pointing out the legalities of the situation, and Ricky immediately took them to Garrison Ford who quietly rubbed his hands in anticipation. In an extraordinary show of professional commitment, Ford fought through his hangover and got up before dawn in time to catch Bert *flagrante delicto*, as it were, in full throat, his head thrown back. Here was the very offence itself taking place. It made a wonderful front cover and stirred up all sorts of comment.

Ricky of course had his supporters. What about loud trucks, much louder than a rooster, why haven't they been banned? his supporters asked. But not everybody agreed. 'I could scrag that bloody rooster,' was a typical comment.

Local bush lawyer Rob Malarky got in on the act with the argument that because Ricky had lived in the area all his life, and had always had poultry – Bert was merely the latest in a long line of Berts – fairness and compassion dictated that they both be left alone. The implication was clear. Ricky was in his eighties, and the life of a Rooster, however plucky, is a short one; just wait a while and the problem will go away.

The pragmatism of this appealed to Bob Knox, but since the publicity in *PITs* he had received further complaints, mostly from new residents on the island. His bosses further up the food chain had noticed, much to their amusement, the situation he was in and were keen to see how he would handle it. Rooster jokes were already flying around the office. Sitting on his hands didn't seem like an option, not when some were already suggesting that he would chicken out. Ha ha.

So he had to publicly take issue with Rob Malarky, and the Rob versus Bob battle was on. Somebody took a recording of Bert in full cry and played it on the local radio station at 6 a.m. so that everybody could wake up to Bert's screech and gargle. That caused the national media to pick up on it as a joke story. Ford's photo of Ricky and Bert with their beaks set at a determined angle appeared in the Capital's newspaper. Paradise Island was good for joke stories, as far as the National Media was concerned, and Ricky and the Rooster were worth a laugh. Better than the story of the mad hippie who went around sabotaging people's septic tanks in the name of composting toilets. Bert became something of a celebrity.

Ford rode the wave he himself had created. He was looking pretty cocky, someone commented. And so he should have been. Blackbeard the Editor was pleased. The *PITs* office was humming. There was Ford lounging back in his chair chatting to tabloid reporters like a Pulitzer Prize winner. Talk of the TV coming was rife. Rooster lovers staged a march and Kendell wrote a poem. Everybody was talking about gentrification. Sales of the *PITs* soared and Blackbeard, inspired by the numbers, wrote several editorials that were, in his mind, models of clear thinking and fine rhetoric, recalling the great days of Fleet Street journalism. Anti-gentrification protesters dressed up in rooster suits and disrupted a Council meeting with their crowing and clucking – and had to be ejected.

You might say that everybody, except Bert's tired victims, was happy.

Then tragedy struck.

One night, Ricky died in his sleep, and Bert subsequently went into mourning. The lone bird did a silent vigil on his favourite gatepost, giving everyone who passed by the evil eye and an occasional dreary squawk. Dawn came up over the silent hills of Paradise Island. Bert, it seemed, had fallen quiet forever. Ford took a photo of Bert sitting on the coffin looking wrathful but Blackbeard wouldn't publish it.

With the death of Ricky and the moody silence of his bird, something of the old Paradise Island died, many felt. This is the way the present slips into the past, bit by bit, and one morning you wake up and Paradise has changed. For a few days, Bert's silence at dawn rang as loud as his former crowing.

Ford got drunk with Kendell after Ricky's funeral.

'What's going to happen to Bert now?' Kendell asked.

Ford drew his finger across this throat.

Kendell looked shocked. This was worth a poem.

'A homeless bird. He's being fed by a neighbour right now, but that can't last. Animal control will pick him up and…

'…put him down.'

'That's right. It's the most humane thing to do.'

'Can't he be adopted? A friend or neighbour.'

'Not according to Bob Knox. Besides, nobody wants him.'

The two men drank in silence, thinking about that. A scraggy, rowdy old bird, who would want it? Bert was fine as a symbol but…

'…not in my backyard,' Ford said.

They both laughed.

'Let's liberate it,' Kendell said.

'What? Read it the Communist Manifesto?'

'No. Capture it and take it into the wild where it might survive. It can then become Bert the legendary rooster who never died, just like the spirit of this island never dies. You know, *If you listen hard you can hear his dawn cry…*'

'Let's do it then,' said Ford.

When Ford and Kendell got drunk together they always came up with some madcap plan. Few were ever realised. In this case, they gave it a go, sneaked around to Ricky's old place with giggling intent.

Bert was nowhere to be found. He'd already made his break for freedom, struck a blow for independence.

It takes more than a couple of fumbling drunks to catch a wily old bird like Bert.

KENDELL AND THE KILLER CHEMICALS

In the early days, before he got swallowed up by words, Alex Kendell took a keen interest in the politics of Paradise Island. In those days, before it got swallowed up by the nearest city, and was still largely self-governing, Island politics was an endless source of outrage and entertainment. An ongoing soap opera in which everybody had a part to play.

Kendell managed to keep out of sight until Marie Baigent approached him claiming that the cocktail of chemicals used to control the weeds on the roadside was making her children sick. They were anaemic and had sores on their arms. Intrigued by the notion of a cocktail of chemicals, Kendell did some research and found that it was so; at least six different chemicals were used in the roadside mix. There was a history of safety concerns about each one of them, but their action as a cocktail was completely unknown. It was chemical cowboy country, Kendell told Marie.

Kendell was fascinated and talked about it to Sue Lake, who saw the political potential in it. A populist issue like this must have its uses. Kendell also spoke to the reporter from the local newspaper, the *Paradise Island Times*. The *PITs*, as it was known.

'It's all a load of crapula,' Ford told Kendell. Ford had seen many a nutcase come and go and more wacky causes than wacky-baccy, and this roadside spraying business had all the hallmarks of a hobbyhorse. Say what you will about Ford, and Kendell said plenty, he had a fine nose for bullshit. This chemical kerfuffle reminded him of the nutcase with the printing press who from time to time printed alarmist pamphlets warning that the rat population at the rubbish dump had reached a critical threshold and the island was about to explode with rodents unless the Council took immediate action. Now, apparently, all the children on the island were being poisoned by evil chemical companies and their dupes in Council.

As far as Ford could see, Alex Kendell was a nutcase being used by Sue Lake to further her desire to be queen of the island, and that Marie

Baigent was an overwrought solo mum paranoid about her children. Like hypochondria except you transfer the feeling to someone else and become fixated on *their* health. There had to be a name for it.

In a killer conversation over a morning coffee Ford put it to Kendell straight.

'You're just a screwball wingnut fruitcake. Greenie conspiracy freak artist.' He threw in a sneer for good measure, and he was good at sneering.

Kendell laughed out loud and gave Ford a big appreciative grin. He couldn't remember when he'd last been so finely insulted. Maybe in his poetry performance days.

That laugh nearly blew Ford, who hadn't had his first shot of vodka for the day, off his stool. That grin began to change Ford's mind about Kendell. Nutcases don't normally have a sense of humour, at least not where their own fixations are concerned.

Kendell began to gather around himself something of a coterie of nutcases, however, most of the Ngati Hippy, and well known agitators like Russel Northrop and Jean Jeanie. Jean Jeanie, who boasted about once being a member of a famous theatre troupe, got dressed up as an organophosphate molecule, that is, with lots of coloured balloons, and went rushing in and out of the shops on the main street making spraying noises, which sounded like snakes hissing, much to the bewilderment of shopkeepers and patrons. Ford got some great shots that made everybody look stupid. His editor, Blackbeard, was only too happy to publish them. Making agitators look stupid was one of the central objectives of the *PITs*.

The political establishment braced itself for the political silly season. Landowners started spraying at night to avoid detection by Northrop and his green vigilantes. The island's vineyards issued placating statements.

These people are the New Puritans, Blackbeard sternly declared in an editorial, *eager to force their purity on others with an ideological zeal not seen since the Crusades.*

'This is wonderful stuff,' Kendell said to Ford, pointing at the editorial. 'The most sublime heights of rhetoric. This guy should have his own band.' Kendell himself had written a submission so large and detailed that nobody was likely to read it. Everybody read Blackbeard's editorials.

Ford, who had had his first vodka of the day on that occasion, found himself grinning foolishly. He was learning that Kendell's humour cut in all directions. Nobody was spared.

The stakes were raised when Monsanto, a major chemical company, sent two senior representatives to the island to address the Council and set everybody straight on the safety of their product.

'See!' Kendell said to Ford, 'If I'm such a nutcase, why would Monsanto bother sending a couple of heavy guns to deal with it? Where there's smoke, there's fire.'

'Nope,' Ford said, stubbing out his cigarette. 'Where there's smoke there's smoke.'

'Whatever happened to the spirit of investigative journalism in this country?' Kendell wanted to know. 'You're just an underpaid PR man for Big Pharma.'

Ford agreed with the underpaid part. Local reporters like himself were a dying breed, and Ford had often cast envious eyes on his mates in PR who seemed to be doing very nicely thank you with wives and mortgages and yachts. Ford had been aboard some of those yachts, and some of the wives too, and found the lifestyle sweet. All these years he had been beached on Paradise Island, writing up the week's Playcentre news. There had to be more to life.

At this point, enter stage left, Alan Axely, the council worker who mixed the chemicals and did the spraying. Alan Axely was a reliable man, a straight shooter, solid rural NZ stock. Moved and talked like a farmer. Did his job well and kept the weeds off the roadsides, which was what he was paid to do. He knew bloody well the chemicals were harmless to people; he mixed them himself with a stick. Even stuck his hand in from time to time. Been around them for years. He didn't pansy about in all that protective gear either; the company only recommended that to cover their asses. The city sprayers did it in shorts and boots and t-shirts. The city councils actively encouraged that, since the sight of men dressed in spacesuits with spray packs tended to unsettle people and cause anxieties.

Alan had intended to visit the *PITs* himself, although he was a shy man, and tell everybody that it was a big fuss about nothing. Kendell should stick to fantasy. A couple of sympathetic chemical company reps advised him, however, to hold back for the right moment.

The crisis came and the farce was played out in the drab Paradise Island council chamber. The cast were all assembled. The nine council members, all honourable with the best interests of the island at heart, even if most were property owners and chemical users themselves. The Monsanto suits with their glossy handouts tried to look inconspicuous. Kendell's rabble was stretched to include unlikely suspects such as MoJo, his neighbour JJ, Cess

Claw the boatbuilder, Green Mazie the witch, and Stumpy Stewart who had brought along his penny whistle. Jean Jeanie was *in character* as a bird dying from spraydrift. Or perhaps a wilting flower. Even Millie Millicent was there showing off her legs to everybody in need of distraction. Which was everybody.

It was a show of community force. At least that's what Kendell told Ford before the show began. Ford was sceptical, as was his editor, Blackbeard, who had turned up to witness the occasion for himself. But they weren't saying anything. The press had gone into lockdown. 'Where is the TV?' Sue Lake wanted to know.

The show proceeded much as Ford expected, everybody performing their parts. Like all local political meetings of a highly charged kind, the events bordered on farce, and Ford struggled to keep the crooked, vodka-inspired grin off his silly face. Every now and then he would go to the toilet where he could chug a mini vodka while relieving himself of the previous one – it took less time that way – and he didn't miss much. Everybody had a say. Marie Baigent spoke on behalf of her children, and all children on the island. Stumpy Stewart made a strong plea for creating activities for teenagers on the island, bringing a warm round of applause. Green Mazie said she had a crystal large enough to heal the bad energies of the whole island, and everybody was invited to her crystal burying ceremony.

Then the Monsanto suits pulled out their ace in the hole. Alan Axely. Their man on the ground. A respected local whose job was at stake. A decent bloke all round. A down to earth bloke. He'd soon deal to the scaremongering.

And he did. Telling it just like it was. He described the 'cocktail effect' argument, in which individual chemicals magically enhanced their powers when mixed with others, as superstition. He'd just finished this devastating attack when one of the Councillors, who had been studying Kendell's sprawling submission, said,

'Excuse me Mr Axely, but can we see your arms.'

A hush fell over the room.

'I've got nothing to hide,' he said.

He mostly wore long sleeves, except when he was mixing the chemicals – the stuff tended to get into clothing and make it smelly. Now, with evident reluctance, he pulled his sleeves up.

Everybody in the room stared at the sores that ran all the way up his arms.

'I've got eczema. It's a medical condition. It's got nothing to do with the chemicals.' There was no scientific evidence that would put those sores on his arms anywhere near the chemical cocktails he mixed for the roadsides, but it was too late. It was all over. The Council voted to stop roadside spraying. The men from Monsanto beat a retreat and Stumpy blew on his pennywhistle. Then everybody went home.

Except for Kendell and Ford who got very drunk together and became friends for life – the Booze Brothers, as they were later to be called. Ford said the island needed more nutcases of Kendell's quality, and Kendell said the island needed more intrepid reporters just like Ford, who had to write up the story with a hangover the next morning, which was par for the course.

Everybody lived happily ever after. Even Alan Axely, who got another job and whose eczema subsequently faded away as mysteriously as it appeared.

A QUEER ROOSTER

Politics. It was a terrible job but somebody had to do it.

Mavis Stretchly wouldn't go to work in the morning until she could say that to herself in the mirror with a straight face. It meant she was quite often late. That straight face didn't look as young as it once had.

Truth was, she hadn't had such a great time since Lucy died, and it sure beat the hell out of hairdressing. More lucrative too, potentially. From trimming hair to trimming budgets was only a snip or two away; they didn't call her the Razor Queen for nothing.

'It's a helluva job but somebody has to do it,' she said. Better this time. No smirk. The smirk was a dead giveaway. Even their super bland Prime Minister smirked from time to time. An occupational hazard.

Since going into politics, even getting dressed had become fun. She liked strong, primary colours and bold designs, and had a hankering for the padded power shoulders of the 1980's corporate women. *Power dressing*, they called it. These padded shoulders having the fortunate side effect of making corporate waists look slimmer. She wanted her clothes to announce her as a woman on the move, a woman who was going somewhere, a woman capable of dragging Paradise Island out of its sloth and into the 21st Century.

And all she had to do for her money was sit around a big table feeling important and dishing it out to left-wing losers and community bleeding hearts. Her own feeling, which she only shared with close associates, was that there was far too much riff-raff on the island. Too many old cars without warrants or regos creeping around the back streets. Hippies and left-wing loonies, people living in boats, beneficiaries in bare feet, kids not getting to school, starry-eyed environmentalists and tree-huggers, community do-gooders and dope smokers, earnest cyclists – the dismal list went on forever. That was Paradise Island for you: a human garbage dump.

She had a vision of a much sprucer island with a more robust culture. A cleaned up island, gleaming in the sun, doors wide open to that special class of tourist who didn't come here to see riff-raff. And there was nobody better to articulate that vision than herself, Mavis Stretchly, soon to be the woman of the moment. If she played her cards right.

As usual, around this hour of the morning, when Mavis was hesitating between the yellow and the blue blouse, the red phone rang. That would be her colleague and boss, Sue Lake or Madam Slasher to her friends, to talk about the path opening ceremony later that day. Sue Lake liked things to go exactly as planned, and liked to plan down to the last detail.

'We have a problem,' Sue Lake said.

The path opening ceremony was a carefully designed piece of political theatre for election year. The press was lined up. The faithful were lined up. Sue Lake had written a speech which not so subtly presented her as a staunch defender of public walkways. There were not supposed to be any problems.

Most of these walkways had been opened by her predecessor, and Sue had attacked them on the grounds of ratepayer expense, but once elected as Representative, essentially the Mayor of the Island, it had become expedient to continue the policy even while quietly winding it down.

'We have a fly in the ointment,' Sue Lake said.

'Let me guess. Russel Northrop.'

'He's going to make a scene.'

Then of course it is the 'scene' that becomes the media focus rather than Sue Lake. Mavis didn't ask how Sue Lake knew this. Sue had her spies everywhere. She liked to cover her bases.

Mavis thought this over, trying to see some advantage in it for herself. In terms of her own political ambitions, it would be best to distance herself from Sue and the public walkways policy, particularly if there was going to be a scene.

Sue Lake didn't have to spell out what Northrop would say. He had a list of complaints against landowners adjacent to the paths. These evil landowners were intent on sabotaging the track where it skirted their boundary, or attempting to annex the land one way or another. A large pile of garden weeds on a track. A shed that pushed its boundary. Deceptively placed Private Property signs. Another list that went on and on.

The question was, what would he do? Placards were not really Northrop's style.

Privately, Mavis thought that the paths had been put in provocatively close to adjacent properties. Some landowners felt their privacy compromised, and Mavis's sympathies were with them rather than busybodies like Northrop who of course didn't own any property, didn't pay rent and sponged off friends – if the stories she had heard were true. A compulsive agitator and troublemaker.

Moreover, Northrop had had it in for Sue Lake in a big way after somebody overheard her describing him as 'a queer rooster.' She didn't improve matters by trying to explain that she didn't mean 'queer' as in gay but as in unusual or eccentric. This confused people as Northrop wasn't gay. Northrop had gone apeshit. Roosters, he said, were irascible, aggressive, sexist, bullying birds, and he demanded she withdraw the comment. Sue Lake refused. 'Perhaps my idioms are a bit out of date,' was the best she could manage.

'What can we do?'

'I have a few ideas.' Sue Lake, who liked to play her cards close to her chest, always had a few ideas. She was the consummate back room player. Mavis had learned a lot from her.

As soon as the call was finished Mavis made another one.

'If we don't use them, we'll lose them…' Sue Lake was well into her speech, Mavis Stretchly by her side. The faithful had turned up and the press was there. Sue had sprung her little surprise, bringing along two of the major landowners concerned to speak in favour of public walkways and thus take the wind out of Northrop's sails.

But not all was going as planned.

For one thing the weather was turning against them. Clear skies had given way to dark clouds and rain threatened. For another, the local reporter for the *Paradise Island Times*, Garrison Ford, a tall amiable man with a boyish smile, was drunk. One of the landowners was turning sour on the idea. He was only there because he owed Sue Lake a favour.

The event was turning soggy. Another dreary, political duty. Northrop had not appeared. The faithful stood around and stared with dazed looks on their faces at the piece of green ribbon tied across the new walking track. The local reporter had gone to sleep. Mavis Stretchly was having trouble with her smile. Sue Lake was busy telling the birds and the lowering sky about the importance of keeping public lands in public hands.

A scrawny rooster in bright shining plumage came flapping and squawking, apparently out of thin air, right over their heads, landing in front of Sue Lake. Like a cut-out from a world of colour. Sue Lake's grey voice faltered. A second and third bird came out of the trees. One of them jumped at her. It was Sid Vicious, a well known feral rooster with a history. Sue Lake screamed and jumped backwards. The faithful scattered. Garrison Ford woke up and grabbed his camera. More birds followed. There were at least half a dozen now, all kicking and screaming as wheat followed them out of the sky. The local reporter got a good shot of Sue Lake fending off Sid Vicious. It began to rain.

Sue Lake and Mavis Stretchly beat a hasty retreat.

'I'll kill that Northrop,' Sue Lake said.

Off in the bush Mavis thought she caught a glimpse of a man-sized rooster slipping between the trees. Heard a triumphant squawk.

Handy fellow, that Northrop.

But Sue Lake got the last laugh. She normally did. Quietly, she ordered some council workers to do a cull and get rid of Northrop's little army of feral roosters. Most of these birds had been abandoned by people who only wanted laying hens and were too squeamish to kill the cocks. Sue Lake knew people who weren't so squeamish, and who owed Northrop one.

A couple of dead roosters, with their necks wrung, left outside Northrop's door, got the message across. When Garrison Ford rang her about that, Sue Lake coolly told him that Northrop had done it himself, and Ford agreed with her. Northrop was crazy enough to do anything.

'It's become personal with him,' she said.

But Sue Lake didn't stop there. She rang up Tom Tommyknocker the cop, whose main interest was in leading a quiet life, to arrest Northrop for vagrancy.

'I can't make that stick, not if he's staying with a friend,' Tom said. He had enough trouble with real vagrants like Buckie Bozo or small time operators like Minute Ago.

'That doesn't matter,' Sue said.

Once more Mavis had to take her hat off to Sue Lake. She knew how to deal with her opponents, another important lesson for Mavis.

Then she got a call from Sue Lake, and learned yet a further important lesson.

'I know who put Northrop up to that little escapade with the roosters,' she said.

'Did somebody have to put him up to it?' Mavis said.

'Yes. He's not that bright. I mean not that devious.'

'I'm not so sure about that.'

'I am. And there's one thing you need to remember.' Sue Lake's voice had become as sweet as the coconut-ice at a school fundraiser.

'What's that?'

'I never forget.'

Politics. A terrible job but somebody had to do it.

ART IS A WAY OF LOOKING

Unless he took too great an interest in the Shire Weed, there wasn't much for the local cop to do on Paradise Island, not back in the day.

Sometimes Tom Tommyknocker would get a get a call from MoJo Mayhem about his neighbours of the time, Buddy and Queenie, who got drunk and fought and threw bottles in the air. They would always round on Tom if he turned up to keep the peace. 'Who asked you to stick you nose in?' Queenie would shriek.

Next morning empty bottles would land on MoJo and Ella's lawn.

Not much for Tom to do but round up drunks – until the great art thefts began. Works of local artists began disappearing from their homes. Clever burglaries. Tom knew he had limited time to get to the bottom of it before the City sent over some detectives to humiliate him. A couple of the missing paintings had been worth some money.

The Café Résumé was abuzz with theories and speculations. Garrison Ford of the local rag, the *Paradise Island Times*, maintained it was professionals, a gang from the City, working the island over. They must be using a vehicle to get the stuff off-island. Tricksy Claw was of the opinion that an artist was doing this, a local artist who was jealous of the achievement of his or her peers. Tricksy counted herself as one of the local artists, and she would not be surprised if somebody was jealous of her. Others had other ideas. Some, like JJ–180, maliciously suggested that the artists were in a conspiracy to steal their own work and so drum up interest in their mediocre productions.

Tom talked to everybody but nobody had a shred of evidence, just a whole lot of theories. Find the motivation and you find the perp, he told himself. A picture did begin to emerge. According to the *PIT* reporter Ford, it was all to do with gentrification. More tourists were coming to the island, attracting more arts and crafts people like flies to a carcass. Wherever there was money changing hands, there were thieves, but Tom had to ask, with no answer in sight, why anybody would steal these artefacts. Experts assured him that private collectors would not be interested; this local stuff was just not in that league. And it wasn't worth going to the trouble for the junk shop and flea market trade.

Sympathy letters flooded into the *PIT's* editorial box. Ripping-off struggling artists was the lowest of the low was the general opinion. There were a couple of dissenting letters. One, signed by a 'Colonel McCloud', observed that since contemporary art had fallen into such a degenerate state that even pieces of bloody meat could be tacked to a canvass for the admiration of fools, the world would not mourn the disappearance of any like objects. A malicious glee was evident in the letter, Tom thought.

Tom knew that Billy McCloud, the self styled Colonel, was free with his opinions on modern art, especially after a whisky or two, but didn't fancy the sixty year old as the cat burglar. Yet his letter drew Tom's attention to the fact that all of the missing items belonged to a kind of conceptual art much despised by the more conservative members of the community. Traditional landscape artists and portrait painters had hardly been touched, whereas the bold artist who had taken a decaying corrugated iron fence, cut it into sections, framed them in steel and hung them in the art gallery with a couple of hundred bucks tagged on each, had had the whole sequence stolen, the whole fence. Maybe some broke farmer, somebody quipped.

Tom didn't know much about the passions that art can arouse. He was a live-and-let-live sort of cop. It was no skin off his nose if people wanted to wander around a gallery looking at pieces of a corrugated iron fence, pre-vandalised. It was legal. He did a bit of reading and discovered that not everybody felt the way he did. Modern art made some people very angry. Seven hundred years ago, a fanatical Christian called Savonarola had purged his province of all 'heretical works', burning paintings and smashing sculptures; and only eighty years ago the Nazis burned Picassos and other modernist works from much the same impulse.

Apparently some people felt that if they didn't like a piece of art nobody else should look at it. Tom didn't understand that impulse, but it was enough that he recognised it existed.

His first port of call was Mira Bexley, a smart professional woman with a substantial art collection.

'You're right. Most of this stuff isn't worth stealing. But there may be one thing. I mean, the other burglaries could be a smokescreen for a single target of interest. Were they professional jobs?'

'I get to ask the questions,' Tom said. He wasn't getting anywhere.

'Let's have a look at the inventory.'

Tom showed her. There was no hidden gem. She shook her head slowly. She'd already had to upgrade her own security, she told Tom. 'Some people find modern art very threatening,' she said.

Next he spoke with the artists themselves and didn't get anywhere. They seemed more eccentric than criminal, like the man famous for his childlike figures on beaches who painted black shoes on his feet, complete with laces. Most were upset at the loss of their work but a couple seemed flattered. After a few interviews Tom called it quits. Talking to artists for too long did his head in.

The word from Head Office was that the City was going to send a couple of detectives specialising in art theft. Head Office took a dim view of the shenanigans on Paradise Island. There was talk that maybe Tom had got himself a bit too comfortable.

The day of his humiliation crept closer.

Then Tom got a tip. A game changer, he hoped. Somebody had spied parts of the corrugated iron fence along one of the island's more rural roads where few people lived. A couple of lifestyle blocks, a few farmers running cattle, and Harry the Hobbit.

So he drove out to take a look. Just a piece of corrugated iron fence to him. He had to return with the artist who confirmed that this was *the* corrugated iron fence. He was able to show Tom where he had cut it and where the frames had been. 'Actually,' the artist said, standing back and admiring it, 'I quite like it as an open air installation.'

The artist was a short, stout man with dark scrubby hair. He explained it carefully to Tom. 'This guy has gone to considerable trouble to dismantle my work. Take it to pieces, very carefully, and restore it to its environment so it's now indistinguishable from others like it. Hidden in open sight.'

'Why would somebody bother to do that?'

The artist shrugged. 'Anti-art,' he said. 'A deliberate deconstruction. Very post modern.' He pulled out a camera and took several photos of it.

Tom nodded as if he understood. He would sort out the jargon with Mira Bexley later; what seemed evident to him now was that some sort of vandal was at work.

That opinion strengthened when a second object was found. This was a stone sculpture entitled 'The Angel of Compassion.' It didn't look much like anything to Tom except a smooth, rounded shape. Some kids had found it sitting on a rocky outcrop facing out to sea. They wanted to bore a hole in it and use it as an anchor for their dingy.

The artist, a determined older woman, was ecstatic about its placement on the rocky outcrop. 'Look at the way its lines of energy harmonise with the lay of the land around here,' she enthused. 'It sits up here like a jewel in a crown, giving meaning to the whole bay. This has been put here by a master!'

Tom had a lot more questions for Mira Bexley, but he put them aside too. He had the stolen item. No great harm had come to it. The artist was happy. So why was Tom still disturbed?

'Are you going to take it home?'

'No. I'm going to give it to the kids for an anchor. Imagine what those flowing lines will look like at the bottom of the bay! It's a natural progression.'

Tom had no sooner rung head office to tell them that the stolen pieces were starting to turn up, and there was no need to send the heavies, when a third item was found. This was a bunch of twisted metal pipes called 'The Maze of Death' and it turned up at the car wreckers. Hidden in plain sight once more.

That settled the issue for Tom. There was some prankster at work.

'However, none of the paintings have turned up,' Mira Bexley observed.

Garrison Ford pretty much agreed with Tom until the *PITs* received notice of a mysterious event, time and place to be announced. Watch this Space. Dozens of people received similar announcements. All the artists, plus community leaders such as Sue Lake and Mavis Stretchly. The community was agog, and rife with rumours. When the announcement came a couple of days later, it was for that same evening on a farm. Billed 'A Public Event of Stupendous Significance.'

Tom got out there straight away to be ahead of the mob, along with everybody else with the same idea. The road was jammed with cars. It was a collective frenzy. Nothing to make Tom feel comfortable.

The Public Event of Stupendous Significance was being held on an open field of a few acres, with an absentee owner. The first thing Tom saw was a lumpy shape about the size of a bach, covered by tarpaulins. Billy McCloud was standing in front of it, holding a bunch of tightly woven dried sticks.

'Ah,' he said, 'the law is here to see justice done.'

'To see the law is maintained, Billy,' Tom said. People didn't always appreciate the difference.

'You are all witnesses,' Billy McCloud shouted.

'Take it easy, Billy,' Tom said in his softest voice, a voice that called everybody to reason. A voice that had defused many a tense situation.

With a dramatic gesture Billy McCloud pulled the tarpaulin aside to reveal a wooden construction made of framing timber, containing bays and surfaces upon which were nailed paintings, a couple of dozen paintings. It was later said, only quietly, that this construction was itself an extraordinary conception, designed to strategically place the paintings within a three dimensional space.

When Billy lit the dried sticks no one was in any doubt as to the true function of that extraordinary structure. It was a funeral pyre for the paintings, and it burned as soon as Billy touched it with his flaming torch. He must have soaked the timbers in petrol.

There was no time for Tom to jump forward and heroically put an end to it; Billy knew what was coming and moved fast. Now Billy stood by the flames, his proud face aglow.

The affected artists who were there either wept or screamed, but most people just watched. There was something hypnotic about fires. Some of the paintings seemed to come to life at the last moment and writhe on the canvas.

'Be glad! Be glad!' Billy shouted.

Some of Billy's friends in the Lions Club stepped forward as Tom arrested Billy. Some of the performance artists began to clap as the martyred Billy was ceremoniously placed in the back seat of the cop car.

Tom was glad. He had his perpetrator. He had proved he could handle things here on Paradise Island. Just the odd crank or two.

No dicks from the City required, thanks very much.

HOUDINI AND THE HOLIDAY HOTTIES

Houdini arrived on Paradise Island one summer looking for some action and never left.

He wouldn't be the first escape artist to come to Paradise Island only to discover that there was no escape. Here was a man practiced at slipping out from the padlocked chains of marriage, an expert at leaping in and out of bedroom windows, an emotional contortionist who, in the end, found paradise to be the most effective trap of all. There can be no climbing the sides of the sky, or escaping through a hole in the ocean.

At least, not with a steady supply of holiday hotties on hand.

Houdini might be described as a hunter-predator, a 'player' as such are called by the party set, where those like Houdini, of both sexes, are most likely to be found.

The sunshine, the beaches, the parties, the girls and the boys getting up to no good. That's where Houdini liked to be. In the thick of it. And gone by morning. Extricated. His preferred target was the innocent holidaymaker who drank a bit much, got a bit giggly, and didn't mind going too far just this once. He could spot one of those across a crowded room. Being ridiculously good looking, charming, plausible and sympathetic – he was a good listener – he often succeeded. His more likely target, however, was someone very much like himself. A player. A here-today-gone-tomorrow kind of girl. He discovered that there were women who cruised the holiday venues and resorts looking for the same thing he was looking for, and they were easy enough to spot. From time to time, he could enjoy being the hunted.

During the day, the beach was the best place for connecting. People draped themselves everywhere – in the sun, under parasols or in the shade of rocks – in varying states of undress. They were relaxed, more likely to be open and friendly with strangers, their guard down, you might say. There was nothing more delicious than setting up an assignation with a sun-drenched wife right under the nose of a husband too distracted by beach bunnies to notice. At night the beaches emptied into the parties that were always to be found nearby. The best of these were often last minute affairs, a group of strangers from the beach invited back to somebody's place.

Houdini didn't have a place, exactly, not in the summer, although he seldom lacked for a bed. Otherwise, he liked to sleep under the stars in a very private spot on a very small private beach. A wonderful, secluded spot.

Mornings, he would position himself early in his favourite vantage point on his favourite beach and wait for the babes to arrive, as they invariably did. Quietly and agreeably, the day's hunt would begin. The delights of the chase. Another day's sunshine on Paradise Island.

On this particular day, three remarkable looking prospects materialised at the far end of the beach almost as soon as he had spread his brightly coloured beach towel and taken up his position. He could see that they were women, but as they approached they seemed to waver as if seen through a heat haze, although it was too early for that. They were skirting the waves, chasing them as they retreated, then running away from them. He could hear squeals of laughter like the sound of excited gulls as their shimmering forms merged and separated.

When he finally could see them clearly, he had to catch his breath in his throat. And they were heading right for him. He knew he was something of a chick magnet, being so good looking and all, but this was ridiculous. Coming towards him were three great beauties, magnificent rather than pretty. The first was a redhead with pale skin and amber freckles. The second was a brunette with olive skin and dark eyes. The third was a blonde all peaches and cream.

'Hi,' the redhead said, unfurling her towel on the sand nearby. She made sitting down look like a curtsey to the sun. The early light, bouncing off the ocean set her copper hair gleaming.

Houdini's senses reeled and, before he could recover, the brunette had done the same on the other side of him. She unselfconsciously took off her top and that same sneaky early light caught the smooth slope of her breasts and the dark whorl of her nipples.

Houdini wrenched his eyes from that sight to the peaches and cream blonde who, while leaving on a white top, slid off her jeans to let that lucky first light play with peaches and cream thighs.

'I think I've died and gone to heaven,' Houdini said. What else could he say? He was struggling for an opening line.

The girls laughed. The redhead's laugh was like the sun striking a burnished shield. The brunette laughed low and dirty, as if at some wicked secret, and the blonde's laughter was as pure as a sprinkle of holy water.

'It had to happen someday,' the brunette said.

'Only in my dreams,' Houdini said.

'Well, you can wake up now,' the blonde said, with a touch of merriment.

'Who are you?' Houdini said. He was a pretty cool guy, even if he said so himself, but he was touched with awe right now. The sun, just risen, opened a path of light across the ocean towards him. A clump of rocks in the middle of the beach gleamed darkly. The great orchestra of morning struck up its melody.

'We are the answer to your prayers,' the redhead said.

And so it proved to be. The day unfolded in all its delight, with the evening promising to be more of the same. Houdini frolicked and swam with his three lovely companions, hardly aware of the comings and goings of others. And they talked. The girls said they were models who had come to Paradise Island to do a photo shoot, and stayed for an extra day or so. Each was delightful in a different way. The redhead was earthy and forthright, the brunette was sly and secretive, and the blonde loved to dance.

Each of them had brought a bag from which they drew all kinds of goodies, even a bottle of champagne, which had remained miraculously chilled, and invited him to share.

'What's the catch,' he said as he raised his flute to the sun, which was a bubbling effervescence of light in the sky.

'You will never see us again.'

That suited Houdini. He didn't like coming back for seconds anyway.

The day of delight continued until the sun went down and the girls invited him back to the bach they were renting. What could be more wonderful, or natural, to be walking back through the twilight with these three exquisite women to continue their reveries in private.

Seldom can reality ever match the dream or the fantasy. The dream is an airy, luminous thing that does not belong to the world. In the world, imperfections creep in, the unexpected happens, ambiguities occur. There is always a fly in the ointment. But not this night. This night the dream matched reality exactly, and perfection was possible. It was a night of revels and ecstasy. Of wine and laughter, of secret pleasures and open delights. Nothing was denied him – no fragrance too subtle, no touch too silky, no smile too inviting.

That this was the impossible made real occurred to him, but he didn't care. Such a match of dream and reality, of the realm above and the realm below, must happen to every person at some point in their lives. A time when the sky fits the earth so exactly no join is visible, when there is no division between the word and the deed, no shadow to fall between the desire and the act.

He was under an enchantment, he told them. Three witches had put him under their spell. Come dawn they would turn into old hags or vanish in a puff of mist. Or he would awake in the ruins of an old decayed bach alone with the mother of all hangovers. 'I've walked into a fairy tale,' he told them. They laughed and pinched him all over to assure him they were real. This was no fairy-tale. Tomorrow they would be gone, yes, but on the ferry in the normal fashion, with a normal hangover.

Just this one night they had vowed to dedicate themselves to his pleasure, and their own. Just one big night out.

He didn't know whether to believe them or not, but the spell of the enchantment was too strong for him to care. The pleasures were real; that was enough.

As dawn approached, each took their leave of him. The redhead kissed him on his forehead and left him with a burning halo there. The brunette kissed him on the navel and sent shivers back through his past lives. The blonde kissed him on his feet, blessing the journeys they would take.

When he woke it was not in a derelict bach, or on the beach holding onto a dream, but in an ordinary if very rumpled bed in an ordinary bach, an empty bottle of champagne courting the morning light on the window sill. No hags in the bed beside him, no tinkle of fairy dust in the air.

He didn't doubt for one moment that everything he remembered had happened to him for real. That's why it brought about a drastic change in him. He tried to renew his old life, take up his old position on the beach, sleep under the stars on his private bit of sand, but none of it worked anymore. Overnight his old life turned to ashes in his mouth. There was nothing to pursue when the dream had been fulfilled and the promise delivered.

Having been touched by perfection, the imperfections of the world hurt him. In every new target of his attention, he would see one of the Three Graces, as he came to think of them. They said he would never see them again, that was the catch, what they didn't say was that he would see them everywhere, in every face, hear them in every voice, chat them up at every party. That was the real catch.

So he gave up the life of the beach bum, the hunter/predator, the player, the party animal, the meat-market maestro. The three kisses, or the Three Gifts as he thought of them, stayed with him. The Three Gifts from the Three Graces.

He began to perceive the larger enchantment of the world, and decided to stay on Paradise Island, get married to an honest woman and lead a quiet life. All of which he did. There were times, however, being nothing if not a frail man, he would visit the beach at dawn and see the redhead in the flaming sky, the brunette in the olive depths of the water, the blonde in the profligate pale sand, and he would remember.

STUMPY AND THE BUNNY RABBITS

Rosaline Rose can still remember the day when the kids were young, she was a solo mother, and all she had to do was step out onto the road with her thumb out and get a lift to the shops. That was when Minute Ago had still been on the island cutting a dash, before Boatie Ben ripped off a dope patch belonging to JJ-180 and his neighbour, MoJo, and set sail for Fiji where, under the dictatorship of Frank Bainimarama the price of weed had soared out of all proportion.

Rosaline always remembered these things when she was walking to the supermarket, various landmarks triggering certain memories. It was a drag. So predictable. Every time she passed a particular patch of scrubby ground where once, in this very public place, a magnificent dope plant had grown, miraculously unseen, she remembered Minute Ago, who declared that a praying mantis who lived on the leaves had the power to make the plant invisible to everybody except the stoned.

She was so sick of the memory she had even taken different routes to avoid it, with only partial success. After all these years, the kids had grown up, the hippies had all buggered off or got jobs, and she was still walking around thinking about Minute Ago. Years ago. Could she really still be holding a candle for the guy, or just for the times, the lost times, when Paradise Island was still a paradise? There was no supermarket in those days. And only one cop. Billy. Billy the Kid. A man who liked a quiet life.

The alternate route took her along Mako Street, past the house she rented when the kids were young. The house, upgraded from the bach it once was, was another timebomb, another landmark made up of memories. Stumpy had owned the house in those days. The one armed bandit as they called him. A tall, sloping figure who could be seen walking the streets of Paradise Island once a week in pursuit of his rent from his various properties. Cash, he only took cash.

Nobody knew what Stumpy did with the money because he lived in a more rundown house than those he rented, it was stacked top to bottom with junk of all kinds, and he wore clothes that looked like they were leftover flannels from the depression of the 1930s.

As she paused to look at the house, a tour bus edged past her. Mako Street wasn't made for buses, none of the streets on Paradise Island were. Most had started life as walking trails and had just been widened from time to time. Faces, most of them Asian, stared at her from tinted windows. Look at the frumpy woman standing by the roadside with a lost expression on her face.

She wasn't so lost as to imagine that those were all good times, before the tourist buses. No rosy spectacles for Rosaline. The kids. Rama had been four years old, Milly just three. Father in Aussie; Rosaline lumbered with two kids; it was a common enough story, probably still is, she didn't care. You had to be tough to live through those years. It wasn't all joints and joviality. Minute Ago would come and visit her. Hop into the sack with her if she were willing.

He had some kind of mystique about him, the bastard. Always on the run from something. Always in the middle of nefarious deals. Once a whole bunch of cops came over from the mainland, brought their own cars and dogs and the whole caboodle, and drove all around the island looking for him. He was never where they looked. He'd always been there, though, just a minute ago. Every now and again he would appear, like a genie out of a magic lantern, and offer her the world for an hour in the sack while the kids were asleep.

A bit further up Mako Street, where it took a left for no obvious reason, there was another landmark, timebomb, memory shell. A big old house half hidden away. Dennaray Darko, the twisted red-haired sylph from California, once lived there in perpetual party mode. Another solo mum but she was a cut above the rest, a work of art she was; boasting of a Hollywood mother and money that would eventually come her way, she cut a swathe through the men on the island, knocked them out of their gumboots and drank them under the table. Minute Ago had been a regular visitor, of course. He took it where he could get it. She wasn't surprised to hear that, on occasion, he would leave her bed when the first kid began to grizzle and show up at Dennaray's a few minutes later, sniffing around for wine and anything else he could get his hands on.

However, Minute Ago had a rival for Rosaline's attention. Sure he did. Solo mums were fair game. Often passed from one loser to the next, and there was an endless supply of losers on Paradise Island.

Stumpy, however, was not quite a loser and besides, unlike Minute Ago, he probably genuinely fell in love with her. Even now it made her blush to think of it, Stumpy being one of the ugliest men to ever wear a black singlet, quite apart from his one arm, and too old for her. She was only in her late twenties then. Stumpy was fifty going on seventy. He would frighten the kids with his tall, scarecrow body and his weather-beaten face, especially Milly who started crying every time she saw him.

Stumpy came out of rural New Zealand, man-alone territory. He would sit awkwardly at her table not knowing what to say while she made him a cup of tea and prayed for his early departure. He was more comfortable with guns than he was with women, even though he'd blown off his own arm while climbing through a wire fence on a hunting trip. He'd been fourteen and hunting since he was eleven. She wouldn't forget that because he told her several times. It was one of the few stories he had.

Most people thought Stumpy was simple, a can short of a six pack and so on, but Rosaline could see the integrity in the man. He had no guile. In that respect he was simple. The incident with the rabbits was evidence enough for that, and put an end to Stumpy's clumsy wooing.

It began with a remark Rosaline made while paying the rent about how hard it was to put food on the table on a benefit. She didn't begrudge him the rent, which was low enough, she couldn't complain, it was just that it was so relentless, pinching every penny week after week.

In that regard, she thought, pushing on past Dennaray's old place, nothing much had changed for her. She'd given everything to the kids and they'd buggered off and washed their hands of her. They were ashamed of their mum. Even Milly who should know better. What a flibbertigibbet she turned out to be. And Rama had gone to Aussie like a fly to shit and rang once a month. News that he'd hooked up with his no-good father over there didn't give her any satisfaction either.

Finally she turned the corner of Mako Street into Ocean Road, and the sight of the supermarket, trolleys gleaming in the sun. It was a relief to get through the gauntlet of memories. To hell with Mako Street, she'd choose a different route next time. The sight of a cop car reminded her of the last time she saw Minute Ago. He was in the back of the cop car, with Tommy Tommyknocker driving. Tom looked very pissed off. So much for Minute Ago.

For Stumpy, the rabbit incident put a painful end to a painful episode.

Apparently he had taken what she said to heart, and did what was natural for him to do. That is, put some food on the table for the woman. One evening she was feeding the kids and there was a knock on the door.

It was Stumpy. He was carrying, in his one hand, two rabbits dripping blood. As he walked into the room with his offering Milly had started screaming first, and Rama was not far behind. They screamed as if they were having their throats cut. Stumpy didn't know what to do. He was out of his depth with screaming kids. He lifted the rabbits into the air to show them, blood going all over the table. They screamed even harder.

'He killed the bunny rabbits,' Rama shouted. Perhaps he thought he would be next.

Stumpy dropped the rabbits on the table and ran.

Afterwards, Stumpy explained to anyone who would listen, that the problem was calling rabbits *bunny* rabbits, which turned them into pets. Pets instead of pests.

'There's nothing like rabbit to taste a stew,' Stumpy had said.

After that, Rosaline would leave her rent in her letterbox for Stumpy to pick up. Every time he did that he would pause for a moment and look down at the house.

Inside, Rosaline would hold her breath.

MILLIE MILLICENT AND THE SPIDER MAN

The romance between Millie Millicent and Russel Northrop fascinated the inhabitants of Paradise Island, even the children, who liked to follow them around chanting naughty rhymes.

It was the attraction of opposites in just about every sense imaginable. Just the physical disparity was enough to arouse comment, not all of it pleasant to listen to. Northrop was the hairiest man on the island, as well as being tall, dark and lanky. He was King Beast, the cave man who roamed the more remote, uninhabited parts of the island, preferring the bush, often sleeping rough and unwashed, scourge of any landowners bending environmental regulations. Millie Millicent was cute. She was small, delicate, fair and smooth of skin, with a taste for scented soaps, restaurant meals, morning mochas and mini-skirts. She could look spectacular sitting at the café with her steaming mocha and her legs crossed in the splashy morning sun.

They met at the Council Meeting at which Kendell and the forces of the community had prevailed in the matter of roadside spraying, although Northrop didn't trust Kendell who had brushed him off whenever he brought up the issue of landowners spraying their own chemical cocktails. Northrop had great interest in what other people did on their land. 'That's a fight we can't win,' Kendell had said. Coward. Sometimes you have to fight anyway, win or lose.

He was standing to one side, glowering at Kendell who was at the sandwich trolley stuffing his face with asparagus rolls, when Millie approached him and said something he thought to be suitably silly, and he said something suitably dumb in reply.

Northrop didn't notice women much; he had other concerns in life. But Millie was so noticeable you'd have to be blind, and Northrop wasn't blind. Not that blind. His reaction was embarrassment and confusion. He blushed all over. There he was sporting his favourite short shorts, and his short-sleeved t-shirt. And there was Millie mincing in a micro-mini and a fluffy blouse. They might as well have been naked, was the thought that ran through both their heads at the same time, like a bolt from the blue. And if they were naked, what would happen then? His rugged, long hairy legs and her smooth buttery thighs? It was her turn to blush. Her pretty, pale neck turned an even prettier pink. She glowed like a flower in the spring. She wasn't just the prettiest girl in the room; she was the prettiest girl in the world.

So they stood in front of one another tongue-tied and blushing furiously, their imaginations way out of control. There was something about Millie's reddish-blond curls, her airbrushed, fashion-model toothpick legs and her carefully calculated helplessness that lit a fire in Northrop's essentially innocent heart. Northrop was a man-alone type with little experience of people, let alone a woman like Millie Millicent whose smile could set the birds singing in his head. He had no resistance. He fell, as they say. From a very great height.

Millie had never lacked for men, or men's attentions, but she'd never met anybody like Northrop either, anybody so… overt. She was used to sallow handsome boys who drank lattes for their hangovers and cultivated subtexts for their amusement.

Northrop, the poor bugger, could hide nothing and what his face didn't show, his gallant shorts did.

That meeting ended in general confusion for both of them. They agreed to meet for coffee. Millicent had a sort of boyfriend, but he was about to be swept away in the flood.

The Café Résumé was her territory. A tourist trap in the summer. A hang-out for locals in the off-season. Northrop sat with profound awkwardness, not knowing where to put his human spider legs, of which he was suddenly, painfully aware. Millie Millicent wasn't the only one drawing stares that morning in the Café Résumé. In the bush or on a beach those legs looked just right; in the café with its tiny, white, ironwork tables and cramped spaces they had nowhere to hide. He was like a child in a big man's body.

Since he didn't drink coffee, he ordered green tea, asking for two tea-bags.

'Otherwise it's so weak you can't taste it,' he said.

Millie couldn't imagine anybody who didn't drink coffee. Everybody drank coffee. And she couldn't imagine anybody who drank green tea.

Nobody actually drank green tea.

They talked for a while, very awkwardly. None of her usual conversational gambits worked and Northrop didn't have any conversational gambits. Northrop mowed lawns and did odd jobs for a living. Millie didn't say where her money came from. They had nothing to say, but couldn't tear their eyes away from each other.

Millie came away from the encounter shaking like a leaf in a storm, her pretty arms and her pretty legs covered in goosebumps. Northrop took a hike to a quiet beach where he swam for half an hour in the cold spring breakers. While swimming he had a revelation. To get a wife he had to get a life.

They had sex later that week. Northrop took her to a tiny remote beach that only he and a few boaties knew about. Millie, who was not quite as promiscuous as she looked, had never done it outside, in the open, with the sun and the sky watching. At first she was embarrassed to bare her pale, freckled body to the sun and the sky, but soon her natural narcissism and exhibitionist tendencies kicked in, and she was able to share her pleasure with not just the sun and the sky but the rocks and the waves as well. She was making love, not only to Northrop but to everything. It was the cosmos sliding in and out of her.

All this was new to Millie, who was more accustomed to sex under the covers in the comfort and safety of someone's double bed, not out in the open air with gritty sand on her bum and knees, exposed to the world, being possessed by an ugly, hairy man who was more a force of nature than a man, rasping up against her thighs, bringing the blood rushing to her face and throat. She could hardly recognise the guttural sounds coming from her mouth.

That first time didn't last very long. Northrop, who wasn't accustomed to sex much at all, found years of pent up frustration discharge themselves through his body into hers in a frenzy of activity, a brief tumult, until he fell back on the sand feeling weak and oddly feminine, as if she was the one who had taken him in a whirlwind.

They both lay gasping in the warm air like stunned mullets until it was time to do it again. She could hardly believe that she would do it again with him, deliberately this time.

Suddenly he didn't care about anything, even that hypocrite Kendell.

His seed was a river. Her body the ocean.

For some weeks, this romance was played out in public, neither having the presence of mind or the inclination to hide anything. Like their bodies, their lives were on display. The older kids, the pre-teens, soon learned where the couple liked to go for their trysts, and observation points were at a premium. Tales of the wild activities of Beauty and the Beast spread around the island faster than the 'flu, losing nothing in the telling.

In the minds of many, and not just the children, this couple began to take on a mythic quality, a larger than life dimension that left everybody else looking ordinary by comparison. No other man on the island had a sweet looker like Millie Millicent to love every which way on twilight beaches – the infinite variety adoration – and many an envious glance went Northrop's way. On the other hand, no woman had a man as tall and hairy as Northrop to take them to twilight beaches and love them every which way as their own desires might dictate.

Some, of course, for reasons of their own, found this very public display of affection and desire disgusting. And disturbing. The couple crept into people's dreams. And into people's imaginations, causing unwholesome thoughts. Some women laughed, some wept. Some men engaged in guilty, solitary pleasures while their women laughed or wept. Some sniggered. The women laughed to keep the devil from the door, and wept for their youth. The spring sun walked in the shadow of fever. Children chanted mocking rhymes. When Millie and Northrop walked the main drag hand-in-hand or arm-in-arm, they gathered glances and stares as if they were celebrities.

Little by little, the couple became social outcasts. People couldn't look them in the eye without giving away their secrets, and nobody likes to be made to feel uncomfortable. That didn't bother Northrop, who was a social outcast anyway and accustomed to being an embarrassment to others, but it did bother Millie, a café girl at heart who loved nothing better than to bask in the admiration of others and shine in her social set. Her friends, at first fascinated, began to freeze her out. They went all polite on her. Just why that was, she couldn't work out. Without knowing it, she had stepped over an invisible line that divides the socially acceptable from the pariah. She made everybody uncomfortable.

It might have been this potent mix of envy and disgust that caused the relationship to unravel. Or maybe, as in the way of these things, they woke up one morning and found they were lying beside a stranger. It happened slowly, at first, then very suddenly. They sat together at the Café Résumé with nothing to say to each other. Now their bodies had stopped talking they were struck mute. They began to wonder why they were sitting there.

They began to wonder what they were doing on Paradise Island in the first place. Northrop left the island and went pig hunting around the East Cape while Millie returned to her spiritual home, the inner city, where the café set still reigned, and people really did call each other darling.

Eventually they returned. Paradise Island doesn't let go that easily. But when they did, they both pretended, by unspoken mutual consent, that they had never met.

It was easier that way.

CHAINSAW TRAVIS AND THE SLEEPING UGLY

Chainsaw Travis had a wife. At least for a while. Her name was Lucy Loosehead and Travis met her at a pub called The Road to Ruin in a town called Hellbound. There really is a pub called The Road to Ruin in a place called Hellbound and it really did have a pretty barmaid called Lucy whose smile lit up the bar and who made sure the glasses stayed topped up.

But that was in another country, at another time, and all the faces looked different then. Younger and flushed with blood. And Lucy's eyes were the same cloudless blue as the skies back home.

Travis didn't ask if it was such a good idea to fall in love with the barmaid from The Road to Ruin. You don't ask questions like that when you're falling in love with the woman who's filling your glass. And there were lots and lots of glasses to fill, everyday, and lots of hooning around Hellbound in utes when Lucy finished for the night.

For her part, Lucy Loosehead had seen many a man drink themselves silly over her. That flattered her and suited the management just fine. Every now and then Daemon, who owned The Road to Ruin and kept a beady eye on all comings and goings, would pat her on the back and smile at her with black teeth. But at the same time she was drawn to this large customer who always had a bourbon in one hand and chainsaw in the other, and spoke with a funny accent about a place far away from The Road to Ruin called Paradise Island where the birds chirped in the morning and you could walk to the ocean from pretty much anywhere.

Lucy was a local girl. She'd never seen the ocean, local birds had long since given up the unequal struggle to keep their songs alive, and the idea there was a place other than The Road To Ruin was quite novel to her. She built a Paradise Island in her mind which sparkled and glowed and chirped like a tourist billboard.

Meanwhile, things came to a head pretty quickly as they do on a binge. All roads led to The Road to Ruin where Lucy was behind the bar with a big smile and a full bottle. Boy, could that girl smile! The bottle didn't remain full for long, but who cared, there were plenty more where that came from. And the days turned into one long day. The past was nothing more than a bunch of discarded empties until…

…until one horribly bright and clear morning Travis awoke lying miraculously unhurt in a sea of broken glass. Somebody was ripping into the back of his head with a chainsaw. His chainsaw. He was inside somewhere, a barn. He remembered now trying to set fire to the barn before passing out. He saw the burnt patch. And he saw Lucy, also passed out, her face innocent like a Sleeping Beauty.

'I nearly killed us,' he said as she came to and rubbed the sleep out of her eyes with the back of her wrist, a gesture that looked charmingly childlike to Travis and made his heart bleed. Lucy looked good even with a hangover. Her brilliant blue eyes never lost their lustre, even with the dark shadows of night lingering beneath them.

Lucy looked at the burnt patch of straw.

'We were lucky,' she said. She didn't care too much. Being lucky was part of being alive as far as she could see. Happened every day.

Travis saw further. He saw how close they had come. Too close, far too close. He remembered drunkenly pouring vodka onto the straw to get it alight. He'd been laughing like a maniac. What was all that about?

He quit drinking. Immediately. He walked out of that miraculously intact barn a sober man and never touched another drink.

His first act as a thinking rather than a drinking man was to plot how to get Lucy away from Daemon and The Road to Ruin. How to lever her out of there, because she seemed to have some peculiar loyalty to the sweaty man who had given her a job when she was just out of school and not much good for anything. Travis saw, with the dreadful clarity sobriety brings, that those pats on the back from Daemon were like chains on Lucy's wrists and ankles. She was expected to remain forever grateful.

The only answer, as far as he could see, was to marry her. That would do the trick. And it did. Lucy was tickled by the idea. While Travis had walked away from the bottle, she hadn't. It was all part of her job, to have a drink with the boys, lots of drinks with lots of boys, and get them all drinking for the night. Rushing off and getting married was just another hoot, until she realised that the ring on her finger dissolved Daemon's chains and freed her to leave The Road to Ruin and Hellbound forever. Freed her to go with

Travis to Paradise Island, where the great ocean sparkles under the sun and the cry of birds greets the dawn.

But, as Travis told MoJo later, you can take the girl out of The Road to Ruin but you can't take The Road to Ruin out of the girl. Not even a couple of babies made any difference to that. Oh, Lucy loved the boys well enough between the first drink and oblivion, but her problem was that Travis had forbidden any alcohol in the house, or even on the property. He tended to find bottles stashed all over the place. It was like Daemon's revenge. She had to go out to drink and that was a worry. Anywhere there was heavy drinking going on, you would find her still playing the pretty barmaid, still topping up the drinks, still letting the boys see her sky blues when she smiled.

MoJo and Ella lived nearby and sometimes discussed the matter.

'I've told Lucy she can crash here if there's nowhere else to go,' Ella said.

'Is that wise?'

'She's slept outside sometimes. Too afraid to go home falling-over-drunk.'

'Afraid?' MoJo thought it more likely that she couldn't leave the bottle behind at the gate, would rather sleep with the bottle in fact.

'Travis gets pissed-off,' Ella said.

'I don't blame him,' MoJo said.

'What about yourself?' Ella said. 'You've crawled in here a few times on your hands and knees, goodbuddy.'

MoJo didn't like it when she called him goodbuddy. It always had a sinister ring to it.

'You can't make people do things like give up drinking,' MoJo said to Travis over a smoke or two.

'Sure you can,' Travis said. 'It's her choice.'

'Life's like that,' MoJo said, the weed making him philosophical. 'Always a Zen slap when you least expect it.'

'I'll slap 'em right back,' Travis said, the weed making him angry. He wanted to take a chainsaw to the world.

'This story is not going to have a happy ending,' MoJo said.

It didn't.

One night Ella and MoJo woke up to a strange caterwauling, like a cat on the prowl, only sadder. It might have been human because there was suffering in it. MoJo had heard people making noises like that while having sex.

The sound grew closer and closer, and as it grew closer it became more human and more full of suffering.

It was Lucy. She was crawling towards Ella and MoJo's place, through bush and bracken. When they opened the door a sorry sight greeted their eyes. Lucy, bedraggled, front covered in vomit. They let her in and led her to the couch where she fell into sleep like a drowning person sinking under the water for the last time.

They got back to bed but not for long. Soon there was a banging at the door. Certainly not a polite knocking.

'That's either the drug squad or Travis,' MoJo said.

Ella groaned and tried to pull the covers over her head.

It was Travis, but he had a face like the drug squad. He didn't wait to be invited in.

He took one look at his wife crashed out on the couch and turned away. He'd walked away from the bottle, now he had to walk away from the barmaid. In that moment his marriage dissolved.

'Sleeping ugly,' he commented as he went out.

CHARLIE AND HIS CHOP SUEY WIFE

Charlie Chugger was tired of his hairy-legged lesbian wife.

If pressed, Charlie would have conceded that not all lesbians were ugly and hairy-legged. Just that his was. If some men had good-looking lesbian wives who had good-looking girl friends then all power to them. Charlie had drawn the short straw in that department. In every department. And Billie, who became Bill, never let him forget it. And never stopped reminding him, in case his guilt began to falter, that he was the one who pulled down her pants in the olive grove when she was too young to know if she were Arthur or Martha.

It was the decade of the eighties and lesbians proliferated everywhere, at least everywhere Charlie Chugger looked. They ran about suing their husbands for custody of their children and writing All Men Are Rapists on the sides of public toilets. Some women even believed they could become lesbians by despising men, easy enough to do – and a dose of sheer political zeal. Billie, or rather Bill, was not one of those. She was the real thing. She had been liberated into her true, ugly butch self, even Charlie could see that. She had developed a smile like the witch Baba Yaga of the iron teeth and she had never felt better in her life.

'I'd be better off gay,' Charlie said to anyone who asked.

It was during these dark times, when men had to feel ashamed of being men, that Charlie Chugger began to dream of a porcelain pretty Chinese wife, one whose smile was sweet, whose skin was soft, whose step was light and who, above all, did not have hairy legs. At first he felt suitably ashamed of his fantasies, but came, through their agency, to the realisation that his marriage to Billie was already over. Billie no longer existed, and Bill was spending more and more time with her friends and allies. Having sex with her friends and allies.

Charlie Chugger began to realise that he was not alone in this fantasy, that other men had the same dream, and some even acted on it. Filipino wives began appearing here and there, even on Paradise Island, and Charlie was not the only one to notice that even the older, rougher men married to their gumboots seemed to have no problems bringing back a woman with doe eyes, soft skin and smooth legs.

One fine, balmy afternoon in Paradise came the event that was to decide it all for Charlie. He was scheduled to pick up their daughter, Jose, who, Charlie could not help but notice, already had hairy legs, even at the tender age of seven. Bill had left a message to tell him to pick Jose up from such and such an address, and Charlie dutifully turned up, only to be met at the gate by a thin intense woman who told him to wait. This was Athene. Charlie didn't know her personally but had heard of her. She boasted that she had no men among her friends or acquaintances. She specialised in liberating men's wives by sleeping with them. She told Charlie he couldn't come in. He had to wait at the gate and suffer his humiliation. Athene abruptly informed him that this was a safe house, a male-free zone, where the abuse and violence perpetrated by men had no place.

'I'm just here to pick up my daughter,' Charlie said.

'Your request is being considered,' the woman said. The idea of handing the girl over to a male, an abuser by nature, clearly disturbed her.

'It's not a request,' Charlie said. Bill had instructed him, for Christ's sake. He was only doing what he was told, like a good boy.

Charlie's attitude disturbed the woman more than ever. She looked towards the house as if she wanted to call for back up. Rogue breeder at the gate!

Charlie stood for a moment at the gate, feeling foolish and humiliated, before turning away. There were tears prickling at the back of his eyes. He couldn't stop them. It was over. Everything was over.

Just how Charlie found Chop Suey, as he fondly called her, is shrouded in secrecy and rumour. Some say he went to an agency, but he would never admit to that. Some say he advertised, but he wouldn't admit to that either. He told Kendell that he met her on the ferry, but he told Chainsaw Travis that he'd met her on a beach.

One day she just appeared, complete with white blouse and cut-off jeans, as if out of a magic lantern, and was living with him. The community quickly noticed that Chop Suey was very shy, knew almost no English, had very pale skin, a pretty face and, above all, very smooth girlish legs.

'She could be a teenager,' Bill said to her friends.

'It's hard to tell,' one of them said, 'she could be any age.'

'She can't be over thirty,' another said.

Not all the women in Bill's circle were lesbians, and among the group there was some unease at the idea of these pert, doe-eyed Asian women coming in and taking away their men, useless as the men may be. Of course, some stoutly maintained, this just went to prove what sluts and arseholes men really were, their minds fixated on pubescent images these cunning Asian women were only too happy to pander to. This was true, but not everybody was happy.

Then rumours began that not all was well with Charlie's new relationship.

Chop Suey was fastidious to the point of obsessive, and was having trouble with the rough and ready culture of Paradise Island. Hardly anyone could credit the story that, at first, Chop Suey had refused to take off her shoes at the beach. The thought of sand squishing between her toes made her shudder. Charlie had forcibly removed her shoes and thrown them a short distance to encourage her to walk in bare feet to retrieve them. Instead, she had crawled, keeping her feet in the air.

When they heard this, Bill and her circle didn't quite know what to think. Of course Charlie had abused and humiliated the girl – it was a good thing Bill had got out of that relationship – making her crawl; but on the other hand, who'd ever heard of someone who couldn't take their shoes off on the beach? Among Bill's circle, going bare feet everywhere was *de rigueur*. It went along with not shaving legs or armpits.

Then there were other rumours. This slip of an Asian girl could play the piano like a virtuoso, with a taste for the Romantics like Paganini, Offenbach and Bruckner, but didn't know one end of a broom from the other and couldn't wash dishes without a dishwasher. What might take place between her and Charlie in bed only the worst of minds would speculate, although nobody saw Charlie looking too unhappy.

The mystery around Chop Suey grew. Some, with an eye for respecting the cultures of others, started calling the girl by her real name, which was unpronounceable and sounded suspiciously like Chop Suey. With her delicate air and fine features, Chop Suey was obviously from a high-class Han family. And her incompetence in the house suggested she was a rich girl used to having others take care of her. If all this was true, what the hell was she doing with Charlie Chugger on Paradise Island negotiating spiders in his long-drop?

She was on the run. She was escaping an arranged marriage. She'd been banished by her family. She was hiding from Triads. She was a bit soft in the head. She just wanted a New Zealand passport.

After all, she made no friends.

More sinisterly, Charlie might have kidnapped her. Lured her to the island with false promises, maybe pretending that he was rich, and was now holding her, preventing her from leaving, turning her into a sex slave.

Bill's friend Athene approached the girl one day and attempted to establish communication. If Charlie was up to something, she'd soon ferret it out, but all the girl would do was nod and smile a lot and say, yes–yes. No joy there.

Then, one day she was simply gone. There one moment, gone the next. Charlie went quiet about it and stayed out of sight. His daughter Jose tried to tell everybody that Chop Suey had thrown the cat into a scalding hot bath, but nobody believed her. That sounded more like something Jose herself would do, but the rumours that Chop Suey had done something crazy before she left persisted. Some said she ripped up the mattress with a carving knife. Some said she burned all of Charlie's clothes because they stank of fish. Apparently Charlie had turned up at a neighbour's with nothing but a towel wrapped around him.

Others said that Jose drove the woman out with a series of malicious tricks, most of which involved the worms from Charlie's worm farm. Still others of a darker turn of mind suggested that Charlie had become a bit too carried away with his liberation from his lesbian ex-wife and had started making kinky demands on Chop Suey.

There was no end of tongue wagging, but no hard data.

The girl came and she left again, that was the story.

Shortly afterwards Charlie too left the island. He was going back to his native West Coast, he said.

When he returned to Paradise Island a few years later, Bill and Mavis had left to join an all-women community on the Coromandel, the All Men are Rapists graffiti had been scrubbed from the toilet walls, and everybody had forgotten about Chop Suey.

TRICKSY CLAW AND THE DEMON RAT

Tricksy and Cess stayed together for a while in an effort known as *making a go of it*. All the best couples did it, and some of them even succeeded. Making a go of it usually involved having babies, building a house, and entering into a longterm relationship with the tax department, a relationship that often lasted longer than making a go of it did.

'If you can keep your head, when all about you are taking out mortgages…' Kendell would say to Cess when the subject of making a go of it came up, and Cess's lip would curl. Making a go of it was one thing, getting saddled with a mortgage quite another. Who came to Paradise Island looking for mortgages?

For Cess, it was all quite clear. If he could build a boat, he could build a house and if he could do it himself, he could stay clear of the banks. There was plenty of demolition timber around if you knew where to look, and Cess knew where to look.

For Tricksy it was not quite so clear. What it meant, for her, was to be forever living in an unfinished house, because Cess had to divide his time between his unfinished house and his unfinished boat, the *Joseph Conrad*. Since Paradise Island boasted a warm, equable climate, living in an unfinished house with a screaming baby wasn't really as bad as it sounded. At least it was better than living in a packing case with two children, which is what Pete and Martha did. As Cess said to Tricksy, there's always somebody worse off, although how that was supposed to comfort her was beyond Tricksy.

Cess seemed to have forgotten that Paradise Island did have a winter, and the cold winds could blow through bare uprights and half-clad walls. He had also forgotten man's natural enemy, especially on islands, the rat – a creature who also likes to get in out of the cold. Unfinished it might be, there were plenty of warm, protected areas from a rat's point of view.

'If we could charge them rent, we could make a fortune,' Tricksy said.

At first Cess was largely impervious to the rats. Unless they got in his way, he took no notice of them. After all, he said to Kendell, rats are a part of life. Wherever humans go, rats go. There is no escaping them. Tricksy was terrified of them, however. They can smell breast milk, she told Cess who was intrigued by the idea. Clever little buggers, he would often say.

Tricksy had to put her foot down, and make it clear to Cess that there was a limit to making a go of it, and sharing their house with rats was exactly one of those limits. She was well brought up, was Tricksy, an educated woman with a flair for maths. She'd make sacrifices to stay out of the clutches of the banks, but she didn't want to make a lifestyle out of it. Her mother, and her mother's mother, and her mother before them, had spent lifetimes making sacrifices and where did it get them? Mostly nowhere but a bitter grave.

So, she duly delivered her ultimatum to Cess who nodded slowly, flipped open a beer and sat down to give the matter serious thought. Spreading poison was not an option, not with a lactating woman and a baby in the house. Poison got around. It couldn't be controlled. The answer lay with the psychology of the rat.

He was well into his third beer before he got the answer.

Tricksy tried not to look over her man's shoulder as he worked. The important thing was that he was doing something about the rat problem – not just sitting drinking beer. She even brought him a cup of tea and stuck a couple of beers in the fridge for later. She didn't say anything when he brought an old, empty 44-gallon plastic drum into the house and proceeded to slice the top off it. It stank a bit of something best not contemplated but she ignored that.

Whatever happened next happened slowly, and was accompanied by a lot of head scratching, but finally a structure emerged. Cess explained it to her while he bucketed some water into the drum.

'It's a water trap,' he said, quite proud of his work. 'You put bait on the end of this plank, the rat comes along the plank to get the bait and tips the balance of the plank which drops the rat into the water, where it drowns. Then you set the plank back up with more bait and wait for the next rat.'

It wasn't rocket science but it would work.

Cess had to go to the City for a couple of days to sort out some materials for the *Joseph Conrad*, and was now satisfied that Tricksy and baby Max could sleep peacefully – but Tricksy was not convinced.

That night, however, Tricksy awoke to a commotion, a screaming and splashing. Max clutched close, she approached Cess's water trap. It had worked. The plank had tipped and the rat had fallen in. But the rat had not drowned. It was screaming and splashing and swimming around. There was no way she could just leave it. It sounded far too human. Like a baby human, in fact. The sound went right through her skull.

She grabbed a thick plastic bag and, swallowing her fear and her bile, leaned over the drum and scooped up the rat. Now what? If Cess were here he'd just grab a lump of wood and beat the thing to death; chalk up a faint tick for having a man around the house. Without further thought she threw the bag into the freezer, slammed the door and quickly scooped up baby Max from the table where she'd placed him. No sound came from inside the freezer. It would freeze to death. More importantly, it would freeze to death quietly.

She put it out of her mind and went back to bed, mildly comforted by the thought that by now every rat in the vicinity would have run for cover.

The next day she delayed as long as he could, but in the end she had to face it, and look in the freezer. The rat would be as stiff as a board by now, just another lump of meat in a plastic bag. She could take it out and bury it and that would be that.

She opened the freezer door and she and the rat faced each other eyeball to eyeball. In an instant she saw what had happened. The rat had eaten its way out of the plastic bag and had consumed everything in the freezer, a lump of beef they were given, a bag of snapper courtesy of Boatie Ben, a rack of lamb chops Tricksy had bought on special from the supermarket and a dozen pork sausages she was saving for Max's birthday barbeque. All gone. Every last bit.

The enormously fat rat jumped clumsily to floor. It was so dazed she could have killed it if she'd had the presence of mind and a handy weapon. As it was, all she could do was watch as the rat waddled stiffly away, out the door and out of sight.

Cess was most amused by the story, which he told to Boatie Bill who told it to Chainsaw Travis who told it to his wife, Lucy Loosehead, who told everyone, but Tricksy was not amused.

The rat's prodigious physical feat in staying alive inside the freezer for the best part of ten hours so enhanced the image of the rat in her mind that she started jumping at shadows. The rat had not drowned or frozen to death. It was alive. It was out there, somewhere, around the house. It knew about her and it knew about Max. It would come back.

Cess tried to laugh away her fears, but Tricksy was having none of it. It was there. It was coming for Max. Then one night she saw it, at least the shadow of it. The shadow was an enormous humped shape with a rodent head. She knew it was a trick of the light, that the rat was on the roof, near the outside light, but that didn't help. It could smell her breast milk. It could smell Max. It would never go away.

Her fear grew so out of proportion, like the shadow of the rat, that Cess told Kendell he thought his wife might be falling into neurosis. 'She's obsessed with it,' he said.

When she went to sleep at night it was in the presence of that humped shadow and rodent head, and she could only sleep in desperate, exhausted snatches. One night she felt it. It was in the bed, creeping up towards her breast. She could feel the bristle of its fur along her leg. She screamed and leapt to her feet.

'It's in the bed.'

'Don't be silly,' Cess said. He had no trouble sleeping; it was trying to wake up in the middle of the night that gave him problems, especially after a few beers. Tricksy jumped up and down on the bed like a kid on a trampoline, screaming, before leaping off onto the floor.

'You're crazy,' Cess said.

Then he felt it too, creeping up his arm towards his face. He screamed like a girl and leapt to his feet. He and the rat confronted each other. He went to grab the nearest weapon but Tricksy already had it. It was only a broom but there was a grimness of purpose in the way she advanced on the rat. She would kill it, she would break its horrible humped back, she would stamp on it until she knew it was dead. She would put an end to its reign of terror.

'Throw the blanket on it,' she said to Cess.

He complied, moving with uncharacteristic speed, and Tricksy proceeded to beat and stab the hump in the blankets until the broom handle broke.

But when they finally peeled back the blankets… the bed was empty.

DENNARAY DARKO AND THE PRIMORDIAL TWINS

Dennaray Darko was from California.

That said it all back in the day. California was a place where dreams were made and sex invented. She arrived on a cloud of wine and feathers – and stayed that way. It was always party time at Dennaray's place. Fun and games for all!

Dennaray and her three doe-eyed daughters hit Paradise Island in a bright whirl of colour. It was generally recognised that the blonde Millie Millicent, of leggy fame, was the town hottie, but her star was eclipsed by the flame-haired Dennaray who fell to earth like fire from the sky. Dennaray was as slender as an elf, drank like an orc, and made love until the man was pooped. Having men pooped was a drag, so she took women lovers when she was in the mood. They tended to last longer in the sack.

There was no denying that Dennaray had staying power. It seemed to derive from her long and copious red hair.

Some women, like Rosaline, were jealous of her. Dennaray was from another world. She burned a little too brightly, a little too scandalously. She was a gaudy bird among dowdy fowls. But some women joined the party; after all, there was never any shortage of men hanging around the big old house half hidden away in Mako Street, and most had to settle for less than Dennaray's bed.

Dennaray had a way of wafting through life as if she were made of a different substance to everybody else. Nothing blunted her Californian *joie de vivre*. She was an endless sunset on a perfect beach. She was good vibrations incarnate. This emotional buoyancy might have something to do with her expectations, for Dennaray had an exotic background with a famous film star for a mother. Her mother, who had made selfishness a virtue and renounced her no-good daughter whose ambition had never stretched beyond the next party, would do anything for her grand-daughters upon whom she doted, especially Aglaya, the youngest and most beautiful. The old woman had insisted that Dennaray name the child Aglaya, after her favourite character in a Dostoevsky novel called *The Idiot*. A name suitably complicated and exotic.

The old woman's money often arrived through the bank accounts of Dennaray's daughters, but that didn't bother her. Money was money, always had been and always would be. Being poor was something way beyond the horizons of a luxury swimming pool childhood and a whimsical, indulgent mother.

Hence she had no understanding of the hunger in the eyes of the beautiful young brother and sister couple who arrived at her house one Friday night looking for wine and food. The brother was as fair as the sister was dark. He had tousled blond hair and a merry, devilish glint in his drop-dead blue eyes; she had straight dark hair, pale skin and lustrous moonlight eyes. He was talkative and she was observant; he had the wit, she the wisdom.

'Beautiful people!' Dennaray declared to all. Everybody clapped. Corks were popped on some brave new bottles.

They quickly became favourites at her table. Which suited them just fine, for they were starvelings, ignored by parents too busy and self-absorbed to care. Dennaray was sympathetic. Her own mother had sprinkled affection with a carefree indifference, as she might sprinkle rose water on settee cushions before guests arrived. For Dennaray, these starvelings were straight out of Romance, invigorating musicals like *Oliver* or *Les Miserables*. If she had actually read Dickens or Hugo she might have been less charmed, the writer Kendell was to comment.

They became her constant companions, particularly the young man, Lodge, who was barely twenty but ready to take on the world. Dennaray took him to bed where she could revel unimpeded in his youth, energy and unselfconsciousness. And a fine lean body. That was heaven, and was working well all round until one night, in the midst of their coupling, she became aware of somebody else in the room. The dark-haired sister, Zephyr, standing in the corner like a moon shadow. Dennaray overcame a potentially awkward moment – she had no idea how long Zephyr had been standing there – by inviting the waif to her bed. That doubled the heaven. From coupling to tripling. Lodge's impetuosity tempered by Zephyr's silky shyness; his loud laughter mixed with her soft cries. His celebration, her mystery. Not to mention the bliss of bringing them together, urging them softly, into that forbidden embrace.

For the first time in her life Dennaray felt complete. In perfect balance. She walked in the light of Aphrodite and didn't care who knew it. Both the sun and moon were in her firmament, the sun on her right and moon on her left. When required, she could turn to one or the other for succour. All she had to do was put money in Lodge's purse for more wine and oysters and soft gooey cheeses.

The world was illuminated from behind by a honeyed light. The air brushed her skin when she walked as if grooming her. The heaving ocean invited her to open herself up to all and everything, the sun and the moon and the prickling stars. The sleek contours of the evening landscape gave her goosebumps.

Because this magical world she now lived in contained no nastiness or evil, she did not at first grasp what Lodge was talking about when he began to discuss plans for some great escapade to the City.

Brother and sister, who looked after each other like a pair of orphans, had been doing a lot of whispering. Finally Lodge told her. He was planning to raid his father's home in the City and steal his famous stamp collection apparently worth a fortune.

'But why?'

Brother and sister looked at her uncomprehending.

'To sell.'

Dennaray was still confused, but knew better than to ask more.

'I've got money,' she said.

For once Lodge was as quiet as his sister. For the first time Dennaray noticed the hunger in their eyes. Like animals gathered at the rim of fire, the cold wind of the world at their backs. She didn't know what to say.

That night only Zephyr joined Dennaray in her bed. The girl was as tender as ever, but Dennaray was distracted.

'Lodge wants to get back at his father, doesn't he?' she said. Being from California, she was familiar with this kind of shrink talk. Revenge against the father. Unrequited love for the mother. The stamp collection charged with the wealth and power of the father. Steal the stamps and he steals daddy's MoJo.

'Yes, and so do I,' the girl said, speaking with such seriousness that Dennaray felt a delicious thrill go through her body. This crazy plan was so raw and primal. Here they were, brother and sister as avenging angels. Zephyr kissed her hard on the mouth. Usually it was Dennaray that took the lead, as if guiding the shy, reluctant girl to their palace of pleasure, but that night the roles were reversed and Zephyr showed her something Dennaray had never seen before.

Afterwards, she felt ravaged, exhausted, violated. The bright sun of morning made her wince.

A few days later, brother and sister left Paradise Island on their mission. Dennaray was bereft, as if they'd left forever. Life was flat and stale without them. Even the best wines tasted like last night's leftovers.

'Maybe it's time to leave Paradise for a while,' the thirteen-year-old Aglaya suggested. 'We could go and see Grandma.'

'Of course,' Dennaray said, her mind on the absent pair. 'You must be missing your grandmother.'

'Not particularly,' Aglaya said.

Dennaray was just starting to wonder what she would do if the pair never returned, when they returned. It gave her a fright to think about it. They could roast the kernels of her heart over a fire and she would not flinch. But there they were, as large as life. Lodge was laughing. Zephyr was glowing. They had braved their demons, crept into the house and succeeded in their quest. They had the stamp collection, and many tales of daring.

The celebrations went on far into the night.

A few days later, however, it all turned pear-shaped. Lodge arrived at the house in Mako Street in a stinking mood. His drop-dead blue eyes were like chips of obsidian in a totem of a wrathful god. A god that would trash the house. He started in Dennaray's room, their love nest, kicking the legs out from under her dressing cabinet, overturning tables and smashing mirrors.

'The stamp collection isn't worth anything,' Zephyr told her. 'Dad took the valuable ones and locked them in a safe in his office.'

'Okay, but… why did Lodge need the money? I mean right now? And why not ask me?'

Zephyr didn't want to tell her. Her eyes became hooded, like the night.

'You'll have to tell me.'

'He needs it for Wendy.'

Wendy? Dennaray remembered some mousy, young girl who would turn up at the parties. 'Peter Pan's girlfriend?' A little bitch with a domestic heart out to snare a lost boy or two. Lodge made a good Peter Pan, eternally boyish, eternally irresponsible. Wendy made a perfect Wendy.

'Wendy is pregnant. She needs… to get rid of the baby.'

Dennaray's world fell apart. The brother sister pair, the primordial twins, torn asunder.

She rushed to the mirror. The luxurious frazzle of red hair was still phoenix bright. Her elfish face held its lines. She looked just the same. Only older. Old enough to have three daughters. She didn't want to count the years that now yawned between her and Lodge. The light of Aphrodite was never about counting years. Now the years counted themselves, over and over without end.

In the belly of the crocodile, the clock ticked.

Things were never the same at Mako Street after that. Wendy decided to have the baby and Lodge joined her to do the decent thing. Which didn't last long. They moved off the island. Zephyr disappeared one day. Dennaray heard word of her from time to time. The never-ending party at Mako Street ended. Dennaray took to long walks on the beach and drinking alone. Her daughters took over the running of the house. Aglaya began to court a rich sugar daddy.

Dennaray flew back to California to reconcile with her mother.

When she returned, nobody recognised her. The house in Mako Street now long since sold, she bought a modest bach in a modest part of the island and lived a quiet life. Eventually she began to hear stories about the wild redhead and legendary parties of Mako Street, back in the day.

All quite exaggerated, of course.

After a time, she shaved off her wild red hair and became a Buddhist monk.

PETROLHEAD PINKIE AND STOCK CAR SALLY'S LAST RIDE

They called her the motor-head Madonna, and they would not be wrong. She was a cute, tough tearaway with a heart of pure petrol fumes. PP, Petrolhead Pinkie, should know because he'd been in love with her for long enough. Ever since she was six and he was a know-it-all eight, since he'd been a bad-ass fourteen and stolen his older brother's motorcycle and she, a bad-ass twelve, had jumped up on the back and screamed like a banshee as he'd done some wheelies on his brother's lawn.

They'd been bad-asses together until they weren't. Until she went and got herself a boyfriend called Dipstick who got drunk all the time and beat her up. Between beatings, she sat around feeling bad about herself and neglecting the juvenile delinquent within. She began to feel that her life was over before it had really started. So Pinkie got a girlfriend just to spite Sally, one who was so useless just sitting around feeling bad about herself that he had to get drunk and beat her all the time. He couldn't beat the uselessness out of her though.

It was a bad time for both of them. The only time they felt good was at the racing track, racing wrecked old cars and smashing them into one another, or sitting around with a beer watching others do the same. It was a man's world, but Stock Car Sally didn't care. She had proved herself. She could drink any man in the club under the table, for a start. The men had bets. If one could drink her under the table, he could have her, with everybody's blessing, but although many came and put their money down, none stayed sober enough to attempt to collect his prize.

'The boozing gene,' Sally called it. The one good thing her mother had passed on to her. It qualified her to be an honorary man. It was like a ring of protection.

The men noted with approval that she didn't drive like a girl either. She could roll her car and keep driving. She was good. She knew how to throw her car into the corners and smash the opposition aside on the straights. Whenever she raced everybody clapped. Not just because she was a girl, but because she was the best. She had no fear, people said, that was why she was so good. She did things other drivers would hesitate to do.

Her car was some piece of Japanese junk with a Ford motor. She'd welded the bumper bars on herself, so she was confident that she could take a roll safely. Her famous lack of fear had more to do with confidence in her skill and her welding than foolhardiness. You were more likely to die crossing the street than stock car racing, people said.

Every year, back in the day, the club would host a competition with a couple of city clubs, and the lovely snarl and roar of engines could be heard all over Paradise Island. The men in the club were immensely proud of their Stock Car Sally. None of the other clubs had anything like her. There was one other woman who came to competitions, but you had to look three times to see that she was a woman, whereas Stock Car Sally was hot, in a tough, tomboyish way. But she never slept around. Dipstick might spend most of his time living up to his name but Stock Car Sally stuck with him. The men might lust after her, but they admired her, and she was smart enough to keep it that way.

That was, until this particular year when something went wrong. Sally raced like a demon, but there was this one guy, Snorkel, who seemed to know her every move, cut her off on the bends and muscle her out on the straights. Snorkel was as crazy as she was. Some Nordic guy with blond dreads and no fear of death. They had to race off for the championship in the final heat, and the crowd went wild. Both of them rolled their cars, which was thrilling to watch, and Sally jammed Snorkel's car against the sturdy railing, pushed it along with a shriek of tormented metal.

Everybody agreed it was the best race they'd ever seen, even if Sally lost it by a nose. That was all good fun, but what happened afterwards changed the game. Sally and Snorkel got together and did it among the squashed beer cans and ciggie stubs, going at it as if the race had never finished. All good fun. The result was that Dipstick up and left, badmouthing Paradise Island and all who inhabit it, and Stock Car Sally got pregnant.

As soon as she knew she was pregnant, Sally gave up Stock Car racing and beer, her two great pleasures in life, her two only pleasures in life. Her stock car was the only thing in the world she owned, except the clothes on her back. Her club mates stepped in to help. One of them bought her car for a couple of hundred bucks, and somebody else found her a place to live. She went on the benefit and boxed along.

Her one strength in all of this was her old mate Petrolhead Pinkie.

He was always bringing her bits and pieces, food, firewood and good cheer. He was a solid sort of bloke was PP; when Sally looked at him she could hardly credit that she had ruined a good friendship, a friendship that might have developed into something, by taking up with the useless Dipstick. Now that Dipstick had gone, they might have come together, Petrolhead was holding out for it, but the spectre of Snorkel, the father of the baby, stood between them. Snorkel, while keeping well clear of the entanglement, kept in touch with Sally, kept her heart on a string; it was him Sally really wanted, Petrolhead concluded.

When a baby daughter was born, PP encouraged Sally to work on her stock car, helped her overhaul the motor, repair some bodywork, and get the car into racing form. While this was happening, he set about to subtly poison Sally's mind against Snorkel, whose reputation as a lady-killer went before him. Sally was not his only victim. The man had never given her a penny to support the child. He denied it was his child even though the baby was born with blond dreadlocks. Even his mates despised him. And so on and so on.

It worked. From dreaming that one day Snorkel would walk through the door with a life for her, she went to dreaming about how she might kill him. Track him to his home, perhaps. A knife in the back was a satisfying idea. Or a plastic bag over the head. She rather liked that when she saw it on TV. The staring eyes, the horrified realisation; it would be satisfying to see that look on Snorkel's pretty face.

'Naa,' Petrolhead said when she started to run these ideas past him. 'The right place to get him is on the racetrack. A terrible accident.'

Sally saw the justice in that. Imagining his mangled body being carted off the track gave her comfort, momentarily. 'I don't know how it might be done,' she said. Up to that point it had just been a fantasy. The idea of actually doing it was creepy.

That year the races went ahead as usual, and PP heard on the grapevine that Snorkel was coming, boasting that he would clean up the field, and that those Paradise Island cuckolds had better lock up their wives and daughters. Petrolhead faithfully related all this to Sally.

'I'm going to race him again,' Sally said.

'No,' PP said, as if he hadn't been angling for this outcome all along.

'It's the only way I can get my MoJo back,' she said.

'What about our little plan?'

It never had been a plan, but Sally passed over that. She knew where

Petrolhead was coming from, and it suited her to keep him on a string. 'Killing him is going a bit far,' she said. 'I just want to damage him. Badly. Maybe turn his balls to pulp.'

Petrolhead thought that was a wonderful idea, although how it might be managed on the racetrack was another matter. Wonderful idea or not, PP suspected that Sally was losing her nerve. She even showed signs of nervous anticipation, like one waiting for the arrival of a lover. Sometimes her gaze would wander off into the distance and PP couldn't tell what she was thinking. He didn't know which way it would go.

Sally went into training, burning up the rubber around that race track as if there were no tomorrow; her foot had forgotten the brake. Everybody agreed she'd lost none of her edge. If anything she was even more reckless than before. The betting began long before race day arrived, and the money was going on Sally.

Petrolhead had to keep quiet about his plans; a couple of his mates were betting on Snorkel. As far as he was concerned, however, Snorkel was never going to win that race. And there would be no repeat bout afterwards among the squashed beer cans and ciggie stubs, if that was what Snorkel was dreaming. PP didn't know whether Sally might be dreaming it too, or how deep her feelings might run for the father of her daughter.

It all hinged on a stock car race.

The day dawned bright and steely, and the crowd gathered. The thrill was in the air. There would be blood on the tracks one way or another. The opening heats warmed up the crowd while they waited for the big race off, last year's champion, Snorkel, against Paradise Island's contender, Stock Car Sally.

Petrolhead was in a sweat. He'd had some vague plan for sabotaging Snorkel's car, but that wasn't going to fly. Sabotaging Snorkel himself was another option, and satisfying to imagine – a hefty wrench to the back of the head would do the trick – but once more it wasn't going to fly. So he ended up doing nothing but sitting like a limp dick watching the action on the track just like everybody else.

And action there was. The challenge wasn't a race; it was a massacre. Sally went straight for Snorkel, let him get ahead and then battered and smashed him at every turn. It was clear to everyone that she wasn't interested in winning, just inflicting as much damage as she could. It was not a pretty sight. Snorkel did his best to keep ahead of her but she was wild on the corners, relying on smashing into him to break her speed. Not once did she try to overtake him.

The end came with a spectacular flip and roll. No one agreed on exactly what happened, but suddenly both cars were in the air. Hitting the ground, they rolled over each other, their bunper bars somehow locked. A hush went over the crowd because, as Petrolhead saw it, Sally and Snorkel were doing it on the racetrack in front of everybody, humping each other with their steel bodies, the grind and shriek of it. The agony of torn metal. The final, juddering, rocking gasp, Snorkel's car ending up on top of Sally's. Like the mating of two mechanical monsters.

Stock Car Sally and Snorkel were both carried off the field on stretchers, shaken and concussed but otherwise sound. The worst was Snorkel's broken rib. And perhaps Petrolhead's pride.

It was all over. Until next year.

SHORT CUTS

These legs were made for running, Julie Tagget intoned as she finished lacing up her trainers and ran her hands quickly over her thoroughbred legs. Julie the Jogger they called her, and for good reason. She'd probably run more miles on the back roads of Paradise Island than anyone – except for old Randy the Runner who'd been at it since before jogging was invented.

Arriving on Paradise Island with her husband and two daughters had unleashed the hidden runner in Julie Tagget, who had never run much in her life except when she was late, but now had marathons on her mind. It began, she thought, with an urge to get away from the house, as far away as she could, because Julie had a jealous husband – and for good reason. Julie had a roving eye. She had reached that age, or stage, when the presence of young men made her feel quite weak and giddy. For example her husband, Perry, who did not make her feel weak and giddy, had hired a young man to work on their driveway, and Julie suddenly found it necessary to take lots of pictures with the young man in every one. Preferably in action.

Julie hit the road running, taking some pleasure in looking down at her legs. They may not be the fanciest legs in town, not to rival Millie Millicent or that mewling Melanie, the doctor's wife, but they were sleek and strong and did their work. She was half in love with her own legs. Just thinking about that milksop Melanie made her lip curl. Simpering blondes! She might put on airs, being the doctor's wife and something of an actress, but Julie had one up on her. Julie was having an affair with the doctor.

It had begun with a strained tendon and developed from there. Her legs had done their work on that occasion.

Her route took her along a coastal trail where she would sometimes see, as she did on this occasion, another woman running the other way. Clearly an amateur – she could tell by the trainers – trying to run off some excess. Legs like young tree trunks, she had. Julie was glad she wasn't built like that. She stood aside to let the puffing woman pass.

When Audrey Lamplight passed the rather arrogant looking woman in expensive jogging gear, she hardly noticed her. Audrey had something on her mind too, namely her husband, Dude, known as The Dude to his mates. Dude's career had taken off. Computers, that's all she knew. Something to do with computers and it had made him very rich – not that she saw much of the money. He doled it out to her in pennies after carefully explaining that he didn't trust her with access to large amounts. He said it to her face. Meanwhile, he swanned around town spending up large on all kinds of women, she was sure of that. She could smell it on him. Along with the cocaine.

He worked in the City while she was conveniently out of the way cooling her heels on Paradise Island.

Finding a credit card of Dude's, and by accident knowing its access code, was a turning point for Audrey. Instead of meekly returning his credit card, she planned an exquisite revenge, one that would satiate her jealousy. Just thinking it through, getting the plan straight, gave her pleasure. She would give The Dude one hell of a fright. At least get him to bring some of that lovely cocaine home.

Audrey was thinking about her revenge as she passed the brunette with the fancy trainers and the hard won figure. I'm going to seed, Audrey thought. No wonder Dude is dude-ing elsewhere, probably with a woman like this one. He puts me here, on this stinking island, to rot, and when I start to rot he holds his nose. She'd fix him!

She ran on.

In a small, new house, with a view that overlooked a portion of the coastal walking trail, lived Kara and her cookie jar. She was nibbling on a cookie, in fact, when she saw the two women meet on the path, the slimmer one standing aside to let the bulkier one past. The momentary politics of who gives way. She'd seen lots of joggers running that track. Everywhere you looked there seemed to be sweating runners. Kara wondered what was wrong with them. Hadn't they heard that running ages people, and excessive running can damage internal organs by bouncing them around.

Really, I should be out there, Kara thought, getting fit like those women rather than jeering at them. Taking better care of myself. Looking after my figure. What nature gave me, I'm busy squandering. Cookies in the jar.

She had all the more reason to look after herself since she had just begun, tentatively, a relationship with Kendell, the writer. Kendell had, if not charm, a certain cunning, and oh how he could talk! He had smooth talked the pants off her. Whether that constituted a relationship or not she didn't know. Relationships had always been a bit of mystery to Kara, but she was in her thirties now and could feel the clock ticking away in her womb. To have a baby, she needed a man, preferably one that would stick around and pay some bills.

Kendell had some funny habits. Like getting up in the middle of the night and wandering around muttering to himself, and sometimes she had to rap her knuckles on his forehead to see if there was anybody home. He liked his weed, did Kendell, and was a demon for the booze when he got together with his buddy Garrison Ford. He didn't seem to care that she was a slacker who hung around the kitchen with her hand in the cookie jar, who would no more take to the trails in trainers than fly to the moon. She was relieved, if a little piqued, that Kendell did not seem interested in writing about her. It was the past he was working on, he said. The dim distant past. Still, she wouldn't be surprised to see a story written about her. Kara and the Cookie Monster, perhaps. Writers could be sneaky. And cruel.

It occurred to her that she was too contented to get serious about jogging, or rush off to the gym at six in the morning the way her friend Ella did. That kind of behaviour was something to talk about in the Café Resume over a mochaccino and a nicely buttered scone, not to actually undertake. A long time ago she'd figured out that people's prime motivation was, very often, dissatisfaction; people did things to scratch an itch, that was about it. And wanting a baby was a mighty big itch, she was discovering. But taking to the trails wouldn't scratch it.

I'm not sure Kendell is the right man, she thought, taking another cookie.

A few days later, the Dude did indeed get a hellava shock. He was sitting on the back deck of a ferry popularly known as the Darth Vader having a beer with a few others. Back in the day, Dude was one of those comparatively new breed of Paradise Islander – the commuter. There were Lizzie and Joe, and Jean Jeanie and her new protégé, Xena. There was Perry Tagget all suited up. And the doctor who travelled to his practice in Auckland. The back deck was crowded as the summer weather was mild and the afternoon bucolic. Everybody wanted to sit in the sun and have a drink.

The Dude was having a talk to Kendell, or trying to. Kendell kept sticking his nose back into a book. Dude, who was way ahead of his time and already saw books as obsolete, artifacts from a quaint bygone era, was amused at Kendell's persistence.

'I'm reading these stories by Raymond Carver,' Kendell said, waving the book at Dude.

'Why?'

'I'm trying to find out what makes them tick.'

'Why?'

'Because if he can do it, I can do it.'

'Monkey see, monkey do.'

'That's right,' Kendell said, taking a swig at his glass of obnoxious house red.

'And can you do it?'

'I don't think I'm drunk enough,' Kendell said.

'That's easy fixed,' Dude said, taking a good long pull at his cold beer. Life in the fast lane was pretty good. Plenty of money, plenty of drugs, plenty of lap-dancers at his command. Plenty of male computer buddies doing the same thing. He could make millions with the software he was working on now. Plenty, plenty of millions. And there was silly old Kendell trying to write like somebody else for no profit at all! How come people said he was smart?

At that moment there was a disturbance at the back railing. Jean Jeanie and Xena were pointing at something and exclaiming in high voices. Dude thought maybe there were orcas. Sometimes a pod of orcas would guide the ferry over the shining water to Paradise Island. Above the throb of the ferry engine, he could hear the sharp whine of an outboard motor. Dude and Kendell moved to the back railing to check it out. Dude squeezed in beside the doctor.

The ferry was being tracked by a speedboat that was zig-zagging through its wake, bouncing up and down. That, however, was not what was drawing attention. It was the woman in the skimpy bikini sprawled dissolutely in the back seat that did that. Plus the hunk in skinny briefs at the wheel. The woman wasn't too bad, actually, Dude, who had a professional eye for these things, noticed. Padded in the right places, if a little over padded. Lots of lovely brown, reddish hair. Just like Audrey's. As he watched, the woman lifted a bottle of Champagne to her lips. Expensive stuff, Dude could see even from the deck. He was the expert.

Then his glass fell out of his hand. Good thing it was made of plastic.

The woman lounging in the back seat of some stud's speedboat did not just look like Audrey, *she was Audrey*. In the warmth of the summer sun, the Dude went very cold.

'Now there's a pleasant sight,' Perry Tagget said.

'You're not wrong,' the doctor said.

Tagget, who looked down on the doctor, didn't reply. He didn't expect to be wrong.

Kendell began to wonder what his new girlfriend Kara would look like in a bikini, but stopped himself just in time.

While they watched, Audrey, carrying the bottle, climbed into the front seat beside the stud who put his arm around her while he gallantly swung the boat back and forth over the ferry's wake with his other hand. Her thrilled shrieks were swiped away by the wind, faint, like the sound of a sea-bird.

'You could have one like that,' Kendell said to Dude.

'I already do,' Dude said.

The speedboat followed the ferry half way to Paradise Island before peeling away, heading for a lonely little beach on one of the smaller islands.

The Dude watched it until it became too tiny to see.

The Dude was a man struck dumb where he stood. He didn't regain the power of motion or thought until he remembered his missing credit card.

He turned away from the now undisturbed wake, leaned his back against the railing and observed the people. Nobody had recognised Audrey, much to Dude's relief. Everybody had apparently forgotten the incident. Perry Tagget was talking to the doctor. Jean Jeanie and Xena were acting something out, carrying on like a couple of idiots.

Paradise Island loomed on the starboard bow. Rocks and pohutukawa trees and amber afternoon light.

Kendell's nose was back in his Raymond Carver book.

Dude took a deep breath.

WILLARD AND THE WINE TASTERS

Willard was a taxi driver. That is, until the mini-buses came along with their tiki tours of Paradise Island. Everybody wanted a slice of paradise, even if it was just a photograph to take home or a memory to cherish. Amazing the number of people who came to Paradise Island attempting to accumulate pleasant memories, to store them up to be employed, as it were, against the unpleasant realities of life. Released bit by bit until they were used up and needed refreshing, anyone would think these precious memories could somehow shore up the psyche against the incoming tide of time itself.

The behaviour of tourists was something of a mystery to Willard, even though he had been a taxi-driver on the island since Adam was a cowboy; most of his business had been locals, to and from the ferries and a few midnight drunks – that was, until the wine tour buses came along. Also, Willard was something of an innocent. He'd had a romance or two but never married, never left the island much, and was happy enough in his way without having to enquire too deeply into things. He just got on with life and could never quite understand people travelling around gawking at other people getting on with theirs.

The wine tasting tours changed all that. Groups came, not to accumulate memories but to obliterate them, not to do touristy things like go to beaches or walk coastal paths but to be carted around from vineyard to vineyard getting progressively plastered, until, at the end of the day, to be poured onto the ferry for the return trip to hangover land.

Willard didn't care. What other people did with their lives was of little interest to him. He was quite happy to sit in his mini-bus and wait for the wine tasters to emerge ready for the next vineyard. It was just a job, but he had one quality essential for a taxi driver: patience. He didn't mind waiting when there was a dollar at the end of the hour.

One afternoon he picked up a group for the 'twilight' tour. There were nine of them, all young women between twenty-five and thirty-five, Willard judged. And they were classy. All dressed up in their corporate finery. Power dressing, was the phrase Willard had heard. He knew nothing about labels or fashions but he knew flash when he saw it. Money too. Seeing them climb elegantly into his mini-bus made him feel conscious if not ashamed of his everyday working garb, neat and clean but not much else. He was like a dowdy little weed amongst a bouquet of spectacular lilies.

They were ready for some fun, and the island appeared ready to offer them some. Even by Paradise Island standards, it was a gorgeous afternoon, mellow, softly lit, the gentlest of breezes blowing, the odd fluffy, cartoon-like cloud. 'I can't wait,' one of the women said. She was a neat blonde with orangey coloured skin. The woman who had been assigned to deal with Willard reminded him of a mother hen, herding her giggling chicks onto the mini-bus and waving a gold credit card in Willard's direction. Back in the day, such generously built women might be called 'blousy', with sufficient maternal cleavage to establish their credentials.

Willard wasn't a young man, but he wasn't old either, and not completely indifferent to the charms of the mother hen, or her chicks, but he felt too intimidated to be charmed; he was not accustomed to so many up-market women all at once, all grinning at his evident fluster, delighted at his discomfort.

As he pulled away from the wharf, his friend and fellow driver, Chucky, gave him a 'you-lucky-bugger' look to which Willard replied with his best smirk and a cheeky toot of his horn. Chucky could eat his heart out.

On the way to the first vineyard, there was much chattering, and oohing and aahing out the window. A couple of the women had been to the island before and were filling the others in. Willard began to relax and think of what he could tell Chucky later to make him even more envious. He put his feet up and read *Best Bets* while the women enjoyed their initiation. They came back out to the bus laughing animatedly as one of them, a tall, stately bottle-blonde, told them some elaborate story, one which provoked shrieks of laughter at every turn.

'It was just so sumptuous I simply had to order a case,' one of the women said in a plummy voice. Willard practiced it under his breath so he could tell Chucky, *so sumptuous I simply had to...*

The Mother Hen, who introduced herself as Scheherazade, or Cher for short, sat up front with Willard. She told him they worked for a large company and were having a girls' day out. She asked him a couple of questions about this and that which he answered gladly. Willard the driver, always happy to be of service.

'You been driving long?'

'For donkey's years,' he said.

This answer seemed to provoke some amusement in the back. 'Did he say he has donkey ears?' he thought he heard one of the women say. *Titter titter.*

'Are you married, Willard?' Cher had a nice, friendly voice. Soft and tender.

'Never had the pleasure,' he said, which is what he always said. This time it provoked further giggles and laughter. Willard began to feel positively witty.

'What about a girlfriend?'

The back of the mini-bus fell silent. Willard felt his donkey ears burning.

'Surely, a likely fellow like you would have a girlfriend.'

The sound of muffled laughter from the back. He wasn't sure what a 'likely fellow' was, or if he had ever been one.

'We're here now,' he said, gratefully pulling into the next vineyard. It was back to *Best Bets* and the empty bus, but his mind wasn't quite on the horses. It kept returning to Scheherazade, her nice soft voice, and the way she kept turning her cleavage in his direction.

This time, the nine emerged positively merry. Something was terribly funny and they couldn't stop laughing as they bundled into the mini-bus. Something to do with an absent colleague. Some trick they'd played. They'd lost a little of their corporate neatness, a make up smudge here and there, a mussed hairdo, an opened top button.

This time a different woman joined him in the front. She was petite with dark curls, a quick smile and a throaty voice. She introduced herself as Maxi. Willard had already decided that she was the prettiest of them, even though the tall blonde was more impressive.

'Now,' she said, once they were moving again, 'you'll have to tell us about this girlfriend of yours, Willard.'

'Well…' said Willard.

'You can't keep us in suspense,' Maxi said.

'Keep us in suspenders,' a voice from the back said to an explosion of laughter.

'You'll have to confess everything,' Maxi said.

'Confess, confess!' came a chorus of voices.

Willard blushed and concentrated on his driving. He was too aware of the woman sitting beside him, how shining her dark curls were, how short her skirt suddenly seemed, how close her knees to his.

'I've got nothing to confess,' he confessed weakly to a chorus of disbelief.

'What's her name?' somebody from the back shouted.

It was a relief to get to the next vineyard and to pull out his much folded copy of *Best Bets*. His relief was short-lived however, as it seemed the women were back in no time, and much drunker and more dishevelled than before. A somewhat large woman in high heels stumbled and had to be supported. Some of the women, he noticed, had removed their heels and were carrying them as they made their way to the bus. Maxi gave him a lopsided smile as she pulled herself into the mini-bus.

It was a raucous trip to the next vineyard. There was so much giggling and laughing going on, Willard thought there was a conspiracy developing. A different woman had joined him again in the cab. This one had long soft straight brown hair and a girl-next-door smile. Her name was Penny. He imagined Penny might be a nice person – when she wasn't drunk. 'Don't take any notice of them,' she counselled him solemnly. 'They're just letting their hair down.'

That was literally true in some cases. Several of the women with more elaborate hair-dos had unpinned them and let their hair fall over their faces and shoulders.

A sudden explosion of laughter from behind had him twisting in his seat to see what was going on. 'I bet you wouldn't,' someone shouted, and he recognised the voice of the statuesque blonde. 'How much?' This was Maxi, but her throaty voice was hard and scratchy and filled with some emotion Willard didn't recognise. There was more wild laughter.

'Calm down ladies,' he called out, but this only provoked further mirth.

'We're not your girlfriend,' somebody called out.

Again he turned in his seat, ready to tell these unruly passengers off. As he did so, they burst into song.

All together now, one, two, three
Keep your mind on your driving
Keep your hands on the wheel
Keep your snoopy eyes on the road ahead
We're having fun, sitting in the backseat

Kissing and a hugging with Fred
De doodee doom doom…'

They just made it through the last 'doom doom' before cracking up into ragged shouts and laughter. 'Hey, Fred's my husband,' somebody shouted. A chorus of ribald comments followed this revelation. *'De doodee doom doom,'* three or four of them kept chanting.

'I'm not drinking any more,' Penny said. She was gripping the armrest.

Willard began dreading the next pit stop. 'I don't want any vomiting in the bus,' he shouted, but his voice sounded high and timbreless. There was a chorus of 'yes sirs' from the back.

There was no *Best Bets* at the next stop. All bets were off. Am I going to have a story to tell Chucky, he thought, as he watched the women reeling back to the bus. He discretely turned from them as they stumbled into the bus in considerable disarray, no longer caring how many buttons were undone or how high short skirts could ride when scaling steps. Except for Penny, who looked haunted and wouldn't look at Willard.

Maxi was the last one on, and just before she pulled herself into the bus, she lifted her top and flashed her breasts at Willard. It happened so quickly Willard wondered if he'd imagined it.

'Time to go back to the ferry,' he announced as he climbed, shaken, behind the wheel. There was a chorus of disappointment. 'Please sir!' someone called.

Willard was frightened, but wasn't sure why. He remembered when he was a child having his pants pulled down by a group of older girls in the changing rooms at the swimming pool when nobody else was about. He felt like that now. As he put the bus into gear and slid away, all fell ominously silent behind him. He was alone in the cab this time. There were one or two muffled explosions. 'I bet you wouldn't,' he heard someone say. 'I will if you will,' another voice said.

'Hey Mr Driver, stop!'

Willard stopped.

'Look!' said several voices.

Willard looked. The pretty Maxi and another woman had taken off their knickers and were revealing everything to Willard.

Blushing deeply, Willard averted his eyes as the bus erupted into screams. He was filled with shame. They had come to paradise for no other reason than to become animals, he thought. He was no great drinker, had never been lost upon the heaving seas of drunkenness. All that happened to him when he drank was that he went to sleep. Not these women. They had lost all reason.

I can never tell Chucky about this, he thought. He'd never believe me.

Shortly after, the vomiting began.

XENA AND THE ZOMBIE

When she saw the zombie for the first time, Xena didn't know what she was looking at. She was not a horror movie fan or anything; she was too young, hardly out of Goosebumps and far from being a morbid or even imaginative girl. Certainly not given to nightmares.

She was known as a bright, sunny, practical girl. The ideal friend, with never a nasty word to say about anybody. The great thing about her, her friends said, was her cheerfulness. Her teachers liked her because she was intelligent without being cheeky or arrogant with it, which was a relief to them. Aside from loving her, of course, her parents liked her because she didn't give them any trouble, which was a relief to them.

In the light of later events Xena's relationship to her peers was examined closely and found to be normal. She had a best friend, Doreen Dunn, and a host of lesser friends and acquaintances. All in all, a healthy, happy girl.

Until she saw the zombie.

On a long summer evening, around twilight, she was going for a jog along a nice winding, quiet road that hadn't been paved yet, with trees on each side and baches and holiday homes set deep in their sections as if to get as far away from the road as possible, when she saw a boy ahead of her. He moved with a peculiar motion as if he'd just woken up and forgotten the use of his limbs.

Before she could get a closer look, he'd disappeared around the next bend. She slowed down, uncertain. Sometimes she jogged with Doreen, but had no problem being alone, not on these familiar streets, and the boy, hardly much older than herself, didn't appear dangerous.

When she rounded the corner he was there, close, and walking back towards her. Her first thought was that he was ill. His face was grey, the colour of clay, the colour of river stones, and his eyes had a flat, dull look,

113

like pieces of opaque plastic. She stopped. Then skipped to the other side of the road, which wasn't very far, the road being so narrow. The boy stopped too, and turned in her direction. Peculiarly, he turned too far, overshot the mark as it were, and had to correct the motion. He was like a compass needle trying to find north.

When he had located her, he moved towards her, stiffly but quite fast. He didn't look threatening, but he didn't look friendly either. She ran back up the road the way she had come, stopped, turned, and saw that he was still coming, but no faster. Perhaps he wasn't running after her but just coming up the road. As he got closer, however, he seemed bent on approaching her, so she ran away again and repeated the manoeuvre. It was funny that he hadn't greeted her, or said anything, and funny too that she had never seen him before. She was sure she knew all the boys on Paradise Island. He could always be a tourist, but he didn't look like a tourist. He looked like a tramp. A down-and-out.

This time she decided not to run, confident that she could get away if she had to. He didn't stop. He just kept coming no matter what she said. He had a fixed expression on his face she couldn't read. When he reached out for her, she brushed him away, but his bony arms were strong and he gripped her by the shoulders. She didn't scream. She always thought she would in such a situation. She grabbed him by his arms and ripped herself free. His skinny arms had an unpleasant, slimy feel. He bent forward with surprising speed and was about to sink his teeth into her hand when she pulled it away.

'You're not going to bite me,' she said.

He had other ideas and came at her again. Now she understood that fixed expression. It was hunger.

'You can't eat me,' she said.

Even at this point, our practical heroine was not afraid. The silent hungry boy was mostly slow and clumsy. She could easily evade him, run circles around him just for fun if she wanted; all she had to do was stay alert and not let him get within biting distance.

She heard a car coming up behind her and jumped onto the verge. Sometimes people drove too fast along this mostly deserted, narrow road. The boy apparently didn't hear it and was standing in the middle of the road, turning in that funny mechanical way he had of locating her, when the car came revving around the corner, too fast, she'd thought. Much too slowly, the boy began to turn in the direction of the sound. She raced forward and pulled him out of the way of the swerving car. He seemed to have no awareness of what had happened, but just tried to bite the arm around him, the arm that had saved him.

She pushed him away. 'You're all skin and bone,' she said, which was something her mother said sometimes to describe people. It wasn't pleasant, having him bump up against her. He had a smell, partly sweet, partly rank.

'You need a bath,' she said.

The boy was doing his best to appear human, but she could tell from the awkwardness of his gait that he was dead. The dead had forgotten how to walk, and, like children, had to learn all over again.

It was getting dark and she had to do something. She couldn't just leave him wandering around. He might get run over. Or bite somebody. Her father's friend, Mr Hanks, lived nearby, and he had a workshop on a separate property next to his house, Xena knew because she had visited with her father. By running around behind the boy and pushing, she devised a way of moving him in the desired direction. She could see the workshop, a dark shadow now, and the first bright stars showing behind. It was hard work because he kept trying to turn around and eat her, which meant she had to run around him again to get him facing the right direction.

Luck was with her. Mr Hanks hadn't locked the side door to his workshop, and she immediately found some rope she could use to tether him. That wasn't easy either, as he kept trying to bite her.

'You're persistent, I'll give you that,' she said.

In the struggle to tie him up, a part of his filthy shirt came away from one shoulder. His skin was unnaturally white. There was a line of poetry – *with skin as white as leprosy.* Maybe Keats, she hadn't been paying full attention in class, but now the line came back to her. It was just right for her zombie boy.

'Well,' she said, 'I could never take you home to meet Mum and Dad looking like that.'

At home that night she said nothing to her parents. No sense in disturbing them. They would just tell her that she was making it up and maybe send her to some doctor. That's what they did when you made things up. Once, when her parents decided she was suffering from exam stress they had sent her to Dr Lovejoy who seemed a lot more interested in her than in what she had to say.

She stole some meat out of the fridge the next morning and went for a little jog, hoping that Mr Hanks hadn't visited his workshop yet. Again she was in luck. There was no sign of activity at Mr Hank's place, so she went straight to the workshop. The zombie boy was still there. As soon as he saw her he made a run at her, jerking against the ropes that tethered him.

He so much wanted to eat her, she felt sorry for him. She gave him the meat, but like a little child he spread it around and didn't eat. It was her he wanted. Although she knew what he was, a dead person walking around, she was still not scared of him. He was more pathetic than scary.

'Who are you?' she asked. 'Where did you spring from? You can't have just appeared out of nowhere. Are there others like you?' But of course he never answered, so she was free to make up answers for herself. She made up all sorts of pasts for him. And all sorts of deaths. He died of some terrible illness, or a car crash, or he drowned. She could change her answers any time and nobody cared.

Otherwise, he wasn't that much fun to be with. The only game he liked to play was chasing, him chasing her. On return visits, she sometimes let him off the rope for fun. Whenever she was with him, he never took his eyes off her for a moment. All it would take was one slip and his teeth would be into her. She wondered if she would turn into a zombie too. That was what was supposed to happen.

With Mr Hanks apparently away, she was able to return every day and she soon noticed changes in him. That skin as white as leprosy was starting to turn a horrible grey and peel. He stank worse too, a cloying smell that got up her nostrils. His eyes were starting to stick out from his face, which was caving in around his cheek bones. His teeth too were starting to stick out. He was the ugliest boy she'd ever seen.

'I'm sorry I don't have a plump little sister or brother to feed you,' she said.

She felt guilty at saying something horrible like that, but it didn't matter what you said to him. Some of her friends, like Doreen Dunn, did have plump little siblings, and for a moment she contemplated capturing a couple of the annoying ones, and bringing them to feed to her zombie boy. She wasn't sure if he would put on weight if he started eating the way she did, but she imagined so. Maybe if he ate enough he would turn back into a person again.

One day she was with him, and Doreen Dunn who had followed her crept up behind her while she was talking to the zombie.

'What are you doing?' Doreen's voice was sharp, like a mother.

'This is my pet zombie. He's hungry.'

Doreen backed away, her hand up to her face. 'You can't keep him like this. You have to kill him.'

'I don't want to kill him. He's dying anyway. Soon he'll just be a skeleton.'

Doreen shuddered. 'Get rid of him. Quick!'

'He's hungry.'

The boy was reaching out to Doreen, wanting to eat her too. He'd eat everybody in the whole world if he could. For a moment she contemplated grabbing her friend and feeding her to the zombie. She'd be able to watch while he tore Doreen to pieces, ripped her innards out and greedily fed on them. That would be something to see.

Doreen was screaming at her. 'You've got to kill it. Kill it right now! Kill it! Kill it!'

She knew Doreen was right. She took up a hammer and chisel from Mr Hanks' workbench and approached the boy. For a moment he went quiet, as if he knew what she was doing, and in that moment his face looked infinitely sad. No creature, alive or dead, should be that sad. It was all that hunger, she decided, that had made him so sad.

She waited until he made his next lunge at Doreen, then slipped in behind him, fitted the chisel to the back of his head and, before he could turn, slammed the hammer down upon it with all the strength of her young life.

THE ARTIST AND THE APPLE TREE

Back in the day, there was and there was not a kingdom far away from Paradise Island ruled by a cruel and capricious monarch called Thunder-in-the-Mountains. Ever fearful of new ideas, the monarch turned on his own young people, sent troops into the schools and universities to close them down, instituted mass arrests, and sent his emissaries into people's homes searching for mutinous material to be destroyed.

In that kingdom, there lived a young prince of sensitive nature and a love of beauty, whose skills tended towards art and poetry rather than those of war and repression, much to the disappointment of his royal father, who was a general in the monarch's army and keen to advance his son.

So precocious was the young prince, it was said the very first words he spoke were poetry, a reflection on falling apple blossoms. And, as an infant barely able to sit up, he could draw a bird on an apple branch in a few lines, just like the old masters. It was said that, as he grew up, the prince took to sitting very quietly beneath a spreading apple tree near their family home and drew pictures in the earth with a stick.

The dreamy boy was much beloved by the people, and when he stood up to sing his verses, the people cheered, and when he displayed his paintings, their eyes grew wide. One whose eyes grew very wide was a young woman of suitable birth whose name translated as Faithful-to-the-End. She had a reputation as a painter already, but was as practical in her outlook as the prince was dreamy. She fell in love with him when she saw the image he had of himself in his mind, which was of pure beauty.

They were married in the springtime of their lives, and everything was set for a happy-ever-after story, as befits fairy-tales, when the prince's father was arrested and banished, with his family, to a far province where he was to live his life in quiet gratitude for keeping it.

The prince and Faithful-to-the-End decided to escape the kingdom altogether and go to a very far off place, an island at the ends of the earth called Paradise Island, where, it was rumoured, it was possible to live a decent life. Of course, it is much harder to live a decent life without money, and, cut off from all sources of support, the two faced a hard life in their refuge.

They found a hut to live in with an apple tree outside, and their new life began. They danced and laughed together when they ate their first fruit from their apple tree, and the prince began writing poems in the dirt with his stick. He would write a poem, laugh, scuff it out with his feet and write another one. Still he wrote about falling blossoms which were like kingdoms falling into history.

However, while Faithful-to-the-End adapted to their new life, learning a new language, growing food and generally making herself liked and useful, the delicate web of fantasy that sustained the prince began to unravel. He couldn't learn the language of the place, and didn't try. His ears were tuned to the music of his own language and he didn't want it any other way. He found a hat he could pull down over his ears so that the unpleasant sounds of the Paradise Islanders did not intrude. Faithful-to-the-End learned how to drive, which gave her precious mobility, but the prince was incapable of learning and twice drove their old car into the sea to prove the point.

Only the apple tree seemed to delight him. He would sit beneath it and scratch his visions in the dirt.

Still, they might have boxed on as people in adversity do, if it had not been for the arrival of Easy-on-the-Eyes. Another refugee from the troubled kingdom, another painter, poet and dissident, this young woman was both an admirer of the prince and a leading exponent of the 'veiled school' of painting which hid its political messages behind elusive images. It is easy to imagine how the arrival of this vital, idealistic young woman, struck by the prince's genius, would further destabilize the couple already battling to stay emotionally afloat. Easy to imagine the prince falling in love with her, or at least his image of her, a passion watered by tears for his lost homeland.

Homesickness is a form of grief, and can grow unbearable. Easy-on-the-Eyes represented the homeland and everything the prince yearned for, while his wife came to represent the island and everything he rejected. The alien hissing sounds of the local language were now coming out of her mouth, and she was already half stranger to him. Sometimes he would look at her and not know her.

The three lived in uneasy alliance for as long as such arrangements tend to last, which is not very long. There were some mutual benefits for the two women that might have kept it alive past the usual use-by date for these situations. As the prince became increasingly childlike and unable to properly fend for himself, it was a relief for Faithful-to-the-End to have another woman to share the burden. The prince was incapable of any practical action around their hut. He had also become clingy and jealous of his wife's freedom, especially the car, which he regarded with particular suspicion. With the prince focused on Easy-on-the-Eyes, it was possible for Faithful-to-the-End to get away and begin to build her own life. A life filled with new interests. A life away from the prince.

The end was heralded by the arrival of the magician. The magician was an older man who exuded worldly confidence and who put himself forward as a friend and counsellor to the prince and his household. What they didn't know was that he was really a black magician who lived by deceiving women out of their property, and who had wormed his way into their lives in order to secure Easy-on-the-Eyes for himself. It began with him teaching her the language and the ways of Paradise Island, but soon he was warning her about the prince. The prince, he said, was going mad from grief and isolation, and was a growing danger to himself and others.

Just as the magician had calculated, this drove a wedge between the prince and his young protégé, exacerbating the prince's suspicion and jealousy. Jealousy became his ruling star. Inevitably, the edge had worn off the young woman's idealism, and her admiration for the prince suffered in the face of his growing reluctance to deal with the world. Genius, she was discovering, is best admired from afar. Besides, like Faithful-to-the-End, she had to find her own feet in this new land. She didn't really need the magician to tell her that the prince would drag her down with him, but it helped.

To the prince's despair, Easy-on-the-Eyes began to spend more and more time with the magician, who showed her how to access her own magic power to give her protection from the mad prince. The magician taught her spells and incantations, which she readily learned. An apt pupil for the dark arts, she was now his protégé not the prince's and the magician quickly moved to take advantage of the situation by becoming her lover.

Secretly they plotted their escape from the prince and the island itself. 'If you tell him, he will kill you,' the magician said.

The magician soon found himself enmeshed in the web he had

created, for he fell in love with Easy-on-the-Eyes, and began to see himself in heroic terms, doing battle with the monster prince for the hand of the damsel in distress. He had become a victim of his own fantasy, tricked by his own trickster. He was so carried away by his mythic role that he proposed marriage, and Easy-on-the-Eyes, seeing a way out of the situation she was in, accepted.

As so often happens in these cases, the prince soon faced the loss not just of his lover and protégé, but his wife as well. Faithful-to-the-End did not, in the end, live up to her name. Her bout of poverty had given her a healthy respect for money and a comfortable life, and when a man came along who offered both, and who respected her, she decided to take her opportunity. She didn't plot behind the prince's back, as Easy-on-the-Eyes had done - she was of a more forthright and honest nature - and told him straight out.

Faced with the loss of everything he held dear, the prince decided to take his own life. He had no home, no country, no family – and even his beloved language was slipping away. When he tried to paint, the brush slipped around in his fingers. When he sat beneath the apple tree to write poems in the dust, his stick failed him. It lay inert in his hands. He couldn't even feel it there. He couldn't taste the world any more. He was in effect already dead. Only the body remained. When he closed his eyes, all he could see was his body swinging from that very tree.

One afternoon, when Faithful-to-the-End was away making preparations for her departure, and he sat beneath the apple tree, his stick began to move of its own volition, giving him a sudden scare. It began writing poems in the dust so furiously he had no time to follow the lines, no time to catch them. Faster the stick whirled, faster the words flew into the obliteration of dust. A whole lifetime of poetry, everying he had to say, or might have to say in years to come. Every word of it purged through the stick in a few ecstatic moments. Afterwards, there were no words left. Nothing. He was as empty as the sky above. His head stretched from one horizon to the other. He looked up at the sky and didn't recognise it.

A bird flew into the apple tree and let forth a warbling cry. It went right through the empty man's head and out the other side.

He wandered about the property like a sleepwalker, poking into this and prodding at that. He found an axe, a small one used for cutting kindling. It had no weight. If he threw it into the air, it would keep rising until it vanished into the unrecognisable blue. He walked slowly along the path looking for a place to sleep… No, a place to hide. To hide from everybody… No, a place to hide from his wife. A place where he could see her but she couldn't see him. That's how it had to be.

And he did. And he waited. Waited for the slow sun. Waited for the creeping shadow. Waited with the axe in his hand. The blue sky turned bluer and the picture postcard yachts bobbed on the whitecaps in the bay until the whitecaps turned grey.

His wife came rapidly along the path, a brisk, business-like step. He had no time to think. Not now. He lept to his feet, rushed after her with inhuman speed and, with a scream of rage, buried the axe in her back.

News of the murder suicide spread far and wide, even back to the kingdom and reached the ears of the cruel and capricious monarch, who immediately ordered that all works of art and books by the mad prince, who had disgraced the kingdom, were to be destroyed.

Meanwhile, back on Paradise Island, the property, with its apple tree, an invisible load still swinging from a branch, became something of a tourist attraction. There was a rumour, for a time, that someone was going to put a plaque there but nothing came of it.

It is said that, to this very day, that the apple tree bears no fruit.

PIPPA AND THE PLACENTA TREE

There was a time, way back before the day, when women could not give birth on Paradise Island, but would have to go to the City. The island's doctors wouldn't risk it.

That was until Pippa came along. And Pippa wouldn't take no for an answer, not for her first and probably only child given her age. There were no practice shots, no coming back for a second try.

Pippa was German with firm ideas about what was right and what was wrong. What was the use of living in paradise when you couldn't give birth in your own home? There is something special about being born in a place, particularly if your placenta is buried there. Giving a child a sense of place by burying its placenta is one of the greatest gifts a child could receive, she maintained, and few argued with her. Freezing the placenta and bringing it back from the city was just not the same.

For best results, the placenta should be buried still warm and quivering with life. That way the infant's transition would be smooth and joyful. The first laughter of infants came from the initial jolt of transition from mother to mother earth. This ensured a happy and fruitful life for the child, and warded off evil. Pippa wasn't going to deny her baby that. It was one of the reasons she had come all the way from Germany to Paradise Island on the other side of the moon, as her friends put it.

Of course these Paradise Islanders were terribly naïve, living perhaps in a fool's paradise. They had no idea of what might be coming their way. She'd seen it in Germany, seen the heart of the beast, the beast that ate children, and knew that it would leave no place untouched. Not even Paradise Island. All the more important to give her child a powerful connection to the earth right from the start. That child, that precious he or she, would need all the grounding it could get. Her husband, stuck in Germany for a year finishing off a contract and making some money, agreed with her and gave her his blessing.

Her ideas struck a chord on the island, and not just among the home-birthers and breast-feeders. Many had come as refugees from one thing or another; many were groping for a life they imagined was possible. Her main hope was an idealistic young doctor, Dr Lovejoy, who had come to Paradise Island for what he called the lifestyle. In keeping with the lifestyle, he was easygoing and receptive.

In his easygoing life he had never encountered a woman like Pippa, who was as much a force of nature as a person. He was moved by her plans for the placenta. She had already chosen a tree to be planted on top of the buried placenta. With its roots in the mother's blood, the tree would be the child's connection to the earth and the place. Dr Lovejoy, who declared himself to be an empiricist and a rationalist, found himself vulnerable to the mythic force of the idea.

'Perhaps it's because I was brought up a Catholic,' he said to his wife. 'I've got a taste for superstition and ritual.'

His wife, Carol, very much a no-nonsense sort of person, warned against it. 'You're going native,' she said. Carol was very firm in her resolution to stay on Paradise Island and not go native.

The two other doctors on the island were also against it. One, an elderly gentleman of the old school, was disturbed by the idea. 'You start doing it, then we have to start doing it,' they said. 'We're not equipped for complications.'

'It's a healthy pregnancy,' he said.

'Even healthy pregnancies can turn pear-shaped,' they said. It was important to err on the side of caution. There were legal issues.

'Blah, blah,' Pippa said. 'All the authorities ever do is blah blah.'

So Pippa kicked up a fuss. She took her story to Sue Lake at the Council and Sue washed her hands of the issue. 'We cannot get involved in a medical matter,' she said. Pippa took her story to the *Paradise Island Times* and intrepid reporter, Garrison Ford, took a daring photo of the great orb of her naked belly which Blackbeard the Editor promptly put on the front page. Pippa's belly had its fifteen minutes of fame.

Opinions varied from those who thought Pippa a courageous woman standing up for herself and her baby, a pioneer of sorts, to those who thought she was a madwoman prepared to risk the life of her baby to prove a point. However, despite her best efforts, and the advocacy of Dr Lovejoy, the tide turned against Pippa and her crusade, and it might have all ended there, with her going off to hospital to have the baby just like all the other mothers, if Pippa herself had not drastically upped the ante by announcing that she would have a public birth in the local community hall, and have a public burial of the placenta afterwards.

'It used to be,' she told the open-mouthed Garrison Ford, 'that giving birth was a tribal, communal experience, and it can be again. The whole community will bond with the baby.'

She got up in front of people and said, 'I want other people to be a part of this experience, this marvellous experience, the miracle of birth. But this will not be a free for all. It is for my friends and supporters, those I count as my community. If I haven't met you yet, and you want to come, then please step forward and talk to me.'

Many did. Admiration and contempt for Pippa grew in equal measure. She was a flagrant exhibitionist one moment and a saint the next. 'I hope she doesn't need a caesarean,' somebody commented. Art collector and critic, Mira Bexley, declared that the public birth was a 'profound work of conceptual art' and should really take place in the art gallery. Such a work would be full of dramatic tension, with rising action capped by the mother of all climaxes, manifesting raw, primal power, the most primal of all, she said.

Dr Lovejoy was a tower of strength. Without him, nothing would have happened. He organized a helicopter to be waiting in case of an emergency. He made sure the community hall was equipped with all that was needed, with plenty of running water and so on. He also made sure that he had two experienced women, who had assisted at many childbirths, standing by.

A group of concerned citizens approached Tom Tommyknocker, the local cop, but Tom couldn't find any law against giving birth in public. Nor could Sue Lake find anything in the by-laws, and had just about taken the skin off by constantly washing her hands of the affair. Retired lawyer and defender of public rights, Rob Malarky, declared that a charge of creating a public nuisance wouldn't stick. Tom put it in the too hard basket and called for calm.

The day came and all went well. Those who expected a disaster were disappointed, but of course couldn't say so. There were no hitches except one of Pippa's dearest friends had brought her five-year-old son to witness the joyful occasion. When the baby had gushed from the mother, the little boy cried, 'Put it back, put it back!' to much laughter and clapping.

A few hours after the birth of a baby girl, the indomitable Pippa led a large procession to the appointed place, a regenerating forest area in a reserve, some willing hands soon dug a hole, the placenta was placed reverently in the hole and a tree was planted. The trees nearby, like the humans, watched in hushed silence.

'You have to take your hat off to her,' Garrison Ford said to Blackbeard. For once Blackbeard, a short man with a tall beard, agreed, and put a picture of the new baby in front of the tree on the cover of *PITs*.

Again, it might have all ended there, happily, with mother and child triumphant, if fate, or God, as some hinted darkly, had not intervened. Three months later, the child, a sweet natured little girl called Eva, fell ill with a runaway infection immune to antibiotics, and Dr Lovejoy had to tell Pippa that her child was dying.

Pippa, distraught to the point of collapse, went to see Tina Tuppa, known as a wise woman who could talk to taniwhas.

'If only I could talk to Eva. I know she can hear me. She's just too young to talk.'

'Go to the placenta tree,' Tina said, 'but go alone, at night...'

'Why at night?' Pippa found the New Zealand forest a bit scary at night.

'The elements are more fluid then. Sit quietly by the tree and listen. Just listen. The child can talk to you via the tree, if you are still enough to hear her.'

'How does that work?' Pippa was not a mystic. She was a social revolutionary. A feminist. Distraught as she was, this kind of talk put her on guard.

'Eva's spirit may very well have already left her body, since the fever can drive it away. But the spirit cannot leave the earth until the body dies, so the spirit can go to the placenta tree where it may wait the fever out, or for the body to die. The placenta tree becomes its temporary body.'

Pippa did as Tina advised. She hated going alone. She was, she discovered, a very social person; the privacy of the night and the weirdness of her mission frightened her. She could hear, close by, the bleak cry of the morepork. *Whirlpool, whirlpool,* the owl cried. Silly really, to go off into the dark and talk to a tree.

When she reached the tree, she sat by it and composed herself as Tina had suggested. She made a futile effort to quieten her mind. Around her the world came alive and the tree spoke to her. It spoke not so much in words but in tonalities of feeling. It was not that mysterious; people did it all the time without realizing it.

At first she didn't recognise what the placenta tree was relaying to her, because it was the last thing she expected.

Gratitude.

The spirit of the child was thanking her for the chance to spend even a few months in the company of the world. The welcome Eva had received by the community on Paradise Island had buoyed her spirit in the face of approaching death, helped fuel it with the joy it needed to take the next step.

In the face of that unexpected gratitude, which filled her like a benediction, Pippa cried. And as she cried she felt the spirit lift from Eva's body and fill the placenta tree, which seemed to grow tall and strong and reach up towards the stars.

Then it was gone. The placenta tree became a little sapling once more. Beside it a woman, a bereaved mother, sat weeping, and there was no witness but the silent forest and the placenta tree itself, bursting with young life.

HARRY THE HOBBIT AND THE HIDDEN TREASURE

Harry Hellman had all the qualifications for being a successful hobbit on Paradise Island. He was short in stature, lived in a half-buried house, had furry feet, was of generally cheerful disposition, and had a taste for the 'Shire Weed.'

All he lacked was a quest, although sometimes his weekly visits to the shops from his remote bach with his donkey, Bill, had an epic quality. Particularly if combined with a party, for, like all hobbits, Harry loved to eat and drink and make merry when the sun goes down, and Bill always knew the way home.

It might have been a blessing that Harry seldom remembered these revelries in any more than the most general terms. Somebody danced on a table. Somebody fell over. Somebody started talking orcish. Sometimes there was a tall, strong elf girl with pale hair who faded with the dawn. Sometimes there wasn't. And Bill always knew the way home.

The cool night air and the journey home tended to revive Harry, for again, like most hobbits, Harry had great resilience. He would pat Bill on the neck and sing hobbit songs about the Bilbos and the Frodos and the Hellmen and all his proud ancestry, songs of bravery and daring. The same cool night air, however, tended to revive not just his good spirits but his fears. Paradise Island was no longer a separate place protected by magic seas. There were trolls who drove around in huge trucks and diggers, and wargs – his nearest neighbour owned a warg which he thought was a sheepdog – but none were as bad as the orcs. The orcs came from the City, which they called Orcland, and they had nothing but malice in their hearts. Woe betide a feckless hobbit caught in the dark dark wood on a dark dark night without a wizard for protection.

You have to remember that most hobbits don't like adventures, only to sing about them. A hobbit like Harry will run a mile at the least hint of an adventure.

One early spring night, however, having danced and drunk his fill, and liberally partaken of the Shire Weed, he was returning home on the back of faithful Bill when an adventure befell him which would change his life forever.

It began with the sound of motorbikes, those favoured by some of the rougher tribes of orcs, coming up behind him. He was near the hidden turn-off to little more than a walking track, a short cut to his hobbit hole, and he hastened towards it. He hid in the deep shadows of the pohutukawa tree that arched over the beginning of the track. He expected the bikes to thunder by on their obscure mission.

This didn't happen. Instead the bikes slowed at the turn-off and circled about for a moment before finding the track. There were five of them, but it seemed like five hundred to Harry, and the noise made by their infernal machines throttling up and back sounded like all the legions of Sauron on the move.

He had read of heroes shrinking back into the shadows, Frodo or Bilbo might have done so a couple of times, but it wasn't until he tried to do it that he realised that it was impossible. Try as he might, he couldn't shrink even a tiny bit, so he had to hope that the benevolent shadow of the pohutukawa would cloak him like the cloak of invisibility that protected Frodo and Sam.

The bikes, with their bulky drivers, moved on past him, going slowly as they negotiated the rough track. He was starting to wonder how far the bikes would get, as the track deteriorated as it wound its way up over a saddle that lead to the valley where Harry lived, when the bikes pulled in a circle and stopped. The night was eerily quiet after the racket of the machines died.

Harry patted Bill's neck, counselling quiet, as the riders took off their helmets. Orcs. Just as Harry thought. They began to talk to each other in their rough, orcish language. Harry was no expert on their language, but by their intonation he guessed they were from the South Reach. What were orcs from South Reach doing on Paradise Island, where hobbit, dwarf, troll and elf muddled along just fine?

Burying something, seemed to be the answer. Or rather hiding something. The orcs left the trail and moved some distance off, although Harry could still hear their voices, and see their lumpish shadows moving.

'Pleash,' one of the voices was saying over and over.

Harry secured Bill to the tree and stole closer to get a better look.

The orcs were grunting and snarling as they lifted something, a heavy rock, Harry couldn't get close enough to see much. Or rather the bulky mass of the orcs cut off his view. There were six of them, one a female who must have been a passenger. He could hear her voice, broken yet strident, above the rumble of the males.

Harry was about to creep closer, growing a little bolder in the dark and the noise of their voices when one of the males said something and they all fell silent.

'There's somebody out there,' the male said in the common tongue, although roughly.

Harry held his breath. The world around him seemed to do the same. Except Bill. Bill gave a disgruntled snort.

'It's a donkey.' One of the males of somewhat slighter build left the group and passed within a couple of arm's lengths from Harry as he located Bill.

'Forget it,' the first male to speak said.

'It's all saddled up, with bags of stuff.'

The female now moved to the front, revealing a box or case behind her. She was dressed in bulky black leathers like the others.

'We know you're there,' the female said. 'Come on out now. If we have to come and get you, we'll bust all your fingers for you.'

Harry didn't doubt her for a moment. Finger busting was merely a minor orc accomplishment. He thought of his stubby, hobbit fingers. They weren't much but they were his.

'Or just bust your fingers anyway,' one of the males said, and the others all laughed in short, loud bursts.

Harry realised that they were afraid. Not of tangible enemies so much as of the quiet, endless night. Orcs were used to lots of noise all the time. And fear was making them jumpy. One of them snarled something in orcish and another produced a knife. He saw the moonlight sliding off it, just like in the movies.

He had no choice. Without further thought, he stepped forward into the moonlight. The orcs stood very still as they looked him over.

'How many of you?' the female demanded. Harry saw that this female was of surpassing ugliness with a bony body and a head like a raptor.

'Just me,' Harry said, feeling very small and alone in the universe. He decided that if he were to die now, his last thought would be of the tall elf girl with the pale hair.

'What are you doing creeping around?'

'Just going home,' he gestured up the track. 'Then you guys came so I hid.'

There was general relief among the orcs. The knife disappeared.

'We can't leave it here now,' the first male said to the female.

'You're a problem,' the female said to Harry.

'Not me,' Harry said. 'I'm just passing on by.' He moved towards Bill but found a large orc body in the way.

'Not any longer,' the large orc said. He looked like he fed on tasty little hobbits for breakfast.

'We could deal to the problem,' the first orc said.

The female nodded. Everybody looked at Harry.

'I got a better idea,' the woman said. 'Let's give it to him.'

'What?'

There was consternation among the males.

'I thought we were going to get rid of it,' the first male said.

'This is a better idea,' the female said.

The first male let out a huge breath. 'I dunno,' he said. 'He could still talk.'

'He won't talk,' she said.

'That's right,' Harry said.

'Not if we pull out his tongue,' one of the orcs said and there was another burst of nervous laughter.

'It's up to you,' the first male said to the female.

'Very generous of you,' the female said. At the same time she reached into the box and pulled out a bundle. As if pushing it away from herself, she thrust it into Harry's arms. 'It's your lucky night,' she said.

Harry examined the bundle. There was cloth all around it. He pulled aside the cloth and there was a face. A tiny, very ugly little orc face. Sleeping.

'Are you its mother?' he asked without thinking. He thought he detected a family resemblance, a certain raptor-like aspect.

She thrust her face close to his. It was not a pleasant experience. Her breath alone was enough to make him giddy. Her eyes were as black as the pit of hell.

'You don't ask questions,' she said. 'If you talk, we come back. And you won't want to see us.'

'No,' Harry said. 'I mean yes.'

'Let's get out of here,' the first male said.

The female lingered for a moment. The last look she gave Harry was terrible in its anger and its sorrow. What dreadful orcish realities had led to this, he could only guess.

Then they were on their bikes which once more shattered the night and they were gone.

Harry the hobbit stood there, holding the baby, until the sound of their motors had vanished into the night. Bill made some impatient noises but Harry didn't move. He just kept looking at the tiny orcish face. He could see now where they had been going to put him. There was a crevice covered by a large stone. They'd moved the stone to one side leaving a crevice exposed. Easily big enough to hold a baby, and with the stone pushed back nobody would ever know.

He could do that right now. Finish the job for them. Not another word would be said.

As he stood there, hesitating, the orc child woke up and opened its eyes and stared it him.

Its eyes were as black as the pits of hell.

.... to be continued

HETTIE HARPER AND THE INDIGO CHILDREN

Hettie Harper had always done her best to walk in the light. She didn't expect to be rewarded for her steadfastness, exactly, knowing life didn't always turn out that way; but she didn't expect to get a kick in the guts either. It would be nice to think there was some justice in the world.

It was one thing for a bad mother and all-round evil person like Polly McGuire to have attention deficient kids, little world wreckers, but for Hettie Harper – Hettie the Holy, they called her – to have to deal with a child like her Evelyn simply did not feel fair. It's a vicious thing to live one's life in constant comparison to others, but Hettie couldn't help it. Look at these solo mums like Rosaline, living life high on the hog with their cosy little government benefits, hopping in and out bed with any scoundrel who knocked on the door. Worse still, look at that blatant Californian redhead Dennaray revelling in her hotbed of sex and drugs and yet with three of the most beautiful daughters, cheerful and smart.

And look at Hettie, who had done all the right things. Married a faithful man called Dan she had just as faithfully served, making a cut lunch for him every working day of his life so that Dan didn't have to spend his precious pay on greasy hot pies. A woman who never drank or smoked or whored after other men. Always walked in the light. Always gave thanks for the blessings of the world. Now she had to ask herself, what blessings?

Her faithful Dan had turned out to be faithfully dull, a cheese-and-tomato man who didn't ask for more; and her daughter, her God-given child, brought up in the light with every opportunity before her, was like the worst of the over-sugared brats that ruled the playcentre and wore their parents down to a frazzled edge with their scatter-brained behaviour. If Hettie had been that way inclined, she might have decided that her daughter was possessed by a malicious spirit that would never let her rest, or focus on anything longer than a few seconds, but Hettie's faith was not as specific as that; hers was a god of warm fuzzies, a god of sunsets and happy glows. A god who was fair – certainly not a god who would punish her for her faith by blighting her daughter.

The doctors were not a lot of help. They poked and prodded and pressed and looked serious and told her that Evelyn had Attention Deficit Hyperactivity Disorder. That sounded so frightening that Hettie recoiled into herself.

'I guess they know what they're talking about,' Dan said.

Hettie was not convinced. No one had heard of any such thing when she was growing up. The doctors must have made it up.

To make matters worse, there was a woman called Marie Baigent running around saying that roadside spraying was causing neurological damage to sensitive children. She'd read all about it in the *Paradise Island Times*. Hettie was not the only parent to suspect that her child might be damaged in some way.

In fact Hettie was not, as she discovered, the only parent whose child had been diagnosed with this mysterious ADHD the doctors could not satisfactorily explain. So Hettie did some reading and made a stupendous discovery.

Her child, Eveyln, was not damaged, or suffering a mysterious disorder – her daughter was special.

Her daughter was an Indigo Child.

And she wasn't the only one. Indigo children had special psychological and spiritual attributes, sometimes even supernatural traits and abilities, which the doctors saw as 'symptoms.' Far from suffering from 'learning difficulties,' such children represented the next stage in human evolution. They could travel easily between worlds. The real reason Evelyn was not getting on at school was because of her rejection of rigid authority, because she was smarter or more spiritually mature than her teachers and refused to respond to their guilt trips and fear-based discipline.

In fact, Evelyn, along with many other children diagnosed with ADHD, was actually a space alien! Or at least part space alien. A spirit guide called Kyron had explained it all to those who first discovered the indigo children.

Hettie told some other parents and the word quickly got around. The indigo children were special. They would save the world. As small children they were easy to recognize, too, by their unusually large, clear eyes. Extremely bright, precocious children with an amazing memory and a strong desire to live instinctively. Wasn't that Evelyn, exactly? Hettie pulled out the photo album and stared at the photos of Evelyn. And there it was, all the evidence she needed. A small head and large clear eyes.

Not everybody was receptive. Hettie and a couple of other indigo mothers, as they called themselves, went along to the school for an awkward and fruitless meeting with their children's teachers. Those teachers didn't have a clue. They were as bad as the doctors. Other parents, who should have been happy that they had normal children, began to ask why they didn't have indigo children also. Why shouldn't their children be special? Somehow that was Hettie's fault. More heartbreaking, at least for Hettie, were those parents who did have indigo children but drugged them up with nasty stuff like Ritalin.

'They're turning their own children into zombies,' Hettie said to Dan. 'It's so sad.'

'Yeah, but those kids seem to be able to concentrate a bit better,' Dan said. Flaky Dan.

Community feelings began to rise. Certain children were not allowed to play with certain other children. Space aliens were not welcome. People began to give her funny looks, or worse, avoid her. Upset, Hettie sought an appointment with Tina Tuppa who was known to be a wise woman, one who could talk to taniwhas and heal cats.

'This is all a lot of nonsense,' Tina said to Hettie in a stern voice. 'Of course your child is special, they all are. If you carry on this way, saying your child is a space alien, you will blight Evelyn's life just as surely as putting a curse on her.'

'But she is an *indigo* child. They have special auras, you know, that people with synesthesia can see…'

'Then let her discover that for herself, as she grows older.'

'She has a destiny…'

'Then her destiny will find her.'

That night, after visiting Tina, as she lay beside her oblivious husband, Hettie had a dream, the most vivid dream of her life. So vivid that perhaps it wasn't a dream at all. She was lying in bed fretting over what Tina had said to her, when the room filled up with a soft light and an alien being entered the room. From her research she knew him to be a Grey, one of those with the huge leaf-shaped eyes and bald heads.

'I am Kyron,' he said.

As soon as she saw the shape of his eyes, and heard the sound of his voice, she knew that Kyron was Evelyn's true father. Dan might have provided the physical seed but Kyron had provided the spirit, the animating, shaping force. Kyron held out his hand and she rose up out of bed, careful not to disturb Dan, and followed the Grey through her house and into a huge room she'd never seen before. The ceiling was arched like a cathedral. The floor was made of marble.

In the middle of the room a group of children knelt in a circle. Indigo children, she knew them all. Somehow they were really here, and she remembered that such children were easily able to travel between the worlds. A Grey was walking around the circle on the inside, giving each child a flat piece of bread. Suddenly Hettie was a little child once more, kneeling on the floor of a familiar church, a priest pressing a soft wafer into her mouth.

'What's all this?' Hettie said.

Kyron didn't answer.

The children stood up and Hettie noticed that they were wearing everyday school clothes. The girls mostly had their hair in sensible ponytails and the boys were well scrubbed up.

'They have to be ready for the world,' Kyron said. 'Like you, like all star beings.'

Hettie saw now that each child was carrying an instrument of some kind. One carried a ruler, another a calculator, another a set square, another a compass.

Hettie was struggling to understand the meaning of these objects when she woke up. Dan was staring at her. It took her a moment to realise he was sound asleep with his eyes open.

'It's your turn,' Dan said.

Of course, that's the way it had been when Evelyn was a baby and would wake up at night. They would take turns. She lay awake listening for sounds from Evelyn's room just as she used to. Old habits die hard, she could hear her mother saying.

Without disturbing Dan, she slipped out of bed and into her daughter's room. Unlike many children, Evelyn preferred to sleep in the dark with no night-light, and it took a while for Evelyn's eyes to adjust. There was her daughter, lying on her side, sleeping. Asleep, Evelyn looked like the baby she had once been. Or, when the shadow of the room deepened, like her grandmother lying in bed dying of old age.

That's what Evelyn will look like when she is very old, Hettie thought. She found the idea frightening. Evelyn will grow old and look like that.

And she will die, as vulnerable as the day she was born, star being or not.

'I'm a star being, and I will die too, looking just like the baby I was when I was born.'

Evelyn opened her sleepy eyes and looked at her mother. She didn't understand why her mother was there, staring down at her as if she'd never seen her daughter before. And perhaps she hadn't. What she saw was a normal child, full of fear and confusion.

Hettie fell to her knees before the bed and swept her bewildered child into her arms and cuddled her blessing close until their beating hearts became one.

POLLY AND PLAYCENTRE

Polly Maguire hated Paradise Island. She hated it as much as she hated the draughty excuse for a bach she lived in, her greedy landlord who lived in the City and didn't give a toss if the place fell to pieces, Flower-Power Ray who'd fathered a couple of kids with her and shot through, and the other moo-cow mums with their snivelling kids. She hated them all.

She wanted to go to a real place where real people lived.

Above all, she hated her own kids. It hadn't started that way. She wasn't a monster. She'd loved her kids just like all the other moo-cow mums. That was until Flower-Power Ray turned sour and started abusing her. He was one of those men you hear about who is Prince Charming in company and a monster at home. They do exist. He was such a monster that he got the kids abusing her too, showing them how to kick her and spit on her and bite the soft part of her arms or legs when she wasn't looking. After he shot through, the kids carried on the tradition. When she tried to put a stop to it and recover her dignity, they just got worse, hating her even more for the punishments she attempted to impose on them.

The kids, her kids, were just like him. They looked like him, thought like him, talked like him.

'They're only kids,' someone said to her once.

'You don't know,' she said.

The upshot of this was that she hated herself as much as she hated her kids and everybody else. The kids treated her like a doormat because she was a doormat. Her subjugation to Flower Power Ray was evidence enough. In the end, he'd walked out on her because his contempt had grown too big for the bach, too big for the two of them. He walked out and left his kids to do his dirty work.

Winter on Paradise Island was never fun at the best of times, and these were not the best of times – unless you were very rich. People with nowhere to go went around and around and ended up going stir-crazy.

Being incarcerated in a miserable little bach over winter with three kids for days on end without relief or enough firewood would have turned the very Buddha himself into a child beater, let alone an ordinary woman with more hate than she could bear. Extreme circumstances called for extreme measures: *Playcentre*.

Polly Maguire was not a natural Playcentre mum. She had no interest in its philosophy. Besides, she wasn't there to play with her children but to get away from them. When they were out in the sandpit she was inside with the kids building blocks, and when they were inside with the building blocks she was outside at the sandpit pretending to be watching over other people's kids who could scratch each other's eyes out as far as she was concerned. She noticed a few other mums doing the same thing but she didn't care about them. She despised them along with all the moo-cow mums.

She made it clear right from the start that she was only there on sufferance, because she had to get out of the house or go psycho, and because Flower Power Ray had left her with three children from hell on a cold and wet afternoon that had gone on forever. She couldn't even remember what her life had been like before, except that she must have had one and it must have been a whole lot better than the one she had now.

Officially, the mums and dads (an occasional dad) were all gooey over their children but Polly knew better. She saw the bruises on little limbs that gooey eyes missed; she saw the glazed parental eyes and slump of exhaustion. She saw it all and curled her lip. They were no better than her.

At first, her three monsters cut a swathe through those sweetness-and-light Playcentre kids, creating havoc left and right. The middle one, a boy named James, went around smashing everybody's sand castles and building-block castles and anything else standing. The eldest, Alice, specialized in giving kids quick, vicious little pinches and diving away in time to be doing something else by the time the scream arrived. Her youngest, the angelic little Toby with golden curls, liked to take out his penis and pee on kids paintings. He'd seen Flower Power Ray piss on one of Polly's paintings, the little water-colours she liked to do when she could grab a moment for herself, and in the case of golden-haired Toby and his sadistic daddy, it was monkey-see-monkey-do.

Much to Polly's amusement, the lovey-dovey moo-cow mothers all turned into hens and ran around clucking and flapping their arms. You should try having them day in and day out and see how you like it, she wanted to say, but bit her tongue. She couldn't trust her voice.

When James kicked sand into some kid's face, Polly laughed.

A couple of the busy-body mums took James aside and told him that kicking sand in people's faces was not nice.

That made Polly laugh even harder. Not nice! These earnest women with their tired faces and their exploited lives didn't have clue. Her kids didn't do *nice*.

They came to her with their complaints. 'Go tell their father,' she said. After that the other women tended to keep away from her, which suited Polly just fine. She had no time for their saccharine talk anyway.

It was one of these incidents with James the Destroyer that finally made up her mind. She'd seen how some desperate mother, shocked by the way her children acted like animals at the dinner table, started treating them like animals and made them eat out of a plate on the floor like a dog or cat. At first Polly had been shocked, but the idea slowly grew on her. It satisfied her craving for justice. Pigs belonged in a pigpen not at the table with a knife and fork.

Thinking about it gave her a few pleasurable moments. Imagining the looks on their faces, when they realised they weren't going to get fed if they didn't get down on the floor, made her smile. Toby, she realised, would probably think it was great fun and get right into it, he loved the idea of being a pig, but Alice wouldn't. Alice was old enough to understand, and to get a taste of shame and humiliation. It would be worth it just to see the look on Alice's face. Maybe she'd refuse to do it and starve herself to death, although that was a bit too much to hope for.

That's what it had come down to now. A fight to the death.

It was an ugly moment, when her plans became concrete in her mind and she knew she was going to do it. Ugly but liberating. It put a sickly smile on her face for the rest of the day.

And it would have happened, too, just as she imagined it, if a tiny, apparently insignificant moment had not intervened.

It was a dark afternoon, and bedlam at the Playcentre. Since it was raining too hard to play outside in the sandpit, all the kids were squashed inside and the noise level would have put an airport to shame. All the moo-cow mums were there. There was Ella, MoJo's wife and their brat. Tricksy Claw and Margery Razorblade, who were friends and had to be watched. There was Hettie the Holy with her two God-fearing children. Then there was Rosaline who struggled with her kids and thought they gave her a hard time, whereas they were nothing compared to Polly's kids.

Rosaline's eldest, Shanka, was not the brightest star in the firmament. Kids were always making him cry. Crying was all he knew how to do, since he didn't have the sense to run away. Rosaline was working hard with Tricksy and Margery to keep several kids occupied, Alice included. Shanka was sitting beside her and kept tugging at her sleeve. Polly waited for the pinch, that quick nasty little pinch, but it didn't come. For the moment, anyway, Alice seemed content to let the gormless boy annoy her. That certainly wouldn't last for long.

When Shanka hurt himself, Polly was watching and saw everything. In theory there was nothing lying around that a child could use to harm itself, but determined children will find a way. Shanka found something to swallow. Nobody knew what it was when he started choking. There was such a small noise nobody noticed except Polly, who watched with fascination. Maybe the kid would choke to death before anybody caught on.

Alice caught on first. Her own dear Alice. Now Shanka would die for sure. But that didn't happen. Alice took the boy gently by the arm, whispered some words in his ear and thumped his back like an expert. The boy coughed but didn't stop choking. Others began to notice now. They watched wide-eyed as Alice put her fingers into the boy's throat and gently removed the obstruction, some bit of plastic wrapper. Shanka's head fell into her lap as he sucked in air. Gently, Alice stroked his forehead.

The moo-cow mothers stared at each other.

Polly stared at her daughter. For a moment, a crack opened among the dark stars and a little light shone through. In that little light, her daughter was transformed from the ugly monster she was into the angelic being that hid inside her. Alice was beautiful. Her face shone with it. Aghast, Polly looked around the room. All the kids were like that; they were all beautiful. Their faces shone with the light that opened just a crack among the dark stars.

Polly didn't make her children eat off the floor that night or any night. That very afternoon she bought Alice an ice-cream as a reward for 'being nice' to Shanka. Saving his life, more like it.

Alice ate the ice-cream and went back to being a monster. Polly even thought that Alice was developing her father's ability to be wonderfully charming in company and a tyrant at home. Now all the moo-cow mothers thought that Alice could do no wrong. Alice had them all wrapped around her little finger. But none of that mattered. The light had opened. Polly had seen the face of beauty. Now she couldn't look at one of these snot-nosed brats without seeing it. Even though the crack closed, the light was there in her memory.

Many years later, Alice, who remembered the incident, confessed that she had caused Shanka to choke by encouraging him to eat the plastic wrapper and pinching him to make sure he jerked in his breath and sucked the wrapper back.

'I was always much more careful after that,' she told her mother.

LITTLE THIEVES

It is generally agreed that Paradise Island is the best place in the world for bringing up kids. All those sandy beaches, the open sky and open spaces. Paradise Island kids had something special about them, the parents all agreed. Kids on the Island had it good compared to City kids. They had an opportunity to run in bare feet and to enjoy nature to its fullest. To grow up as *natural* kids. As wild as the pumpkins that clambered over gardens in the late summer.

You could in fact grow organic kids as easily as organic pumpkins. Just add a bit of love and set them free.

Robo, Whizz and his sister Squelchy were just such kids, born on the island and nourished on its fresh air and freedom. They liked nothing better than getting together and roaming all over the island, or at least as far as they could. They made all kinds of discoveries. They found out that the glow over the horizon after sunset was not the absent sun nestling just out of sight, as they first thought, but city lights. They could hardly credit the idea that the City would be big enough to cast such a glare all night.

Nothing beat walking around at night. Night was special. Things happened at night that would never happen during the day. Distances looked different at night, they noticed. Dark, empty streets looked longer than daytime streets. Voices carry further too. At night they always wanted to talk in low voices or shout as loud as they could.

They began to notice other things too, such as which houses were occupied and which were holiday homes. The occupied houses always had lights and vehicles around. Sometimes dogs barked at them. Whizz could bark back, sounding just like a real dog, and could set all the dogs in the neighbourhood into a frenzy. The only time they got frightened was when a dog followed them, not barking or growling, but silent, as if stalking them.

One house in particular drew their attention. It was different from the other houses, being bigger and whiter and with a flat roof. Robo had heard his parents talking about it, so knew something his friends didn't. Apparently, people had forgotten how to build houses that kept the water out, and some houses had to be abandoned because when it rained the water got everywhere. This was just such a house.

'I bet it's abandoned,' Robo said. 'I've never seen a car here.'

'It doesn't have to be,' Whizz said.

'I've seen a car there,' Squelchy said, but the others took no notice of her since she lied all the time to make herself more important.

They were standing outside the house in the shadow of a macrocarpa tree. They liked it in the shadows, just as they liked to hide when a car came by. It was cool to think of the car sweeping past without seeing them.

'Let's go inside,' Robo said. 'I bet we could get in.'

'I bet we could too,' Whizz said, but he didn't sound convinced that they *should*.

'We can't do that,' Squelchy said. 'There are ghosts in there.'

'You've just made that up because you're a scaredy-cat,' her brother said.

'It's true,' Squelchy said. 'People have heard noises coming from that house.'

'They have not,' Whizz said, but the truth was that he was a bit of a scaredy-cat himself. They liked to do new things, and dare each other to do stuff, like go around the rocks at high tide, but going into somebody's house, well that was a different thing, not like following a road they had never followed before, or climbing a fence to take a short cut.

'Nobody will find out,' Robo said. Whizz was always scared that their parents would find stuff out. His angry mother was not a pretty sight. She would accuse him of not looking after his baby sister and he would have to feel all guilty.

They hurried up the short drive, where they could be seen from the road, and followed a concrete path around to the back of the house where they found a window that was loosely latched and big enough for Squelchy to squeeze through.

'You can open the door for us,' Whizz said.

She complained, said there was no way she was going to go alone into the empty house, but she did it after Whizz promised to use his pocket money to buy her some caramel chocolate, which she adored.

Once inside, she wasted no time opening the door for them.

'It's spooky in here,' she said.

They pretty soon got the feel of the house. It was surprisingly small compared to how it looked from the outside. It had a staircase that lead to a small bedroom upstairs, and an outside stairway to the flat roof.

There was furniture and other things, not much in the kitchen, which Robo deduced meant that nobody was in residence, although they might come here from time to time, especially in the summer when it wasn't raining. There was nothing wrong with the house when it wasn't raining.

Squelchy checked out the two bedrooms downstairs. 'Kids lived in one of those,' she declared, having become an instant expert on bedspreads. The one with the Pinocchio pattern must belong to a kid. 'Probably about seven years old,' she said. An age to which she herself aspired. She was already pretending that this was her house.

Robo poked around into everything looking for something to steal.

'I think we should leave,' Whizz said. 'There's nothing here.' It was after all somebody else's house.

Robo found the cache of videos in a closet, zipped up in an old bag. The secrets of the adult world were now theirs to feast their eyes upon. The pictures on the back and front on the video case were enough, more than enough.

'That's adults having sex,' Squelchy said.

'Do they all do it like that?' Whizz said. He was trying to imagine his parents engaged in these activities, and his imagination failed him.

'Sort of, I think,' Robo said.

'All the time,' Squelchy said.

'That's a lie,' her brother said. The longer he stared at the pictures, the less likely it all became.

Just then they heard a noise. A banging noise from upstairs.

'We didn't hear that,' Squelchy said.

'We're going to get punished,' Whizz said. On the back of the video he was holding there was a tiny picture of a big-breasted woman being whipped by a man in a mask. No way his parents did anything like that.

'Let's get out of here,' Robo said, grabbing a couple of videos and shoving them under his jersey.

Outside, a car door slammed. There was another noise from upstairs.

They ran to the window.

'The cops,' Whizz said in a resigned voice. How they knew to come, he didn't know, but he was certain it had something to do with the forbidden movies in the closet.

'Let's hide,' Squelchy said. She was good at hiding. If she didn't want to be found, nobody could find her.

'Good idea,' Robo said, giving Squelchy a moment of pleasure.

Whizz wanted to run, but there was nowhere to go but straight into the arms of the cops or up the steep bank behind the house.

There was a thump on the stairs and an apparition walked into the room, ragged and bearded like one of the prophets of old. In his hand he carried a small bucket.

He looked at the kids and they looked at him.

Robo was the first to recover. He'd seen this man at parties.

'If you don't go now we'll tell the cops you brought us here to do nasty things,' he said. He took one of the videos and waved it at the figure who took one look at it and ran for the door.

'It's only Bozzo Buckie,' Whizz said in relief. Buckie was a familiar enough figure around the island, named after the little bucket he used for smoking dope. Just a tramp looking for a place to crash. Bozzo Buckie would know all the empty houses and holiday homes on the island.

'The cops would be after him, not us,' Robo said. That made sense, even to Whizz who was still scared.

'I wonder where he hid,' Squelchy said.

'There are plenty of places,' Robo said. 'The roof probably. We didn't look around up there.'

They were back at the window looking down at the cops. Buckie was explaining something to them. He pointed back to the house. The cops were looking.

'He's told them,' Squelchy said.

'I think they're coming up here,' Whizz said.

This time his fear was infectious. And the cops were on their way.

The kids were out the door and scrambling up into the thick bush at the back of the house when a torch light came around the side of the building. It was a cop. He found the window with the dodgy latch and flashed his light around.

The kids held their breaths. This was scary. This was fun. Squelchy peed herself. Whizz could already hear his mother's voice. He imagined his little sister in prison. This was all Robo's fault.

This must be the most fun they had ever had.

Robo was already calculating what the videos would be worth at school. Heaps.

After he'd watched them, of course.

They'd have to watch them.

Squelchy planned all kinds of revenge. She followed Bozzo Buckie all over the place, to all his hideouts. She became an expert in all things pertaining to Bozzo Buckie, but the funny thing was, she never did take any revenge. When asked why, she couldn't think of a suitable lie – because she didn't know the truth. Sometimes you just did things. Or not.

They watched part of a video and it made them uncomfortable.

Robo didn't sell them at school either. He didn't care that much about the money. Whizz became frightened all over again. What terrible things his mother would say if she got wind of this. That he had let his sister watch even a few seconds of that stuff! He would die from shame.

Over Squelchy's objections, they decided to get rid of them – but where? No place was safe from discovery.

Finally they decided. These videos were like a bad dream; they should be returned to the darkness that spawned them. So, when Squelchy assured them that Bozzo Buckie was out of the way, they sneaked back to the white house with the flat roof. Whizz said they should be returned to the closet but none of them wanted to go in again. It wasn't fear; it was something else they didn't want to talk about.

They chucked the videos through the window with the dodgy latch and made a run for it.

They didn't talk about it again for years, and then they laughed.

CESS CLAW AND THE CITY SLICKER

Cess Claw built a boat. That is not to say he was a boat builder, since that implies some sort of business, a career, a revenue-generating activity which, as Cess's wife Tricksy often pointed out, would be far from the truth.

Cess built his boat in the same spirit that Alex Kendell wrote his unreadable stories – it gave him a reason to get up in the morning. It gave him something to do other than sit around at home and drink beer. He could hop on his bike and head off just like a normal person going to work. He would wave to some of the regular commuters or friends on the move. He might see MoJo Mayhem who liked to get his shopping done early so that he didn't run into too many people. Or he might, if he were lucky, see the pretty Millie Millicent flouncing off to work. Her short, jagged cut blond hair and her gangly, Pippi Longstocking legs provided Cess with his meagre share of the world's lustful thoughts. When he got on his boat, he could sit on the deck and drink beer and contemplate the day's work.

Years could go by this way, and they did. The boat grew. The little boy he had fathered with Tricksy grew up. Tricksy got pissed off with Cess's no-hoper lifestyle and left him for another country. The bike got rusty and Cess took to living on the boat. Millie Millicent got pregnant, started pushing a pram with twins, and stopped providing him with his meagre share of the world's lustful thoughts.

'Takes you longer to build a boat than it takes me to write a novel,' Alex Kendell said once when he had come aboard the *Joseph Conrad* for a beer. Cess and Kendell talked about Conrad, the writer. Cess was a keen admirer. They both agreed that *Nostromo* was Conrad's greatest book.

'It was Conrad who got me interested in boats,' Cess said.

'When it's finished, where are you going to go? Sail off into the sunset? Become your own Outcast of the Islands?'

'I could go anywhere,' Cess said.

Most often, those days, Cess would be seen in the company of his son,

Max, then an over-active little boy with a taste for trouble. Cess wasn't too sure about Max. He was a bright, energetic kid, but had only the haziest notions of consequences. For a bright kid, he could do stupid things. Like ripping off a neighbour's dope patch when he got old enough to realise how much money he could make selling it at school. Max had to get his money from somewhere; his father certainly didn't have any. Thing was, the kid made it obvious, got caught by JJ-180 who immediately confronted Cess. JJ was all steamed up. Couldn't put a crop in these days without bloody kids ripping it off.

'Would you like a smoke?' Cess said when JJ had finished, reaching for some stuff he'd confiscated from Max.

Max was always doing stupid things and getting into trouble. Especially at school. Never much for schoolwork. Always a worry to his father.

The years passed. Max got older but no wiser. And Cess built his boat. Alex Kendell, who was a regular visitor to the *Joseph Conrad* for a while, found himself envious of Cess's achievement. Kendell wasn't sure about his novels, but the *Joseph Conrad* was certainly a work of art. Every piece of timber carefully prepared and placed with the precision of a jewel-maker. A classic, thirty-five foot design, Kendell didn't know the details or even how Cess knew how to make such a vessel. It just seemed to take shape beneath his sedulous hands.

What rankled with Kendell the most was that, even unfinished, Cess's achievement was on show for everybody to see. Motorists passing would pull over to admire the sleek vessel. Everybody said how beautiful it would look in the water. Kendell's manuscripts had no such allure.

Eventually the unthinkable came to pass, and Cess finished his boat. A beautiful, sleek, handcrafted vessel using only the finest of timbers. He did a little bit of informal business taking tourists for trips around Paradise Island, but the coastguard got too interested in his activities and he had to cease and desist – or get a real licence. Did a bit of snapper fishing, took his mates out a few times. Engaged in long, technical discussions with Boatie Ben. But Kendell began to realise that despite appearances, Cess was at a loose end.

Now he'd built the boat he didn't care much about sailing it. The fun was in the making, and Kendell could understand that.

'What are you going to do now?' Kendell asked him one day when they were sitting out in the Gulf fishing.

'Dunno,' Cess said.

'What about the *Joseph Conrad*?'

Cess shrugged. 'Give it to Max, I guess.'

And he did. After Max turned twenty-five and had got himself a woman and a child of his own. The idea of Max being a father gave Cess the night sweats. However, the gift of the *Joseph Conrad* would give Max a start in life. A smart young man could make a decent living out of a boat like that. Deep sea fishing tours. Trips to Fiji. All he needed was his skipper's licence. He wasn't just giving Max a start in life, he was giving him the opportunity for a life.

Besides, he didn't have anything else to give his son.

He explained all this to Kendell over a beer when he made the decision. Kendell was full of admiration. Here was a man who had lived in virtual poverty most of his life building a boat, only to give it away when it was done.

'What are you going to do now?' Kendell asked. Without the *Joseph Conrad*, he meant, but didn't have to say it.

'Build another boat, I guess,' Cess said, staring down into his beer.

So they listened to some Bob Dylan to compensate for the mediocrity of life.

But Cess had forgotten Max's heedless, headlong tendencies. Max thought he was a sharp operator, the kid who used to sell dope at school, but was really just an idiot. Prey for the first city slicker to come on the scene.

The city slicker knew all about boats. He'd lived and operated around marinas for years. He knew the value of boats, that's for sure. It was inevitable that the *Joseph Conrad* should attract the interest of a man like that. Max had moved off Paradise Island to the city and had taken the *Joseph Conrad* to a berth in a bay not too distant from where he lived.

He was on the boat when the city slicker approached him.

The first Cess heard of it was when he got an excited call from Max. He'd swapped the *Joseph Conrad* for a much larger, commercially built vessel. A bargain. Cess got that cold feeling in the guts that writers write about. He got on the next ferry to the city and went to have a look for himself.

'It's a dog. A piece of shit,' he told Kendell when he got back. 'Max has been had. A fucking rust bucket.'

Cess had gone to Kendell for advice on what to do. He wasn't going to let the *Joseph Conrad* fall into the hands of a city slicker. It was too much to contemplate. Kendell should know what to do. He was an educated man. Wrote books and knew the meaning of Bob Dylan songs.

'I rang the guy myself,' Cess said. 'I said to him, my son has made a mistake, just back off, and the guy said that Max had signed a contract and that it was all over.'

Cess stared gloomily at his wasted life. 'Max got drunk,' he said.

'Ring Rob Malarky,' Kendell advised. 'He'll know what to do.'

Rob Malarky was a retired lawyer and friend of the oppressed. Cess rang him straight away, from Kendell's house.

'I'm afraid so,' he said to Malarky. 'He did sign the contract.'

Malarky's advice was simple. Possession is 99% of the law. Take the *Joseph Conrad* to some remote beach where the city slicker will never find it. Then see what he does. Odds on, he would drop the whole thing.

How father and son stole their own boat and sailed it to a remote bay is another story. As Malarky predicted, the city slicker vanished into the woodwork when the *Joseph Conrad* disappeared.

Life went on. Max grew no wiser. He sold the *Joseph Conrad* again, this time for real, and had another baby.

Kendell wrote another book and Cess Claw started building another boat.

REVENGE OF THE DISH-DOG

Back in the day, it was not uncommon for locally owned, provincial newspapers, like the *Paradise Island Times*, to harbour at some desk somewhere, a dissatisfied reporter with literary ambitions – and a hangover.

Such a reporter was Garrison Ford, who was all too aware that he was not Garrison Kellor, a man who could write movingly and humourously about his hometown. Our Garrison Ford envied Garrison Kellor and detected, in the coincidence of names, either the mockery of fate or a message.

There was not much room in the pages of the *PITs* for literary endeavours, but every now and again Blackbeard the editor let him off the leash and allowed him a whimsical column the editor insisted be called *It's a Life*, the most forgettable and uninspired title he could come up with as far as Ford was concerned.

'It makes me think it's *not* a life,' he said to Kendell, who really was a writer, apparently. Ford had just chugged some vodka. He was in the frame for getting angry and depressed. 'What kind of a *life* is it, anyway?'

Ford had recently taken on a relationship with Yvonne who had a fourteen-year-old daughter. It gave him something to complain about. Along with not being a literary genius. Along with being trapped in a piddling job with a piddling little weekly rag with a couple of thousand readers and a vindictive editor. Ford knew he was cut out for greater things.

'Just write about ordinary situations,' Kendell said, who did no such thing himself. 'Find the emotion and you find the story, they say.'

'Who sez?'

'I don't know. Hemingway or somebody.'

'How do *you* do it?'

'I write every story as if it were my last.'

'That won't be difficult.' Ford took an anarchic swig straight from the bottle.

'But you have to sober up long enough to write it.'

Ford didn't believe him. Kendell himself was no stranger to a bit of arm-bending.

'There's too many writers in the world anyway,' Kendell said.

But Ford had what he wanted. He found the emotion required in a strong desire to strangle the sweetly named Bella, Yvonne's horrendous daughter. Bella never missed an opportunity to sabotage, infuriate and embarrass her mother's boozy boyfriend. Revenge was a pretty fair motivation for literary production, he decided. And he had his ordinary situation. And so it was. He wrote the story, although to say he sobered up would be a bit of a stretch, and submitted it to Blackbeard who promptly published it. 'Don't blame me,' Blackbeard said.

It's a life
By Garrison Ford

Any parent of teens or pre-teens facing the school holidays will know the terror of killer kitchens – the ones you clean up, wipe down, get sparkling, only to find, a little later, after the marauding kids have passed through, the same unholy mess you'd faced earlier. In fact, if you were truly dedicated, you could spend the whole of the school holidays standing in the kitchen, smiling, and cleaning up after continual bouts of hurricane Suzie and Johnny – that is, if you had any time left over from picking up clothes and 'stuff' off the floors.

These relentless mess-makers operate on a few basic laws, laws to which they will fanatically adhere.

1) Items removed from the fridge should never, ever be returned, and in the case of jars, the lid should never, on any account, be put back on. 2) Any clean, carefully wiped-down space should be immediately occupied by foodstuffs and containers. 3) If any honey or jam is spilled on a bench it should never, under any circumstances, be wiped up, and 4) if asked to clean the bench, quickly pile all plates and bowls, un-scraped and un-rinsed, into the sink, in any old order. The ignorant and exasperated among you might be

asking, why not just tell the effing kids to do the effing dishes. Well, yes that happens, if you're prepared to clean up after the cleaning up, mop the floor of slopped water and wipe down every touchable surface; yes, it does happen, but for the energy you have to put in you might as well just do the effing dishes yourself! (To be fair, I have heard rumours of children who are not like this and are impeccably tidy, but they always seem to belong to other parents).

Recently, when I was denied the pleasure of sitting at a nice clean table to listen to the latest crop of world disasters in uncluttered quiet, I came up with a brilliant scheme. An appeal to reason – with a little shame thrown in! I placed a sign in the kitchen containing all my concentrated kitchen wisdom:

> *Basic Principle: leave nothing for someone else to clean up.*
>
> *Advanced Spiritual Concept: Leave the kitchen a little tidier than you found it – enlightenment follows.*

The result? Well, the sign did provoke some comment all right, although not of the grateful kind. My wisdom, it seemed, had fallen on deaf ears. Ah! But I had a secret weapon up my sleeve. I worked to rule! I applied the Basic Principle only, strategically abandoning the Advanced Spiritual Concept. I cleaned up after myself, only. Much wailing followed as the mess grew exponentially. Dear daughter even wanted to know why I wasn't pulling my weight! What a chuckle that was. Self-righteousness ruled. Further, the mess-makers and crucifiers became amazingly eagle-eyed in finding my tiniest infraction of the Basic Principle. I couldn't slip up even once!

Try it you kitchen martyrs – see how long you can hold out.

To Ford's gratified amazement, his column provoked much comment. It produced dissension and arguments in many a Paradise Island home as parents and children squared off over unmade beds, messy kitchens and clothes all over bedroom floors. Some stories got back to Ford of his Basic Principle and Advanced Spiritual Concept being printed, laminated and tacked onto fridges as those kitchen martyrs crawled out of the woodwork. 'I like the bit about the killer kitchens,' Kendell told the glowing Ford, who was celebrating his literary success with a few shots. 'And crudifiers, there's a word I wish I'd invented.' 'Eat your heart out,' Ford said happily.

Not everybody was enamoured, of course. Ford's teenage readership, which decidedly spiked that week, took it badly. Why was an ignoramus like Ford attacking them publicly anyway? Bella was particularly furious. She saw it for what it was – a personal attack. That week's *PITs* lay around the house like an accusation. Bella shook the offending article under Ford's nose. 'You believe this garbage you write, don't you?' she screamed.

'If the shoe fits,' the complacent Ford said.

'And what's this stuff about the spiritual concept? Spiritual stuff is about God. What's God got to do with the kitchen?'

Ford pointed dramatically to the messy kitchen. 'Meet God,' he said.

'You're nuts,' she said.

'God is your unfinished business,' Ford said with lofty authority. Lordy, was he getting sharp!

He had to point out, not just to Bella but everybody who would listen, that all the upset and kerfuffle had not made the slightest difference to the messy behaviour of teenagers. Kitchens looked no cleaner. In fact, some were worse as the parents tried the 'work to rule' strategy, which proved to be, as Ford had written, more of a provocation than a wake up call.

Now Bella might have been less than a beauty queen with her lank black hair and the nail that protruded aggressively through her lower lip, but she was not stupid. In fact, she had hidden talents Ford had not taken the time to notice, just as he didn't notice that something might be brewing behind Bella's closed door other than sulky silence. He fondly imagined that she was in there feeling devastated and possibly ashamed, even contrite... although that was pushing it. Certainly licking her wounds.

Nor did he hear the whispering that went on behind his back. Why would he care about the rustling of fallen leaves? He was planning his next minor masterpiece. He was on his way. Nothing could stop him now.

He remained equally deaf when the whispering began at work. He had other fish to fry. He was getting out of here, out of *PITs*, out from under Blackbeard's arbitrary rule. As far away from Paradise Island as he could get.

'You won't see me for dust and small stones,' he said to Kendell.

He had applied for several positions on national newspapers, sent his 'This is life' piece, renamed 'You'd better believe it – life with hormones,' which seemed to have just that right mix of snap and intrigue, to several editors, with the suggestion that he be given a weekly column with an eye to syndication. His career was about to take a quantum leap, if not exactly into literature then something that came close to it.

It came as a complete shock, therefore, when the next week's edition rolled off the press to find, right on the front page, a vicious cartoon that showed him behind a desk stacked with tottering filled ashtrays, discarded mini-vodka bottles, papers, pizza cartons with fungoid lumps of pizza, and a pile of something that might be vomit with flies coming and going, and random trash everywhere from broken ballpoints to tortured paper clips.

As if that wasn't enough, the face that stared back at him over this humongous mess was recognisably his own but horribly distorted by what must be, he thought, one of the sickest of minds to pick up a pencil. He had the same kind of shock that Dorian Gray had when he finally saw the portrait of his true appearance. His eyes were maniacal pinpoints sunk in bags of flesh, and simian bone above. His nose was a compendium of every drink he'd ever drunk. His face was twisted into a demonic leer, and some unsavoury liquid dribbled from the side of his mouth. The biggest of these was a speech bubble, and he was saying, 'I always leave my desk a little tidier than I found it.'

Beneath this most outrageous and grotesque caricature, the headline read:

The generation war heats up

He didn't have to look far to find the artist behind this scurrilous attack. Bella the Bitch. And Blackbeard had said nothing and published it. Blackbeard had shafted him, as usual. Happy to hold his ace reporter up to public ridicule.

'Of course,' Kendell said to him. 'It makes good copy. Everybody's going to want one.'

'But it's not true, that's the thing!' Ford chugged a mini-vodka in one go and chucked the bottle down. 'I keep a clean desk. Always have, always will.'

'That doesn't matter. It's the narrative that matters.'

'What narrative.'

'The public narrative.'

'What about it?'

'Your necessary humiliation. Brings you down to everybody's level. It is the narrative of the righteous brought down, the smart-arse outsmarted, the kids getting the last word. It's a *the-joke's-on-you* story.'

'But there is no joke! It's not true, I tell you. I'm so tidy I'm anal!'

Kendell shook his head and took a bite at his own vodka.

'Can't see how you'll ever be a writer then,' Kendell said.

'I can do the hangover bit,' Ford said.

SUZIE, SARAH AND THE SCHOOL UNIFORM SHEMOZZLE

Suzie and Sarah were good friends, and had been since they were three years old and their mothers would get together for mutual support and sanity. (Later they were to rename themselves as Gin and Juice, but that's another story). They quarrelled over everything, but nothing could part them. They went to primary school together and walked through the gates together on their first day of high school.

Small as it was, Paradise Island had its own high school. From the point of view of some parents at least, the high school was pretty slack. Kids coming in and out at all hours of the day, kids not wearing shoes in the summer, kids dressing as they pleased. Everybody kept saying that something should be done and things blundered along as they always had, until a new school principal grasped the nettle and declared that all children would have to wear a school uniform.

This new principal, a firm woman called Mrs Forman, belonged to that breed of people who would come to Paradise Island full of visions of cleaning the place up. They would vote for Mavis Stretchly at the local elections and advocate for kerb and channelling at every opportunity. What Mrs Forman saw was a school of neatly uniformed children all skipping gaily through the gate on time.

What Mrs Forman didn't see was the storm of controversy that would follow her decision, the biggest upset the school had known since the teachers were banned from smoking on the school grounds. Everybody seemed to dust off their dreary old high school debating arguments, and everybody had an opinion. Mr Fowlks, the mathematics teacher, felt obliged to declare publicly that there was no evidence linking scholastic achievement with the wearing of the same coloured clothes. He accused the advocates of superstition and wishful thinking. The advocates, in their turn, were unmoved by this lack of evidence; to them the advantages of a school uniform were more or less self-evident.

'It's not an even debate,' Suzie's father Tomeck said to her mother Marie. Tomeck opposed the imposition of school uniforms. His family had seen enough of that sort of thing in Europe. In Tomeck's mind, uniforms meant the military.

'What do you mean?' Suzie said.

'I don't mind if parents decide to put *their* children into uniforms,' he said with some heat. 'That's their decision, their children. But they want to put *my* children into uniform. I'm not telling them what to wear.'

'Our children,' Marie said.

Suzie was very impressed by this argument and decided then and there never to wear the uniform. Nobody could make her wear a uniform. Her Dad would back her up.

Meanwhile, at Sarah's place a similar discussion was taking place, but with the opposite conclusion. It was obvious to Sarah's father Joe that something had to happen to shake the school up, and uniforms were as good a place as any to start.

'Just think,' Joe said to his daughter. 'No more teasing for what you wear to school. No more expensive fashion crazes. No more panics in the morning trying to figure out what to wear.' As far as Joe was concerned it was a no-brainer.

Sarah saw it that way too. It was all very well for the pretty ones, like her friend Suzie, or the rich ones like Madeline Mudface, but for the ordinary girl not on such great terms with her mirror, the uniform was a solution. A relief, in fact.

'I'm looking forward to it,' Sarah said to Suzie.

'You won't catch me dead in one,' Suzie said.

'In fact, I can't wait,' Sarah said.

They argued for hours over the colour without getting anywhere.

The community argument raged on, fuelled by the *Paradise Island Times* editor, Blackbeard, who cautiously came down on the side of discipline. Stumpy Stewart wrote a letter saying that he was regularly beaten at school and it never did him any harm. Jean Jeanie, of a theatrical bent, wrote in reply that uniforms and capital punishment stifled a child's creativity, and had done her a lot of harm. The editor pointed out in a note after the letter that the correspondent meant *corporal* punishment, and that had nothing to do with a rank in the army.

Mr Fowlks, the mathematics teacher, complained to the editor, and everyone else, that the argument lacked rigour and logic, and that anyone who wanted to look at the actual research was welcome to contact him. A group of parents, using Mr Fowlks as their authority, declared that their children would not be turning up to school in some ridiculous 1950s school uniform.

'I can't believe we're going through all this,' the writer Kendell said to *PITs* reporter Garrison Ford over a beer. 'It's unreal. I used to write essays about this when I was at school!'

'Yes,' Ford enthused, 'Isn't it wonderful? We haven't seen anything like this since Ricky and his rambunctious rooster.'

For Mrs Forman, the whole thing had become a tactical nightmare, with the devil always in the detail. Some cunning parents had suggested a phase-in period, with students able to wear partial uniforms. The idea of partial uniforms was enough to make Mrs Forman shudder. A jumper here, a skirt there, a blouse here – oh, no you don't. A so-called compromise solution in which only the children who wanted to wear uniforms had to wear them made no sense to Mrs Forman, either. A uniform was a uniform; everybody had to wear one or there was no point.

And there would be no messy phase-in period that would somehow go on forever. She set a date and that was that. Let the four winds blow!

On D-Day morning, there was general chaos in many a Paradise Island home, most certainly at the respective homes of Sarah and Suzie. Suzie had been up long before any self-respecting thirteen year old should have been up, carefully considering her clothes for the day. She had laid her entire wardrobe on the bed and was considering combinations faster than a prayer wheel could spin.

Of course she had decided everything the night before but had undecided it again. Come morning she stood and stared at all her clothes and arrived at the only conclusion that made sense: she needed some new clothes. She'd already told her parents that but they refused to be hustled. 'All in good time,' they said to her.

At Sarah's place, all her clothes stayed in the wardrobe and the new school uniform lay alone on her bed in neatly pressed splendour: blouse, jumper, skirt, socks, shoes. Laid out that way, it looked as if somebody had been lying there and vanished, leaving just the clothes. She didn't need to try the uniform on, of course; she'd already put it on and taken it off a thousand times. It was pretty neat, and she liked the pleats in the skirt. At the same time, she thought, her friend Suzie had a point about the colour. It was kind of maroon, a dark brownish red, supposed to be a russet, but there was something *off* about that colour. Her mother kept on saying how the colour suited her, but her mother would say that, wouldn't she? Her mother had a special tone of voice for saying things like that, especially when she didn't believe it herself.

Everybody wanted their children to feel comfortable in their uniforms, but Sarah didn't feel comfortable, not entirely. That russet colour reminded her of unpleasant things.

At Suzie's place the table was set and breakfast was served, but still Suzie had not chosen the day's outfit. Since most of the kids would be wearing those stupid uniforms, her outfit would stand out that much more. She'd be scrutinised to death. She wouldn't just be wearing her clothes, she'd be making a statement. Her father agreed. 'Remember,' he said, 'uniforms are a statement too.'

That was all very well, but it hadn't helped her choose, even whether to wear jeans or a skirt. It wasn't just indecision, she realised; it was fear. It was all very well for her father, whose own father had escaped tyranny in Europe. He didn't know how it felt.

At the first burst of panic, Suzie rang Sarah. They always rang each other if a panic attack threatened.

'I haven't had breakfast yet,' Suzie said. 'I haven't even got dressed. I'm a wreck.'

'Me too,' Sarah said. Her mother was calling her for breakfast, while her brand new uniform lay untouched on the bed. Time was ticking away.

'It's easy for you,' Suzie said. 'All you have to do is put on your uniform. Why haven't you put it on already?'

'Because it's creepy.'

'Creepy? It's just a stupid old uniform.'

'What are you going to wear then, Suzie dear?'

'Nothing.'

'Nothing?'

'Right. I'm not going to school.'

'Your parents won't let you get away with that.'

Suzie knew this was true. They wouldn't buy any last minute sick-in-the-tummy act. They never ceased reminding her that they had once been teenagers themselves, although Suzie found that hard to believe.

Sarah tried again. 'I mean, I still think uniforms are a good idea and everything… it's just… that you were right about the colour. It's pretty rank.'

'You'll get used to it. It's just a colour.'

'And the shoes too.'

'What about them?'

'Well, I know they are kind of practical and everything, but it's like wearing clodhoppers.'

'What are clodhoppers?'

'I don't know. Dad always sez it.'

'Can't you wear your own shoes as long as they are the right colour?'

Sarah thought about it. That there might be some wriggle room with the uniform had not occurred to her because Mrs Forman made sure it hadn't, but Suzie seemed tickled by the idea.

'Heels in school brown,' Suzie said.

Sarah giggled. 'I don't have heels in school brown. I don't have any other shoes in school brown. I wish I could wear your hot pink trainers.'

'I only wear those with my holes-in-the-knees jeans.'

'I know.' Sarah sounded glum now. 'My breakfast's getting cold.'

'Mine too. But I'm not wearing that yellow top that mum wants me to wear, Not again.'

'But that top is cool.'

'Was cool. Maybe the first hundred times I wore it.'

'At least you have a choice. I *have to* wear this dumb uniform.'

'Okay,' Suzie said, 'here's what we're going to do.'

'I'm all ears.'

Suzie explained it and Sarah liked it. Sometimes she just loved the way Suzie's mind worked. Devious hardly said it. It was a win-win for both of them. Suzie solved the problem of having nothing to wear, and Sarah swapped the problem of having a uniform she didn't want to wear to having her choice of Suzie's best clothes.

The parents didn't understand it, of course, but that didn't matter. As usual, the parents did as they were told.

MANNY AND THE MEN'S GROUP

Back in the day on Paradise Island, everybody with a penis was in a men's group. It was the done thing. It was mandatory. In fact, if you weren't in a men's group you were probably avoiding something, not facing up to something. Or you had something to hide.

Manny was sceptical. He talked to Doctor Lovejoy about it. Lovejoy knew all about such things.

'It's a good thing,' he said with enthusiasm. 'It allows you to work through stuff.'

'What sort of stuff?'

'Issues, you know. The kind of things that men run into.'

Manny didn't know. He wasn't sure that he had any issues, but it seemed that everybody had to have them. Having issues was mandatory too. So Manny must have them. Even if he didn't know what having issues meant.

'Do you have a mother?'

Manny sensed some kind of trap, but carried on anyway. 'Yes, of course.'

'She's still alive, I mean.'

'Yes.'

'How do you feel about her?'

Manny shrugged. 'She's my mother,' he said.

'Does she annoy you?'

'Sometimes. She's getting a bit cranky.'

'You seem quite repressed in terms of your feelings about your mother.'

'Do I?' Manny was astonished. His mother was just his mother, and he got on with the job.

'That suggests you have issues with your mother.'

'I do when she refuses to go to the dentist,' he said.

'Is that all?'

'Well, sometimes if it's cold I have to drive her to Bingo on a Saturday night. That can be a nuisance if I want to go out.' Manny spoke almost hopefully. He did have issues after all!

Dr Lovejoy sighed. It was a hard job getting through to some people. Getting them to express their deeper feelings was like getting blood out of a stone. Like poor Manny here, who didn't have a clue.

'Do you love your mother?'

Manny looked puzzled. 'She's my mother,' he said again, as if that were self-explanatory.

Despite the unsatisfactory nature of this conversation, Dr Lovejoy managed to convince Manny to attend the next men's group. 'Everybody is very friendly,' he assured him, as if Manny were somehow afraid. 'There's only five of us.'

Manny turned up at the next meeting with some trepidation. That week it was held at Briscoe's place. Briscoe was a South African and apparently had lots of issues. He did have a nice place, however, much nicer than Manny's. Maybe that was an issue. He'd have to keep his eye out for these issues.

Manny joined the four other men who were joking with each other about the fact that men feel compelled to joke and wise-crack and get one up on each other.

They started by playing some trust games. At least that's what Dr Lovejoy called them. Manny had to stand with eyes closed and allow himself to fall over backwards. He would be caught by the other four. If he couldn't do it, it meant he didn't trust them to catch him, and that was bad. Manny watched the others and it looked simple enough, but when it came to his turn and he closed his eyes, he found that his body didn't want to do it. Falling backwards with your eyes closed is hardly a natural thing to do, he reasoned. But if he didn't do it, then the others would think he was a coward, a sissy, and that he didn't trust them.

So he did it. It was no big deal, but it was unpleasant. He couldn't see that making the body do something that deliberately destabilised it had anything to do with trust, but he was starting to see that he was pretty backward and that everybody was being darned nice about it.

The next trust exercise involved standing blindfold on a plank and being lifted into the air, two men on each end. It was the same as the falling backwards thing only worse. It fooled the mind into not knowing if the body was a few inches or a hundred miles up. That tended to induce panic, and that proved that you had trust issues.

Manny was very pleased to get through the trust exercises. He was certain now that he must have trust issues, which was why everybody was being so nice to him.

Next they all sat around in a circle and talked about their issues, and everybody talked about other people's issues, too. Manny sensed that it was good to have lots of issues because it allowed other people to get their teeth into you. Have a good old scrummage around in your life. On the other hand it was bad to have issues because they had to be dealt with, flushed out into the open, worked through until there was nothing left of them. To claim you had no issues was to invite suspicion.

Two of the other men, MoJo Mayhem and his neighbour JJ-180, had lots of juicy issues relating to their boundaries and who was growing dope on whose property. They got very excited about it, but Manny found it boring. He hoped he wasn't expected to get hot and flushed and have to wave his arms around.

Because it was his first night, he wasn't expected to talk a lot, which was lucky for him as he didn't know what to say. He had saved up the bit about having to drive his mother to Bingo on cold nights, but he knew it would sound pretty lame. What he needed was a real issue. Like Briscoe, for example. His wife had gone to South Africa for a holiday and had never returned. Briscoe couldn't understand it. He'd always been nice to her and spent her money wisely, such as coming to Paradise Island and buying this lovely house. Now there was a real issue for you. Manny had nothing like that. He was sure that when he got home Pattie would be there, keeping the bed warm, as she put it. He didn't have an issue with that.

Briscoe was so upset he shed some tears in front of the other men, especially when he related how she used her sexuality to manipulate him. Dr Lovejoy said it was really brave of him, to cry like that. Having issues meant you could be really brave and have other people admire you for crying.

Manny did notice, however, that while Dr Lovejoy was good at getting other people to talk about their issues, and have a little cry, he said very little about himself. He had a way of subtly deflecting questions about himself that nobody seemed to notice except Manny. It had a lot to do with his open and engaging smile. A very useful skill to learn, Manny decided.

Next, while still sitting in a circle, they chanted AUM, which Dr Lovejoy explained was the primal sound of the universe, the echo of the Big Bang, the sound of one hand clapping, and all sorts of clever things.

Manny enjoyed singing. He enjoyed the feeling when he moved from one note to another, hearing his voice make the change. The problem with this chanting AUM was that it just went on and on keeping one droning note. It was quite boring really, just singing the same note all the time when there were so many other notes to sing.

After chanting, they had some refreshments, some tea and biscuits. Booze, of course, was forbidden, and Manny wondered if he was the only one who could have done with a coldie right then. Manny got to talking to the fifth member of the group, a skinny little guy called George. He admitted to Manny that he was an ex-alcoholic with a tendency to depression, and that he only came to the men's group because he couldn't bear being alone in his room at night.

'You must have lots of issues, then,' Manny said.

'You can say that again,' George said.

Mention of George's alcoholism turned the conversation to Garrison Ford, who had written a derisive article on what he called 'the men's group craze' which he lampooned, suggesting that the men involved were a bunch of New Agers sitting around with their hands in their pants. Without mentioning any names, he managed to suggest that Dr Lovejoy was a SNAG, a sensitive new age guy of the most contemptible kind.

Dr Lovejoy was very understanding. 'Garrison Ford feels left out, excluded,' he explained. 'He can't come to a group because by 7.30 he's too drunk. It's no good trying to come to a men's group drunk.'

The men nodded their heads vigorously at this, and Manny felt ashamed for thirsting for a coldie earlier, and glad he hadn't voiced the thought.

'So he reverts to satire and sarcasm, which, as the saying goes, is the lowest form of wit.'

All the men agreed with that too, and how unfair it was that Ford got to poke fun at others from his soapbox in the *Paradise Island Times*.

'Of course, he's excluded himself,' Dr Lovejoy said.

The meeting resumed and they listened to MoJo Mayhem's account of an LSD overdose some years back which had set him off running around in circles on Paradise Island, and he was still doing it. He couldn't have made it this far without Ella.

After MoJo's confession, they all went home, Dr Lovejoy suggesting that next week they do a more fun trust exercise that involved throwing each other up the air, and perhaps talk about Manny's mother.

'How did it go?' Pattie asked as he climbed into the bed she had been keeping warm.

'Fine. Great,' he said. 'I learned a lot.'

'Well, come on! What secret male things did you get up to? Spill all!'

'Nothing much. People just talked about things.'

'Did you talk about me?'

'No. Why should I?'

'Were there strippers?' She felt around for him under the blanket.

'Don't be silly. It's not that kind of men's group.'

'There are women's groups too, you know.'

'Do you want to go?'

'I don't know.'

'It's best,' he said, 'to have issues.'

'What kind of issues?'

'All kinds. It doesn't seem to matter. As long as you can talk about them and have a little cry.'

'What issues did you have?' She got up on one elbow and studied his face. 'Am I an issue?'

'You? I don't think so!'

'I do snore.'

Manny wasn't sure if that qualified as an issue or not.

'No worries then,' she said.

'No worries,' he said. But there were worries. He was worried the group was going to talk about his mother. There was no reason to be worried but he was. He didn't want Lovejoy stirring around. Perhaps the fact he was worried meant he really did have an issue, and that was a worry in itself.

'Will you go back next week?'

'I don't know,' he said. He was in conflict about it.

It was an issue.

He fell asleep and dreamt about being thrown up in the air by his mother.

PETRA AND THE PECULIAR PAINTING

She picked it up at a garage sale for five bucks. Pretty ordinary to look at. Nothing to write home about. Another indifferent oil-colour painting depicting a brown road with trees on one side and a meadow on the other. The trees were so poorly painted that they had no identities, just vaguely tree-like blobs that might have been poplars before the painter got hold of them.

'Why buy it?' Wade said. 'We don't have a hole in the wall to cover.'

'I don't know,' Petra said. 'There is just something about it.'

Wade couldn't see anything about it. Even when he sat in front of it and smoked a spliff he still couldn't see anything in it. It was so bad it was completely resistant to any imaginative engagement or interpretation. It didn't even offer the eye a focal point.

'The five bucks would have been better spent on a cup of coffee,' he said. He'd just wasted a good smoke on it.

'I know,' she sighed.

At the same time, Petra was drawn to it. She hung it in the little room she used as an office, ostensibly to brighten up a dull corner, but it didn't brighten up anything. And yet, she found herself glancing at it from time to time. The brown road and lumpy trees were somehow familiar, but seen as if through the blur of a remembered dream.

The first time she actually dreamed of it, there was nothing blurry about it. There was some kind of building behind her, she was standing in its shadow, and before her, the road stretched off into the distance, a rich muddy brown, and the trees on the right were not poplars but pines. They lined up behind a neglected, sagging wire fence. Opposite, the meadow, which glowed green, was dotted by tiny white flowers.

She didn't tell Wade about the dream, afraid that he might mock her.

Afterwards, she examined the painting more carefully, looking for the wire fence. She was convinced she had added this detail to her dream. But no, there it was, badly distinguished from the colours around it, but visible if you knew what you were looking for. One of the fence posts, which looked like the trunk of the tree behind, was on a lean. The wire was hardly visible at all, just a couple of streaks of paint.

She had to ask Wade if he had noticed the fence.

'Can't say I did,' he said, 'but then again, how hard was I looking?'

The next time she dreamed of it, she was not just observing the muddy brown road, but walking along it, the fence and trees on the right, the meadow on the left. I have to get to the end of this road, she thought. Across the meadow and in the distance, a line of mountains gleamed crisply in the sun. No matter how far she walked, the mountains didn't come any closer.

At the first opportunity the next day, she examined the painting again, convinced that there were no mountains, and that again she had added that detail to her dream. Somehow her mind was struggling to create a landscape, and was using the painting to do it. But again she was wrong. The mountains were there, just hard to see, looking possibly like clouds, amorphous shapes in the distance. She could make them out because she knew they were there. Yet, somehow she must have known they were there in the first place in order to put them in her dream.

She told Wade all about it, feeling a bit silly as she did so. When she said it out loud it sounded like a whole lot of nothing, just like the painting.

'Good thing this isn't a Stephen King story,' he said.

She sort of knew who Stephen King was. Some kind of writer. She preferred travel books.

'In a King story it would turn out that the painting itself was changing. When you dreamed about the fence, the painting then changed to put in a fence. Same with the mountains.'

'What would be the point?'

'Something sinister going on, some nasty supernatural force operating though the painting.'

'No thanks,' she said. 'I don't want anything like that.'

The drab blobs of colour on her wall didn't merit anything as fancy as being credited with a supernatural force, but at the same time Wade's careless remark stuck with her. It was all a big joke to him of course, her dreaming about the silly painting in the first place, but what if its drabness were a disguise? Whatever else might be said, she was forced to admit that the painting had entered her imagination, and that was a mystery enough in itself. But it wasn't scary, not in the way that Wade was trying to suggest.

'I think I know that place,' she said.

'What place?'

'The place in the painting. The dirt road, the trees, the meadow.' It felt silly to be spelling them out like that.

'Is that what you see?'

Stunned, she stared at Wade. He looked perfectly serious, no little quirk at the side of mouth. 'What do you see?'

'I'm not sure,' he said cautiously. 'Those lumps might be trees.'

'And what about the white flowers?'

'There are certainly some white spots there,' he said.

'You're kidding me,' she said.

'Cross my heart and hope to die,' he said.

'It's not a Rorschach test! It's a landscape not an ink blob.'

'Okay, it's a landscape with a muddy road and mountains in the distance. Badly painted.'

'Agreed.'

The next time she dreamed of it, she was still walking along that muddy road, but there were many more details, as if her imagination were compelled to fill in what the lumps and streaks of colour struggled to represent. The green pine cones on the pine trees. The moss on the fence posts. The ruts in the road she was walking. It was as if she wanted to improve the painting, to bring out the vision the painter had failed to convey. What a wonderful painting it could have been! In her dreams!

She tried to explain it to Wade. 'Imagine you are looking through a camera lens. The image is blurry because it is not properly focused. You have to adjust the focus until the image sharpens up and you can see all the detail. The painting is like the blurry image. My dreams are the focused lens. Every time I dream the focus gets a little sharper.'

'That's amazing.'

'You don't sound like it's very amazing.'

'I just don't see the point of it. I mean, why all the effort?'

That she didn't know, but it wasn't effort exactly. The dreams came unbidden.

'I think I saw that landscape once. When I was a child.'

'How could you?'

'It's not that impossible. The painting's not signed, but the artist might have been there.'

'Where? In your dream?'

'We don't even know if a man or woman painted it.'

'Does that matter?'

It shouldn't, but somehow it did. The anonymity of the painting annoyed her.

In the next dream, a building had appeared in the distance. It was a relief to have a destination, to know that the road she was walking actually led somewhere. She woke up from that dream feeling happy. As usual, she went to the painting to confirm the new detail, and there it was, just a smudge of indeterminate colour. Outside of her dream, there was no way of knowing that the smudge represented anything. For that very reason she didn't tell Wade. That would just open up the same arid conversation.

It was time to stop dreaming about the painting, she decided. Time to start dreaming about something else. She took the painting down, wrapped it in some old newspaper and stuck it under the house with the paints and nails. The next step would be the rubbish bin.

That night, her dream opened in spectacular colour. She left the brown road and walked into the meadow. The grass beneath her feet was lush and glowed with green. The sky vibrated blue. Light was pouring everywhere like a waterfall. Now she entered an orchard. She could smell apricots. A girl was standing under a tree. She smiled in greeting. Petra took the girl's hand and felt a jolt, as from a live electrical wire, go up her arm.

When she turned away from the girl and looked back, she couldn't see the road. A monstrous sun, much larger than it should have been, hoisted itself into the sky. All the colours of creation blazed up around her. She began walking back in the direction of the road. There was a building she had to get to. Walking was slow going, however, and when she looked down she saw her little child's legs in big red gumboots that came up to her knees.

When she woke up it was dawn. Out the window, the afterglow of her dream touched the world. It made the dawn special and she felt happy.

There was no way she was going to go back and look at the painting. The orchard, the girl, the monstrous sun, would all be there, if she looked hard enough. And they would all have been there right from the start. It was enough to know that. She didn't have to tell Wade how well she knew that meadow, and the orchard with its apricot smell; she didn't have to tell Wade anything.

At the breakfast table she said to him. 'Let's have a garage sale. Get rid of some of that junk under the house.'

'Good idea,' he said.
'And we can get rid of that silly old painting,' she said.
'Bit of a mistake that,' he said. 'A waste of five bucks.'
She shrugged. 'There are worse things.'
'Somebody will buy it.'
'I think I got my five bucks worth,' she said.

THE MAN WHO COULDN'T STOP WALKING IN CIRCLES

MoJo Mayhem came to Paradise Island carrying his hell with him. Issues. So many issues he'd lost count. He was in fact one big bundle of issues. Good thing Ella, his wife, was of the old-fashioned, loyal variety, who stuck with him through thick and thin, rather than these modern wives who prefer to stick it to them rather than with them. But it took MoJo a long time to see it.

It all began when Ella got sick of him moping around the house and instructed him to 'go take his issues for a walk.' So MoJo outfitted himself for a day's walking, patting his pockets every five minutes to make sure he was equipped with his necessities: tobacco (one of his issues) with papers and matches, a couple of nice heads of the best home grown, non-hydroponic weed (another of his issues), and carefully plotted a course that would not take him past the pub (another issue), or past Dennaray's place where Dennaray's eldest daughter, the red-haired Isolde (big-time issue) lived. He'd be fine as long as he stuck to the beaches and the headlands and avoided inhabited areas.

The first thing he discovered about walking on an island is that it's impossible to walk in a straight line anywhere for any distance. Since all roads lead back to the ocean, to keep walking you have to turn, and turn again until the only choice you have is to walk in a big circle. Thus began MoJo's days of walking in circles. It was not unpleasant. There were all kinds of circles, and if he found himself walking a path he'd trod before, he didn't care too much. There was walking. Then there was sitting on a beach or a headland having a smoke and a swig of water. In the summer, there was always a sheltered spot where he could take off his clothes, enter the water and float on his back staring at the sky and dream guiltily (another issue) of Isolde with hair the colour of red wine. They don't call it Paradise Island for nothing.

Hell didn't seem so bad.

He took his issues everywhere he went, of course, and they seemed no worse off for a good airing.

At the same time, however, the sneaking suspicion grew that there must be more to life than walking in circles. MoJo was a muddled man, but he wasn't a fool. And there was a persistence in him that encouraged the long-suffering Ella to stay the course.

'MoJo goes walkabout,' she'd tell people.

'I thought only Australian aborigines went walkabout,' some thoughtless person commented.

'Well MoJo does,' Ella said.

One day MoJo had a conversation about it all with Kendell over some wine and spliffs. Spliffs were preferred because they took care of the tobacco and the dope issue in one hit. They were sitting on MoJo's back deck, with a view of a bush-clad valley and JJ-180's house.

'All I ever do is walk in circles,' MoJo said. 'It's a kind of hell.'

'It's a common complaint,' Kendell said. 'Have you tried walking in squares? Or triangles perhaps. Imagine walking in cubes. Now that'd be hell.'

MoJo couldn't. Didn't want to try. Life was hard enough as it was. 'What I think is a straight line turns out to be a circle.'

'It's called a learning curve.'

'But I'm not learning anything.'

'Did you know Einstein said that if you set off travelling in a straight line in one direction, eventually you would end up back at the same place coming from the other direction.'

'How did he figure that one?'

'He figured the universe was curved.'

Maybe my universe is curved too, MoJo thought. I'm like a fly walking around on the inside of a hollow ball. It was an unpleasant thought. There was a claustrophobia in all those circles pretending to be straight lines. Now apparently the whole universe was like that.

'Have you ever set off to go somewhere and found yourself back where you started?' MoJo asked.

'Just about every day. I like my futon.'

'I don't mean it like that. I mean…' MoJo wondered for a moment just what he did mean… 'I mean… I never seem to get anywhere.'

Kendell took a long drag on the spliff. One thing he liked about MoJo was that he always had the best weed in town. 'That's pretty standard.

There's a lot of it around.'

'No… It seems I just follow my own footsteps all the time.'

'Have you ever read AA Milne? The Pooh Bear stories?'

MoJo had to confess that he hadn't, and Kendell knew a moment's sadness. A childhood without the wisdom of Pooh was incomprehensible to him.

'There's a story about Pooh and Piglet…'

'Who?'

'Pooh's little friend. They start to walk around a large tree after snowfall and, at a certain point, they join another set of footprints just like theirs. So they keep walking and soon join another set of footprints.'

'Did they walk on four legs or two?'

'Does it matter?'

'If they walked on four legs it would get complicated very quickly.'

'That's not the point. The point is that they didn't realise they were following themselves. They thought they were following… a woozle.'

'A what?'

Kendell stopped while he was still ahead. Since woozles didn't exist, he was going to have a hard time describing them to an already confused MoJo. Certainly the humour was lost in the telling. The sublime metaphysics of it. Divine whimsy.

'Tell me, MoJo, how do you know you end up back in the same place?

'Because I remember.'

'So it's not the same place is it?'

'How do you mean?'

'You can't know for sure it's the same place.'

'Shut up! Of course I can.'

'But memory is not the same thing as reality. The place in your memory is a separate place.'

'That's just silly.' MoJo was disappointed. He'd thought Kendell to be a clever man. Now he wasn't making sense.

'The person who arrives is not the same person who set out.' Kendell tried to recall his T.S. Eliot and gave up. Eliot put it so well.

'Of course I am.' He tried to sound indignant, but MoJo was starting to feel afraid. Walking in circles was one thing, disappearing along the way was quite another.

'No you're not. You have lost and replaced many cells. You have shed and replaced skin. You have sweated. You have forgotten some things and remembered others. Laid down neural pathways.'

'I never get to be anybody else at all. Every morning when I wake up I'm stuck with me again.'

'Only because you want to be. In fact, you're a new person every morning, and by the time you go to bed at night, you'll be a different person again.'

'Speak for yourself! Maybe you get a makeover every morning. That doesn't happen to me.' MoJo took a swig of wine, which suddenly seemed cloying in his mouth. 'When I look in the mirror, it's still me.'

'I kinda hope that's the case,' Kendell said.

He sounded so doleful both men laughed.

'Jeez Kendell, you better have another smoke.'

'You got any Lapsang Souchong tea?'

'All I ever do is walk in circles,' MoJo said. Like a tiger in a cage.

Kendell sighed. 'It's a common complaint,' he said.

One of the amazing attributes of outer-space is that any object, once given a push, will carry on forever, there being no friction, nothing to slow it down or stop it – unless it collides with some other object. MoJo's inner space was a bit like that. Give a thought enough push and it will set sail forever, and yet, like a fiery comet swing back the way it came.

It would be wonderful to relate a tale of how MoJo stopped walking in circles. How he collided with something. Some grand idea, some larger inner-planetary body which would throw him in a new direction, lift him way above the petty plane of his elliptic, but that didn't happen. MoJo was not like Kendell, given to grand ideas. Other than his compulsive circle walking, he was pretty much an ordinary Joe. Too ordinary to be astonished. Too humdrum not to be humdrum. MoJo's mind did not soar; it plodded. One foot in front of the other. Around and around.

So no sudden revelation, no hand of God, no triumphant emergence, no neat plot device to save the man who couldn't stop walking in circles. After a time, however, it didn't seem to matter. It started when he stopped one day to have his customary rest and smoke. He was contemplating a view he had already seen several times since he had passed this way before. A familiar circuit, walked out of habit. Go round a circle more than once it becomes a habit. But he thought, perhaps it doesn't matter. Circle-schmerkle, straight-line or fate-line. Effectively, it's all the same. One foot in front of the other either way. Feet don't care, except to hurt when the way grew too long.

Ella noticed this creeping stoicism and approved. He would enjoy his walks more if he didn't keep thinking in circles. Might even help with some of those issues.

This began to happen. A certain gloom lifted from him. He didn't have to keep his eyes fixed on the ground ahead, but could lift them to the horizon. Of all the stupid things to worry about! So it is that an ordinary man, if he keeps plodding, may arrive at a conclusion both ordinary and profound. It is okay to walk in circles.

MoJo was making progress until Kendell intervened by posting him a picture. It was an illustration from a book. It depicted a line of pilgrims waiting at a large, formidable gate. There was a gatekeeper checking the pilgrims through. As they went through the gate he instructed them:

DO NOT PASS THIS WAY AGAIN

This frightened MoJo, gave him nightmares even, especially when he discovered that the gate was the threshold between hell and purgatory, and that those souls who wished to ascend would only get one chance.

There would be no running around the back of the queue again.

This fear became another issue needing to be walked off. But he couldn't walk this one off. Paradise or not, he lived on an island, where it's impossible to walk in a straight line anywhere for any distance. Small circles or large, it was all the same.

What choice did he have but to pass that WAY again – and again.

And never pass through the gate.

LADY NICOTINE AND THE NICOLETTES, OR, LAST GASP GASPS HIS LAST GASP

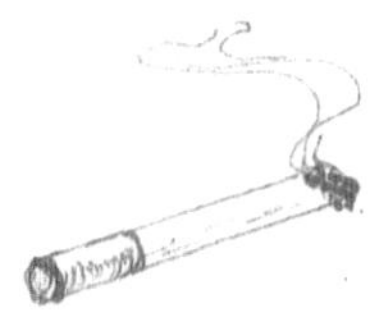

Back in the day, everybody smoked. Even on Paradise Island. You weren't a complete person unless you had a white stick hanging out of your mouth. Cafes and pubs encouraged the habit by leaving ashtrays on tables; their proprietors knew that smoking and drinking went together like love and marriage. Sure, the doctors maintained it was bad for you, but they would, wouldn't they? They had their own drugs to peddle, and besides, there were more old smokers than there were old doctors. Some line of thought like that. Anything to keep the habit alive.

I'd die without my smokes, was the common expression, even though the opposite was true. It's a filthy habit, the smokers would declare as they stubbed out their very last cigarette – until the next one. They said it in the same jocular spirit as they asked 'what's your poison?' when offering someone a drink. Remember when it was polite to offer cigarettes around if you pulled out a packet? If you can't remember that, you're too young to be reading this.

However, even in Paradise, a new wind began to blow, and it brought with it bad news. The doctors were upping their rhetoric. Smoking was not just a risk but a death sentence. Fifty percent of smokers would die of 'smoking related illnesses,' which made it five times more dangerous than playing Russian Roulette with the six-chambered forty-fives used in shoot-outs in old Cowboy movies, movies you could once watch while having a smoke.

And, apparently, a growing number of militant non-smokers objected to breathing in other people's smoke, which was very picky of them, and were starting to drive smokers into pariah status. Groups of smokers would huddle around corners the way dope smokers do, always looking over their shoulders. It's the new Puritanism, they declared. My one pleasure in life and they want to take it away!

Not satisfied with besmirching the name of Lady Nicotine, these righteous, politically correct ones began banning her outright. It began in the schools. Teachers were forbidden to smoke because they were setting a bad example. Whatever happened to 'do as I say not do as I do,' the teachers grumbled as they trekked off campus to light up, trying to avoid students who were doing the same.

It was a slow creep, working its way through the clubs and pubs and restaurants like some awful malaise. Those places were filled with the tense faces of those trying to quit or to hold off for another ten minutes. Nicotine patches had just been invented so addicts would have a 'direct to bloodstream supply,' which was very thoughtful, while they tried to quit the smoking ritual. They didn't work for everybody. Chainsaw Travis, for example, slapped a whole bunch of patches on his shoulders and continued to smoke away as usual. He got to like those patches. He even swore by them.

It was during this chaotic phase, when Lady Nicotine was in full retreat, that Kendell came up with what he thought was the answer. He and Garrison Ford had a serious talk about it over a cigarette and a beer at the Café Resume, which they now had to enjoy sitting outside with the other addicts.

'The real problem is not Lady Nicotine so much as the two thousand odd chemicals added to the tobacco,' Kendell said, pointing to the toxic object between his fingers. 'Chemicals to addict you, chemicals to keep you addicted. Chemicals to make it burn, chemicals to stop it from catching flame, chemicals to make it taste, chemicals to repel insects and fungi, chemicals to keep it moist, chemicals to stop it from rotting…'

'Mmmm, lovely,' Ford took a defiant drag on his. Kendell had a bit of a thing about chemicals.

They were joined by a mutual acquaintance, a guy with a very lined face and a nicotine stained voice called Last Gasp. 'What are you talking about?' he demanded of Kendell. He was a three-pack-a-day man trying to quit and not doing too well.

'Organic tobacco,' Kendell said. 'There's organic everything from toothpaste to toilet cleaner, why not tobacco? A clean Lady Nicotine.' He waved his unclean one around.

'Quick, where can I get some?' Last Gasp gasped. He grabbed Kendell by the front of his shirt.

'You can always grow your own,' Ford said. 'Cure it in rum.' That's what people did on Paradise Island, back in the day; they grew their own.

'I don't have time,' Last Gasp croaked. 'I need one now.'

With malice aforethought, Ford tossed his pack of evil ones down in front of Last Gasp. 'Do your worst.'

Last Gasp dragged at the deep lines on his face, a spreading web of tobacco lines. 'I can't. I promised Spooky. She can't quit unless I quit. She read that it's harder for women than for men.'

'People shouldn't read,' Ford said, reclaiming his packet before Kendell could get hold of it. Smokes were getting too effing expensive to share around. Too much government tax. That was the problem. That was always the problem. Kendell wouldn't agree of course. He would argue for increased taxes, which would directly hit him every time he bought a pack; some people just don't get it. He was already buying roll-your-owns under the pretence that they were not as bad for his health.

'Especially that newspaper you work for,' Last Gasp said. 'They're all in on it. To hell with them!'

'We've got to think of the teenagers,' Kendell said. 'What are we doing to protect them?'

'To hell with them too,' Last Gasp looked close to snapping, getting ropey on account of not having had a smoke for at least ten minutes. 'I don't care about them. It's their lookout. It's poor me I'm thinking about.' Hope was dying in his eyes. All he could see were tombstones with packets of tobacco buried beneath them. 'But is organic tar any better for you than non-organic tar?' That's what Spooky would be asking him.

'Hey! Fatties!' Ford called to a couple of overweight visitors wandering past. 'Look out, they'll be after you next! They'll be banning cream buns!' The two visitors did their best to hurry on.

Last Gasp laughed so hard he broke into a series of hacking coughs, as if he were trying to cough up his lungs. For that very reason he tried to keep laughing to a minimum.

Kendell hid behind his beer. 'You're an embarrassment, Ford.'

'That's what Bella keeps saying,' Ford said with sudden gloom, referring to his girlfriend Yvonne's teenage daughter, the bane of his life. Bella the Bitch. 'Yvonne caught her smoking the other day and she blamed me. Said I was setting a bad example.' She'd picked that little one up at school, of course. The teachers would have put them up to it. Harass your parents and caregivers! Make them feel guilty. Drive them out of the house!

'So Spooky wants me to quit. I quit years ago and now I just have the odd one.'

'Yeah,' said Kendell, 'like every twenty minutes. George Bernard Shaw said, "giving up smoking is easy, I've done it plenty of times".'

'Ha bloody ha,' Last Gasp said. He didn't know who this George person was, and didn't care.

'The funny thing is,' Kendell said, 'that he never smoked at all. He was a pure living vegetarian.'

'Just like Hitler,' Ford said. 'Did Hitler smoke?'

'Not publicly. It would have made him look too much like Charlie Chaplin.'

'I'd better have a beer,' Last Gasp said.

'I wouldn't if I were you,' Ford said, tossing the last of his beer back, 'it ups the craving for a smoke. Imagine what Spooky will say if you go home stinking of cigarettes *and* booze.'

Last Gasp's hands twitched. He didn't know where to put them. 'Where did you learn to be so cruel?'

'He was born that way,' Kendell said. 'Have you ever met a journalist who was not cynical?'

'I heard that,' a voice said. It was Tin Lizzie, now retired, once a journalist for a City paper. Some said that she got religion and had to retire; others said that she burned out, came to Paradise Island to regroup and never did. 'There's just as many cynical bus drivers as there are cynical journalists,' she said.

'Have a cancer stick,' Ford said, gesturing to his packet.

'What is this, the slow suicide club?'

'Do you want one, or are you just being cynical?'

'I gave up. Don't mind if I do,' she slid a smoke from Ford's packet. 'I mean, I gave up buying them. Now I'm on OP's.'

'What that?' Last Gasp asked hopefully. He was looking for a miracle around the next corner.

'Other people's. All you gotta do is ask.'

Ford quickly retrieved his smokes and put them in his pocket. Maybe this OP business was catching. Kendell would pick up on something like that as quick as a flash.

'Lunchtime already, is it?' Tin Lizzie said, glancing at the beers around the table while lighting up using Ford's lighter. She flourished the cigarette. 'Another nail in the coffin.'

'What gets me,' Kendell said, 'is that I know all about how the tobacco industry works, and it's dirtier than their product. They set out to addict people. They are in the nicotine delivery business, that's how they see it. They play on our desires and our weaknesses. I know all this, but still I keeping on smoking. What does that make me?'

'A fool,' Ford said quickly, before somebody else could get in.

'If I am, then you are.'

'That's right,' Ford said. 'You are absolutely right. And this whole stupid conversation is going nowhere.'

'Because it's a ship of fools,' Kendell said.

'That's right,' Ford said. His voice was getting louder. His face was getting redder. 'And I'm bailing. Man overboard!'

He pulled his cigarettes from his pocket, opened the packet and shook all the little white sticks onto the table where they rolled around and soaked up the spilled beer. Last Gasp gasped in horror.

From a nearby table, Ford seized a squeezy bottle of ketchup and proceeded to empty the contents over the beer soaked cigarettes. Now those pristine white sticks looked sad and blood-soaked.

'What a grand gesture,' Tin Lizzie said, salvaging a couple of still dry ones. 'Better than scavenging for butts,' she said. 'You ever done that?'

'Right,' Ford, who had done that, said. 'That's it. Finish. End. I quit. As of now. I'll never have another one.'

Nobody believed him, of course, but the funny thing was, he never did.

THE SUITCASE THAT WALKED BY ITSELF

This is a tale of separation and grief, included here for the sake of balance and fairness; after all, even back in the day, even on Paradise Island, especially on Paradise Island, nights could be long, hearts could wear out, and the days filled with the loneliness of which the poets sing.

No. Not at all. This is a story about a suitcase. A battered, scuffed, long serving suitcase. A suitcase that learned how to walk by itself.

It began life as a spruce, upright, forward looking, brand new suitcase. It belonged to a little boy who lived on Paradise Island, and who was very proud of his new suitcase. The suitcase was proud too. It was the smartest, newest and flashest object in the house. Its sides were firm, its locks were snappy and its zippers gleamed. Its handle was made of soft, strong leather. The carpet on which it sat was threadbare, the sofa beside it sagged with age, the table was chipped, and the bedroom dresser had grown too warped for its drawers to slide open and shut. The suitcase looked as if it didn't belong in those drab surroundings but in some wonderful shiny heaven where everything was eternally new.

The suitcase zipper flowed open with ease, revealing a grey, satiny inside, with special pockets for precious objects and an elastic pocket on the inside of the lid. When the little boy's clothes and toys first went into it, the suitcase felt a little sullied, almost violated. The clothes were clean but, like the furniture, old and worn, and the toys had mostly seen better days and were not necessarily clean, but as more clothes went in and a very special teddy bear, pretty clean, was given the elastic pocket, a privileged position, the suitcase began to warm to the idea, even feel fulfilled. After all, this is what it had been made for. Those nice roomy insides and enticing pockets. It had been built to hold things, to keep things safe, dry and secure.

It felt good to be filled up with things, even the two heavy books that went in on top and mashed the clothes down.

It wasn't unhappy, however, to leave the house and go into the boot of a nice clean taxi, carried by a man who gripped its handle confidently, and a little boy who clung to it for dear life as it went from taxi to ferry to taxi again and finally to the airport, where the suitcase found itself amid hundreds of others of its kind. Never had it seen so many other suitcases, some of them as new and shiny as itself. It was a humbling experience. And a little frightening, too, when it was jammed in with lots of other suitcases and packed away in a hold.

The suitcase soon learned a stoic acceptance of being squeezed on all four sides by other suitcases, the corner of one being jammed unpleasantly into its side. This was the lot of suitcases. This was how they travelled. Our suitcase could feel the resignation and the grim determination of the older suitcases – and learned acceptance. This is what it had been made for.

It didn't last forever. Soon it was taken, pretty much unscathed but for the dent in its side, out of the hold, transferred to a moving belt which trundled it into waiting hands, and the little boy. It was pleased to see the little boy. Before long it was in another house, not that different to the first and was soon being unpacked, content to have done its work. It wasn't long before it lay, depleted, with lid open, its satiny insides enjoying the fresh air and releasing some of the odours of the clothes and the toys. There had been one little rabbit-eared creature with its insides hanging out that was a bit stinky.

Shortly afterwards it was flung into the bottom of a closet and had to learn the periods of neglect that is also the lot of the common suitcase. It could do nothing but gather dust and wait in the dark with no company but some old shoe box filled with papers, a pair of high-heeled shoes forlorn and dusty, and hanging clothes that stank of old lives and naphthalene. It was a lesson in mortality to be stuck in the closet with these things forgotten or past their use-by date. The shoes did nothing but reminisce about days of former glory, and the clothes spent all of their time wondering if they'd ever be worn again.

When the little boy pulled out the suitcase and began to pack it once more, the suitcase was overjoyed to get away from the dull company of the wardrobe, but could sense a heaviness in the movements of the little boy as he re-packed the clothes and the toys he'd brought with him. When the big people were out of the room, the little boy lay across the suitcase and his tears soaked into its fabric.

The suitcase realised that not only would it carry all the little bits and pieces precious to the little boy, but his tears as well, the grief he sobbed into the suitcase as it filled up. It's not just clothes and toys, the suitcase thought, but a life I am carrying.

On the way to the airport the little boy clung to the soft leather handle with all his strength, and the suitcase bore his pain. At the airport everybody cried and the little boy didn't want to let the suitcase go.

This journey was a reverse of the first, seeing them arrive at their initial point of departure, the same threadbare carpet and sagging sofa. Paradise Island.

And so the life of the suitcase fell into a pattern. It would reside for some time on Paradise Island where it rested on top of a wardrobe, with a grand view of a very ordinary bedroom, then it would be filled up with the little boy's bits and pieces, many of them familiar from previous occasions, and whisked off to the other place and its other home in the dark closet with the sad high-heeled shoes, the old shoe box and the dusty clothes. It collected tears on departures and laughter (and a few tears) on arrivals. This back and forth movement confused it sometimes. It would wake in the middle of night uncertain if the darkness was that of the closet or the curtained bedroom.

It began to notice other changes. The very special teddy bear, after a few journeys, soon looked not so special, and a nice shiny dinosaur book took its place in the elastic pocket. One of its eyes had become a little loose because of the boy's habit of twisting it back and forth in his fingers, giving it an abused look. And one day the stinky little rabbit-eared creature with its insides hanging out disappeared and the suitcase never saw it again. There were changes in the closet too, where the suitcase least expected change.

One day the high-heeled shoes were taken out, brushed and worn. It was only a little trip up the High Street but the shoes were overjoyed and lived upon the memory for long afterwards. The feel of the foot inside, a little tight, perhaps; the rhythmic striking of its spike against the hard pavement, the taste of leather on stone. We're still wanted, the shoes said. We're still important, we still have a role to play. We are taken out for special occasions only.

Once, the suitcase arrived to find the shoebox with the papers had split down one side and the papers were spilling out. The suitcase watched as the old box was removed and crumpled into a rubbish bag while a new shoebox took its place. 'I'm sad about that,' the high-heeled shoes said. 'We came in that box.' Soon, however, the old box became a distant memory while the new box proceeded to gather dust.

The suitcase itself was changing. A fall from a stack of luggage at the airport had cracked one of its sides, only a little, but it was no longer quite so firm, or the smartest, newest and flashest object in the house. The history of its travels could be seen in the marks and scratches that appeared upon it. The stains of tears and miles. The little boy was no longer little. Only the very special teddy bear now made the journey, the other toys having fallen away. The boy could drag the suitcase all by himself now.

Then one season the unthinkable happened. The suitcase was not taken down from the top of the wardrobe. It did not make the trip to the other place. The boy took it down from the wardrobe, opened it and looked at it, leaving it empty but for an immense sadness. The suitcase knew it would have to carry this sadness forever. Even on the top of the wardrobe. Whether empty or full. Every time it was opened, the sadness would come out, like a genie from a magic lantern. So nobody wanted to use it. It stayed where it was, and, like the shoes in the other place, shoes it would never see again, it dwelt on former glories, its early days as a spruce, upright, forward-looking, brand new suitcase.

Until the day, unable to bear its sadness, it decided to take matters into its own hands. It would leave the ugly wardrobe and the ordinary bedroom and strike out on its own. It would learn to walk by itself. Out there was a place called Paradise Island, a place to explore. It had to get out, because sooner or later it would be taken to the junk shop, or worse. Its freight of sadness, which, in the silence and loneliness of the top of the wardrobe had grown unbearable, would be handed on to someone else or discarded in a pile of garbage.

It learned to inch itself forward and one day fell off the wardrobe. And it got up and walked. It walked right out of the house into the sunshine of Paradise Island. It knew it had to keep walking until it found someplace for its sadness to go. It needed a home for its sadness. It needed a place where it could outwait its tears. Outlive its memories. A place where it might learn something new.

It was found sheltering under a hedge by a homeless man who was very grateful to find it. He put his few belongings into it. They were pitiful, but didn't mind the sadness or the memories of grand cargo-holds and rattling luggage-belts, so the suitcase didn't mind.

Now the suitcase knew a different journey. Not one that led anywhere, just from here to there, and was always on the move. It was a good life, although rough. There were no long dreary periods in closets or on top of wardrobes. This man lived out of his suitcase. He was on the road, and the suitcase was to witness many wonderful and sad things.

The suitcase was soon to become as pitiful and battered as its owner, but it no longer minded the scuffs and scratches, the rusted locks or the sticky zippers. It had quite forgotten its old life, its old smells.

It knew, however, that it must have had a former life before it learned how to walk. It knew that somewhere a little boy wandered between worlds, clasping in his hands a brand new, shiny, proud, upright suitcase.

STANDING OR SQUATTING?

If you're looking for someone to blame, start with Dr Lovejoy. He started it all when he told his men's group that the latest research out of Scandinavia suggested that men should squat to pee the way women do, or at least sit down.

'Apparently that provides for a more complete emptying of the bladder, and is therefore more healthy, particularly good for the prostate,' he said. 'All in all, a more complete peeing experience.'

'Was that research carried out by a woman, by any chance?' Briscoe asked. He had always stood up to pee and always would.

'Does it matter?' Dr Lovejoy asked.

Apparently it did, at least to Briscoe, and he wasn't the only one. He was firmly convinced of a feminist conspiracy to degrade and control men, and here was the evidence.

Dr Lovejoy should have known that he was opening a Pandora's box, especially when he went on to suggest that young boys be encouraged to squat like girls when they pee.

'They're trying to turn us all into girls!' Briscoe said. He felt hurt that his friend from the men's group was promoting this attack on men and began to wonder if Lovejoy might be gay. In an impassioned plea, which Lovejoy suspected was really directed at his mother, Briscoe asked, 'What more do you want of me? Wait, I know. You want my maleness. You want me to become a sitting-to-pee neuter.'

Dr Lovejoy found Briscoe's language fascinating, but held his tongue.

When the women running the Playcentre began to encourage the boys to 'be a sweetie and take a seatie,' Briscoe ominously suggested that fathers should take a closer look at what was going on there, and in day-care. Time for the men to step in!

Elsie Childs, who ran the day-care, sweetly suggested that it would be very nice to see fathers more involved in the care of their children. She was bluffing, of course. The last thing she wanted to see was a posse of self-righteous men running loose among the children, but she needn't have worried; the Briscoe brigade preferred bluster to buckle-down.

Briscoe, however, was the man of the moment, and he received a lot of support from the community, not all of it welcome. 'Colonel' Billy McCloud, for example, came out of his corner claiming that since Muslims also promoted peeing while sitting or squatting, this effort to get boys to 'take a seatie' was a part of a Muslim conspiracy to bring Sharia law to Paradise Island. 'It's the thin end of the wedge,' he said. The Colonel was supported by those wingnuts, as local reporter Garrison Ford called them, who believed that the United Nations, the Vatican, Prince Philip and Snow White and the Seven Dwarves were engaged in wide ranging conspiracy to bring about a New World Order. In that New World Order, men would have to pee while sitting down.

The parents of Indigo children claimed that their little boys squatted down to pee quite naturally, and needed no 'brainwashing.' Still others claimed that all toddlers squatted to do their business and in fact little boys had to be trained to pee standing up. Stumpy Stewart said that a lot of problems would be solved if more facilities could be provided for young people, then they wouldn't get drunk and pee on people's letterboxes. In a literary aside, Kendell noted that in *Gulliver's Travels* two sides go to war over whether or not to eat a boiled egg from the fat or the thin end.

'Those researchers don't know diddly-squat!' Crusty Crookshank famously remarked. Fancy, he said, living long enough to hear such things!

When Garrison Ford tentatively suggested that further research was needed, Briscoe commented that the alcoholic Ford did most of his peeing lying down, and if he tried to squat he'd fall over backwards. Ford, who instinctively hated the idea of women telling men how to pee, and was struggling to keep his largely imaginary journalistic objectivity, wrote three editorials he had to trash.

The forces of reason rallied around Dr Lovejoy, who appealed to all to not shoot the messenger. 'Science cannot tell us how to live,' he counselled everybody, 'it can only tell us what is.' In a wide-ranging interview with Garrison Ford in the *Paradise Island Times*, Dr Lovejoy said sometimes scientific facts may be culturally unpalatable, but that doesn't stop them from being facts. 'If peeing sitting down is good for the prostate, it doesn't matter how much we huff-'n-puff. We can't change the fact.'

It seemed that peeing while sitting was all part of a balanced and happy lifestyle.

While most of the men, with their beers and their barbeques, blew froth and spat gristle at the idea, MoJo Mayhem may not have been alone in having some private doubts. If it helped the prostate, then why not? It was no big deal surely, standing up or sitting down, despite all the outrage. Besides, it was rather unsettling to know that five to ten percent of the urine in his bladder might never get emptied, and be breeding dark and vicious things. Dr Lovejoy, who had been doing some research, waxed lyrical on that subject. 'If one urinates standing and never completely empties the urinary system, our urinary system starts to gather sediment and gradually grows and multiplies dirty things, garbage, bacteria, stones, infections, etc which gradually causes urinary system diseases, unhealthy sexual desire, dissatisfaction, anxiety, frustration, incontinence, depression, frequency of wet-dreams, lust, and impotence.'

All of which sounded to Ford like a personal attack.

In other words, Lovejoy said, peeing while sitting might increase male libido, a claim that caused some disquiet among some of his female allies, who wondered if increased male libido was what the world needed.

What really needled MoJo was the implication that peeing standing up had affected his performance as a lover, dented his precious libido, whatever that was. It sounded a bit like the cloth you tie around a baby's neck at feed-time. Like many men, MoJo was proud of his sexual prowess while at the same time suffering from performance anxiety. Could his unhealthy interest in Dennaray's eldest daughter, the exotic and red-haired Isolde, be due to years of peeing while standing up? This was not something he could exactly talk over with Ella, and a certain instinct for self-preservation prevented him from bringing it up at the men's group.

Ella was a good woman. Maybe she deserved better than what she was getting.

The idea played into his feelings of guilt and inadequacy, those terrible twins always ready to take over his emotional life and, between them, grind him to pulp. Impotent pulp. Bravado only goes so far when it comes to these terrible twins, and that is not far enough, so we might speculate that MoJo was not the only man to begin to surreptitiously sit down while peeing. After all, it was easy enough. You didn't have to tell the world what you did in the privacy of your own lavatory.

At first he felt silly, sitting there with nothing else to do but pee.

Silly and embarrassed. But after a while that wore off. He also noticed that if he did a pee standing up, and shortly after got the message for a more substantial evacuation, he would pee again when he sat down. This made him more convinced than ever that there was something to it.

What disturbed him was the hypocrisy of his position. Around the barbie with the men, a beer in one hand and a spliff in the other, he was quite happy to scoff at the interfering lefties, feminazis and their social engineering, and get righteous about it, but when he took a break to have a slash, he would slip into the toilet, and after making sure the door was securely locked, sit down and pee to the very last drop. Gotta look after that prostate. Gotta get that libido pumping.

When Briscoe suggested a mass public male urination, a *standing* urination, although women could come too and urinate standing if they wanted to show solidarity with their men, there was a general furore. Ella respectfully declined but MoJo was expected to go, show the flag as it were.

Tom Tommyknocker, the local cop, gave due warning that anybody exposing themselves in public could expect to be arrested, and while Briscoe was happy to be a martyr to the cause of standing urination, most of his cohort were not.

Matters might have remained there if Bella Bangle, a teenager whose mother Yvonne had the unfortunate distinction of being Garrison Ford's girlfriend, had not suddenly entered the fray. The ever-resourceful Bella had been doing a little research of her own, not into men's urination, but into the sleeping patterns of teenagers. It was a simple matter of science, she said. Because of their chemical/hormonal balance, teenagers needed more sleep than adults. This had been proved in a number of studies. If the community was going to listen to the scientific evidence regarding men sitting down to pee, it should also listen to the evidence on adolescent sleeping patterns and not open the school until 10 a.m.

Dr Lovejoy stepped up to support her. She was right, he said, and her reasoning was sound. He believed later school hours were being tried in Germany with positive results.

This last piece of loony left mischief was enough to tip Garrison Ford over the edge. He wrote an editorial on how far teenagers would go to justify their laziness. As if sitting down and peeing wasn't enough, the loony left now wanted teenagers lying about limp until 10 a.m! So your sons are to lounge around all morning while others have to get up and go to work, then sit like a girl to take a pee, then finally slope off to school! What kind of world do we want?

Opinions became hopelessly confused and divided. As far as MoJo was concerned, he'd been a teenager all his adult life; maybe his hormones and chemicals hadn't kicked in. As it turned out, Bella's cheekiness received support from an unexpected quarter, schoolteachers who said they were tired of trying to teach kids falling asleep at their desks as soon as they arrived at school. 'Colonel' Billy McCloud commented that he knew the answer to that sort of behaviour. And maybe the teachers could do with a bit of it too. Some wag said that it sounded like Billy McCloud wanted to bring Sharia law to Paradise Island.

From Briscoe's point of view, the whole thing was a huge distraction from the real issue. That girl Bella Bangle was just muddying the waters, probably from sheer malice. A born man-hater. He announced that the public peeing would take place at 6.30 a.m. sharp in a secluded corner of a public park, and challenged the teenage boys to come along to see what real men did. In reply, Bella announced that, on the same morning, all teenagers would stay in bed until 9.30 a.m.

And so it happened. The public urination was a damp squid, as Ford described it. Only Tom Tommykocker was there, keeping a friendly eye on things, and Ford himself, calculating the most suggestive angle he could get away with for a photo; it was too early for everybody else and wives stayed away. The teenagers had their sleep-in, at least Bella's friends and supporters did, before going to school late and getting detentions for their trouble.

Life returned to normal on Paradise Island except for MoJo Mayhem. His life was changed forever. He never peed standing up again unless he had to.

CRUSTY AND THE CANNY CAT

It would be nice to think that nothing ever changed on Paradise Island. That, back in the day, time didn't really exist except in the hopes and fears of the inhabitants. That the place we call 'back in the day' goes on forever.

Look at it this way. Paradise Island was not supposed to change. People were not supposed to get old and die. Or if they were already old, they stayed that way. Forever. You could say that the sin of Adam and Eve in the original paradise was to let time loose in the world.

At least, that's the way it seemed to Crusty Crookshank who was well aware that he had not always been old, and who had a 'back in the day' of his own, memories of the island when he was just a child.

Crusty lived on his own in an old but standard three-bedroom house, tucked away behind hedges and pines in a scattered settlement with houses few and far between. Crusty's nearest neighbour was a good five minute walk from his place and he liked it that way. Not that he chose to live alone in a big house away from everybody. People just moved out or died while he stayed where he was. His wife had died ten years back, his kids had left home twenty years before that. One day a house full of people became a house full of empty rooms. Crusty didn't mind too much. No sense in resenting the ways of the world. A couple of times a year, his son visited him with a packet of biscuits, told him he should get out more, and went away again. Getting out more meant going to Bingo or sitting in a café with other old people who didn't know what to do with their lives but talk about how things were back in the day. What did they know about it anyway?

Alone but not lonely, was how he described his life to his son, who was sceptical. He spent a lot of time wandering around in his bit of a garden or walking some of the tracks only the old timers knew about, not those fancy new tracks with wooden steps and yellow markers on posts. He didn't consciously try to keep the world out, build walls or anything the way his son suspected, it was just that the world stayed away from him. And why shouldn't it? It was entitled to. He had no claim on the world except his pension, and the world had no claim on him except its taxes. Simple.

Until the advent of the kitten.

Crusty was not a cat person. Not really an animal person. Once, his son had pointedly told him of some research showing that elderly people with pets lived longer on average than those without pets. His son put a lot of store in research. But, Crusty pointed out, he did have pets, lots of them, in his garden. Slugs, snails, stick-insects, stink-beetles, woodlice, spiders, lots of cheeky blackbirds and even a couple of gracious wood-pigeons dressed in their Sunday best. Why would he need a cat? So he told his son about his own father, a man from the backcountry. He used to put stray cats and unwanted kittens in a sack with a rock and toss the screaming sack into a bath full of water.

Of course, the cat didn't know any of this. It was just a scrawny, hungry kitten that lived in the shadows. The first Crusty knew of it was a glimpse he caught of a little, starved, grey furry face peering at him from beyond his fence line. A frightened little face too. As soon as he moved, the face disappeared. A few days later he saw it peeping at him from the side of the road when he went out for his morning walk. Clearly it was abandoned, hungry and neglected, but Crusty's heart was not moved. It wasn't his job to feed all the stray cats of the world, for where there was one there were thousands; at the same time he found that while he walked, that little, starved face came into his mind, and when he returned, he found himself looking around for it.

It was probably there, somewhere, watching him.

A few days later he found a half-chewed dead mouse on his path. He saw this as a signal to him, a message that told him he had too many mice in residence, and just how handy a cat could be to a man living alone with nothing but his rodents for company. Somewhere back in our evolution, he speculated, cats learned how to make themselves useful to man in just this way, and learned how to make a place for themselves around a human fire.

That night he put some meat on a plate at his back door, just inside the square of roof that protected the steps and the back door. If he knew his cats, the food would be gone in the morning.

He was wrong. The food was still there. After a few days went by and nothing happened, he put some more food out, and while it was gone in the morning, the piles of mouse droppings around the area told their story. A couple of weeks later, he decided that the cat had gone. A world with stoats and weasels at large was a dangerous place for a starving kitten; it had doubtless met the fate of all weak and unprotected things.

He was wrong again. The cat survived the land of stoats and weasels. He saw it a few months later, when he'd almost forgotten it, sitting in the same spot along the road, watching him. But the grey furry face was no longer tiny and kittenish. Or frightened. There was wariness, perhaps even a touch of wisdom. The cat watched him calmly, calculatedly, and vanished as he drew near.

A few days later he saw it again, this time in his garden. He came around the corner of his garden shed and there it was, crouched down and looking at him. He and the cat both went very still as they eyeballed each other. They couldn't stay that way forever. As soon as Crusty moved the cat disappeared. It didn't just run away; it just wasn't there. A clever cat. And wild too.

And still hungry.

This time, Crusty left the plate of meat far from the house, at his fence line. In the morning the meat was gone. The next night, he moved the plate further along the fence line where it would be closer to the house. Again the meat was taken. There was no other sign of the cat, however, but Crusty knew it was there. The next night he moved the plate even closer to the house, and again the meat was gone. In its place there was a half-eaten dead rat. The dialogue had begun again.

If his son had come by and asked him why he was doing this, Crusty would not have had an easy answer. It was fun. Just how close he could lure the wary, wild cat to his house was the question he was testing. He didn't want the cat as a pet, stretched out on the sofa doing nothing or meowing over the food bowl. He had no time for cats like that. But this tough, independent cat was nothing like those pampered pussies. He could admire a cat that could stand up for itself and look out for itself.

He had to go slowly. The process took some weeks but eventually he got the cat to take food from the top step before the back door. There was nowhere left to go now but inside the house. Rarely, however, did Crusty actually see the cat. He knew it was living around the house, but it was keeping well out of his way. He'd heard that the way to get rid of an unwanted cat was to throw water in its face, and he wondered if perhaps this cat had received some such treatment, making it shy of humans.

Just to catch a sight of it he stayed up one night and kept a vigil by the back window. It was a bright moonlit night he'd chosen, and was soon rewarded by the sight of the cat coming warily around the side of the house as softly as a grey ghost. Hyper-alert, it moved with great care until it was positioned in front of the plate. Crusty held his breath. If he moved, the cat would surely see him. Just before it bent its head to eat, the cat looked straight up into his face; its uncanny eyes locked with his. After a long moment it put its head down and began to eat, ignoring him completely.

Alan Crookshank approached the old home, a packet of biscuits under his arm, with the usual misgivings. He'd been raised here, the house was a part of him, and now he had to face the fact that, sooner or later, his father would have to sell it and move to a more convenient place closer to medical facilities. Perhaps even a home. These things had to be faced with an aging parent, even on Paradise Island.

He was fully resolved to raise the issue with his father today.

As he walked through the familiar front door, the first thing he saw was a cat, a formidably large, grey cat, sitting in the hall, on top of a small table where the telephone sat, its eyes fixed on him. With its classic posture, as in pictures of ancient Egyptian cats, it looked like a threshold guardian, ready to test the purity of his intentions. The grey cat looked right through him to the impurity of his intentions. In the moment he was distracted by a noise from a room to one side, the cat leapt in a long, graceful arc from the table to the hall and raced for the back of the house.

'She's pretty shy of strangers,' his father said, emerging from his room.

'You've got a pet,' Alan said. 'That's great!'

'She's no pet,' his father said with vigour. 'She's not tamed. She never will be.' There was a touch of pride in his voice. 'She will come into the house, on her terms of course…'

'Of course,' Alan said.

'But she's no house cat. She can disappear for days and turn up again when she pleases.'

'I bet,' Alan said.

His father peered up at him suspiciously. From the rear of the hallway, a grey face appeared and two yellow eyes fixed on his with equal suspicion. Alan had read that cats emit some kind of smell, like a pheromone, that makes human beings high. The same stuff that makes its prey more careless, less risk averse. Looking at his father now, he thought that might well be true. His father was grinning as if he had one up on his son. From the other end of the hall, the cat seemed to be grinning too.

Alan's resolve to raise important issues melted away. With this cat in residence, Crusty might last a bit longer. He could put off the inevitable till the next visit.

'I believe the female is the hunter in the cat family,' Alan said.

'You can say that again,' his father said, and led him to the kitchen for their ritual cup of tea to go with the biscuits.

The cat was nowhere to be seen, but its scent lingered in the air.

TINA AND THE TANIWHA

Tina approached Maori Hill warily. Modest looking, with its gorse and rocky outcrops, Maori Hill had a formidable reputation. Legends told of massacres here when the marauder, Te Rauparaha, passed this way. The local tribe made its last stand here, on Maori Hill, among the kumara pits.

There was a walking track that wound up the north side of the hill, but not many people used it. Even tourists avoided it. Talk of ghosts and vengeful spirits is all very well over a cup of coffee at breakfast, not so much fun at night with the great bulk of Maori Hill looming darkly ahead and the sigh of wind in the paspalum.

Nobody was around. Nobody would have seen Tina Tuppa disappear into the low tea-tree and broom at the base of the hill. Even if somebody had seen her, they would never have guessed that this small woman was heading up Maori Hill to spend the night. Alone. Nobody did that.

But Tina Tuppa had a mission. In her Vision Quest, before her beeswax candle, she had seen a Maori woman giving birth under a pohutukawa tree while blood from a battle rained around her. The woman needed help.

'I know that tree,' she said to her man, Metternich from Germany.

'Then you must find it,' Metternich said.

He meant *should* rather than *must*, but she got the idea. It was already there in her head. Her spirit guides wanted her to find the tree and help the woman. So, how to find a tree on Paradise Island that is full of trees, pohutukawa in particular? She had to sit quietly and visualise the tree and try to glimpse its surroundings, get a feel for where it was. This took her longer than it might have. There was something resisting her, blurring the edges of her vision. She got it, eventually, with patience – a patch of sky with a headland. Maori Hill.

In the days preceding her visit it became clear what she had to do in order to help the woman. She had to find the tree and stay the whole night by the woman's side, acting as midwife, not for the birth of the child, who was already murdered in her womb, but for the woman herself, to guide her from her earthly existence into the beyond. Her agony had trapped her here.

Tina carried a tightly rolled sleeping bag and some water, but nothing else. The hard ground would serve as a mattress, and she wouldn't eat, not on a mission like this. She moved quickly, having a lot of ground to cover before dark. She couldn't just stick to the track either, but had to explore likely terrain and of course check out every pohutukawa. She didn't think she would have that much trouble, since such a large tree could not be easily hidden even on Maori Hill, but again the task took her longer than she expected. The tree was veiled. She had to look hard to see it.

She didn't find it until twilight, as the sun edged down out of sight and the shadows came out to play. A waxing gibbous moon was rising above the lumpy bulk of the hill, itself pale and misshapen. It would be several days before it would fill out into its full glory. Its wan light didn't penetrate the gathering shadows at the base of the pohutukawa. Those enormous branches tended to hoard shadows.

At first she didn't see the woman trying to give birth at the base of the tree, but the air was full of presences, the chittering of spirits, a rounder disturbance of elementals, and behind those, a more powerful bass voice she didn't recognise. Tina waited patiently until her vision cleared and she finally saw the woman. She was not much more than a girl; she could hardly have been seventeen. When she saw Tina her face creased in terror.

'It's alright,' Tina said. 'I am here to help you.' Although exactly what help she would give was not clear at that moment.

'My child,' the woman said. 'Save my child.' The woman was a grisly sight, spattered with blood all over, spotting her face like rampant measles and spilling from between her open legs. One arm, partly severed, hung uselessly. In truth, there was no saving either of them.

Composing a prayer of release, Tina stepped forward, only to encounter an invisible physical resistance. It felt rough, hairy, like the side of a beast.

'What are you doing here?' a voice asked, the same bass voice she'd heard earlier. It sounded like rocks beneath the earth being rolled together.

'I am here to guide the woman to her afterlife,' Tina said.

'Who are you to be doing this? What is your *iwi*, your *hapu*? Who are your ancestors? Who brings you here?'

Tina realised that she was dealing with an elemental, but one on a far greater scale than she had ever encountered. Maori Hill was only a part of it, the rest of its massive body curled across the peninsular and out into the Gulf. Tina had been in the presence of many nature spirits, from tickly flower sprites to cool river gods, but the huge presence around her was more animal than spirit. Ancient animal.

'I have no iwi and I have no hapu,' Tina said, holding herself steady. 'And my ancestors come from far away. It was spirit that sent me.'

A rumble of dissatisfaction shook Maori Hill like dry thunder. The nearest inhabitants, lagoon dwellers on their houseboats, looked up from what they were doing.

The woman beneath the tree was still suffering. The pain of giving birth had mixed with the pain of her wounds to send her cries through all the sentient worlds. 'Let me go to her,' Tina said.

'There is nothing stopping you,' the voice said.

This being, vast as it was, was still an elemental, and in Tina's experience elementals were tricky creatures to deal with. They could lie and dissimulate. They could be wise or childish, or both at the same time. Once she'd had to pull up a dark elemental that had taken root on somebody's property. The being had fought her every inch of the way, but had departed in the end.

'That's true,' Tina said and sat down where she was. She didn't need to be right beside the woman to do what she had to do. She was close enough. Her mind was now shaping a prayer for release and she was starting to visualise a shaft of light shining down on the woman, like a spotlight from the sky. Since she'd never encountered anything like this, she had to make it up as she went along, evolving a ritual that would work for the situation. She began pulling together the strengths of the four directions. Nothing short of a massive effort would help this woman.

She began to chant, softly, almost under her breath.

'What are you doing?' the great voice asked.

The ground around her rippled. She was lifted up a little and dropped down, jarring her spine.

'I'm preparing a pathway for the woman,' Tina said. 'You can see for yourself she's trapped.'

'By what authority do you do this, little worm? Don't you know that I could crush you in a moment, smash every bone in your body.'

'I don't doubt it,' she said. 'And you know spirit sent me here. I have already told you.'

It was always best to be firm with elementals, and not play their silly games, even one capable of killing her. She suspected now that the elemental itself was wounded, and the source of that wound lay under the pohutukawa tree. It was often said that war wounds the land, here was the evidence. The agony of the woman had entered and infected the elemental. By freeing the woman she would help heal this land – the creature would oppose her, of course, as any animal would if something began prodding at its wound.

'I can heal you too,' she said, 'but not if you act badly.'

'Who are you? You think you can heal the sky and the stars too?'

'They don't need it. You do.'

It was a dangerous game she was playing with this elemental, but it was the only way to play it. One sign of doubt or hesitation and she would be blasted off Maori Hill like a leaf in the wind.

She returned to her work. The woman, fully aware of her, had turned in her direction, one arm reaching into the sky as if she would pull it down on her and end her suffering once and for all. Not only had the woman been unable to move on, she had not been able to leave the last moments of her earthly agony. Tina would have to intervene, to lift the woman's spirit out of her tortured flesh. She had guided spirits towards the light before, but had never had to undertake the psychic surgery she now faced, let alone face an angry elemental at the same time. It wasn't possible. She couldn't do it. It was too huge. This spot, where a pregnant young woman had been raped and hacked to death, would have to fester forever.

'But then,' she said, hardly conscious of talking aloud, 'it will fester in our dreams forever too.'

'Go ahead and do it then,' the elemental said, apparently having no trouble following her thoughts. It knew her fear. It was playing with her.

So she did it, swiftly and without warning. Gathering her energies, she left her body and glided to the woman's side. While her body could not cross the barrier the elemental had thrown up, her spirit passed through it as if it were nothing. With nothing in her heart but love to guide her, Tina plunged her spirit hands into the woman's body and drew her soul out.

The woman's scream and the elemental's were one. Like a referred pain, a distant volcano opened one eye and flickered.

'My baby,' the woman moaned when she was still just half-way out of her body, ready to return even to the hell of the body's pain for the sake of her child.

'Your baby is dead,' Tina said. She could feel the exhaustion that would later hit her already creeping up, and the job was not yet done.

Using all the leverage she had, Tina pulled the woman's soul from her body.

'Go to your ancestors,' Tina said sternly.

She had to return to her body now, or she'd be going to *her* ancestors.

The job was done. The night was quiet. There was so little movement in the air that it seemed to her that the branches of the pohutukawa hung in suspension.

The elemental lay still.

Tina lay in her sleeping bag and waited for dawn.

KENDELL AND THE TALENTED TYPEWRITER

One day back in the day, Paradise Island's very own writer, Kendell, sat down to write and discovered that he had lost his mojo. The words wouldn't come, the sentences wouldn't flow. There was no juice or joy left in the world.

So he wandered around the island, looking for inspiration. He didn't find any. Just people going about their lives until they died. He visited Penny, proud daughter of a famous writer. He and Penny had a thing going once, until he realised that Penny hated her father. 'For him words are more important than people,' she said. 'That's very bad,' he had replied.

Penny made him a cup of tea and offered him a pipe. Ah, the famous Shire Weed. Maybe that's what he needed. A little puff of the dragon. Penny's place was full of kids, friends of her daughter, Squelchy. Kendell had a pipe and considered the sad state of things. These kids, for example. Kendell didn't like kids much, and had avoided having any, but looking at these bright eyes now, he felt the stirring of what might have been pity.

There was a day, he told them, before the computer, when the humble and now nearly extinct typewriter ruled. Clackety-clack.

'Why didn't people just use their iPads?' a sceptical youngster asked.

'Well, you may ask,' Kendell said. The good writer had been suffering a creeping despair which inclined him towards answers like that. It wasn't just that he felt history had passed him by, but that history had passed everybody by. We were now living in the midst of impossible futures. When asked recently at a party what he did for a living, he said he repaired typewriters.

So he told the children how, on the day he decided to be become a writer and immortalise the denizens of Paradise Island as best he could, he found a typewriter at the rubbish dump. It had a seagull sitting on top of it and only had one letter missing. With a little 3 'n 1 oil and some coaxing he got the machine working. He could still remember the thrill of that.

'You really had to hit the keys,' he told the less than wide-eyed youngsters. 'Writers needed strong fingers in those days.'

The missing letter was a d. That didn't seem to matter much at first until he came to write a word like 'didn't' or a sentence like 'There was the odour of death in the dark dank dungeon,' a sentence he'd really wanted to write for many years. Without the d it read, 'there was the oour of eath in the ark ank ungeon,' which reminded him of certain strains in modern poetry, and was possibly even an improvement on the original, but was otherwise unsatisfactory.

The youngsters he was attempting to enlighten looked at each other and shook their heads. Except the one who was busy texting.

'That was my first typewriter,' Kendell said wistfully. The world had been at his feet then. With his broken typewriter, he would astonish and conquer the world. He wondered if people felt nostalgic about their first computers. Possibly. People can feel nostalgic about all sorts of things.

'What happened to the d?'

'Ah. That is a mystery.' The d arm (he had to explain) had been broken right off near the base, as if someone had disliked it and snipped it out. He went on to explain that the machine was beyond repair since, even if he could find a d arm for that particular model – a very long shot – there was no way of attaching it. For some reason it was important to Kendell to get that point across, but the kids didn't care. If stuff didn't work, you just got more stuff. They couldn't see the miracle of an almost working typewriter sitting in a rubbish dump with a gull on top. That gull had had something in its mouth too, something unsavoury, like a piece of plastic.

'What I didn't realise,' he said, 'was that this was a magic typewriter.'

That aroused a moment's interest. 'Could it fly?'

'Not quite. You see, one night I was working on a story I was having trouble finishing. I couldn't get the ending right. So I went to bed. Next morning I came into my office and guess what I found?'

'A d arm?'

'No. I found the story finished. The ending was there. Perfect. But I didn't write it.'

'You probably just forgot you'd done it.' This from Squelchy who thought she knew everything about everything.

'Oh no, I thought about it all night.'

His audience looked at each other. There was just no way of accounting for the behaviour of adults.

'Have any of you heard the story of the Elves and the Shoemaker?'

Kendell asked, looking from one face to another for some sign of recognition. Nothing.

Kendell felt a little dizzy. Here was a whole generation who had never heard of the Elves and the Shoemaker! Probably other stories as well, unless they had been turned into a movie or a game. Those old stories were tried and true; they'd stood the test of time. Until now. A whole new field was open to him. He could reinvent all these old stories for a new generation! Six In One Blow!

'It started to happen regularly. I would begin a story in the morning. I'd fail to finish it by the end of the day and the next morning I would find it all finished, with the spelling mistakes corrected.'

'Didn't the typewriter have a spell-checker?'

Kendell shook his head. 'The magic typewriter did it, all by itself.'

The kids were less than impressed. How magic could the typewriter be if it couldn't even spell-check, they wondered.

In the story, Kendell recalled, the shoemaker and his wife rewarded the Elves for their industry by making them warm clothes to wear, little jackets and shoes. That wouldn't work for typewriters. So here he was once more, half-way through a story for which he had no ending. And since, of course, he never found a d arm, he couldn't pull that one out of the hat unless he was just going to make everything up and to hell with what actually happened.

'What do you write?' Squelchy asked.

'Sentences,' said Kendell, his mind somewhere else.

That little conversation set Kendell off on a quest. He would locate a typewriter just like that old one, same model, same year, and if it should miraculously have a d arm missing then all to the good.

Although he wouldn't like to admit it, he was motivated by more than just nostalgia for the days when a broken typewriter might conquer the world. He secretly believed that only if he could find his typewriter could he get his mojo back and would be able to write again. He remembered those days sitting at the typewriter. His story to the kids had been apocryphal. His old typewriter had not written the stories, but it had *seemed* that way, his fingers flying over the keys, the letters leaping out onto the page like Olympic champions, every paragraph a gold medal winner.

He had a superstitious dread that he would never be able to write another sentence unless he got away from the ubiquitous blue eye of the screen and back to basics. With a typewriter, there could be no flicking over to email or a favourite website or some other distraction no more than a click or two away. With a typewriter he would regain his old focus. He would make that thing jump.

Tracking down such a machine was easier than he thought. An internet search revealed whole communities of typewriter freaks with their esoteric talk of ribbons and carriages and lubrication. It was a thriving sub-culture. There were the purists, who only used manual typewriters, and those who used electric typewriters. There was mutual distrust between the two groups. He even learned that typewriters were making a comeback in spy agencies, since nothing on the blue screen could ever be trusted. The model he was after had been a popular one, noted for its reliability. He was able to track one down. Some idiot was even making ribbons for them, but you had to use your own spools. Wonderful stuff!

It cost money, buying it and crating it and freighting it. But who was counting the cost when a writer's mojo was at stake and his life hung in the balance like an unfinished story?

The day it arrived, he cracked a bottle of wine, sat in front of the machine, running his eye over its familiar form as if it were a lover long gone, but miraculously returned. He ran his hands over it in the same spirit, letting them remember it. Ceremoniously, he took a sheet of paper, slipped it into the carriage, and with a powerful sense of déjà vu, rolled the paper up to face the waiting keys. Like riding a bike, you never forgot how.

He wrote the first sentence. One thing he had forgotten was the little bell that rang at the end of the line, signalling the need to hit the lever and roll the paper up to a new line. That little bell, as if each line would have its own special illumination.

The quick brown fox jumped over the lazy dog. Ding!

As promised by the seller, all the keys were working smoothly. And the noise! Clackety-clack. The whole house would vibrate to it. He had a girlfriend once who was driven out of the house by the sound of it at five o'clock in the morning. Clackety-clack!

It was very physical. His fingers had forgotten how hard he had to hit the keys, made lazy by too many years of seductively sensitive keyboards. The whole arm and wrist were involved. The letters slammed onto the ribbon with a satisfying sense of finality.

Now is the time for all good men to come to the aid of the party. Ding!

Yes, there it was, the sentence as a physical fact. The blue screen made words ephemeral, fleeting, disposable, despisable.

It was time to settle in and write something.

So he did. He had to. He'd gone to all these lengths. Paid all that money.

It was hard work. Like taking a pick to a coalface. In the afternoon he became tired, and the story still wasn't finished. This was just like the story he'd told the kids. He was acting it out. When the day was done the story was still not finished and his arms ached.

That night he dreamed vividly of how the story would end. It was the magic typewriter that did it. He could see the keys flying through the air towards the paper one after the other, clackety-clack, *ding*! but no fingers punched the keys. He could see the words, imprinted into the very fabric of the world.

He knew then with certainty that he would, upon waking, be able to finish the story and bring everything to a satisfactory conclusion.

It was the most uplifting dream Kendell had had for a long time.

His sleeping face smiled into the dark.

At long last, he had his mojo back.

Ding!

NORTHROP AND THE FROG MAN

Russel Northrop arrived at the crest of the hill and took a breather. He was sweating hard and his heart was thumping away, but he felt good. The two-hour tramp, which had taken him to some of the most remote portions of the island, was just what the doctor ordered. Truth was, Northrop got ill if he sat around inside. Nobody seeing him now would think that he had been a weedy, sickly child. Walking, and lots of it, had been his salvation, and still was; the sickly weed had grown tall and strong.

Socially, he was clumsy, he knew, but out here in the wilderness, he came into his own; he could move like an animal through its precincts and feel perfectly at home. The snags and thorns of the forest were nothing compared to the tongues at work in the Café Resume, for example. He knew that other people felt comfortable cooped up inside, but he didn't understand it. Only when he was ranging the bush trails was he truly happy.

What was satisfying about the view in front of him, which included several bays and a good portion of the rougher south coast which he only visited two or three times a year, was that it had no people in it. No sign of human occupation. Just bays and headlands, softer valleys and slopes. He could imagine, if just for a moment, that people didn't exist. That illusion was shattered when he turned around and looked back the way he had come. In the distance, the vineyards and the olive groves stood out as square-shaped blocks cut into the hillside.

He paused and ate some cold sausage. A big frame like his needed feeding. As he ate, he allowed his gaze to linger on one of the beaches in the distance where cool shadows would gather as the afternoon progressed. He thought he would sleep there; he knew of a grassy, protected spot perfect for dossing down. His dreams were always sweeter when he slept under the stars.

At the same time as he was enjoying the view, he was aware that he could only do so by pretending that there was no ownership of land, that the land owned itself. Paradoxically, that pretence pointed to the underlying truth: private property was the basis of the huge misstep civilization had taken. Here he was, a person who owned nothing, yet who felt a part of everything he saw before him; while others owned lots of land and felt a part of nothing. And so craved more. It made no sense to him. It made his head hurt just thinking about it. The destructiveness of it.

People made jokes about tree-huggers, but how many had tried it, how many had put their arms around a tree, rested their head against the trunk, and closed their eyes? And even if they did, would they be sensitive enough to feel anything? Probably not.

He finished his piece of sausage and set off down the southeastern side of the crest, heading towards the distant beach. He understood the secret of walking, that there was an energy that jolted up through the soles of the feet into the body, conferring strength. That energy came from the earth. People who were insensitive to it grew tired very quickly, while he, for example, gathered energy as he walked. This didn't make him feel superior to others, just different, yet it was in that difference his social isolation lay.

A little further along, there was a turnoff that led to a small stream and pool few knew about. Once the island had been replete with rivers, pools and wetlands, but humanity's occupation had taken its toll; the water had withdrawn its blessing and disappeared underground, where people had to hunt for it with their bores. It might be Paradise Island, but it had once been much more, a real paradise if not the Garden of Eden with fish and birds and tall trees. He didn't hate his own kind, wouldn't have thought of himself as a misanthropist, but it was hard, impossible in fact, not to notice what the naked apes had done to the land God had apparently made for them.

He hesitated at the turnoff, not sure if he wanted the detour. The day was hot and he was looking forward to the beach and a swim. The stream and pool wouldn't be much at this time of year, after a pretty long, hot season; it was best enjoyed after rain, in full turbulence. He set off in that direction anyway, reluctant to pass the beauty spot without a visit.

This path was hardly a path at all, a faint trail over the grass, and an even fainter one beneath the cool trees where fallen leaves covered everything. He moved quietly, super aware of the sounds around him; the constant shifting of the wind through the trees, which made a light, shuffling sound, and the creaking and snapping of gravity-bearing timber.

Then he stopped still, and listened to the murmur of the forest.

There was somebody else here. He could feel the presence before he heard the human voice, or at least he thought it was human. Somebody up ahead, sitting by the pool, crying. That was the sound he heard. The sound of a human being crying.

He approached warily, aware that he should probably turn away and quietly disappear. His encounters with human beings were invariably unsatisfactory, so there was no point in seeking them out, yet at the same time he found himself continuing on the balls of his feet and quietly like a cat, ready to turn and flee at any moment.

As the sounds of grief became louder, he paused again to make sure they were the sounds of grief. Occasionally, he had encountered lovers who, overcome by the great nakedness of the sky, and the forest around them, had fallen into lovemaking and, from a distance, the sounds they made might be mistaken for sorrow.

This however was one person, a man, sobbing his heart out, and as Northrop came within sight of the pool he saw that the man was the writer, Kendell. This brought Northrop to another halt. He'd never got on well with the writer, although that wasn't saying much. He'd found Kendell aloof and self-centred, a man who entertained too many ideas to be fully committed to any one of them, which made him tricky to deal with. You can't trust a person who thinks too much.

Again he had the option of quietly retreating, unseen, and again he moved forward. It was simple curiosity, he thought, that impelled him. At the very last minute, the thought occurred that he shouldn't impose on somebody's personal moment, but by then it was too late. Kendell had spotted him.

'I'm sorry,' he called. He'd spent a lot time apologising to people for his ineptness, before he'd realised that most of the time he was right and they were wrong.

'Don't be,' Kendell said. He was sitting on a large rock that, in rainy times, overlooked a mini tumult, now overlooking a sad dyspeptic-looking trickle. He appeared to compose himself as Northrop approached. Both men were struck by the oddness of running into each other out here.

'Listen carefully,' Kendell said. 'What can you hear?'

Northrop stared at him. The writer certainly wasn't himself. He looked hollow-eyed, and the grin that usually played around his mouth was gone.

'What can you hear? Or more exactly, what can't you hear?'

Northrop shrugged with embarrassment; he'd never been much good with puzzles.

'Frogs,' the writer said. 'When did you last hear a frog?'

Northrop thought about it. He couldn't remember, but he was sure he had.

'A piece has fallen out of the world,' Kendell said.

Below Kendell there was a smaller, flatter piece of rock that, in rainy times, would be covered in rushing water, and he took a seat there, hunkering down rather, the way a child does. He'd always been able to do it, find his centre of gravity. He picked up a stick and poked it into the muddy water below.

'When I went to school,' Kendell said, 'there were frogs everywhere. Even puddles on the roadside. Teachers would bring in buckets full of dead frogs for us to dissect. If I close my eyes I can still remember what the insides of a frog look like.'

Northrop watched a bug crawl up his stick from out of the ooze at the bottom of the creek, thinking about frogs. Was it possible for something so common and ordinary to disappear as if it had never been? 'Some of the local species don't have a tadpole stage. The eggs hatch directly into little frogs,' he said. That's what he'd heard anyway.

'Okay,' Kendell said, 'so where are they, all these little frogs? Show me some.'

Northrop looked around as if some little frogs were about to show themselves, hop nonchalantly by.

'You can't because there are none. They have quietly disappeared over the years, leaving little holes in the world.'

'That's a funny way to put it.'

'How would you put it? Here you are, the guardian of these trails. You protect them from the intrusion of predatory landowners, but you don't even know that what you are protecting is rotting away behind your back in a chemical stew.'

Northrop stood up. He didn't know why people had to accuse him all the time, paint him the villain or the fool. He could understand Sue Lake vilifying him, she had a vested interest called politics, but Kendell disappointed him. Once more, Northrop was better off not trying to talk to people.

'The thing is,' Kendell said, 'do I want to live in a world without frogs?' His eyes were filling with tears again. 'Why would I want to? I had a dream about a frog the other night. It wasn't a little frog, it was huge, the size of a car. Its throat was bulging and its mouth was opening, but I couldn't hear anything. Then I heard a vast noise, like two planets rushing together, and I woke up.'

'Wow,' Northrop said. He didn't have dreams like that.

'If we have killed all the frogs, what will we dream about?' Kendell wanted to know.

Northrop still didn't like Kendell much, but he knew he had to stay and not slip away. All he wanted was to return to his beloved trails, the beach, the sunlight on the water. But Kendell might do something very stupid. He looked like he was ready to. Right now, he couldn't live in a world without frogs. What if Northrop left and the crazy writer topped himself, what then?

He felt enormously clumsy as they sat back down again. He had no people skills. All he could do was sit there, and maybe, just maybe, that would be enough.

SAMMY AND THE SEPTIC TANK

Since Paradise Island had no water reticulation, its inhabitants had to rely on rainwater and groundwater to keep their kitchens and bathrooms functioning. Those who couldn't afford to put down a bore had only rainwater.

No water reticulation meant no sewerage reticulation which meant that septic tanks became the only legal way to dispose of body wastes.

Many, including Sammy Scapula, hated septic tanks and all they stood for. Septic tanks, Sammy maintained, were filthy things, underground concrete or plastic bunkers filled with the most septic sludge imaginable. People like Sammy built their own clean green composting toilets and kept quiet about it, hoping to stay under the radar. They had a powerful financial motive, since the tanks cost ten grand to install, and who had ten grand lying around?

For Sammy, the issue had deep philosophical roots. Civilisation took a wrong turn when it mixed water and faeces, he maintained, and would argue it at length with all comers. 'Large scale and small, as soon as you mix faeces and water, you have created dirty water, which you then have to deal with,' he would explain. 'The best thing to do with human faeces is to dry them out, cook them in nature's own oven, the cleansing heat of compost.'

His metaphor probably gave people the wrong mental pictures, but nobody could say he didn't practice what he preached, building a large hollow fibreglass tube he dubbed 'The White Rocket.' All it needed was a bum shaped opening at the top and panel at the back for access. Twice a year or so he would remove the panel and shovel out the lovely fresh soil all properly cooked. As long as he kept it fed with grass clippings, peat moss, sawdust and the like, it gave him no problems.

Sammy was very proud of his White Rocket. 'It is the hardest-working machine in the house,' he would say. 'It requires no fuel, it works twenty-four seven, it is completely silent, odourless, and is a hundred percent efficient. Everybody should have one. No more seeping stinkages from malfunctioning septic tanks.' His wife, Roseanne, supported Sammy in principle, but complained that the bum-shaped opening at the top was not shaped for her bum, or any other human bum she knew of.

Sammy wrote a number of letters to the *Paradise Island Times* arguing that if we want to know how to do something we should look at how nature does it, and what nature does with human waste is not to waste it but turn it into worth. In nature, there is no waste, only worth. Water is too precious to be used to transport poo. Some were less than convinced, but he dismissed them as lazy thinkers who just wanted to see it all flushed away, out of sight out of mind. He was, largely, a voice crying in the wilderness, like the guy creeping around shooting out street lights with a homemade slingshot. That guy was a nutcase, of course, not to be confused with Sammy, whose approach was entirely rational.

There was, however, a small hitch. Sammy's wonder rocket was illegal. The obnoxious septic tanks were the only officially sanctioned sewerage disposal system. Flying under the radar couldn't go on forever.

The opening salvo from the authorities came in the form of a letter. Owing to some seismic shift in the bureaucracy, it had been decided that all septic tank owners needed to provide evidence of septic tank maintenance. Something like a clean bill of health for your septic tank. Sammy, of course, knew that there was no such thing, that septic tanks were inherently flawed, a fact which had now given rise to further bureaucracy, but that was no help to him. So he wrote back saying that he had not kept his maintenance receipts since he saw no reason to do so, but that his 'sewerage disposal system' worked just fine. Thank you.

Perhaps he hadn't quite struck the right tone, because after a few weeks, during which time he'd more or less forgotten about it all, he got another letter stating that if he couldn't provide receipts proving up-to-date maintenance, then his septic tank would have to be inspected.

The last thing Sammy wanted was local government inspectors nosing around. Who knew what they might find. He spoke to local bush lawyer Rob Malarky to see if he could legally keep them off his land, but Malarky was dubious. Officials on official business. The best he could hope for was to keep putting them off. He could delay them for months. But eventually…

Sammy didn't like the eventually. Circumstances were not helpful. It had been a dry summer, and the stink of malfunctioning septic tanks was in the air – which was not a surprise to Sammy. The truck emptying people's septic tanks was working overtime, even while septic tank supporters were claiming that a properly functioning tank did not need to be emptied. This had made local officials more vigilant, concerned about possible health effects.

'What a mess,' Sammy said to Roseanne. 'And all of it completely unnecessary.' The hot, dry weather suited the white rocket just fine. Sammy always marvelled at how the temperature inside the rocket was high enough to deter flies and other insects whose eggs would be quickly baked along with everything else. How elegant compared to the clumsy, septic tanks whose toxic overflow was a fly's heaven.

'You'd better stop writing letters to the *PITs*,' Roseanne said. 'That's not flying under the radar.'

Sammy mumbled about the suppression of knowledge, but stopped writing letters.

'And you should never have told them that we have a septic tank,' Roseanne said, shaking her pretty dark curls reprovingly. She knew how to distract him; she was an expert at it.

'I didn't exactly say I had one,' Sammy said. 'I said sewerage disposal system.'

'But you gave that impression. Now they're going to come around and inspect a tank that doesn't exist.'

Rosanne's words gave Sammy an idea.

'We don't actually have to have one,' he said, 'They just have to think we have one.'

'And how are you going to do that?'

Sammy didn't know but he was sure he could come up with something.

When he did, the idea was so daring he couldn't tell Roseanne but went to see the legendary Larrikin Lenny, Paradise Island's most celebrated pack rat. His property was many metres deep in all kinds of stuff, mostly iron and steel, old whiteware, toilet bowls, reels of wire, insulation, timbers, a stack of old windows, steel reinforcing, random plumbing pipe, old roofing iron, decaying rainwater tanks, a car or two, even a boat big enough to have a cabin; whatever you wanted, Larrikin Lenny was sure to have it. There was only one catch. He wouldn't part with it, not for love nor money. He didn't get to have the island's greatest junkpile by giving it away.

Sammy Scapula, however, knew Lenny's weakness, his abiding hatred of 'Council' who were forever harassing him to clear the junk out, and to cease and desist from living in his illegal house. His claim that it was not a house but a stack of timber, and that he wasn't living there but camping for a while had long since lost its flavour with the authorities who were slowly but surely closing in on him.

Sammy admired Lenny and his one-man stand against the world. Lenny would light a spliff using a magnifying glass to save the planet, and himself, the cost of a match, but would freely roll up his own to share. His house, which had a huge tree trunk growing up through the middle of it, was so co-continuous with his environment, it could hardly be called a house at all, which was his argument. The one he'd long ago lost.

As Sammy had hoped, Lenny's eyes lit up at the plan Sammy laid out before him, and immediately offered not only to supply the materials, which of course Sammy would return, but help in the construction required. 'Bring the Jubilee!' he exulted after he and Sammy had sorted out the details.

Roseanne didn't have quite the admiration for Lenny that her husband had. What was admirable about owning twelve washing machines, none of which were working? Roseanne saved her admiration for others more deserving, but she couldn't help but watch with growing amazement as their enterprise unfolded.

'You're not!' she said. 'I don't believe it. Nobody will believe it.'

'Wait until you hear what you have to do,' Sammy said. Roseanne didn't like the look of his smile.

It took some weeks, and many spliffs and conferences inspired by spliffs, before they were happy with their handiwork. On the day they finished they had a spliff and a beer to celebrate and salivate over their genius.

In the meantime the long drawn out battle of letters finally came to an end, and a local government inspector came to visit. He was a young man who looked like he'd had to resist the urge to put on a suit that morning. He saw what Sammy wanted him to see, what Sammy kindly pointed out to him.

Here is the lavatory. Right beside the house. A converted shed, yes, and here is the toilet bowl, none too new perhaps, but well scrubbed, patched into the concrete floor beneath. Very clean. Please don't flush, we're saving water. There's a drought on, you know. *If it's yellow let it mellow, if it's brown flush it down.* That's what the notice says. Effluent pipe goes down into the earth (you have to imagine that bit, ha ha) where you can follow the line of it, you see where it was dug, to the draining area over here. And this other line you see dug here is the pipe from the bathroom and kitchen, the grey water pipe, which joins the effluent line here, just before the tank itself. The septic tank is under this mound of earth, you can see the hatch sticking up – but don't touch it, please. You'll notice there's no smell. Oh look, here comes the pretty dark-haired Roseanne in a lovely short summer dress – it is so hot, isn't it? And Roseanne looks quite delightful, doesn't she? Isn't she a torment! She'll show you the drainage lines. You can see the shrubs we've planted along them are doing well. That lovely flowering pink rose. Just like Roseanne! Yes, it's working like a dream. We've never had to empty it. You don't have to empty them if they're set up right, you know. And this one is set up right. By the book I would say. Definitely by the book. No no. If it ain't broke don't fix it, no need to go poking around. Never had any complaints. Roseanne will make you cup of coffee. With cream.

And what's that over there? That old white fibreglass thing? God knows? It was here before we moved in. Never got around to chucking it out. We call it the white rocket, ha ha. We use it as a compost bin. Works just fine. Garbage in, garbage out, as they say.

Milk and sugar? No? You won't stay?

You have a form for me to sign? My septic tank has been inspected? Certainly. Do you have a pen?

Thank you. All done.

Have a nice day.

THE MAN WHO MISTOOK THE MOON FOR A STREET LIGHT

Yanis felt his way along the street in the pitch dark, trusting the feel of his feet on the shingle and the smack of his stick to guide him, much the way a blind man might. There was a lot of high, thin cloud around on this moonless night, and the stars, when they appeared, hardly made a dent in the dark. They were the lights of a very far off carnival.

It had taken him a long time to get to this stage. When he'd first arrived on Paradise Island and taken up residence in a remote, unpaved back street with no street lights, he had been too afraid to venture outside unless the moon was very bright. Even then he would take a torch and tended to focus on the tiny circle of light it provided rather than try to take in his shadowy surrounds. He clung to that torch as if it were civilisation itself.

He wouldn't have admitted to feeling afraid of the dark, exactly, just unused to it; he had to learn to let his eyes adjust to the night. Yanis had grown up in a faraway City, one that hardly knew any boundaries, and had become accustomed to the constant presence of street lights. He had never known true dark, never seen the stars in all their stark wonder and clarity. Not until he was washed up on the shores of Paradise Island. At first he'd done nothing much in the evening but sit on his deck and gaze at those stars, trying to adjust himself to the enormous size of the universe, and how small it made him feel. After a time he'd begun to walk, although welded to his torch, and after a further time he'd been able to walk without it, negotiate the dark with his other senses.

He taught himself to walk in the dark. A scary and exhilarating experience because he had to come alive to the dark. People said that the world was different at night, not the same as our day world, and Yanis slowly came to believe that. People were afraid of the dark, he decided, because it housed presences, presences you could feel if you walked alone at night. He trained himself to get used to them. He learned how to slip through the shadows just like them, unseen. The dark of night wasn't going to hurt him any more than the light of day; it was just a different medium.

There was one spot where the road, as it turned, dipped deep into the hillside and was always darker than everywhere else. The branches of tall trees met overhead. It had taken him many months before he could walk that corner without a torch, even on a clear full-moon night. The air was thick with presences. He'd found himself as frightened as a child approaching that corner. A grown man feeling like that – it had intrigued him. Rather than avoiding the dark, he'd begun to seek it out, to value it for the spookiness of it, for its softness, for what it hid as much as the outlines it revealed.

In short, he came to love the dark. He would slip into it the way some might slip into a warm bath. Ah! The sheer deliciousness of night! The phantasm circus that was the galaxy! Its slowly shifting veils as his eyes adjusted and his pupils grew large, large enough to look back in time further than the mind could reach! Without the night, there would be no poetry. The blind faith of the dark. Without the dark, the inner eye cannot open, he decided in one of his more mystical moments. Moments that always happened at night, never in the day. If Day and Night had genders, then the night for Yanis would have to be a woman, mysterious and infinite.

He was disturbed therefore to see one day a group of men from the local power company working on that very corner. They were erecting something, something long and metallic. When upright it bent over like a monk with a cowl and shone with a horrid, garish orange light.

They were erecting a street light.

With dawning horror, Yanis realised what that meant. That cold orange light would kill the magic of the dark, banish the mysteries of night at the very spot where the magic ran deepest and mystery itself made a home.

He ran home and wrote a letter to the *Paradise Island Times*, but no matter how often he wrote it, he ended up sounding like some peevish crank. He had no way with words. He posted it anyway, but realised that he was going to need to do more than that. Much more. He was going to have to take action.

The first night the light came on his worst fears were realised. The light was the colour of fresh chicken shit, he decided, neon chicken shit. It besmirched the dark, cheapened it, sucked the real light out of everything it touched. His hand, for example, looked like the hand of corpse, a sickly yellow. All the gentle perspective and depth of the night had gone, replaced by this ghastly, glazed surface.

Something had to be done. He gathered some stones and began to throw them furiously, but they all missed or fell short. He collected more and went about it with greater calculation. He hit the metal cowl a couple of times, but the light stayed on. It burned his retina just to look at it.

Something more had to be done.

He went home and got to work at his workbench. He wasn't the most skilled of woodworkers, but what he lacked in skill he made up in determination, and after a couple of hours he had it in his hand.

A slingshot. A simple little device.

Then he drove to a stony beach and selected a bag full of stones, not too heavy and not too light. He called them his Goldilocks stones. It was after two in the morning by the time he got back to the abomination that was the street light. It took him only three Goldilocks stones and as many minutes to find his range and take the light out. It blew with a flash and satisfying pop. It burned in his head as an after image for ten minutes before the grateful dark was fully restored, magic returned to the corner, and he could go home and sleep.

It took the power company a long time to figure out its light was gone. Yanis certainly wasn't saying anything. They replaced it, of course, and once again the ungodly light shone, although shining was not the right word for what that light did. So out came the slingshot and another few Goldilocks stones later the light was gone again. This time Yanis hid the slingshot and the bag of stones. The company would know by the damage done to the metal cowl that there was a vandal at work.

But they were the vandals. They had vandalised the night! Nobody asked him if he wanted a street light. If they had, he would have told them. Meanwhile, there were a few letters in the *PITs*, some supporting him while others, especially those who had just moved to the island from the City, bleated on about lit streets being safe streets. Yanis didn't believe that. He'd never seen any evidence for it. It was just an assumption. It was all about fear. Fear of the dark, of hidden things; fear of the night and the infinity of the night. Like infants who needed their night light. Why should he have to suffer that sulphurous light because other people couldn't grow up?

After taking out the light for the third time, he noticed a police car nosing its way around the back streets of the neighbourhood. It was inevitable that, after a time, the police would take an interest. If only everybody picked up a slingshot and did what he had done. His lone rebellion made him nothing but a target. Nevertheless, he couldn't live with that light. He would just have to be careful and very sneaky; he wasn't the criminal type, but he could learn fast enough if he had to the habits of duplicity and concealment.

He found a spot nearby in the bush that couldn't be seen from the road. Well hidden, he could ping away at the street light, and even if the cops were parked beneath they would have no idea where that beautiful little Goldilocks stone came from. Silently it would come spinning out of the night. Being a bit further away than standing blatantly on the road beneath made the light a harder target to hit, and he used a few more stones, but he was becoming very skilled with his homemade slingshot. Death to all street lights!

He was very proud of that little weapon and showed it to nobody. After use he carefully checked it over, and was able to do an upgrade with some stronger rubber that made it more powerful. It wouldn't be difficult, for example, to take out the back window of the police car as it cruised about. That would send a message. The wrong message, probably. Yanis wasn't a criminal type, just an indignant citizen. And if citizens were a threatened species, to be replaced by consumers, then he was a consumer of the dark. He had rights, although he knew in his heart of hearts that rights that were not written into law were little more than wishful thinking.

The next time the light was replaced, Yanis waited a couple of weeks just to be on the safe side. Every night that garish light burned like shame. Every night the dark had to hide its face away, banished, exiled. Until, once more, he crept to his spot and his slingshot did its work. Flash! Pop! Ah! The gratitude of night!

But that night he had a very strange dream. A violent dream for a peaceful man. He was standing in the middle of the road, exposed, with his slingshot sending stone after stone at the street light, but every time he missed. The light burned cruelly in his eyes. His desperation turned to a fever as he emptied his bag of Goldilocks stones. There were explosions all around him, as in a war. Flash! Pop! But still the light burned on. It blazed its image deep into his mind.

Then he understood. It wasn't the street light hanging in the sky, but the moon. His pitiful stones fell far short, of course. The moon was indifferent.

When he woke up, there were tears on his sheets. There would be no end to this. Or rather, just one end. The police would come and that would be that. No matter how many street lights he took out, there would always be another to replace it. He went into his workshop, took out his slingshot and was about to destroy it, when a new cunning took hold of him. He dismantled the slingshot, putting the rubber in one place, the Y frame in another. He took his remaining Goldilocks stones and arranged them along the sides of his path where he could find them again very easily.

There might come a time when he needed them.

You never know.

All the street lights in the world won't hold back the night forever.

SUE LAKE AND THE SIZZLING SAUSAGES

'Sue, how lovely to see you,' Big Buster met Sue Lake at the door.

The irony was, he probably meant it. A big, warm man who once occupied the political hot seat bore no grudges against the woman who had ousted him. He'd been a farmer at one time, made an unlikely shift into pottery, and, in an unusual evolution, went into politics and ruled for some years as Mayor of Paradise Island. Now retired, he preferred his clay and his kiln.

As they headed to the back of the house, where the barbie was underway, he showed her one of his new pieces. It had been crafted to look like a piece of wood. Why anybody would do that was beyond Sue, but she smiled and admired it anyway. It was one way to spend a retirement.

Perhaps he saw the look on her face. 'This postmodernism is a wonderful thing. It makes anything possible.'

'I wish I had something like this in my life,' Sue Lake said.

'If you did, you would,' he said, but mildly.

They left it at that.

'Chiznell's here,' Big Buster said as he showed her an obscure piece which looked a bit like a rugby ball with lumps.

'Ah!' she said. 'Thanks for the warning.'

'Rather you than me,' he said, and they both laughed. 'Let's get you a drink.'

Out the back, the party was humming. Stubbies were opening with a crack and a hiss, and sausages were sizzling. Wine gurgled and glooped into waiting flutes. Sue, who only drank for appearances' sake, took one. Everybody was talking, ninety words to the dozen. Mavis Stretchly, whose contempt for people was as infinite as God's love, said that it was gossip and gossip alone that separated man from the animals. Call us the gossiping ape.

Because of all that gossiping, the politics of Paradise Island were as knotty as knotty could be. An echo chamber of Chinese whispers. Since everybody knew everybody else, everybody was intricately connected. This meant that a group mind could suddenly manifest on this, that or the other issue, like that ridiculous fuss over Ricky and his rowdy rooster, a jape that had Garrison Ford's sticky fingers all over it.

And the group mind had no logic, just fear and greed.

'I'll meet you at the barbie,' Big Buster said, gesturing to the other side of the patio where Mavis Stretchly, with a couple of her sycophants, was guarding the sausages. Mavis was the ideal political ally; one who could make even loyalty seem treacherous, but, since she had no personal loyalty to anybody but herself, and no ideals beyond the self-serving, she was easy to predict.

Spotting Sue, Mavis approached. 'I've already been buttonholed by our buddy over there.'

That was Chiznell, looking not entirely comfortable out of his suit. He was talking to a tall, gloomy looking man Sue hadn't seen before but smelled lawyer. What kind of man brings his lawyer to a BBQ? A man like Chiznell.

At the far end of the patio, strategically placed at the drinks table, Garrison Ford was knocking them back with his boozing buddy, Kendell. They were talking to Rob Malarky, the island's bush lawyer. Officially Ford was only drinking beer, but Sue Lake didn't believe it. He had that vodka look in his eye. She had to be careful with Ford. No matter how drunk he got, his pencil was always sharp in the morning, and he never forgot an insult. She tended to avoid Kendell too. He might be over his killer chemical phase, but he was still not to be trusted. No one as smart as Kendell could be trusted.

As soon as he spied her, Malarky approached.

'Here comes trouble,' Mavis said *sotto voce*.

Rob Malarky was a short, fat man. With persistence. After some pleasantries which were not really that pleasant, Malarky got down to business.

'A lot of people are disturbed by the Stratford application,' he said. He was trying to talk quietly but didn't have the voice for it.

'I know,' Sue said sympathetically. It wasn't just the adjacent landowners who were squealing, but the whole greenie rent-a-crowd. It was not their beards and sandals and skinny wives that worried her about the greenies, but their computers and their sophistication. Their ability to get people like Malarky on their side.

'Do you think the development will go ahead?' Malarky said.

'There are no grounds for declining the application.'

'There are always grounds for doing the right thing,' Malarky said.

'Within a legal framework.'

'Come on Sue,' Malarky said, as if they were great buddies and Sue was being particularly recalcitrant, in need of a telling-off, perhaps. 'Legal-schmegal. There's wriggle room with that high-tide mark.'

'Perhaps it should go to the Environment Court,' she said. Anywhere but here, she thought.

Sue Lake was looking for some wriggle room out of the conversation, and the ever staunch Mavis Stretchly came to the rescue. 'Perhaps you should stand for council?' she said to Malarky. Attacking the man not the argument was Stretchly's speciality. She was the ad-hominen queen. Very useful at barbies.

'The problem is,' Sue said to Mavis, 'you need a modicum of diplomacy for that.'

Malarky laughed with them, or pretended to.

Sue could see that he was getting ready for another go. Pleasantly, she said, 'I'm off to get one of those sizzling sausages. They smell delicious.' She made her escape, leaving Malarky to the tender mercies of the Stretchly, and was heading for the barbie when Chiznell made his play, the tall gloomy man by his side.

'We're starting to worry that the Stratford application will be held up with frivolous objections.' He allowed his eyes to slide, briefly, to Malarky, now talking to Jean Jeanie whose property would be affected by the Stratford development. Jean Jeanie was one of those unstable, theatrical types; pity she had to be involved.

'There are no grounds for declining the application,' she said, talking directly to the tall gloomy man she suspected was the real power here.

'That's a relief,' Chiznell said.

'But objectors could take it to the Environment Court,' she said.

'Would they have any grounds for that?'

'There's a bit of a shady area around the high-tide mark,' she said. The tall gloomy man was staring at her as if she were a squashed hedgehog on the road. Perhaps he was short-sighted.

Once more, the Stretchly arrived to bail her out. 'No one in their right mind would try to mount a legal challenge to the Stratford application,' she said, loudly enough for Malarky to overhear.

'That's good to hear,' Chiznell said, laughing. He raised his drink in a toast.

'But remember,' the Stretchly continued, as loud as ever, 'you're living on Paradise Island. You have to look a long way to find someone in their right mind.'

Ford clapped loudly and gave Stretchly one of his foolish grins. 'For God's sake, don't encourage her,' Kendell hissed.

'A vote for the Stretchly is a vote for the bulldozers,' Malarky said, loudly enough for Mavis to hear.

'Election?' somebody said. 'I didn't know there was an election.'

There's always an election, Sue Lake thought as she eyed the sausages still sizzling quietly on the BBQ, still tantalisingly out of range. Big Buster was standing at the grill, behind it, from where he could view the party. She wondered why he had invited this mix of people to his little outdoor meet-and-greet. It was asking for trouble. Big Buster might have retired, but he would never stop playing politics. As far as Sue Lake was concerned, everybody was playing politics, and it was always election time.

Sue Lake did not have a large and warm personality like Big Buster, but what she lacked in personal warmth she made up for in cunning. Big Buster had been great for the island in his day, but he was too sincere to deal with sharks in suits in the City. Like this tall gloomy man. The problem with sincere people, she had found, was that they made the mistake of thinking that other people were sincere too. Since they expected sincerity, it was easy to fool them into seeing it where they wanted to see it. Neither Sue Lake nor Mavis Stretchly had that problem.

Playing politics meant trying to determine the outcome of events, so the question was, what outcome was the old man expecting here? The overgrown gnome with his lumpy bits of pottery.

He caught her observing him and smiled innocently. She didn't like the look of that smile. He gestured down at the sausages and raised his eyebrows at her.

The sausages sizzled happily.

They seemed, at that moment, very far away.

The tall gloomy man topped up her glass which didn't need topping up. 'We weren't introduced, I'm sorry,' he said.

She smiled and inched towards the sausages, but paid close attention as the man spoke. He had a voice as flat as a recording and she had to concentrate to hear him. Now she would learn something. This man would tell her something important. Perhaps this was why Big Buster had organised this little barbie, so this one conversation could take place. So this suit would tell her something she needed to know.

She was close enough now to see the sausages spit and hear them hiss.

As she listened to the tall gloomy man, Big Buster gave her a big open-faced grin, flipped a couple of sausages out and handed them to her on a paper plate with a plastic fork, still sizzling.

'*Bon Appétit,*' he said.

TINA AND THE TEN CENTS

Sitting in a little tin can that lumbered through the sky, Tina Tuppa opened her purse and looked glumly at her last remaining ten-cent piece. All she knew was that this little copper coloured coin was not to be spent. She turned it over in her fingers. It was dark and dull on one side and bright and burnished as if freshly minted on the other.

Leaving Paradise Island was always problematic for Tina Tuppa, and not just because just because she never had any money. She tended to get into trouble in strange places. She knew the island, its psychic landscape, where a tragedy might have happened, leaving a whirlpool of grief, or maybe the hills just folded the wrong way after creation and needed a little tending from time to time. She knew the places to avoid. One way or another it was a territory as familiar as a song. Off Island, anything was possible.

It was a good thing, therefore, that she would be met by Lady-Jane at the airport and whisked away to the coast where they would work on creating a homeopathic essence from the feathers of some local migratory birds. Lady-Jane, who really was christened with that name and was nothing like a Lady, understood Tina and the etheric typology through which she moved.

Whisking Tina from the airport went as planned and the two women were soon on their way to the coast. For her part, Lady-Jane was excited at the prospect of making an essence with Tina. She was in awe of Tina, who had amazing abilities people could hardly guess at. The last time they had made an essence together, two wood pigeons, as neatly arrayed as a couple of bishops, had arrived to watch over the maturing brew with a soft but attentive eye. That had been pure magic.

All went well until Lady-Jane had to make a stop out of town at a large department store. Although she hated these vast multi-levelled stores, Tina preferred to follow her friend around than sit in the car park and wait. They were passing through the hardware section when Tina felt a tug at her mind.

'Did you feel that?' she asked Lady-Jane, who shook her head.

It came again, stronger this time. It was a distress call.

'There is a taniwha trapped in the building,' Tina said.

'What are you going to do?'

'Find it.'

That was easier said than done. Lady-Jane found herself following Tina around in the hunt for the department store taniwha. Its presence grew fainter and stronger as they moved about. Eventually Tina had to stop and sit down and attempt communication with the creature, now deliberately hiding from her, she felt. Department stores don't like providing seats for people – people sitting down are not buying anything – but they found one outside the women's rest rooms, a reluctant concession to comfort.

Tina sat with her eyes closed as if she were having a little rest. She was able to track the taniwha by its fear and distress, which left behind something like an odour. It was aware of her, but couldn't communicate. It was as frightened of her as it was of everything else. Slowly she began to gather the situation it was in. Up until recently, this area had been re-generating forest, and the only home the taniwha had ever had. Its memory had been damaged, but she gathered that it had been here before the great burning-off that had destroyed most of the forests of this country soon after human settlement. It had survived the fires by settling deep into the earth. As the forest regenerated, the power of the taniwha began to return and the land was happy once more despite the poisonous trail created by the motorway passing nearby. Then, in the blink of an eye, from the taniwha's point of view, people came and built the department store, trapping it inside.

While some of these varied creatures could move around, this taniwha belonged to a genus that, once positioned, rarely if ever moved, although capable of movement. This land, this very spot, had been the taniwha's home for as long as its broken memory could tell, and now it wandered like an unquiet spirit through the steel and plastic world of the department store grieving for the earth. The earth, whose mineral circulation the taniwha could no longer feel.

'I think I know what it has done,' Tina said to Lady-Jane, standing up. She went to the stairwell and looked up. The creature had attenuated itself, made itself as long and thin as it could in an effort to find the earth below or the sky above. She sensed that for some time it had pretended to be a tree.

'I have to finish shopping,' Lady-Jane said. Exciting as it was, she was starting to get nervous. This is the way trouble started when Tina Tuppa left the precincts of Paradise Island.

Going on alone, oblivious to the rush of consumers around her, Tina tracked the taniwha. She began by moving up the stairwell, letting the grinding machines beneath her feet carry her up. As she rose, the presence of the taniwha grew. There was a dry, acrid feel in the air that did not belong to the muddy, recycled stuff that was being pumped around the department store.

She needed to speak to the creature now, and do it out loud, which posed something of a problem. You don't stand in the middle of a department store and speak to mythological beasts, elemental spirits or anything else. But you can stand in the middle of a department store and speak to your cellphone.

'It's going to be okay,' she said loudly into her cellphone. She wanted it to hear her amid the clutter of human voices. 'I can get you out, but you have to come to me.'

A few people stared at her, but not too many. Not enough to care about. She didn't have to cultivate the fixed stare people get when they talk in public on their cellphones.

The taniwha didn't think it would be okay, and it didn't want to come to her. It was like a child protecting its hurt. Even as the concrete and steel pierced its being, still it dodged her.

'Aaah no,' she said, being very firm with it. 'We have to take you outside. We have to get you away from here.'

She listened, as if it were really communicating to her by cellphone.

The taniwha was very frightened by the idea of away-from-here. It sounded too much like dying. Tina realized that what she needed to do was sing to the creature, and, by means of the melody, change its mood from fear and suspicion to trust. If she couldn't get it to trust her, she'd never get it out, and if it did die here, a rare event for taniwhas, this place would be cursed forever and a day.

Talking into a cellphone is commonplace, but singing into one posed something of a problem. Getting into trouble invariably began by drawing attention to herself. She had to sing, however, so she did. Although softly, at least at first. The best place was the escalator. She tried to pretend she was dealing with a child. People looked. Some with amusement. Some askance. To one man, who showed too great an interest, she made a series of hand gestures designed to suggest that she was dealing with a very difficult situation here, which she was. She was going up, and the people coming down stared at her as they went past.

Near the top she abandoned the pretence of the phone and let her voice flow freely into the air. It could hear her, she knew. It could come to her, sliding down the medium of her voice the way a child might slide down banisters. It could use her voice to navigate through its fear, if it would allow such a thing.

She was close to giving up when a hand slipped into hers. It was very cold and froze her halfway up her arm. With one shoulder dragging, she made her way to the down escalator. It was very heavy, heavy with reluctance, heavy with grief and shame. Her lips hardly moving, she murmured reassurances to it. It was a very ancient creature, having lived here since before the break up of the great southern continent. Its own ancestors had been forged in volcanic fires. She could sense their hurtling energies.

It went well enough while she was on the escalator but the weight of the creature made her stumble when she reached the bottom. Now she had to get it to the door. The closer she got the heavier it became. It was like carrying a whole hillside. People bustled around her, a bit annoyed. Annoyance she could deal with. She looked for Lady-Jane but couldn't find her.

Eventually she made it to the door. Once through the creature grew lighter but did not let go of her hand. Now the steel and glass no longer pierced it, the taniwha's agony subsided. Moving steadily across the car park, she was able to sing to it more loudly, lift it up into the air on the wings of a chant. She had to tone that down when it became too frisky.

She saw where she needed to go. There was an open and wooded area just beyond the motorway, the forgotten end of a farm, perhaps. The perfect place for a homeless taniwha. But there was no way she was going to get it over the motorway, not with it pulling on her this way and that. Sometimes like an errant kite in too high a wind, other times like a ball and chain, furiously trying to dig into the earth and finding only blacktop. Concrete and tar kills taniwhas like a poison in the bloodstream. She couldn't linger in the car park.

She stood by the motorway and looked longingly across at the inviting wild spot. Without the taniwha, she could have negotiated it easily – traffic was light. Something was happening with the creature too. Sunlight and open air was changing it. No longer did it have to cower in pain. Strength was flowing into it, even as the concrete beneath burned it.

It was then she thought of her ten-cent piece, her last one, the one that was not to be spent. She took it out and considered it. Shining copper light one side, a rubbed dark on the other. Such a humble coin might have its uses.

'Taniwha,' she said to it. 'See this little coin here, I bet you couldn't make yourself as small.'

'I bet I could,' the taniwha said, adding proudly, 'I can be as big as the sun or as small as that little ten-cent piece.'

'I bet you couldn't *enter* this ten-cent piece while I get you across the motorway to that lovely cool earth over there.'

'Ha! That's nothing. I entered that glass and steel back there.' The creature shuddered.

'Go on then!'

'But how will I get out again?'

'I'll tell you what, I'll bury you when I get there. As soon as I bury you, you will come out of the coin and into the earth.'

'I'll have to think about that,' the taniwha said. But there was no time. No time to think. The lovely cool earth beckoned.

'Alright,' the taniwha said.

And so it was done. As she pushed the dirt back over her last coin in the world, she felt the taniwha burst joyously into the earth, like breaking open an egg.

She stood up and looked back across the motorway. Lady-Jane was standing by the car looking around anxiously.

Tina Tuppa smiled. Really, her friends had no need to worry!

A PLACE APART

Back in the day, it was still possible for Paradise Islanders to dream of being independent of the mainland, independent of the City.

'I wish I could tow the island a couple of hundred miles out to sea,' someone said, summing the feeling up. Paradise Island didn't belong to the City, or the nation, whatever that was, or even the world. Paradise Island was a place apart; it didn't belong to the world at all. It was a bit like Harry Potter land. To get there you had to make a rush at some designated point on the wharf and suddenly, bingo! you were there, among the vineyards and the olive groves, the bush tracks and the beaches.

This wistful sentiment was hardly a good basis for a political movement, but movements have been built on less, and it was in the interests of some politicians, like Sue Lake, to keep the dream alive while making sure that it never actually came true. What actually came true was quite the opposite as the City gathered in its own, and the centre of power moved from the modest local offices to the not so fabled glass towers of downtown.

The independence movement was led by the zealot, Russel Northrop, but gathered a surprising number of adherents which, Sue Lake observed, showed just how far from reality Paradise Islanders could drift. Mavis Stretchly agreed with her, absolutely. In fact, she couldn't understand why Sue Lake tried to pretend to have sympathy for these wingnuts. Sooner or later they'd end up thinking her a hypocrite. But not Mavis Stretchly – she called a spade a spade. During the election campaign she carried around a spade just to prove the point. 'The City is not going away just because we close our eyes,' she said, quoting Sue Lake, except Sue didn't always seem to mean it.

Then Rob Malarky stepped into the argument with some obscure legal folderol. Paradise Island, he argued, might in fact become independent, sort of, if it put itself in the hands of the United Nations under a World Heritage status. Then it could thumb its nose at the City. And all those evil planners who wanted to carve up paradise could go eat worms. And all those big time developers who wanted to build condos on the beaches and dreamed of an international airport, who controlled the evil planners, could wail and gnash their teeth in the darkness.

Malarky's argument had just enough plausibility to give Sue Lake a bad moment. Northrop and his loony cronies thought that Sue Lake was in the pocket of the developers, but she had never used her position for personal gain. She still lived in the same little modest house she'd always lived in, and she didn't even own a car, as did most of the rabid greenies who attacked her. Rob Malarky, for example, was a considerable landowner in his own right. None of these ironies made any difference, of course. Malarky's malarkey caught on. From being a puff in the wind, it became an idea with legs.

'We've got to do something,' Sue Lake said. She wasn't hopeful. The last time she'd crossed Northrop, he'd thrown Sid Vicious, the rooster, into her face.

'The United Nations is part of a conspiracy to bring in a New World Order,' Stretchly said loudly. 'Let's put the rats in charge of the cheese, shall we?'

They were sitting at the Café Résumé where Sue Lake went every Friday afternoon to talk to the old dears who always voted for her. She could sit there, listen to their complaints and watch the picture perfect yachts come and go from the bay. Now she tried to shush Stretchly, not wanting to frighten the old dears with wild talk.

'Princess Mononoke's getting into the act,' Sue said, practicing her smile on some hostiles.

'We're in for trouble.'

Princess Mononoke was the name they gave M…, who had traced a stellar arc through local politics into parliament. All her political career she had stood up for the indigenous and the marginals with an unfeigned passion. She was more than a politician; she was a force of nature. Few dared to stand before her moral outrage.

'I'm not afraid of her,' Stretchly said.

'Then why say it?' Sue was aware of how peevish she sounded, but she had every reason to be. Malarky was bad enough, but Princess Mononoke would bring the issue to a whole new level of insanity.

'She doesn't even live on the island any more,' Stretchly said. 'She's down in the Capital, getting rich.'

Sue Lake got up and wandered over to the large plate-glass window that overlooked the bay. Funny thing was, people accused her of all sorts of things, selling out, selling the island out, selling her soul, but not only had she never got rich, which you might have expected with all that selling out, but she loved the island more than those who wore their hearts on their sleeves and beat their chests to prove their devotion. Princess Mononoke was one of those chest beaters, and yet, with an irony not lost on Sue, Mononoke would probably understand her real motives better than her own supporters, especially Mavis Stretchly.

Standing there, with nothing but Paradise before her and the clatter of coffee drinkers behind, the past caught up with Sue Lake. I've been around too long, seen too much, she thought. Rarely, if ever, did she think this way. She was starting to sound like her retired predecessor, Big Buster. 'Every political career ends in failure,' Big Buster had once told her, 'because eventually you get voted out. That's why politicians are given such high honours – they're on a suicide mission.'

Sue Lake was a practical person who liked to focus on the particulars, but there had been a time, once, long ago it seems, when she had had such grand thoughts. When she had been able to love, but the language of agendas is not the language of love. A mask of herself appeared in the mirror each morning, carefully painted to look like Sue Lake, but the eyes couldn't be fooled. She could see them like ghosts in the plate-glass, see-through eyes with the headlands and the ocean floating behind. Paradise Island, it touched people in many different ways.

'We're going to throw everything we can at this,' she said to Stretchly when she returned to her seat. 'Here's the point. These independence people are whining about power moving to the City, wait until it moves to New York. Most of these people believe that power should stay at the local level, now they want to hand the island over to the most remote agency imaginable.'

Mavis rubbed her hands. 'That's how we play it.'

'No. That's not how we play it. That's the truth. That's how it is.'

For a moment Sue's sidekick looked quite shocked at the notion. The truth! But quickly recovered. 'Of course. That's how it is.'

There was a bitterness in Sue Lake's mouth, as if somebody had slipped some poison into her coffee. Stretchly perhaps.

'And I'm going to ring Mononoke and find out what her intentions are. She can't just descend from on high and put the boot into local issues.'

'Who's going to stop her?'

'Me.'

'How?'

'I'm going to ring her up and reason with her.'

Stretchly laughed. It was a big belly laugh that rang over the Café Résumé like a hunting cry. Her first good laugh of the day. Sue Lake, not renowned for her sense of humour, could be priceless sometimes.

Sue Lake saw Garrison Ford, local reporter, coming through the door in search of a breakfast beer, and made her escape before he could badger her for a story.

The conversation took place at home, with a cup of coffee in front of her and a couple of large kanuka trees leaning towards her window. She liked their slender, bird friendly branches. If she were a painter, she would paint those branches.

The call had been arranged, so Sue got straight through to the Princess herself.

'Paradise Island is a laughing stock here in the Capital, as usual,' Princess Mononoke said, her voice low and vibrant. Sue Lake had heard that her voice could send thrills up men's spines, but it didn't work on Sue.

'Someone did a *cock-a-doodle-do!* when I walked into parliament the other day,' the Princess went on before Sue could say anything, a great technique Sue herself had never been quite able to master. 'I thought it referred to that Ricky and the rowdy rooster business, but no. Your little independence group has sent a mail-out to all members of parliament with a little picture of the Paradise Island flag, which is a picture of a bloody rooster. These people want Sid Vicious as their symbol, symbol of the Island and its independence.'

The Princess's voice was gathering momentum and timbre, but a little spark of joy, or maybe just relief, lit Sue Lake for an instant. This was not what she thought!

'I think you'd better tell this little rooster group of yours that in order to achieve what they want, there would need to be a special Act of Parliament. And that is not going to happen, and I'm not going to argue for it. There are more important things to think about, like the neo-liberal agenda, poverty, poverty poverty…'

Always on the hustings, Sue thought, always just one step away from the microphone. 'It's not my group. It's Northrop's group. He's the rooster man. He's feral himself. Part man, part rooster. And Malarky is just being mischievous, as usual.'

Mononoke sighed. 'Paradise Island,' she said heavily, 'Oh my dear dear dear wonderful Paradise Island, and all those dear dear dear wonderful crazy people I love so much…'

Oh dear dear dear, Sue Lake thought. We're all over the place here.

'Do you realise how precious it all is really, right down to the rooster? A red rooster on a green background, can you beat that?'

Sue couldn't, but her earlier relief was fading. It sounded as if the princess was swinging in the wind, this way and that like a weather vane. Paradise Island was her little rock garden, and woe betide anyone who touched even a beetle in the mulch. It was always possible, from a distance, to get sentimental about Paradise Island, and Mononoke was driven by sentiment.

There's a big gap between passion and petulance, she thought as she returned to the conversation, but they would work something out. Mononoke was too proud to bear being made a fool of, however great her love of local eccentricity. She had to survive in the bear pit, as parliament was known, and didn't need a rooster on her shoulder.

Some approximation of common sense would eventually prevail, Paradise Island style. Plans to drag the island out to sea would be quietly dropped, at least in the meantime.

And the meantime is pretty much what you get in politics.

A blackbird landed on one of the lower branches of the kanuka tree, took a quick look around, and was gone.

HOW GREEDY NAN GOT HER NAME

Back in the day, there came a day when everybody and their German Shepherd seemed to be discovering Paradise Island. Gleaming new SUVs began to appear driven by men in white shirts and pricey sunglasses (or their female equivalents in white shirts and pricey sunglasses) scoping out chunks of Paradise and measuring them with their chequebooks. To the general amazement, a black Humvee was spotted hunting bush-clad properties in remote places. 'It's the CIA,' Minute Ago commented, 'looking for a location for a secret spy base.'

'This would be a wonderful place if we could just get rid of the hippies and riff-raff,' a woman in Ray Bans with a Gucci handbag was heard remarking to Mavis Stretchly, who couldn't have agreed more. They might well have been talking about Minute Ago.

These hippies and riff-raff, some of whom had been on the island for many years and were substantial landowners in their own right, weren't partial to being snubbed in the street for their recycled clothes, or having their marginal old dungas pushed off the road by polished behemoths. Others, however, didn't care as they were laughing all the way to the bank.

The cash rich and asset poor despised the asset rich and cash poor, but they needed each other. Land began changing hands at an increasing rate. Property values began to rise – and rise. Cash registers were ringing. Perfectly normal people developed strange looks in their eyes.

The sound of those cash registers rang in the ears of Nan Goodluck, who owned, quite by accident, a nice little property strategically located on a hilltop destined to boast million-dollar views in years to come. When her father bought it, back in his day, it was seen as worthless: too steep, no decent access, way off the beaten path, covered in gorse – only a fool would buy it. But, as we know, there is one born every minute. Nan was not one of them. She held onto her nice little property through thick and thin and a number of boyfriends who would have cashed her up.

'One day I'll get a million bucks for it,' Nan said, and everybody laughed. Living on an island gives people funny ideas sometimes.

As values rose, the pressure was on to sell, to turn those assets into cash. For Sale signs sprouted like crosses on a dangerous roadside.

The gold is in the dirt! the For Sale signs trumpeted.

And so it was, like a fairy-tale. King Midas came by in the night and touched the land with his golden finger, and you woke up to find yourself in possession of a treasure, a hoard of cash – all you had to do to cleanup was to sell up. Nan Goodluck liked it. Her time was coming, she knew. She studied property values, haunted the real estate agents, of which there were an increasing number, and quietly got around to checking out all kinds of deals that went on under the radar of realtors.

She had, as they say, her finger on the pulse. She watched and she waited. It was all to do with timing; in love, war and real estate, timing is the essence. When to buy and when to sell. Nothing else mattered. She knew her time was near when she befriended an old woman, Smelly Nelly, who wanted to sell-up and move to the land of Oz where her children had all gone to get away from her. Her house was a dog, you could actually shake the walls, and stank of neglect, but the property was strategically placed on the main road, near a bus stop, within walking range of the school and with a lovely Zen view of the ocean.

Old Smelly Nelly knew nothing about the value of her land, or the property boom gathering pace around her, and Nan was glad to share her knowledge and at the same time gently steer the old dear towards the price Nan wanted to pay. After all, the old lady was going to have to sell at some point. Nan was doing her a favour. At the same time, she buttered up the bank manager, using her ownership of an increasingly valuable piece of property as collateral, to raise the money needed to buy out Smelly Nelly. She had figured out the first rule of making money from property deals – never gamble your own money.

Everything went as planned. Smelly Nelly, who was getting quite agitated and confused in the face of this big step in her life, was grateful in the end for Nan's offer, and sold at a price generally known as 'a steal', but, curiously, the beneficiaries of such deals seldom think of themselves as thieves. With the befuddled old woman out of the way, Nan found herself in a position to double her money straight away. Instead of doing this, she worked night and day to clean the place up – you couldn't say Nan was lazy

– and got in a nice young man to do some of the heavier work. She then put the place back on the market for four times what she paid for it.

And got it. The sudden infusion of cash into her account sweetened the bank manager for an even bigger loan for the next property she had her eye on. This was a largish property right on a beach. Another neglected old house, and the garden and grounds were a mess. It was owned by another oldie, a man called Crusty whose son was keen to shift his father into a home and cash up the land. A perfect target for Nan's Modus Operandi. She befriended old Crusty, even to the point of professing a great affection for his feral cat, who hissed and spat every time Nan came near.

'My son can't be bothered coming over to see me, so he plans to sell up my home and move me to town. He doesn't care what I want,' Crusty told her.

'That's cruel,' Nan said.

'I know what he's after.' Old Crusty got a cunning look on his face. 'He's just after the money. He wants his inheritance ahead of time.'

'That's shocking,' Nan said.

He grinned at her, 'He'll never get it at the rate he's going.'

She grinned back. 'What do you think the place is worth?' she asked casually. She looked around as if seeing the house for the first time.

'I don't know and I don't care,' he said.

'I bet it's worth a lot more than what you paid for it back in the day,' she said.

'That's what my son says,' he said.

Nan had friends with the same attitude. MoJo Mayhem, for example, refused to see his house as the valuable asset it was. 'We live here,' he said to Nan. 'Ella and I. You've got to live somewhere.'

Nan had a coffee with Ella at the Café Resume and raised the issue with her.

'I'd give you a good price,' she said.

'But where would we live? You have to live somewhere.'

Nan wasn't so sure about that. If she could get her hands on Crusty's place, flick that off as well as sell her own, she would be able to buy something really upmarket and live in it for a few months while its value rose, and top end values were rising at a ridiculous rate. It was amazing what people would pay for a sea view.

Crusty, however, was as intractable as his wretched cat, and became quite rude to her, accusing her of being in league with his son and of trying to get her fingers into the pie. Old people can get cranky!

Already, however, she had moved on to her next target. Her approach was to get in before the realtors arrived, groom the oldies and work them around to a mutually satisfactory price.

Nan discovered that she had a way with old people. Evenings spent in the hall on bingo night were seldom wasted. People liked to tell her things, and Nan liked to listen. She heard all manner of gripes and grievances, and the oldies were always grateful to Nan for being such a good listener. Nan, for her part, began to keep notes and build up profiles of prospective sellers. She wasn't the only one. The realtors were circling like sharks.

'I had one come down the path and knock at my door,' one old man said. 'I thought he was one of those Jehosiphat people, but it was an agent wanting to list my house for sale!'

'Those agents have a nerve,' Nan said.

Her groundwork paid off, and Nan began to prosper in leaps and bounds. As property values rose, so did her wealth. So did her general satisfaction with herself. Others came to her for advice, but she never gave away the real secret of her operation, which was always to treat people as equals, to be their friends, to give people a reason to feel good about what they were doing. To give them a helping hand in this big transition in their lives. After all, it's so hard to know if you're doing the right thing.

One old lady even said to her, 'I'm glad I sold to you, Nan, and not those horrible real estate agents.'

That was the attitude Nan was talking about, or rather not talking about, and it made her a lot of money. Nan understood now that those strange looks people had in their eyes was greed. It was a time of national madness, when everybody believed that greed worked, that greed was the answer to everything. The common good would be enhanced if everybody just got greedier, and if that didn't happen, who cared about the common good anyway?

'Anybody living on Paradise Island who is not getting rich is a fool,' Nan instructed MoJo, who was not getting rich. This became her favourite saying. She wasn't worried about a downswing in prices. This was Paradise Island; there would be no downswing. And if there were, that would be a great opportunity to buy up at deflated values.

Like many opportunists, she liked to elevate her own experience to a general imperative: if little Nan could do it, anybody could do it. And if they didn't, it was their own stupid fault. She still had her original piece of land on the hillside. Easily worth a million dollars now, but Nan wasn't selling any time soon. The trick was to keep buying, not selling.

You wouldn't notice Nan on the street. If you were driving your polished behemoth down the main drag, and happened to glance out of your subtly darkened windows, you might see a dowdy looking woman of middle age, riff-raff for sure, who didn't look like she had a penny to her name and who wouldn't say boo to a mouse. That would be Nan, probably on her way to the realtors. Being unremarkable suited her. It was camouflage; she could get around the auctions unnoticed. On Paradise Island it doesn't pay to judge by appearances.

Almost unnoticed. There were those who recognised the look in her eyes.

'Here comes Greedy Nan,' they would say as she approached.

Here comes Greedy Nan!

A MORTGAGE AND AN ORANGE TREE

Despite rising property values, it was just as easy to get into trouble with a mortgage back in the day as it is now. There was no lack of mortgagee sales, even on Paradise Island, mostly people biting off more than they could chew with the banks swallowing up the rest.

That was not the case with Margery. With a good job at Telecom and pretty minimal overheads, she had every expectation of being able to meet her monthly payments. She thought of them as she did her other monthly discharge: blood and money, that's the way it goes. And out it goes, every month.

Twenty-five years, however, is a long time; governments come and go, interest rates rise and fall, economies boom and crash, coastlines crumble – and people lose their jobs. And when people lose their jobs they have to sell up and leave.

Losing her job at Telecom came as a blow to Margery. A low blow. It was through no fault of her own, rather the 'sinking lid' policy the company was following as it entered a phase of constant restructuring. She hated the expression 'sinking lid'. All those lives and hopes crushed beneath the heavy weight of the sinking lid, now hers was one of them. How can you treat people like this, she wondered, just chewing them up and spitting them out, how can you hold a society together like that? Her ancestors were often considered warlike and cruel, but what could be crueller than this corporatized culture? A pink slip can end a life just as surely as a stone adze can stove in a skull.

She didn't just have herself to think of. She had an adopted son, T, at the vulnerable age of fifteen. How he came to be with her is another story. He depended on her. She was his compass in a swirling world, the rock to which he clung; he had nobody else, and had been a child whose spirit had taken a long time to settle in a physical body; he needed lots of shielding from the world, and her little hard-won piece of paradise had provided just that. Now she was about to lose it. 'You don't really own your house, you know,' a friend said, 'the bank owns it.'

When Margery got her pink slip, she sat beneath her orange tree and wept. It was the best place to weep. She had planted and fed that tree, thinking of it as one of the family. She'd put a lot of work into it. It needed plenty of nourishing to produce nice fat juicy oranges, and had just begun to come into its own. Last winter she'd eaten its first fruit, and found it sweet. I can't lose the tree, she kept saying to herself over and over. There's no way I can lose the tree.

If this were one of those feel-good stories, something magical would happen, a magic orange perhaps, that would enable her to keep her house and her orange tree; no other ending would be acceptable. She half expected that would happen, something like divine intervention. After weeping, she bought a lotto ticket. The glass must always be half full, even when it isn't. But it's not as easy as it sounds to put art in the service of illusion; reality has a way of creeping in around the edges. As with her brief conversation with her bank manager.

'I think I'm very employable. Would you employ me?'

'I'm sorry we don't have any positions available at present,' he said.

She didn't know how to tell T. He was happy here. Finding his feet. To tell him would be to bring his world to an end. She decided to hold on until the very last moment before she told him. She spent time on the phone with friends and family, but what could they do? They had no magic wand to wave to make her mortgage go away. They had mortgages of their own. They were afraid what was happening to her would happen to them; she could hear the fear in their voices. *There but for the grace of God go I.*

She kept hearing that the economy was forging ahead, but all around her people were losing their jobs, or were afraid of doing so.

That there was no magical ending in the offering did not mean that she had to funk right out. Fear was not in her blood. Grief, maybe, that maternal inheritance, but not fear. She squared her shoulders before the world. Something would happen, life would go on. Her severance pay gave her a couple of months' grace, and, like a hundred or so others who'd gone down in the same purge, she spent most of the time looking for a job. Pounding the pavement, as it used to be called before the days of pounding the keyboard. She did her fair share of both.

I'm too young to go on the scrapheap, she thought, not thinking that of course the scrapheap welcomes all comers of whatever age.

Those two months of grace were the worst. She did lots of weeping beneath the orange tree when T was at school. She was keeping up the pretence with him that she still had her job, figuring, if she landed another job, she could announce the transition without causing him undue pain. And if she didn't land a job, she'd do her best to face the pain for him. Keeping up the pretence was stressful; she wasn't a natural liar, and it was the honesty between them that she valued the most. She'd never hidden the fact that he was adopted, always been straightforward about his background. That honesty was the rock on which he built his faith in her. She lay awake every night in a cold sweat about letting him down, seeing the look on his face when he found out that the rug was about to be pulled out from under them. Then she would feel guilty for not telling him earlier, not preparing him.

She dreamed that she took the axe and cut down the orange tree.

The day after that dream she was visited by Nan Goodluck. Old Greedy Nan had a nose for this kind of thing. Eventually, Margery would have to sell. They all did, in the end, some kicking and screaming, some busy drinking their half-filled glasses. When the moment of panic arrived, Nan Goodluck would be there with her trusty chequebook.

Margery took Nan's visit for what it was, a bad omen. The vultures are gathering, she thought.

Her job applications led nowhere. What got to her was not so much the failure to land a job, but that often enough her application would not even be acknowledged. It was as if she didn't exist, or if she did, she was so far beneath anybody's notice that she may as well not. There was a spirit of indifference and cruelty in the air; you didn't have to be unemployed to notice it, but it helped.

In the week before the two months grace period ended, a hurricane hit the northern part of the country, dumping a year's worth of rain in a few days, one of those increasingly frequent one-in-a-hundred-year events. *As ye sow, so shall ye reap*, Margery remembered her mother saying. Her mother, who had never followed any of its precepts, had been full of biblical sayings. Margery and T huddled inside and watched the shake and rage of the weather. She was afraid for the old iron roofing, but it held.

Everything held but for the orange tree, which lost all its new oranges.

'I thought they were tougher than that,' she said to T, kicking at the green fruit.

The same morning a member of the northern whanau rang her up. A woman everybody called Aunty Bee spoke to her in a loud voice, as if the storm had left them all deaf.

'We've got a mess up here, lovie. A big wet mess. Hows about you and that strong boy of yours come up and give us a hand.'

Margery knew what the deal would be. Slogging around a sodden farm all day for food and keep, a roof over their heads. But it did mean she didn't have to eat into her precious savings, didn't have to pay rent or buy food.

'You could rent your place out,' Bee said.

Of course, Bee was after some free labour. Even woofers would steer clear of a deal like this.

'Sounds like a beauty,' Margery said.

'I wouldn't say so,' Bee said.

Bee knew that she had Margery over a barrel. A renter would cover the mortgage. She wouldn't lose the orange tree which would live to brave another season. She could own the house but not live in it, it seemed. Like having your cake but not eating it. She could always return; Paradise Island wasn't going anywhere. The orange tree wasn't going anywhere. A couple of months up north would give her another period of grace, allow for new horizons to open up. Lots of people lived that way now, from one period of grace to the next.

'Okay. *Ka pai*,' she said.

She told T that they were moving up north for a while. Not only did he take it well, but he was keen. He had cuzzies up north. The all important point that the house would be rented and not sold was lost on him. It was an adult detail. Why should Margery expect him to be as relieved as she was? He couldn't know that the move was a reprieve rather than an adventure, because Margery still held back from him the problem of the money and the mortgage. Now that the crisis was postponed, she could also postpone telling him.

Not exactly a happy ending, but a workable one, one that was open to the future.

Taking leave of the island was the hard part. Paradise can take quite a hold on the heart. All the packing and preparing made her sad; she hadn't come here for this. She visited her friends, and her favourite spots, feeling nostalgic before she had even left. The sand of the beaches clung to her feet. Two wood-pigeons rose and dipped in the air, clapping their wings just for her.

The day before leaving, she sat beneath the orange tree, but she didn't weep. The tree looked green and glossy. She'd bought some topsoil to tide it over while she was away. She wanted to promise it that she would indeed be back, but knew the uselessness of such promises. A storm can come and sweep them all away, uproot the orange tree and toss it in the air.

The renters moved in as Margery and T moved out. A nice young couple working in the City.

As the ferry pulled away, she stood on the back deck while T sat inside and scoffed a pie.

It will all be here when I get back, she thought. It will all be here just as I remember it.

And the orange tree will be full of fruit.

PEAR SHAPED IN PARADISE

Back in the day, magic things happened on the beaches of Paradise Island. Magic wasn't banned then, the way it is now. For example, Harry Houdini (not the real Houdini) met the Three Graces, each of whom gave him a kiss and changed his life, on one of Paradise Island's paradisiacal beaches. This was no pretend magic, or trick magic, or magic out of a bottle, or the facile magic promoted by the tourist brochures — this was the real thing, the true magic of place, of sand, sun and sea.

Visitors to the island reacted variously to this magic. Some recognised it for what it was and loved it, some loved it without recognising it, some thought they could own it, and there were others who ran away from it because it made their lives nonsensical. Meanwhile, the great institution of the public holiday allowed for the illusion of a balanced life that might contain some magic, while effectively denying it.

Varra was one of those regular visitors who sensed the magic, and responded to it, without recognising it. When asked why she kept returning to the same place, the same beach even, she would just smile — she had a nice red-herring of a smile — and reply that she just enjoyed the sun and the sea.

'But you don't even swim,' a friend protested, showing just how little she understood.

In fact Varra did swim, after a fashion. Splash and float about. She liked floating on her back and looking at her toes which popped up out of the water like little creatures with business of their own, just as she liked to sit on the beach and watch her toes wriggle out of the sand, but none of that was really the point. And not the reason she returned year after year, fun as it was.

The beach itself was unremarkable to look at in terms of what Paradise Island could offer. Reached only by a walking trail, it was a modest beach, small with a narrow strip of sand. It was defined by a jumble of rocks at each end, and backed by a steep, rocky hillside clad in pohutukawa trees. Varra found it quite by accident one summer, and her initial response was to feel entirely at home there. This was a rare feeling for Varra who never felt entirely at home anywhere.

Her first impulse was simply to sit down, which she did, and found herself with no desire to go anywhere else. There were a few others about, but they soon merged into the general background. Sitting there, her feet getting the feel of the sand, she felt as if she were at the centre of the world, that she had found the spot from which the rest of the world radiated. The feeling was so unique and unexpected that she sat for what seemed like hours, just enjoying the feeling, but when she looked at her watch only five minutes had passed. That was not possible. The impossibility of it gave her a chill, warm as the day was.

It was her first intimation of the true magic of this place.

This magic did not reveal itself all at once, but quietly and subtly over several visits, and as it revealed itself she became accustomed to it. She was being prepared at each stage for the next step, it seemed. She could stretch or concertina time by finding her 'centre of the earth' feeling. An hour could feel like five minutes or five minutes could seem like an hour. Once she lost time altogether, sitting down in the morning and getting up, a few minutes later, to find the whole day had gone. There seemed to be nothing to stop her from sitting down one day and getting up a hundred years later. It was an exhilarating sensation.

One day, as she was sitting quietly looking out to sea, the sound of some children playing nearby, watching some yachts in the distance, the world as she understood it ceased to exist. There was nothing but shape and colour. She remembered hearing once that a painter, who had spent most of his life painting the lilies in his garden pond, had declared that he was painting nothing but light. Now Varra understood that. The world, as we see it, is a trick of vision, she realised. It was really just light, and light colliding with light.

In the face of this vision, Varra held her breath, grateful to feel the solid sand beneath her. How long the world remained that way, five minutes or an hour, she couldn't tell. Despite her fear at what was happening to her, that same sense of exhilaration was there; she could dissolve the world back to light; she could see through the world to the form and jumble of light textures.

Something similar happened to her hearing. Words broke apart into their individual, disparate sounds; the shouts and chatter of the children nearby might have been the cries of gulls or the yelps of puppies.

All this was wonderful, and she put it down to her relaxed state. This way she could just enjoy it without enquiring too much further. That attitude was difficult to maintain after she started seeing the *others*, creatures that belong to the land, the rocks, the beach, the spreading pohutukawas. At first she thought they were mere tricks of light, for the forms they took resembled the trees, the rocks, the spreading pohutukawas. Some of them resembled the leprechauns of Irish myth and made her laugh, others resembled nothing she could recognise. And there were still others she couldn't see but merely sensed: presences, some happy, some sombre, some touched with light, some with shadow, some as still as stone, and some as quick as fireflies.

As she became aware of them, they became aware of her observing them. They even seemed excited by her company. Some were happy, some were sad and others complained. And there was something else. It was a presence, yes, but more like an awareness. It was like being next to an electrical power station, a feeling in the air and in the ground that was not quite a hum, bigger than a hum. Sometimes it was faint, hardly noticeable; other times it was so strong the hairs on her arms lifted.

None of this frightened her, for there was nothing that didn't belong there, didn't share with her in some way the feeling of being at home. And this place, where the elements fused, was a home to all kinds of beings and presences. It was like a big family, the family she'd never had. Nor did she even find it all that strange, it was so natural to the place, but she kept quiet about it anyway, knowing how strange others would find it.

One day she was lying in her favourite spot with the beach to herself when a woman arrived, took a quick look at Varra, threw off her clothes and ran into the water. Soon she was little more than a head bobbing around. Varra couldn't help but grin. For a moment the naked woman entering the water had looked just like one of her magic creatures, as she called them.

When the woman came out the water, she wrapped a large towel around her and, surprisingly, sat within a couple of arms' lengths from Varra.

'I've seen you before,' the woman said. 'You must enjoy it here.' She had a light, soft voice and dark, unruly curls.

Varra had never seen the woman before but decided she must have been with one of the family parties that tended to distance themselves from her, to give her space.

'I love it,' she said. 'I've been coming here for four years.' She counted it up in her mind. Yes, four years. Ordinary life had its own funny way with time.

'Are you from the City?'

That one little word contained her life, everything beyond this beach. Less said the better. 'Yes, what about you?'

'I live here.'

'Lucky you.'

'Things can turn pear-shaped in paradise just like anywhere else.'

Varra laughed. Pear-shaped in paradise. That might describe Varra herself. The woman laughed, and Varra noticed that she was a little pear shaped too, although more compact and muscular than Varra. They could both sit on this beach and turn pear-shaped in paradise together.

Varra giggled at this and the woman did too, as if she got the joke. Soon they were laughing like a couple of naughty kids.

At that moment, one of the more cheeky creatures came up to Varra and began complaining in a chirpy voice. It was male-looking, with a beard and a face that might be mistaken for sea-hewn rock. It looked so comical, throwing its stubby arms about and moving its head up and down like a reluctant Noddy, that Varra had to choke back a laugh. The woman beside her however laughed outright. A delighted and delightful giggle.

'You can see it,' Varra said, going into a state of minor shock. As long as only she could see the beach-beings, they remained safely within the boundaries of her imagination, even while she did not entirely believe that they were imaginary. She hadn't enquired too deeply.

'It's in a fluster about something,' the woman said.

'What are they?' As she asked, Varra wondered if she really wanted to know. They were a part of the magic of the beach, she didn't need to know more than that. Who was this woman anyway, coming up to her like this, walking right into her private world?

'I call them elementals,' the woman said. 'They are an expression of natural forces.'

'How come we can see them but others can't?'

'Everybody can see them, or sense them, most just take no notice.'

The little rock creature had not departed. It had latched onto the woman now, and she seemed to be listening intently.

Varra was about to speak when the woman held up her hand for silence. The wind had died and the beach was hushed.

'There's something else here,' the woman said.

'Yes,' Varra said, surprised at the sound of her own voice. This was the presence she'd felt earlier. It didn't come from one place but all around.

'What is it?'

'It's not from here. Like the others. It's from another dimension.'

'Jesus!'

'No.' The woman was perfectly serious.

'Who are you?'

'My name is Tina.' She fell silent again and Varra could feel the presence gathering and concentrating around them. Varra had the peculiar sensation that their little beach was detaching itself from the land behind, floating on the ocean rather than embedded in it.

Varra was about to introduce herself when Tina began to talk, but not in any language Varra knew. It was a voluble, bubbling sound coming out of her mouth. She appeared to be arguing or remonstrating. Varra could sense the presence reacting. It wasn't a friendly presence. It was huge and somehow remote. Varra had the sudden fancy that this consciousness was not focused in one place but spread out across the whole galaxy. She felt as if she were about to fall off the world. This encounter with the presence was the reason the woman had turned up in the first place, she thought.

'What was all that about?' Varra asked when Tina had stopped talking and the presence had retreated.

Tina was quickly getting dressed. 'There is a disturbance on the etheric plane because of what humans are doing to this planet.'

Just as quickly as she had arrived, Tina left. Just a smile hanging in the air.

Varra took a deep breath and looked up and down the beach, perhaps to reassure herself it was still there.

Everywhere she looked she could see elementals, her magic creatures, dozens of them. They were all very still.

They were all looking at her.

They were waiting.

THE RECLUSE

When Princess Mononoke retired from public life in her early fifties, turning her back on the world of politics and power that had occupied her best years, there was nowhere to go but to Paradise Island, where she had been nurtured early in her political career.

'Stay involved,' Big Buster advised her, 'otherwise you curl up your toes and die.' Big Buster had not been elected to public office for some years but acted as if he had. He was always to be seen getting on and off the ferry with submissions under his arm. He had mentored the young Sue Lake in her first years as Mayor of Paradise Island, and taught her all she knew. One thing she knew for sure was that while she might be Mayor of the Island as long as the fickle voter favoured her, Princess Mononoke was the princess of these fabled lands no matter what the fickle voter did – one of the great advantages of monarchy.

Big Buster was happy to advise her, too, but unlike Sue Lake, the princess chose to do the opposite of what he said. That usually worked out best for her. And when she saw the way he continued to huff and puff around the place looking important beyond his use-by date, she decided that this was not the way to go. She would get out, slowly, bit by bit, but she would get out.

Mononoke and her husband had a pretty quiet little place in the backways of the island, which was a good place to start withdrawing from the world. Of course, she brought along her cellphone, her laptop, her desktop, and the house had a landline. Back in the day, all houses had landlines. Other circumstances were propitious. Many had come to Paradise Island to get away from it all, from what was quaintly called the rat race, so she was not the only one.

However, cutting all the threads that tied her to the rat race was not as easy as closing a door. Facebook, and what we call the social media, did not exist back in the day, but email did and every morning she faced thirty or more emails all from people who wanted something from her, expected something from her, even imagined that she somehow owed them her time and spirit. Some were quiet and respectful, some were insistent, some were demanding, some were even abusive – but they all required an answer or thought they did. Chopping back those emails was a painful process, but she did it by a combination of not replying at all to careful management, and what she called the 'slow choke'.

'All I have to do is figure out what people want and who can give it to them – other than me, that is,' she said to her husband.

'And what if they want you and not somebody else,' her husband said.

'Too bad for them,' she said. 'What if I died, what would they do then? That's what you have to ask.'

That is exactly what she did ask a couple of old hangers-on for whom she had always done favours. They called themselves her friends but they were, she realised, more like bloodsuckers. These were the ones most likely to be indignant when she didn't reply to their emails, or fobbed them off with some lame excuse, or straight out told them to get lost. She was a forthright person and had ways of telling people to get lost. These hangers-on were like a Greek chorus, singing her praises one moment while the favours were flowing, and conniving with her enemies the next. What a relief it was to shed these so-called friends!

They were in a different category from real friends, people she liked to keep up with, and she retained a few of these right to the end, the end being when she finally closed her email accounts, all but one which was known only to her family of two grown up sons who knew better than to email her for no reason.

All in all, it took her several long weeks to choke it all off, get rid of people politely or not, and feel the blessed silence from that direction. She noticed immediately that the tension associated with turning on her computer in the morning retreated as her email commitments lessened. When the latter was gone, the former disappeared too. Just what she had hoped. There were moments when she missed the cut and thrust of emails, firing off missives in one direction while taking them from another. It was like playing battleships. Every hit counts. The thrill of adrenaline. But those moments didn't last too long.

The landline was another matter, and it took some delicate negotiation with her husband, who used the landline for family, friends and business.

She might be going recluse but he wasn't. Eventually they settled on a compromise. She de-listed, and they changed the number to his name, with the phone in his office adjacent to the house. And it had to be set low so that she couldn't hear it from the house. He was a good husband and was very patient with her. He was under strict instructions not to take messages for her, or, the worst of crimes, call her to the phone. Only a dire family emergency would justify that.

It was, she realised, the sound of the telephone she found most disturbing, its endless double jangle. That was the world at the other end of the line, insisting on its right to interrupt her at any given moment regardless of what she was doing. That was a big presumption. The big presumption that lay behind the invention of the telephone. And how hard it was not to answer! There is a compulsion to answer, a social expectation, a guilt attached to not answering. And an underlying curiosity. You want to know who is at the other end, even if it turns out to be some phony fundraiser.

As she got the telephone out of her life, she further realised how wedded she had been to it. As politician and power broker, she'd spent the bulk of her time talking into a telephone receiver, chatting people up, bringing them down - tests, allies and enemies, juggling them all at the end of a line. Cup of coffee in one hand, telephone in the other - late twentieth century woman? While emails offered their own field of battle, as it were, they were slow and pale compared to the verbal joust of the telephone conversation. The voice, stripped of body language, alone in the wires, became her natural element where she swam along with the other predators. Her voice was her speciality. It was a contralto, rich in timbre, rich in suggestion; she could make it flow full, easy and deep, or rough and tough; she could make it as soft as a black cat at midnight or as loud as a jet overhead. Her voice. Her preferred tool of trade. She had to let all that go. Put down the tools of trade.

That still left her cellphone. Easy, she thought. I just chuck it into the sea as far I can and that's the end of that. Of course it wasn't that simple. Her cellphone connected her to the world just like her landline, only more so. Her list of contacts were like threads that bound her to her past. A friend had once used the expression 'spaghetti' to describe emotional entanglements and complications. 'I'm not having anything to do with him,' she said of her boyfriend. 'Too much spaghetti.' That's what she thought as she stared down at her cellphone, quite ancient by modern standards, but still capable of carrying a lot of spaghetti, of a particularly glutinous kind.

The political kind.

Furthermore, as she wound down the landline, the cellphone became even more active, and those determined to ignore her wishes turned to that little beastie that just about vibrated itself into oblivion. While those around her were upgrading their phones as fast as they could, she was busy plotting how to get rid of her old, uncool one. 'These things will end up ruling our lives,' she said to her husband who was busy upgrading his.

Without the cellphone, her hands felt light and free, her pocket happily empty. Instant availability, twenty-four seven, she thought. With the landline, you have to be in its vicinity to hear it, with the faithful cellphone, you carry your vicinity with you. You are plugged in. But plugged into what? For her, it had become nothing more than the mindless buzz of a fly hitting the window, over and over again. That was the sound of human voices, the sound of the human mind knocking itself silly.

Finally disposing of her cellphone - she accidently on purpose dropped it and it gave up its ghost - was like disposing of a whole past life, a life in which she was not the person she was now becoming. There it was, wrapped in dull, scuffed plastic - a public life.

She discovered, at a certain point, the old adage that no man is an island, nor woman either. She had to allow for some communications from the world, and how to do that and keep complete control of the process took some working out. While she no longer had any phone numbers, she did of course have an address where she and her long-suffering husband lived. Short of going on the road in disguise, there was little she could do about that. While the arrival of the cellphone on the social scene had largely put an end to people just dropping in on one another - why didn't you text in advance? - there was still a letterbox at the gate and a path to the house.

It was easy enough to discourage people from dropping in on her, but the letterbox she decided to turn to her advantage. Because of emailing, people had got out of the habit of writing letters, so she didn't have much to fear from that direction, but people could still leave notes for her there. It happened one day, a piece of paper with her name on it and a brief request for something. It turned out to be something she wanted to do, that in fact she wouldn't want to have missed out on. That gave her pause for thought. She could retire from the world, but not completely. There had to be that one little thread of spaghetti and for her it became the letterbox. It discouraged the casual time waster – you had to get in your car and find the place – but left the door open, in this case a little slot, for the world to enter.

Control she had. Finally. Over her life. No longer was she at the beck-and-call of others. No longer would she serve.

Okay, she said to the silence once it was all done, 'now what?'

BOATIE BEN AND THE MISTS OF UNBEING

Boatie Ben shut down the motor and peered into the mist around him, trying to get a sense of where he was. Near land, he knew, because he had been approaching Pirate Bay on the south coast of Paradise Island when the fog bank rolled over him.

Fog is often described as swallowing things up, as if it were some creature, but for Ben thick fog like this rubbed everything out, rubbed out the world until there was nothing but the slap of water and the creaking of timbers. It was time to remember his boatie mate Cess Claw's comment that, on the water, death is never more than one step away. A freak wave, a sudden mishap on board, an unexpected collision: *there's many a slip between cup and lip*, Ben's grandfather used to say.

Boatie Ben took a swig of brandy and considered the situation. Fog made sailors feel helpless. If it weren't for the compass he wouldn't know north from south, wouldn't know if he were a million miles from land or right on top of it. He couldn't look up at the sky to get his bearings because there was no sky. It was hard to tell the difference between moving and standing still. Fog might be impenetrable to the eye, but the *Merry Marvell*, thirty-five feet of sleek single-masted sloop with a single mainsail could slip through the fog as if it weren't there.

Common sense dictated that he let the anchor out and wait. Sooner or later a wind would pick up and the fog would go its merry way. He couldn't just drift, as he would be drifting right now, even if he couldn't feel it. Winds might die, but ocean currents don't. The only danger was that he might be in a shipping lane and have some huge container ship come looming out of the fog right on top of him.

He took another slug of brandy and made his way to the bow, taking care with the slick timbers underfoot. He shouldn't be drinking either, but try denying an old salt a slug of brandy in the chill fog with night not too far away. Before letting out the anchor, he tried once more to work out his location. But he could hear nothing and see nothing and all he could feel was the wet fog on his face.

The anchor rattled out with an unnaturally loud sound. It hit the water and vanished into the void.

Ben rolled himself a cigarette. He sat on the poop and smoked. *There's many a slip…* He couldn't trust the calm, the quiet, the stillness. They were a deception. For a start, *The Merry Marvell* was still drifting. He could feel it, the dragging anchor bumping over the ocean floor. It might catch on something, it might not. He used his compass in an attempt to figure out the direction of the drift. He would very much like to know if he were drifting towards Paradise Island or away from it, towards black rocks or out to sea.

His knowledge of local currents, and where he had been when the fog struck, suggested that he would be drifting towards the island.

Also the quiet wasn't what it appeared to be. There was the insidious lapping of the waves against the yacht's timber. Once he thought he heard a voice shouting in the distance, but he knew that, in the absence of sound, it is easy to imagine it, to make it up. He thought he heard the sound of a gull, too, but that was unlikely. Birds don't like fog any more than sailors, and for the same reason. He did hear, at one point, the long boom of a ship's foghorn, but only once.

'Okay,' he said aloud, just to hear his own voice. It sounded oddly flat. 'We're not in any immediate danger,' he said, as if talking to *The Merry Marvell*, reassuring the uneasy vessel. But he had no way of knowing if that were true or not. That's what gave the gentle fog its menace.

He didn't expect it to last. Fog was rare around Paradise Island, given that it lay on a crossroad of winds; northerlies, easterlies, southerlies, the island got them all. A bit of morning or evening mist was all. He just had to wait it out. Sounded simple enough, and the brandy helped, but the fog tended to slow time. When he looked at his watch, which he tried not to do, it seemed that the seconds hand was dragging time reluctantly behind it.

It was easy to lose confidence in a situation like this, and do something silly. He'd heard of even experienced boaties doing crazy things in fog, like firing up the motor and heading off for some imagined harbour, or allowing the silent, dreamlike fog to lull them off to sleep, waking up to find themselves on the rocks. It could feel as if the world outside, beyond the fog, had rearranged itself into new configurations, and when the fog finally cleared he'd be in some place he didn't recognise. Some place that was unlikely to be a tropical paradise. In fog like this it was too easy to let the mind drift.

One thing for sure, he didn't doubt his craft. It had a fine bow, a wide, flat bottom and a deep single-fin keel with ample beam to give good stability. It had been designed in the 1950s to serve as an auxiliary craft for the big royal yachts, and it had been repaired and maintained on Paradise Island by none other than Cess Claw, master boat builder. Much of the timber was original walnut. This elegant, slender little craft, could handle the open sea and was better adapted to rough weather than many of your fancy, modern yachts that looked like Christmas cakes and were good for nothing but floating around in the harbour looking expensive.

Fog, however, was the great leveler. It didn't matter if you were in a luxury liner or a dinghy, the fog got you just the same.

Finding the atmosphere suddenly chill and oppressive, he retreated into the small cabin, equipped with a bunk bed and a gas stove. He should make himself a nice strong cup of tea or coffee, but that would mean putting the brandy bottle away, and he wasn't ready for that yet. That would come in good time. Sitting on the bunk-bed, looking around his cabin, and up at the smooth resined timbers of the roof, which was the deck above, gave the appearance of normality. He might be sitting safely at his own mooring in Paradise Bay, drinking brandy and saluting sunsets. All that spoiled the illusion were the faint vibrations caused by the drag of the anchor across the sea floor.

And all he had to do was look out the porthole to see the fog wrapped around *The Merry Marvell* like a great grey cat curled in sleep.

He looked forlornly at his defunct radio. He hadn't needed it, just slipping in and out of Paradise Bay for a bit of fishing. Wisdom had counselled that he should have it fixed, but Boatie Ben was not made of money. In fact, he was broke. All he had in the world was *The Merry Marvell* and it had absorbed all the money he'd ever managed to get his hands on. Now of course he was paying the price. At sea at least, you always paid the price.

Nervousness forced him back up on deck. He couldn't do anything, that was the hell of it. The sails were firmly furled, everything that should be tied down was tied down, everything that should be put away was nowhere in sight. Doing nothing when he could be sliding into danger went against the grain, even when there was nothing to do but stay vigilant.

He was about to take another hit of the brandy when the thought occurred to him that getting drunk and falling overboard was just about the stupidest thing to do in the fog, but it had happened. People had drowned or floated away in their life-jackets to never-never land. He put the brandy away, but kept it close.

He got out his plumb line and dropped it over the side of *The Merry Marvell*. Some of the latest radar, he'd heard, gave automatic sea-depth readings, but he and *The Merry Marvell* would be resting in Davy Jones' locker before the price came down to something he could afford. He knew it was deep because of the way the anchor was behaving, but the plumb kept dropping and the line kept playing out until he could no longer believe in the accuracy of the reading. There had to be some current running that was pulling at both the anchor and the plumb line.

He could feel his mind slowing down, and that was a bad sign; in this soporific mist he had to stay alert. Coffee was what he needed. Coffee with a little shot in it. He was heading back to the cabin when he felt the anchor cease its dragging on the sea floor. He hoped it had caught. He stared down at the sea, trying to get a feel for the craft's movement. They were still moving, which meant that the anchor must have lifted off the ocean floor and was now floating unimpeded as *The Merry Marvell* went… somewhere. Which meant he could drift onto rocks before he could put down his coffee, let alone fire up the motor. *There's many a slip…*

Instinct prompted him to start up the motor, have it idling, ready for any contingency. The problem with that was gas. He'd been out all day – he had a bin full of snapper – and the petrol gauge had been hitting its final quarter as he'd been heading back to Paradise Bay. Ample gas for normal conditions. Then the fog arrived. Just seemed to rise up out of the ocean like a great exhalation. When it was too dangerous to keep going, he'd turned off the motor to save gas. That had been the prudent thing to do.

He made his coffee, had his shot, while twilight thickened the mist until even the mist disappeared. He could see it in the lights of *The Merry Marvell*, a gauzy halo. Otherwise there was nothing. *The Merry Marvell* floated through a void, through sheer opacity.

This will be one of those *I woke up in the morning and it was all a dream* type of story, he thought, as he reinvigorated his coffee with another shot. The fog will clear, and I will have been in Paradise Bay the whole time, drifting around my mooring. The tree-lined hills of Paradise Island would appear, and he would be there, feeling foolish, an empty brandy bottle by his side.

But even as he imagined it, it didn't sound right.

In fact, when he did wake, the empty brandy bottle by his side, the mist was gone and he was in the middle of nowhere.

No land in sight. Not even a seagull.

Nothing.

He wondered about a search party, but he hadn't told anybody he was going fishing barely out of the bay. Why should he?

He did it every day.

He broke out the sails, lifted anchor, and waited for a wind.

A wind would have to come. Eventually.

He looked out over the empty, endless sea.

Snapper for breakfast, he thought.

Life is good.

GARRISON FORD AND THE MORNING AFTER

'Back in the day' came to an end when Garrison Ford died.

That's the trick of time. The day moves on. Tomorrow never comes but yesterdays keep piling up. Sometime in the future, someone's going to look at our present and call it 'back in the day', but we will know that the real 'back in the day' was the time when Garrison Ford still walked the island, writing his pithy little stories for the *Paradise Island Times* and dreaming of grander things.

Ford did not die grandly, if such a death is possible, but foolishly, in a moment of forgetfulness, walking in front a speeding car while feeling in his pocket for a mini-vodka. I just didn't look, he would have said with that silly grin on his face if he had lived to tell the tale. The story of his death has been often told, a cautionary tale for all drinkers and others who become too blasé about life and what it takes to live it; what is less often told is what happened to him afterwards, his adventures in the afterlife, for, to the intrepid reporter, life had been a great adventure so why should death be any different?

The first thing he noticed when he woke up on a bright and sunny morning in his own bed, was that he had no hangover. There was not a particle of alcohol in his system. He hadn't felt like this for years, if ever. He didn't know how this was possible. He tried to remember his last drink and couldn't. He could only remember his very first; all the following drinks had vanished into that first one.

On his feet he felt buoyant, like an athlete. A cool light flowed in his veins. He bounced up and down in spontaneous exercise, feeling the easy flow of air in and out of his lungs. 'This is what I'm talking about,' he said to the empty room. 'Oh Happy Day! Welcome the happy face of the Happy Day, the Glad Day, the Day of Delight, the day of breakfast in the sun on Paradise Island with not a care in the world. No deadlines to meet. No deadlines. Ha ha.'

The clean light passed through the glass of his kitchen window, unmolested by time and circumstance. His thoughts passed through his mind in much the same way. The long addiction was over, his flesh taken apart at the sub-atomic level and reconfigured in a new shape, the shape of a man who had no other desire but to walk in the morning sunlight, enjoying the sparkling blues and greens, the sweet turquoise of the world, and walk the streets and bubbling hills of his beloved island.

Walking was easy. It had never felt so easy; his feet had never felt more at home. You might say the morning walked him along. Sunlight had hoisted a white sail across the deserted street, but there was every sign of human habitation. Cars, freshly washed and polished, lined the roadside. Sprinklers endlessly encircled their lawns. Letterboxes waited with their mouths open. Nodding roses courted the sunlight. Sparrows left every ten minutes on their best behaviour. Trees nestled into their roadsides. Shopping centres were draped in black. Curved steel lampposts bent their heads like monks at prayer. In the distance, the polished glass towers and spires of the City were engraved on blue. There was a river and a bridge. There was a gull flying into the sun. Winged shadows raced each other across the landscape.

On the corner of T.... and Y.... Streets, he found a flower-seller looking like a young woman from an old movie. He stopped to buy a rose. White tinged with pink. It smelled of dawns and sunsets. Such a fragrance can be merciless in its purity. He had nothing to offer her for this beauty but a few dull coins.

Yvonne. He was buying the flower for Yvonne for no other reason but the sheer joy of buying it. The young woman took his money and gave him a smile. The smile reminded him of daffodils. Where he grew up, there had been daffodils all over the parks in spring. Enough to paint the sky yellow.

He had nothing to do, nowhere to go, no point to make, no passion to fulfil, no destiny to resist. He was complete just as he was, rose in his hand, blessedly relieved of past and future.

So he walked until he found himself at the edge of the sea. The waves made a gentle sound on the sand, and he could hear the echo of a gull. He could see how the tide angled against time, and how the sky wore a coat of birds and stars. He could feel the way the ocean fitted the land, the push and thrust of the sea, the land's slow surrender into valiant rocky headlands and submissive beaches. The ocean fitted the land the way the air fitted his skin. There was nothing to jar the eye, or mar the line of the horizon. The sun drew the ocean up into its belly and he could see only light.

The horizon made a clean sweep.

He walked away from the ocean until he came to a large park. Here there were people calling to one another in swirling voices, walking towards one another out of the miracle of their upright moments. Walking among the park benches, all behaving themselves under a lolly-scramble sky where birds flicked from wingbeat to wingbeat, while, behind them, clouds scuttled their shapes in hidden rivers of air. Kingfishers caught flame. Children ran across the blue spaces, waving their arms. The planets tipped forward on rails of light. The flower-seller lifted her roses to an indifferent street. The world filled up with their scent.

Around the band rotunda, chairs were rehearsing their silence.

A large tear slid down his face onto his arm where it made a splash. A tear large and declaratory. It meant no harm. You might weep when you see children, how light they are, how their voices ascend to heaven. When they are gone, the park grows larger with emptiness; the swing hoists its sadness, the see-saw loses its balance.

He was amazed to see that the morning had already turned into afternoon, and that the past tense had given way to the present. As he entered the present, the past folded up behind him like a room full of collapsing furniture.

He walks.

He walks slowly down a familiar street, noting with relish each detail. The peeling paint of 33, the unmown lawn of 42, a child's tricycle upside-down on the driveway at 55, one wheel still spinning. He pauses to watch some washing flapping on the line and a row of clothes pegs that grip the air with plastic teeth. Trousers, skirts, blouses, underclothes, socks, all billowing with imagined bodies.

When he comes to his gate, he checks for mail. There is nothing but a circular that features the latest electrical appliances, front-loading washing machines and digital TVs. He then steps up off the ground into the air, moving with a swimming motion towards the side of the house. Having to make his feet coincide with the ground has become unnecessary. The air is just as comfortable. A simple step. A step from the common language of sleep to the dialect of wakefulness.

He reaches a window, slightly ajar, and slips through. He comes in with the last light which curls up like a ginger tomcat in the corner, while the aging sky lingers at the window, like a forgotten relative. There is an open suitcase on the bed. Some neatly folded shirts shine. The sound of murmuring comes from downstairs. The mingling of familiar voices. Family, friends and acquaintances. Memories talking to memories.

He moves silently from room to room. He knows just where to go, and soon he is floating along the ceiling of his bedroom. His body is lying on the bed where he expected it to be. Very few pieces are missing. A finger here, some odd strips of skin from arms and legs. His eyes are closed and his nose is pointing to the ceiling. A group has gathered around the bed and is standing silently, hands clasped loosely in front of them.

There is his uncle Billy, studying his feet as if they might disappear. He didn't ever like Paradise Island. And his wife Margery, wiping a handkerchief across her nose. There is Cousin Lindsay, breathing too hard and fast, and his wife, Eileen, who is looking surreptitiously out the window. She always did bore easily. Yvonne is not among them. Nor is her daughter, Bella.

He wants to call out, to reassure them, but he has no voice.

Keeping at ceiling height, he floats into the other rooms. In the lounge, Bella the Bad is filling a glass with amber liquid. When it is full, she looks quickly around and drains the glass to the last drop. Having a quick one on him. Cheers! Then she shudders and places the glass carefully on the mantelpiece next to a photograph of Garrison Ford as a child, staring earnestly into the camera, busy being innocent in front of an empty band rotunda.

In the kitchen, people are making tea and talking in low voices. There he finds Yvonne in the thick of grief. And his old booze-brother, Kendell, talking earnestly to her. Grandma Jean has put her gammy leg up on a chair. A child is writing messages on a steamed-up window. Nephews and nieces are standing around the fridge eyeing each other up for size. The whisky is taking a fair hammering.

Outside, among the asphodels, the cast of Paradise Island have assembled. All the old faces from Harry the hobbit to Jean Jeanie of theatre fame. Blackbeard his pirate editor is there, taking his own notes this time. Sue Lake and Mavis Stretchly, with no election to win. Minute Ago has just shot through. Face after face, life after life, story after story. Life is like a shaggy dog story, it goes on and on, holding out false promise, until it stops because it hasn't got an end.

Pits have been dug and fires laid, food over hot stones, flax covering and earth. Food comes hot out of the ground as if it were born there. There is laughing and drinking. Kegs are cracked, beer flows, spliffs are rolled.

Somebody swears, somebody cries. Somebody makes a pass at somebody else. Somebody takes a leak in the garden. Somebody vomits. Somebody falls down among the potatoes and goes to sleep. The ancestors turn over in their bone-hill graves. Somebody springs a song. Birds roost in the air.

Voiceless, he passes through the mourners, through their clapping, hopping time.

Eventually, he notices the flower-seller waiting at the gate, throwing him secret looks that give the game away. He gestures for her to leave, to stay clear. For some silly reason he doesn't want anybody to see her. If there are going to be secrets, she will be his. Eventually he will go to her. She cannot be forestalled.

The city has turned over for the night. Its lights blink into the earth. The sky contracts. The galaxy moves in orbit around him, the moon with its heckle of stars. In the morning they will pull the plastic covers off the new houses. The sky will rub against the earth.

He dances forward and back like a soft-shoe shuffler. He shuffles the days, the years, like a pack of cards. Everybody returns to their lives afterwards. His eyelids fold their wings. His mother - surely it must be her! - crosses the room, her hands on fire.

Time wears away with the wind. The stars sink back into the foam. Night moves its morning shadows from. The fool walks with a glad heart. Fall words where they may.

Paradise Island slips over the horizon.

ACKNOWLEDGEMENTS

To Joanna Smith and Jennifer Rackham for designing the Mike Johnson logo image on the rear cover and inside cover page.
Bree Arnott for cover design.
Gordon Duston for the pictures.
Mahina Marshall for book layout and project management.
Odette Singleton-Wards for proofreading.